WICKED GAMES

A. D. JUSTICE

WICKED GAMES

*Steele Security Series,
Book 1*

A.D. JUSTICE

PROLOGUE

Present Day

The beads of sweat glistened in the early morning sun, running down her forehead and along her hairline before reaching her neck. Her eyes scanned the landscape around her, constantly cognizant of her surroundings. Her rhythmic breathing matched the thumping of her feet as she ran along the familiar trail. She wore her earbuds and an iPhone on her upper arm, but she rarely listened to the music. She'd discovered when others thought she was listening to music, they rarely tried to start up a conversation with her. It had become her diversionary tactic to avoid strangers, to appear to be engrossed in her own world, but still allowed her to make quick assessments of potential problems.

She ran every day, regardless of the weather, but not for the reasons most others did. She didn't want the recognition and satisfaction of completing marathons. She didn't care about fundraisers or health awareness campaigns. She was health-conscious but knew better than anyone that she needed to push herself to her limits every day. Running had become her addiction and her only way to deal with the pain inside. She pushed and punished her body with exercise to try to keep the depressive thoughts at bay. The punishment could only last for so long, though. She couldn't run day and night, but she definitely made her time count.

Boulder, Colorado, normally had mild high temperatures with lots of sunshine in early May, but today the way the dark clouds rolled in felt very ominous. She eyed the horizon while she kept her anxiety level in check internally. The approaching storm held a forewarning, and the emotions that bombarded her from every direction seemed to confirm.

Her thoughts strayed to the place she considered home. She thought, *"Damn, I miss Florida,"* as she continued to pound the pavement relentlessly. Thunderstorms were nothing new to her since she grew up in Atlanta and later moved to Miami. She actually loved storms—the rolling thunder, striking lightning, the sound of a hard rain, and the power of it all combined.

The colder Colorado spring weather had taken some acclimation, and she still wasn't crazy about it. She loved the beach, the water, and the warmth. After she'd lived in the landlocked state for three years, she'd decided that was enough to make someone crazy. Winter was absolutely depressing in every way. Miami winters were mild, to say the least, and it never snowed. However, in Boulder, there was always winter snow, and the white fluff covered everything of color. She'd recently decided to learn to snow ski in an effort to develop a new appreciation for winter weather. She knew most of her dislike stemmed from a severe case of homesickness, added to the fact that she'd never really given the city a fair chance.

She'd had an uneasy feeling for the last few days, but she couldn't pinpoint any specific incident that would account for it. She just knew to trust her instincts. They'd served her well in the past. As she continued along the trail, the hair on the back of her neck suddenly stood at full alert, and she knew someone watched her. She allowed her eyes to slowly scan the area as nonchalantly as possible. She only saw other runners and families enjoying the spring weather in the grassy areas but no obvious bad guys lurking about.

They don't usually wear a big sign to announce themselves, though, she thought sarcastically.

She'd been through too much in her twenty-seven years to dismiss the feeling as nothing. *Something* was wrong, even if she didn't know what just yet. She continued her run, intent on finishing before the rain started. She ticked off in her head each errand she needed to complete and the bills she needed to pay, but her eyes scanned the scenery as she continued on her path.

She rounded the corner of the trail and backtracked toward her townhouse. When the thoughts tried to crowd into her head, as they did now, she pushed her body harder and faster. She dug deeper, increased her pace, and controlled her breathing. She continued until the jogging trail ended then she crossed the street and continued up the sidewalk, not slowing until she reached home.

Home This isn't home. I can never really go home, she thought.

She walked the short distance from the sidewalk, up her driveway, and toward her front door. Her neighbor, Mrs. Elizabeth Stanton, called her name to get her attention, just as she did every morning after her runs. She knew the older lady was probably lonely and had very few visitors to keep her company. Mrs. Stanton's husband had died of a heart attack several years ago. She had grown children and grandchildren, but they were all busy with their lives. They didn't take much time out of their lives to visit her. In her mid-sixties, Mrs. Stanton still looked and acted like she was in her forties. She had such spunk and a zest for life.

"Hello, Kris! Out for your morning run again, I see!" Mrs. Stanton always had such a friendly tone, never prying or nosy.

"Yes, ma'am. I think it may rain soon, and you've fussed at me enough for running in the rain." No matter how long she lived here, she knew she could never get rid of her Southern drawl and slang. Her accent was evident to everyone, but so far, no one had really pushed her on why she had moved here. She genuinely liked Mrs. Stanton and often wished they'd met under better circumstances.

"Glad *someone* listens to me," she replied with the laughing tone she always used.

Kris bent over to pick up the morning paper lying in the

driveway as Mrs. Stanton continued to talk to her about how she hoped the rain came soon to water her newly planted flowers and shrubs. She was naming the various newly planted flowers as Kris absently removed the rubber band from the newspaper and unrolled it. She smiled and nodded at Mrs. Stanton, trying to keep up with all the names of her landscaping, when she looked down at the headline and pictures glaring back at her.

Oh. My. God. It's him! It can't be!

Richard Hollingsworth.

Kris tried to quickly gain her composure as her heart beat so hard against her chest that she would've sworn Mrs. Stanton could hear it. She could barely hear Mrs. Stanton's jabbering over the loud swishing sound in her ears from her elevated blood pressure and pulse rate. Her eyes darted from point to point as she tried to locate the source of her anxiety. She recalled the feeling that pricked the back of her neck and thoughts that eyes watched her as she ran just mere minutes before. She knew she'd been found.

Mrs. Stanton abruptly quit talking about her flowers and gasped. "Kris! Are you all right?"

Breathe! She mentally commanded her body to comply.

"Yes, yes. I just feel a little sick all of a sudden. I think I need to eat a little and maybe lie down. I'm sorry to hurry off."

With a worried look, Mrs. Stanton offered her food, but Kris politely refused and excused herself. Mrs. Stanton promised to check on her later.

Kris entered her townhouse and closed the door as quietly as possible, leaving the front door unlocked in case she needed to get away quickly. Directly in front of the door were the stairs leading to the second level. With an open floor plan, the living room and kitchen actually looked like one big room with a bar and barstools acting as the room divider. To the right, just past the staircase, a short hallway led to the master bedroom and bath. Upstairs, there were two more bedrooms and a hall bath.

She quietly moved through each room, silently checking off in her mind that everything was where it should be. She turned toward the short hallway that led under the stairs. It was always dark under there, regardless of the time of day. She inwardly cursed the builder who designed it this way. She reached in, flicked the light switch, and slowly walked into her bedroom.

When she turned on her bedroom light, she saw a sheet of paper lying on her pillow. Her eyes quickly scanned the room to make sure she was alone. Her feet fell lightly as she searched her closet and under her bed. She didn't really know what she would've done had someone actually been hiding in there. Her nerves were on edge as she gingerly picked up the paper. There was only one word written on it: *"Brianna."* Her heart skipped a beat, and her breath caught in the back of her throat.

She finished her search of the rest of the house with a butcher knife in her hand. She realized if a man wanted to overpower her, he could do so even though she had a knife. It still made her feel better to have it ready. Satisfied she was in her house alone, she quickly locked the front door and grabbed her cell phone. She scrolled through her contacts until she found the name she needed and hit send.

On the second ring, she heard a familiar voice. "Stevens."

"What the *fuck*, Stevens?"

No introductions were needed. After she'd read the headlines splashed across the front page of the newspaper and found the note in her bedroom, she decided no pleasantries were needed either.

"We're still assessing the situation."

"*Assessing the situation?* That's government speak for *'we fucked up and don't know how to explain it!'* Do you have any idea what this means?" She knew that screaming and crying like—well, like a girl, would get her nowhere with a hardened US Marshal. So she used her anger to keep her voice low and serious. She was practically growling at the man.

Mocked by the pictures on the front page of the newspaper, she stared at the man who was *thought* to be dead by everyone except her. This man was the reason she had entered the WITSEC program and left her entire life behind three years ago. He was also a very bad man with a very good reputation and had worked hard to hide his sins. Sins she had uncovered as an investigative reporter but never shared with the media. Very few people knew she had discovered his illegal dealings, but he was one of them. Here he was, alive and well, and *home*.

Home…

~

"Look, I know how you must feel. He claims he was abducted just before getting to the airport that day. Says he's been a prisoner for the last three years and finally escaped from his captors. Could be true, could be a lie. I'm looking into his story. Just sit tight until I figure out what is going on."

She had already read the same story in the paper. He didn't tell her anything that any other person across the country couldn't readily access. With her anger at the boiling point, she kept her voice controlled but allowed the anger to flow freely. "You have no damn clue what is going on! *Think* about it, Stevens. Look at him! First of all, did his captors trim his beard and his hair for him? Don't you think it should be a little longer, if he was a *'prisoner'* for *three* years?

"Second, does he look the least bit emaciated to you? What, did his captors run out of filet mignon and caviar, so he had to survive on rib eyes instead? And then there's his appearance in general. Even Tom Hanks was dirtier in Castaway than *he* is after supposedly spending three years as a prisoner in a third world country!"

Taking a deep breath, she continued. "Third—" She could hardly get these words out. "Do you really believe he would suddenly show up, out of the blue, if he didn't already know *exactly* where I am?"

"Just stay put until you hear from me." His voice held no emotion in it—no concern, no surprise, and no intention of helping her.

"Stevens, there was a note on my bed when I got home. It has my *real name* on it."

Stevens had tried to calm her fears, but he finally admitted the situation could be dangerous, and the way it all came about was very suspicious. He didn't want her to make any rash moves that would draw attention. She knew the feelings of being watched earlier were no coincidence. She didn't believe in coincidences anyway. The note was left while she was out running. Whoever left it had been watching her, waited until she left her home, and then slipped into her house undetected.

A professional.

After hanging up with Stevens, she quickly showered and dressed. She packed a backpack with enough clothes and toiletries to last for several days. She opened a small hidden area in the wood floor and retrieved a small fireproof safe she'd hidden there three years before. It contained her alternate identification, complete with a driver's license, birth certificate, passport, credit cards, and cash. She'd prepared the stash ahead of time in the event her identity was ever compromised and she had to run with a moment's notice.

In the back of her walk-in closet, she found the small black duffel bag that contained the rest of her new identity—the hair cap, wig, adhesive, black brow pencil, and colored contacts. She pulled her long blond hair into a pile on the top of her head, pulled the head cap over her hair, tucked in any loose strands, and then put on the black wig. After making sure it was straight and looked natural, she applied the adhesive to the underside of the edges to help keep it in place.

Using the brow pencil, she applied a small amount to each eyebrow to match her new, short hair. The brown-eyed contacts covered her cobalt-blue eyes. She then applied eye makeup, using her eyeliner to reshape her eyes. She applied a dark burgundy eye shadow and thick fake eyelashes to complete her transformation. She looked in the mirror at her new image for several long minutes.

It was still midmorning yet, on a Saturday, and most of her neighbors were working in their yards. She stood to the side of the window and looked at each person. The trees behind the row of houses across the street from her townhouse were dense. She looked carefully along the line of trees, trying to spot any movement that would symbolize someone watching her. Her inner thoughts were on overload.

Is anyone out of place?

Is anyone pretending to be someone they aren't—besides me, that is?

She glanced around her townhouse and was suddenly more aware than ever that it held nothing personal that could be related to her or anyone she cared about. She'd left that all behind three long years ago. The truth was, she still saw all the pictures, faces, and smiles in her mind. She heard the laughs and voices. She felt the warmth of the hugs and kisses. Everyone she loved believed she died three years ago in a plane crash, along with Richard Hollingsworth.

Only three people in the world knew she hadn't been on that plane three years ago.

Kristina Miller, her current alias.

US Marshal Stevens.

And Richard Hollingsworth.

❧

"Bosco here. She went in a while ago and hasn't left her townhouse since. No, she didn't see me. Okay."

The man, dressed in all black, gave short, clipped answers into the burner phone. He was accustomed to waiting out his targets and knew how to be invisible when he needed to be. He'd noticed she was suddenly on edge when she returned from her run, but she had been more relaxed when she first left. Something along the way spooked her. When she opened the paper, he could visibly see the panic rising in her.

He had been outside her home, watching her for a few days now, and knew she ran in the same area even though she never used the same route. She varied her routine from day to day so she could tell if someone was following her.

Smart girl. Just not smart enough, evidently. He smirked.

She hadn't seen him watching from behind the trees in the park or from his tree stand in the woods across the street from her townhouse. But from her demeanor at the end of her run, he concluded that she knew something was off. From years of watching people, gathering intelligence on them, and using that intelligence against them, he'd learned to sense when his presence had been detected.

He saw the curtains move ever so slightly in the upstairs window and knew she was looking along the tree line. Maybe if she had just looked a little higher, she would have spotted him. But for now, luck was on his side. She had no clue where he was, and he was prepared to stay there as long as needed. He'd been in worse conditions than this, even with the threat of rain. This job was a piece of cake. He straightened his legs to rest on a nearby tree branch, folded his arms behind his head, and waited.

In Miami, Richard Hollingsworth hung up the hotel phone after his call to Bosco and smiled. Soon, all the loose ends from the past would be taken care of. Three long years, he'd looked for her. That nosy, investigative reporter bitch wouldn't quit digging until she'd discovered his secret life and made him go into hiding. He'd figured out that she was onto him just in time—just before he was arrested and sent to prison for life, or worse, hung for treason.

Vengeance would soon be his.

A knock on his hotel door drew his attention. As he opened the door, he was drawn into a hug by a grizzly of a man, his best friend from years ago.

"Noah Steele, so good to see you, brother," Richard welcomed him.

1

CHAPTER ONE

Five Years Earlier

"Mom! I can't find my sunglasses!" Brianna yelled from her bedroom.

Diana stopped at her doorway. "They're on your head, Brianna."

Her hands flew to the top of her head. Finding them there, she smiled ruefully. "Oh. There they are."

"Relax, sweetheart. Your father has made sure you'll be very well guarded while you're away. The best soldiers will surround you in our military." Diana tried to reassure Brianna, even though, inwardly, she felt anything but happy about her daughter's choice.

"I know." She plopped down on her bed. "It's just that it'll be such a huge change. I won't be able to run to the store and get whatever I need, no takeout food. I'm leaving behind so many of the things I take for granted now."

"It'll definitely be a change of pace for you," Diana agreed as she sat beside her daughter.

Evan, Brianna's dad, walked up to the doorway, leaned against the doorframe, and watched his oldest daughter. It seemed like only yesterday when she was born. Looking back over the past few months, he was astonished at how effectively her powers of persuasion had worked on him. Somehow, she had convinced him that her true calling was in investigative reporting—in the Middle East.

Evan and Diana Tate owned a chain of luxury hotels across the United States. Their home and headquarters were in the Atlanta area, but Evan often traveled to Washington, DC to secure hotel contracts, negotiate rates, and maintain his hotel's security clearance for the VIP visits. During those visits, he made many friends who had contacts in every imaginable branch of the government.

When Brianna first approached him with her request for a special assignment to interview the elite Delta Force unit of the Army at a ghost base in the Middle East, Evan feared she'd made an immature, rash decision. Watching her pack, check items off her list, and recheck again, he saw the maturity of a determined young lady.

Still, he was her father, and he worried about his daughter's safety. "Don't make me regret this, young lady," he warned.

"Never, Daddy." Her smile beamed back at him. "This is the trip and the chance of a lifetime!"

"I can't believe you're leaving us in a week. You'll be gone for six weeks," Evan complained.

"It'll fly by, and I'll be back before you know it. I guarantee it." Brianna replied confidently, even though she hid her trepidations at leaving the comfort and security of her life.

At twenty-two, she had recently graduated with a dual bachelor's degree in communications and journalism with big plans for her future career. While in college, Brianna threw herself into her studies, taking extra classes and pushing herself so she could get out into the world and start living as soon as possible. Using this assignment as her career springboard was a gamble, but it was one she knew was right for her. The thrill of the story, getting out into the field, and putting her feet to the street was where her heart knew she belonged.

The following night, Brianna's sisters, Missy, Jessie, and Ashley, coordinated a surprise going-away party to celebrate her first big assignment and freelance job since graduating college. Missy had just turned twenty-one and was closest to Brianna in every way. Growing up not quite two years apart in age had them sharing everything from clothes to toys to boys. Missy's job was to bring Brianna to the party without giving away the surprise.

"Get ready, sis! I'm taking you out for a drink or ten. We need some quality sister time before you go jetting off to the godforsaken desert," Missy demanded as she barged into Brianna's room. "You're depriving me of six weeks of quality time, so I expect you to make it up to me tonight."

"Fine. But only because I know you won't leave me alone until I do," Brianna replied with a smile.

"You know me so well."

Once in the car, Missy and Brianna chatted casually until they reached their destination. Brianna was bouncing with excitement as they entered their favorite sports bar. Talking animatedly with Missy about her upcoming assignment, she completely missed the room full of people gathered to see her off.

"Surprise," the crowd yelled in unison.

Brianna jumped, let out a shriek, and quickly clasped her hands over her mouth. Her eyes were wide open, the shock evident on her face, and she was stunned speechless. Missy wrapped her arm around Brianna's shoulder and, leaning into her, asked, "Did I do good? Or did I do good?"

Brianna nodded before she spoke. "You definitely did well. I had no idea!"

Finally moving her feet, she made her way around the room to greet each partygoer individually. Virtually everyone she knew was there to wish her well. The party was in full swing with a packed dance floor and drinks flowing freely. By the end of the night, Brianna had lost count of how many drinks she'd fulfilled on her IOU to Missy.

When Evan approached her, his eyes conveyed his concern over her leaving. He held out his arms, and she rushed into them for a final father-daughter dance before they closed the bar. Swaying slowly in her father's arms, Brianna felt like a little girl again. She couldn't imagine not having him in her life every day, but moving on with her independence was like a siren's call. She couldn't ignore it, and she couldn't resist it.

Early one morning the following week, Evan and Diana drove Brianna to a secure military airfield. With tears in her eyes, Diana hugged her daughter tightly to her a little longer than a typical goodbye.

"I know you're in good hands, but you won't be in my hands," she said as she released Brianna and wiped her eyes.

"Don't worry, Mom." Brianna smiled reassuringly. "I'm all grown up now. I can take care of myself."

"It doesn't matter how old you are, young lady. You'll always be my baby," Diana replied. "Don't wander off alone. Stay with your escorts. Stay safe. Don't do anything stupid."

Chuckling, Brianna nodded. "You've told me that about fifty times this morning already, and the sun isn't even up yet. Not that I'll have much choice, but I'll stay close to my military escorts, and I won't wander off alone. I'll be back before you know it."

Diana dabbed her watery eyes again and drew in a ragged breath as she watched the soldiers begin to board the large military aircraft. Evan stepped forward, pulling Brianna into a bear hug, and whispered into her ear, "Come back home to us safe and in one piece. I love you, little girl."

"I love you, too, Daddy," she replied, her voice cracking. "I'd better go now."

Releasing her from his embrace, Evan and Diana watched as she boarded a C-17 military transport plane leaving out of the Atlanta area and bound for the ghost base in the Middle East. A deep feeling of dread settled in Evan's gut. He worried about his daughters enough as it was, but not knowing exactly where Brianna would be for the next six weeks made him physically ache.

As Brianna stepped aboard the plane, she immediately knew her days of pampered and comfortable living were coming to a screeching halt. A new respect for the men and women of the military grew in her mind. She decided to capitalize on that and spread it to every news outlet that would pick up her story. Ignoring the headache that threatened to make it a rough trip, she pulled out her notebook and started making notes on the topics she wanted to cover.

Since Delta Force operators are considered so clandestine that the government didn't even acknowledge their existence, her approval was granted only because the Department of Defense confidential contact was a former Delta Force operative himself and wanted the team to receive the accolades they deserved. He had already given her a list of topics that were off-limits to discuss with civilians. She knew if she asked anything classified, no one would answer her anyway. He was merely trying to save her a little trouble and frustration and help get her started on the right foot.

Settling into the uncomfortable seat for the twenty-hour flight, Brianna inserted the earplugs she'd tucked into her pocket. Knowing the planes were known to be noisy inside, she'd already researched the best methods for surviving the long flight. Many of the seats had been removed to make room for the cargo being delivered, allowing the couple dozen people onboard to spread out. Some brought blow-up mats and sleeping bags to help them pass the time after takeoff.

Brianna was too focused on her own mission and how well her article would be received once she returned home to sleep now. She considered what the public would want to know about the team. She wanted to give them due credit for their skills, the intense training they survived, and the improvised ways they kept their skills sharp. She planned to describe the less-than-desirable conditions they lived in so far from home and the lack of creature comforts most people took for granted.

But most of all, she wanted her article to remind people that, at the end of the day, these battle-hardened warriors were still just men. Courage didn't mean there was a lack of fear—it meant they carried on in spite of their fear. They had dreams and lives outside the military. They had families, wives, girlfriends, and friends they didn't see for long stretches of time.

When the plane reached cruising altitude, several people created makeshift beds on the floor of the aircraft and made themselves comfortable. Anxious to get started, Brianna briefly considered changing seats to begin talking to the service men and women on the plane with her but changed her mind when she realized the engine noise alone would prevent a lengthy conversation.

Brianna decided that a detailed diary of everything she saw, heard, felt, and experienced on her journey would help her to create the most descriptive article she could produce. With that thought, she began the arduous task of detailing every thought, decision, and conversation that led up to this assignment.

Spending most of the flight time filling the blank pages with her thoughts and feelings, Brianna began to see a story forming as her words flowed from her fingers. When she could no longer keep her eyes open or hold the pen with her cramped hand, she reclined the seat as far back as it would go and slept for the remainder of the flight.

The pilot's voice booming over the intercom and the flashing lights alerting the crew of an impending landing woke her. Gathering and stowing her things in her backpack, she couldn't stop her legs from bouncing with nervous energy as she waited to begin her exciting adventure. By the time it came to a halt and she was able to deplane, she could hardly stand the anticipation.

As she was easily recognizable in her civilian clothing, the escort team immediately picked her out of the crowd. "Miss Tate?" One of the young soldiers addressed her.

"Yes, I'm Brianna Tate." She smiled.

"Come with us, ma'am. We have strict orders to deliver you right away," he replied.

She noticed he wore the military police left armband and insignia. His name band read Roberts. "Okay, Lieutenant Roberts, lead the way."

He smiled politely as three other MPs surrounded her and led her to the waiting Humvee. Once they were securely seated inside, one of the men tied a black blindfold around her head. "Sorry, ma'am. Orders."

"It's fine. I've already been warned about the security measures." She smiled.

Brianna attempted to stay alert to the subtle noises, shifts in the vehicle, and stilted conversations inside the vehicle. She made mental notes of everything she needed to document in her diary. The vehicle slowed to a stop after several minutes of riding, and she heard three doors open and close. She had to consciously fight back the panic that tried to settle in when she heard more male voices in her near proximity, but no one spoke directly to her.

Lieutenant Roberts's voice startled her when he spoke close to her ear. "Miss Tate, I'm getting you out of the vehicle now and transferring you to another one. This is as far as I'm allowed to take you. These guys will take good care of you from here."

"Okay," she replied, knowing she had no other choice.

After changing vehicles and driving for another hour, she finally felt the vehicle come to a stop and then heard the engine cut off. An unseen person opened her door and helped her out of the vehicle.

When her blindfold was removed, the bright sun blinded her momentarily. Shielding her eyes with her hand as she absently dug her sunglasses out of her bag, she stood motionless for a moment to take in her surroundings. Her initial reaction was that the compound resembled the old TV show *MASH*, only this one had sand-colored tents instead of the standard Army green.

Large tents were scattered throughout the base. Humvees, Jeeps, and large trucks moved slowly through the streets. Troops were spread out in units of three to five. Each team handled different functions to keep the small city running smoothly.

The sun was high overhead and incredibly hot, hotter than Atlanta ever thought of being. Beads of sweat immediately sprang to the surface of her skin. She retrieved one of her notebooks from her backpack and began fanning herself to try to relieve the intense heat. One of her first questions for the men who'd agreed to an interview had already formed in her mind. How do you condition your body to stand this intense heat?

"This way, ma'am," the private carrying her luggage instructed. "Since you're our guest, you'll have your own private tent. It's right over here."

She strode toward the tent her escort pointed out with purpose, feeling both grateful and guilty for receiving special treatment. She began to mentally prepare herself for how she should approach the band of elusive soldiers. Delta Force operators were known for being the quiet professionals. They didn't boast about their missions to anyone. Handling the most extreme cases, they got in and out of a volatile area without anyone knowing they'd even been there.

As they rounded the corner of a tent, Brianna's feet halted involuntarily as her eyes drank in the sight of the men directly in front of her. One man sat in a folding chair, wearing his government-issued hat, Oakley sunglasses, no shirt, and his fatigue pants rolled up to his knees. He was working on his tan, but she couldn't tear her eyes from his chiseled chest, the muscles in his shoulders, his arms and… oh wow, his six-pack abs. She was glad she was wearing her sunglasses because she did not doubt that her eyes were as big as saucers.

His thighs were apparently just as cut as the top half of him from the form of his pants. Brianna's eyes drifted up to his face, and she instantly turned an even deeper shade of red than she already was from the heat of the scorching sun. From his megawatt smile, she knew she had been busted practically drooling over the man.

"Are you our new recruit?" There was a smile in his deep voice, teasing her, and clearly pleased that she liked what she saw.

"Um…I'm…uh…Brianna." There wasn't a coherent thought in her mind. She had no idea how she even strung those words together.

He continued smiling as he stood. Brianna couldn't hide her shock as she drew in a sharp breath. The man was huge. He had muscles bulging everywhere, and he towered over her five-foot-six-inch frame. She knew he had to be at least six-foot-four and every inch of him was rock solid.

He had short black hair, a strong, square jawline, and high cheekbones. Even though Bri couldn't see his eyes, she could feel them piercing through her. She knew she must look like an idiot just standing and staring at him, but she had literally never seen anyone like him in real life.

So much for making a good first impression, she thought to herself ruefully.

"Well, Brianna," he continued, still smiling. "Good to meet you. I'm Reaper. Meet the rest of the team." He gestured to the other men sitting in the ragged lawn chairs strewn around the outside of the tent. "This is Rebel. This here's Bull. That one is Shadow—watch out for him, and this is Judge."

Each man nodded and smiled as she said hello after Reaper introduced each of them.

Looking at the group, she smiled. "No real names. Got it."

"Maybe we can keep this one, Reap," the one called Shadow replied. "Be nice if you didn't have to hide another body today."

"The day is still young. He may have to help me hide your body before long," Brianna retorted with a playful smile.

"Oh yeah, we're keeping her all right," Rebel replied with a laugh. "Already putting Shadow in his place. I love it."

Sharing a laugh seemed to quickly break the ice between all of them, except one. Bull was the quietest man of the group and didn't smile at all. Sensing that she'd have a hard time cracking his exterior shell, she resolved to win his trust and get him to talk to her before she left this secret camp.

As she looked around at the men surrounding her, she realized that every one of them was built like a linebacker. Every inch of their bodies was covered in muscles. Every man was tall, had a thick, muscular body, and seemed to be entirely at home in these harsh surroundings.

She quickly realized these specially trained operators were able to assimilate anywhere they went because of the rigorous training they had to complete. They all also obviously took exercise and staying healthy very seriously, judging from the looks of these men.

The private cleared his throat, reminding them that he was still waiting with her belongings. Instantly feeling bad over forgetting about him, Brianna quickly finished her own introduction. "As I said, I'm Brianna Tate. I'm here on assignment to interview you and shed light on what you do for your country, why you do it, what your life out here is like, and to promote support for you to the general public.

"I'll get unpacked, and we can get started if that's okay with you."

"Sounds great," Reaper replied. After Reaper gave the private a quick nod, Brianna noticed that he turned and quickly deposited her luggage in her tent without a verbal command.

Her assignment would take the entire six weeks, and she planned to spend the majority of that time asking a lot of questions and generally getting to know each soldier. They seemed to understand her assignment and that she genuinely wanted to give them credit for the work they were doing.

Thirty minutes later, she walked back to the area where she'd left them and found everyone still there, except for Bull.

"So, who wants to go first?" she asked with a smile.

"I will," Reaper replied, removing his sunglasses and flashing his perfect smile. "Let's go over here so we can be more comfortable."

Brianna and Reaper moved to a picnic-style table in a shaded area of the camp. It was far enough away from the others that she could comfortably ask probing questions without making anyone uncomfortable. She hoped it would also ensure more in-depth answers from her participants.

"So, Reaper, huh? How'd you get that nickname?" she asked as they took a seat.

"My squadron's nicknames come from our personalities and things we're good at," he answered evasively.

"They also keep your identity secret, especially between assignments, right?" Brianna asked.

"That's right," Reaper replied.

"Am I going to have a difficult time getting to know you?" Brianna asked, trying to throw him off guard.

No such luck.

His smile slowly crawled across his face. His white teeth sparkled even in the shade, along with the mirth dancing in his blue eyes. "Most likely."

"I assume you're the leader of this squadron?"

"I am," he confirmed. "We're all officers, but I'm the ranking officer. If you tell anyone, I'll deny it and then kill you in your sleep."

"Your secret is safe with me." Brianna crossed her heart. "No need to get all scary on me."

Reaper laughed and relaxed a little. "Occupational hazard."

"I literally can't imagine. That's why I'm here. There are obviously things you can't tell me, but I'd love to tell others about you and the rest of the team to make them understand your sacrifices," Brianna replied earnestly.

Reaper carefully watched Brianna, taking in every detail of her face, posture, and body language. His training and field experience in counterterrorism, counter-surveillance, and reading micro-expressions taught him how to read and decipher a person in record time. From his assessment, she was a trusting, honest, and naïve young lady, who sincerely wanted to do a good job with her first assignment.

Plus, he'd already received a detailed background report on her before she ever boarded the plane in Atlanta. He already knew every detail of her life and anyone remotely acquainted with her. Too much was on the line for circumstances to be any different. Lives were at stake, his best friends' lives, and he wouldn't allow anyone to risk them any more than absolutely necessary.

"Okay, Brianna, fair enough. I'm sure you were briefed on what we won't discuss, but we'll help you as much as we can with your article. I'll make sure the other guys in my squadron actively participate, too. We get to read and approve it before it goes to print, though."

"Thank you so much. You have no idea how much this means to me," she gushed before smiling brightly at him.

When Brianna's eyes met his, Reaper's response was completely foreign to him. He remained calm and collected when an enemy fired a high-powered rifle at him. He could single-handedly take out multiple terrorists in a hostage situation without batting an eye or harming one hostage in the process.

But when Brianna gave him her most sincere, appreciative smile, he couldn't catch his breath. His heart sped up, skipped beats, and fluttered wildly in his chest. The warmth spread throughout his body, and his senses tingled strangely. She was definitely different from anyone he'd ever met.

"I'm looking forward to getting to know you much better over the next several weeks, Miss Tate," Reaper stated, crossing his muscular arms across his body.

Her eyes followed their movement, mesmerized by both the size and fluidity of his muscles. Darting her tongue out to wet her lips as her eyes slowly rose first to his mouth then met his gaze, she sharply inhaled when she felt his gaze physically touch her.

"I thought I was doing the interviewing here," she uttered, barely above a whisper.

"We'll just have to see about that. Won't we?"

2

CHAPTER TWO

The first week in the desert was the roughest week of Brianna's life. The intense heat in the triple digits during the day barely dropped below ninety degrees at night. Acclimating to the harshness was a slow process for her. She developed yet another new level of appreciation for the men and women who didn't have the luxury of time for their bodies to accept the changes.

She'd spent the majority of the week being Reaper's personal shadow. She followed him around the base, took notes of his actions, behaviors, and reactions, and she tried to build a character profile of him. She knew she wouldn't be allowed to use his nickname in her article, but she could give him a fake name and accurately describe him for her readers.

He was well-liked by everyone they encountered. Other than occasionally wearing BDUs, he was never in full uniform. After several days of watching his nonconformity to routine Army regulations, she finally garnered the nerve to ask him about it.

"Reaper, why do you not wear the standard-issue uniform?"

"My job doesn't require it. We have more lax rules than the average soldier because of the duties we're expected to perform. If I had to leave quickly to handle an issue in a large city, I have to be able to get in and out without giving away my real identity," he explains with a shrug.

"So what other regulations are you allowed to break?" she asked, intrigued.

Reaper cut his eyes to meet hers, considered what he should say, before finally answering. "Most all of them. Whatever it takes to get the job done."

She already knew Reaper was the leader of the squadron since he'd already confirmed as much. She thought she'd caught a lucky break when she overheard another soldier refer to him as Captain. Unfortunately, the private didn't follow up with his last name, and Reaper quickly shut him down from referring to him with that title again.

"I thought I was about to get lucky," Brianna blurted out.

Reaper tilted his head, humor alight in his eyes, and wore a smirk as he contemplated his reply. "I'm pretty sure that's supposed to be my line."

Her face burned with embarrassment as she gasped and buried her face in her hands. "You know what I mean," she insisted. "I thought the private was about to give away your name," she clarified, raising her eyes to meet his.

Reaper chuckled and nodded. "You may be right. But I guess it's not time for your turn yet." He grinned.

Brianna stared at him for as long as she could suppress her laugh. "Fine. You win this round. I'll have my turn, though."

"One can hope." Reaper smiled broadly.

"Yep. You're trouble. No doubt about it." Brianna shook her head but returned his smile. He was more than charming and witty, and she already knew she was getting in over her head with him.

"It's sexy when you blush. Especially when I'm the one who made you do it."

She blushed again and tucked her chin to her chest in an attempt to hide her smile. His chuckle rumbled through his chest and forced her to close her eyes as it rippled through her body.

Reaper didn't have to be telepathic to know what images flashed through her mind.

"Come on. You can go with me today," Reaper offered.

"Really? Where are we going?" Brianna perked up. Her eyes widened, her lips slightly parted, and her smile engulfed her face.

She pictured going on a special operation with him. One where she was hidden behind a thick, armored car and was safe from any harm, and it provided her with a bird's-eye view of the action. Realistically, she knew that would never happen, but an aspiring journalist could dream.

"To the shooting range."

"On a first date? That's a little forward, don't you think?" Brianna joked. "I bet you take all the girls there."

"Nope. Only the ones that I'm fairly certain won't use me as the target," he deadpanned.

"Oh, so you trust me with a gun?"

"Have you ever shot one?" Reaper raised one eyebrow as his all-seeing eyes assessed her.

"Only a BB gun when I was a kid," she admitted.

"That's why I'm fairly certain you won't shoot me. I don't think you could hit me."

"Oh, you! Every time I think you're being a nice guy, you have to talk more and totally ruin it." She laughed as she playfully hit his arm.

"Come on. I'll teach you how to shoot so you can protect yourself," Reaper said. He hooked his arm around Bri's neck and pulled her with him.

The simple fact was Brianna enjoyed the time she spent with Reaper. He had an outgoing personality that made him easy to get along with, but she'd also seen the dominant, take-no-prisoners side of him. She felt sorry for anyone who had to face that part of him in a dark alley because only one would walk away in one piece. She was positive that would be Reaper.

"Wait here." Reaper released his hold on her just outside the door of the command tent. "I'll grab the keys and be right back."

When he returned with the keys, he also had a long, black cloth to use as a blindfold for Brianna.

"Really? You still don't trust me?" Her face fell, and she quickly tried to recover. From the knowing glance he gave her, she realized she didn't entirely hide the disappointment evident in her voice.

Reaper gave her a small, understanding smile. "It's not that I don't trust you, Brianna. But if you fell into the enemy's hands, they would get the location of this camp out of you. Then every life here would be in jeopardy. I have to do everything I can to help protect the integrity of this base."

"I understand," she conceded. "I wouldn't want to be responsible for putting anyone else in danger."

"That's my girl." Reaper smiled. "Hop in, and I'll blindfold you." He waggled his eyebrows suggestively at her.

"Such a sweet-talker," she mumbled as she climbed into the Humvee.

Reaper stood at her door and secured the blindfold around her eyes. "That's not too tight, is it?"

"No, it's fine."

"Okay, let's go, then."

Brianna felt the movement of the Humvee as Reaper drove them to the shooting range. She had a distinct feeling there were unnecessary turns and stops along the way. Bri had no doubt it was a tactic to throw off her sense of direction. She decided to keep it to herself that he was wasting his time. She was merely glad to spend time with him and wasn't paying too much attention to the direction they were heading.

When the vehicle finally came to a stop, Reaper killed the engine and helped Brianna to get out. Removing her blindfold, she finally got a good look at her surroundings. The rock ledges that encircled them were covered in sand but gave them some shade and natural cover. A small, makeshift shooting range had been erected with the targets clearly marked at intervals between fifteen and fifty yards.

After he removed his handgun from the holster, Reaper gave Brianna instructions on how to hold it, how to chamber a round, and how to squeeze the trigger while maintaining her aim on the target. After she'd spent several rounds, Brianna learned that she was a natural at sharpshooting.

"We may have to sign you up," Reaper praised her.

"This part is fun. I'm not sure I'd make it through the rest of basic training," Brianna chuckled.

"I'll bet you're stronger than you give yourself credit for." Reaper's ordinarily teasing tone had disappeared, replaced with sincerity.

The chemistry between Brianna and Reaper became a living, breathing being. Accidental touches that would normally be dismissed with someone else suddenly became cause for sparks to fly. While showing her how to stand and hold the gun, Reaper had to wrap his arms around her and adjust her body stance with his hands.

If I were teaching a man, I'd find a different way to show him, Reaper thought to himself. The fact that he knew he permitted himself to touch her didn't help his resolve to keep it professional. Her personality and beauty quickly got under his skin.

"So, tell me about Reaper," Brianna asked when they took a break.

"What do you want to know?" Reaper drew up to his full height, his muscles tensed, and his eyes narrowed at her.

"For starters, where are you from?"

"The vicinity of Miami." His eyes scanned the horizon as he shrugged nonchalantly.

"Do you have family there?"

"Yes. But I don't have a relationship with them anymore," he admitted. He didn't speak of his family with anyone, and he wasn't sure why he even confided that to Brianna.

"I'm sorry to hear that. It must be hard for you." She unconsciously placed her hand on his arm as she spoke.

"I've gotten used to it. What about you?" he asked, ready to be the interviewer and not the one interviewed.

"Atlanta." She tilted her head and gave him a small smile. "And yes, my family is there. I'm close to my mom, dad, and my three sisters, Missy, Jessie, and Ashley. I'm the oldest of the four. Missy is less than two years younger than me, so we've always been very close."

"What do they think about you traveling halfway around the world to come hang out with me?"

"They worry, but they're supportive. My dad actually helped me get this assignment. Your squadron isn't exactly the easiest to find." She smiled.

"No, I guess we're not. I'm glad you did, though."

"So, what else do you like to do besides shoot guns?" Brianna changed the subject abruptly.

"When I'm home, I like to go out with my friends, hang out at this club not far from my stomping grounds, and maybe dance a song or two with a hot girl."

"Do you have a girlfriend or wife waiting at home for you?" Brianna held her breath and inwardly cringed as she waited for his answer.

"No, nothing like that," he replied easily. "Even though the Army prefers that operators are married, I've somehow managed to avoid that so far."

"How old are you?"

"Twenty-nine. You?"

"Twenty-two," she replied.

"And do you have a boyfriend back home, Brianna?" Reaper stepped into her personal space as he pierced her with his gaze.

"No, no boyfriend. Not anymore anyway."

"Good." He nodded. He stood rooted to the ground, soaking in her sweet scent as it enveloped him. The urge to touch her suddenly overwhelmed his senses. He took a step back as he quickly checked his watch. "I should get you back to the base now."

He checked their surroundings carefully before he walked her back to the vehicle, secured her blindfold, and began the drive back to the base in silence. The personal conversation felt foreign to Reaper. He'd been one of the youngest operators ever to make it into the team, and it had become his life, the only way of life he knew how to live. One thing he thought he knew for sure was that he wasn't cut out for a serious relationship.

Spending an afternoon with Brianna, simply shooting at targets and talking about any and everything, was starting to make him rethink his position on the subject. He had never been able to picture having a wife and family before now. She was precisely the type of person that could make him want that very thing. The very kind of woman that could make him look forward to leaving this line of work behind just to be home with her every night.

In his mind, that very line of thinking was what would get an operator killed quicker than anything. It was true that the Army preferred married operators since they were less likely to be entrapped by a female enemy. But in Reaper's view, having his mind on his family back home and not solely on the mission at hand was even more dangerous.

When they reached the camp, Reaper removed the blindfold and called Rebel over to them.

"Your turn, man," Reaper said. "Hope you had fun today, Brianna."

She felt the sting of his sudden departure to her core. Her mouth dropped open momentarily before she caught herself. She swallowed hard and stammered out her reply. "Yeah, I did. Thanks for taking me to the shooting range, Reaper. I really appreciate it."

He heard the confused tone in her voice, gritted his teeth together, and simply nodded at her. "Anytime."

With that, he left her alone with Rebel. And he left her very confused.

She turned to face Rebel and decided to jump right into why she was there in the first place. "So, Rebel, where'd your nickname come from?"

He gave a good-natured chuckle at her question. Rebel thought about his answer for a few seconds.

"It's what I am—a rebel. I go against the grain of what most others do and say. They say I always play devil's advocate and argue the opposite view, even if I inwardly agree with them.

"The truth is, I just like to look at all the angles and make sure everyone else does, too. I'm what you'd call the most level-headed of the group. I can easily see the pros and cons of any situation and help bring balance to the team."

Brianna thought about his self-description and agreed with his assessment. Rebel was tall, had a light beard and a completely shaved head. He was obviously in great physical shape with his thick, muscular arms and chest. His broad chest tapered down to his waist, his six-pack abs showing through the tight cotton T-shirt he wore. His legs were also muscular, indicating he was thorough with his workouts. Evidence of tattoos occasionally tried to peek out from under the cuffs of his sleeves.

"How old are you?" she asked, truly interested.

"I'm thirty," he answered easily.

"Is that close to an average age for operators?"

"It's actually a little younger than the average age. It takes several years of service and training to become a full-fledged operator. Our boy Reaper is as smart as he is tough, so he was one of the youngest ever to make it. I think he had a lot to prove to himself and others, though. That helped drive him to where he is today," Rebel explained.

Brianna didn't ask, but she had a strong feeling that Reaper felt like he needed to prove himself to his family. The one he wouldn't talk about.

"Do you have a girlfriend or wife back home?" Brianna asked.

"No one to speak of," Rebel replied. "I have family—my parents and my brother."

"I have my parents and my three sisters," Brianna shared.

"Reaper mentioned he took you to the shooting range?" Rebel asked.

"Yeah, he did. Taught me how to shoot his handgun—how to chamber the bullet, hit the target, and quickly recycle. I did pretty well."

"I'm sure you did. While you're here, I can show you some hand-to-hand techniques that can save you. We try to avoid the close-quarter skirmishes, but when we have to take someone down that way, we're the best at it."

"I'd like that. You never know when I'll be walking through a dark parking garage and some freak comes up behind me," Brianna replied.

"Exactly. And I can show you how to make that bastard wish he'd never laid eyes on you."

"Sounds great. Right after we finish our interview questions," Brianna negotiated.

With a groan of disapproval, Rebel finally relented. "You should know by now that operators don't talk about themselves much. This is painful."

"If you can handle all the training you've been through, you can answer a few personal questions for me," Brianna countered.

"Let's get this over with," Rebel agreed, leading her to a more private area to share his personal information. "What do you want to know?"

"Where do you call home?"

Rebel grinned mischievously. "Wherever I hang my hat."

"Oh no, you don't. I want real answers," Brianna challenged, pointing her finger at him in a mock show of authority.

Rebel threw his head back and laughed out loud at her bravado. "Okay, okay. I'm originally from Houston, Texas."

"How long have you been in the military?"

"Since just after I turned eighteen, so twelve years."

"Do you still go home to Texas when you're on leave?" Brianna asked, genuinely interested in how he transitioned from soldier to citizen.

"Sometimes." He dropped his eyes to the ground. "I actually moved a couple of years ago and have an apartment close to Reaper."

Brianna realized there was something personal there that he didn't want to talk about, so she decided to change her line of questioning.

"Would it be easier for you to talk about the other men in your group rather than yourself? I can ask you questions about them, and you can dish all the dirt to me." Brianna's smile was playful, but she had a method to her madness. If they agreed to this, she knew she'd find out much more than if each man gave the information about himself.

"Actually, I think that's a great idea." Rebel stroked his beard with his thumb and forefinger. His eyes were cast to a faraway spot as he considered the option. "Let me talk to the other guys, make sure we're all okay with it first."

Brianna's stomach picked that moment to growl loudly. Rebel's hand slowly dropped from his face as his eyes floated to meet hers. The question in them was unmistakable, causing Brianna to blush for the hundredth time in the same day.

"Good timing," she muttered as her eyes roamed around, looking for anywhere else to land but on Rebel's amused gaze. "Guess that's my cue to go get something to eat. Let me know if they agree. If they do, you can give me the inside scoop on all of them."

"Okay." He nodded, his tone still holding amusement as he rose. "Come on. I'll walk with you to the mess hall."

3

CHAPTER THREE

Before Brianna had finished her meal, the four men suddenly disappeared. Without being told, she knew they'd been called out on a secret mission, and it would probably be quite a while before she saw them again. She sighed heavily with disappointment as she solemnly put her tray away and retreated to her tent. Sitting on her cot, she separated her notes into different piles to begin working on her article.

She had made several personal notes about the men she hadn't had a chance to interview thoroughly yet. Though she'd spent time around all of them as a group, she tried to focus on one at a time when she was in interview mode.

Bull was as big as a bull, though his build was somewhat different from the others. Bull's muscles weren't as cut as Reaper's, but he was taller and thicker. With those that he knew well, he was easy-going and liked to joke around. He was more reserved around outsiders, and it took longer for her to break through his wall than with the others. Once she finally did get through that tough exterior, she felt she'd have a friend for life. However, her instincts told her never to take that friendship for granted. Once his trust was betrayed, there would be no gaining it back.

Shadow often snuck up behind her, without making a sound, and scared the shit out of her. She wondered how men that big could move as stealthily as a typical house cat. He couldn't even scratch his own back because his muscles were too big for him to reach around, but he could move silently behind his unsuspecting victims. His booming laugh when she jumped out of her skin, repeatedly, was infectious, and she could never stay mad at him.

And then there was Judge. He had been Reaper's best friend in high school, and even though he wasn't part of Reaper's direct team, the remnants of their old friendship were still evident. Judge also was built like the others, but he had blond hair, blue-green eyes, and had a much more cynical personality. Where Bull was hard to get to know, Judge was hard to like. His character didn't seem to mesh with the group overall, which forced Reaper to run interference frequently.

Brianna made a quick note to ask if that was the reason why Judge wasn't on Reaper's team.

After several hours passed, she heard a small commotion outside and moved to the door to investigate. In small groups, people scurried to the Delta tent. One of the soldiers she'd met earlier passed by, smiled, and motioned for her to join them. She quickly slipped her shoes on, fell in with the others, and stepped into the large tent.

The chairs and cots had been moved to the sides, and a makeshift dance floor was prominently displayed in the middle of the tent. One man used his phone to act as a DJ, changing songs to match the mood of the partygoers. They used their footlockers as coolers, with beer bottles chilling on ice, and others began arranging tables with snacks in various locations throughout the tent.

More and more people from the base joined in the revelry and enjoyed a "night on the town" in the middle of nowhere. The impromptu party brought everyone on the base together as friends, brothers, and sisters, giving them a feeling of being at home. Two by two, couples moved to the dance floor and moved in tandem to the music.

The music was rocking, and everyone was having a great time. Brianna's eyes roamed around the tent, taking in the scene, but she still felt out of place. Her breath seized in her chest when she saw Reaper leaned against a post inside the tent, holding his chilled beer bottle. He laughed at someone's weak attempt at a popular dance move, but his gorgeous smile, tall, muscular physique, black hair, and chocolate brown eyes were all she could see.

Their playful flirting over the past couple of weeks had tortured her in her dreams. Repeatedly seeing Reaper every night made the days with him harder to bear without giving away her thoughts. Feeling his presence inside the tent overpowered her senses.

After the first song ended, the slow, sensual melody of Def Leppard's "Love Bites" immediately streamed through the speakers. Brianna was talking with one of the female soldiers, trying to keep her attention on the conversation, but her eyes involuntarily grazed over the crowd.

She silently gasped when she realized Reaper had been watching her. His lips curled into a sensuous smile, while mischief danced in his beautiful brown eyes. She felt a flutter in her chest that settled low in her abdomen, but she couldn't tear her eyes away from his. She felt a smile creep across her face, despite any attempt to keep it inside. From the fire in his eyes, he knew what he did to her insides. He turned them into molten liquid.

By the time she fully comprehended his sights were set on her, he had already pushed against the pole and walked halfway across the floor, directly toward her. She stood still as if rooted to the floor, unable to move as he cut through the densely packed dance floor with ease.

Just like a panther on the prowl, she thought.

"Want to dance?" His sensual voice soothed her nerves while his eyes saw straight through the cool façade she tried to portray.

"Sure." She hoped she at least sounded calm and collected, because inside she was anything but calm. Her heart pounded in her chest, her eyes widened when he touched her hand, and her lips parted with her sharp intake of breath.

He took her hand and led her to the dance floor, then wrapped his strong arms around her waist. She hooked her hands behind his neck as he pulled her closer to his massive body. She liked the way she fit against him, pliable under his touch, and seemed to meld with his body. She tried to think of something else—anything else—before she made a complete fool of herself.

She glanced up and realized he had been watching her intently. She felt like he could read her every thought, like a book that was laid open on full display. The heat that rose in her face was as hot as the sun, and she had the sudden urge to look away from his probing eyes.

She felt the low rumble of his chuckle vibrate in his chest more than she heard it. She looked back up and asked, innocently enough, "What?"

"I love to see you blush. It's so damn sexy."

Well, hell, so much for playing it off, she thought.

She desperately wanted to say something witty back, but she couldn't think of a single comeback.

"Hmmm…I must make you nervous. Nothing to say to that?"

"I'm not nervous. Just not giving in to your mind games!" She reasoned that comeback was only slightly better than just blurting out, *"I want you. Now!"*

"We'll see about that." His sexy smirk told her he knew exactly how much he affected her.

Shadow appeared out of nowhere, per his usual MO, and tried to cut in on their dance. Reaper narrowed his eyes, and his jaw muscles flexed before he quickly masked it. Shadow nonchalantly moved around them to dance with another girl. Brianna realized she just got her first glance at how this team was so effective. She knew they used hand signals to keep from speaking and giving away their location while out on a mission, but they also had their facial cues down to a science.

"What was that look?" she asked Reaper.

"What look?" He didn't even have the decency to look like she'd busted him in the act.

"Yeah. Exactly."

Reaper chuckled easily, and that was the end of that line of questioning.

After several more dances, beer, and ribbing between the

soldiers, Brianna thanked everyone for including her and said she was heading back to her tent. Reaper threw his empty beer bottle in the garbage. "I'll walk you back to your tent," he offered.

She knew that, technically, she wasn't allowed to move around the base after dark without a military escort. But the fact that it was Reaper walking her made her as giddy as a middle school girl with her first boyfriend. She'd felt the spark between them from the moment they first met. She knew all too well that she was only on assignment for a short time. That fact was the sole reason she didn't allow herself to think of him too much.

As they walked along the sand road to her tent, she found it so easy to talk to him about anything and everything. The abrupt ending of their time together earlier that day had been forgotten. His warm, charming side was back in full force, and she was no match for it. He was the one asking all the questions now.

"Do you miss your family yet?"

"Not to sound cold, but not really. I love them, and I'll be glad to see them again, but I'm really enjoying getting to know you and the guys," she explained.

"So, tell me about this ex-boyfriend of yours."

"What ex-boyfriend?" Her eyes whipped to meet his, her feet halted in her steps, and her mind raced with possibilities. Had he looked into her background that thoroughly? Did he have someone check on her ex-boyfriend?

"You said 'no, not anymore.' So, you had one. What happened to him?"

"Oh. Well, it didn't end well, so I don't think about him anymore," Brianna stated matter-of-factly.

"Caught him with someone else, did you?"

She tilted her head to the side, narrowed her eyes, and crossed her arms over her chest as she stared Reaper down for a moment. "How did you know that?"

"Whoa, now." He chuckled, putting his arms up in mock surrender. "Of course, you were thoroughly checked out before you were allowed on base, but remember, I'm a highly trained operative. Besides, it doesn't take a rocket scientist to know from your tone that he did something pretty bad. You're not one to give up on someone so easily."

She relaxed her arms and nodded slowly. "Yes, he cheated on me. I walked in on him and his coworker in bed together. As it turns out, I may not be as sweet and harmless as you think I am."

"Oh, why's that?" Reaper's eyes danced with amusement.

"I'm pleading the Fifth to protect myself. So I can't confirm or deny that I snatched her up by the hair on her head and dragged her out of his apartment. Naked. And threw her into the hallway."

Reaper's laugh echoed through the quiet camp. "And what'd you do to him?"

"Again, I can't confirm or deny my actions. He ran out of the apartment right after I, uh, she left. I may or may not have secretly replaced his shampoo with Nair hair remover. His clothes may or may not have ended up in the garbage can…on fire. And, apparently, he subscribed to every gay, transgender, and cross-dresser dating service known to the internet."

She walked slowly and answered all of his questions about her sisters and her parents. He wanted to know everything about her life growing up, her college years, and what she liked to do for fun. Questions about college led to questions about how she got into journalism.

She explained she didn't want to be an anchorwoman because it was too stuffy and boring for her. Out in the field, with the excitement, was where she saw herself. He also correctly guessed that her parents were not thrilled with her decision to avoid the hotel management career.

It occurred to her he could garner any information he wanted from her in just the phrasing and timing of his questions. She wondered if he learned that from his advanced training or if it just came naturally to him. She knew there was no point in asking. He wouldn't answer any questions about specific training courses anyway.

Just as they reached the entrance of her tent, he grasped her elbow and stopped her in her tracks. As she turned to ask him what was wrong, he wrapped his arms around her waist. She willingly stepped into his arms as he pulled her closer. When he bent to brush his lips against hers, he pulled back for just a second to look into her eyes. She couldn't hide the same desire there that burned in his. He sensed it and covered her mouth with his with a deep, demanding kiss.

His tongue ran across her lips as he teased and tempted her to open her mouth to him. When she did, he dipped his tongue in to caress and dance with hers. Her hands locked behind his neck as she pulled her whole body up close to his. She felt his massive hand run up the back of her neck, grasp her hair in his fist, and tilt her head slightly for him to deepen the kiss even more.

He breathed heavily as he tentatively pulled back from their sensual embrace. He looked around to ensure they were still alone and unseen, then turned back to Brianna. The intensity in his eyes was palpable. It pulled her into him and made her want to succumb to desires she'd never wanted before.

"Reaper, I need to tell you something. As badly as I want this to happen, and believe me when I say I do, I don't do one-night stands."

"Noah Steele."

"What?"

"My name. It's Noah."

"Oh." She wasn't sure what to say at first. No real names were allowed because there was just too much at stake. But he told her without being asked. She didn't know what to make of that. "Noah, I don't mean to lead you on. Really."

"We won't do anything you don't want to do." His voice was low, deep, and so seductive.

"I didn't say I didn't want to…" There was that chuckle that rumbled through his chest again.

"Okay, then, no pressure. I will stop whenever you say." He brushed light kisses along her jawline, to her ear, and down her neck. She knew he must have felt her pulse increase because she could feel her heart pounding.

Barely able to speak now, she almost whispered, "Hmmm…and if I can't say when?"

"I'm here to protect you…even from yourself." He walked her backward into her tent. Then his mouth reclaimed hers with an intense desire and need. Her fingers rested on his massive shoulders, and suddenly her hands ran across his chest, down his stomach, and then around to his back. She couldn't get enough of him. Then she felt his hand splayed across her stomach, underneath her shirt. The heat from his touch seared her skin.

First, his hands traveled up her body, cupping her breast through her bra, the pad of his callused thumb rubbing her sensitive nipple. The traitorous nipple was already hard from his embrace but puckered even more at his touch. A moan escaped her mouth, and he caught it as he deepened the kiss. Then his other hand cupped her ass and pulled her even tighter to him, and she felt his erection pressed against her lower abdomen.

He deftly unhooked her front-clasp bra and ran his hands over her bare breasts, heating the desire that had pooled between her legs even more. He walked her backward, until she was against a pole, and bent his mouth to take her nipple in it. He licked and sucked on it, then drew his teeth over the sensitive skin and ran his hands over her entire midsection.

His hands made their way down her stomach to the button on her jeans. He deftly unbuttoned it with one hand and slowly slid his hand inside. She realized he was giving her ample time to stop him, but she could no more stop him than she could stop breathing. His long fingers reached the top of her lacy panties, and she was instantly glad she was at least wearing attractive ones.

His fingers lightly brushed across the top of the lace and against her stomach, as her fingers dug deeper into his shoulder muscles and the butterflies grew stronger in her stomach. He flattened his hand, and his fingers slipped under the lace, covering her mound and lightly stroking just above where she really needed his hand to be right now.

When she again didn't stop him, she felt his finger reach the mound of ultra-sensitive nerves in her clit, causing intense starbursts behind her eyelids. He rubbed in small circles, making her want him more and more. Then one of his massive fingers stroked along her sensitive folds and suddenly pushed inside her. She moaned deeply, and he pulled back to watch her face. She tried to lean into him, but he wouldn't allow her.

"I want to see you." His low, rumbling voice sounded almost pained with desire.

Even though she felt completely self-conscious and exposed, she trusted him with this intimate moment. He moved his finger slowly in and out of her, torturously slow, as her desire built higher and higher. When she didn't think she could take it anymore, his fingers stopped for a split second as he pushed his index finger and thumb together. He quickly pushed inside her again, rubbing against her most sensitive area as he increased his speed.

"Just let go. Let me watch you come apart in my arms." He was whispering in her ear now, and it was so damn sexy, she couldn't stop. She dug her fists into his shoulders, leaned her head back, and his gaze remained constant on her face. She climaxed with his fingers in her as she released a moan that relayed her complete pleasure. As she lifted her head, his mouth found hers again. But this time, the kiss wasn't urgent or demanding. It was gentle and almost sweet.

She opened her eyes to see him watching her again. "Damn, Bri. You just don't know what you do to me."

Before she could respond, a call came across his radio, ordering the team to the command center. He kissed her again,

"Duty calls."

He stopped at the opening of her tent and turned to look at her. "Don't think this was a one-night stand, Bri. It's not by a long shot." He flashed her that heart-stopping smile of his then he was gone in an instant.

"*What I do to him?*" she thought incredulously.

She spent the rest of the night thinking of Noah. The man had just taken her to a new high, and they hadn't even removed their clothes. Her rational mind immediately went to the fact that this could never work. A long-distance relationship rarely worked under normal circumstances, and this was far from ordinary. He was a man who was stationed half a world away from her. He lived on a little-known, top-secret base, and carried out top-secret missions. She didn't even know precisely where in the world she was.

She decided this wasn't the time for rational thinking. She wanted whatever this was between them to run its course. She didn't want rhyme or reason to take over and complicate things. She'd just enjoy his company while she could. If they weren't meant to be once she returned home, she'd at least have this time and these memories. And she'd never regret them.

4

CHAPTER FOUR

When the team wasn't out on an assignment, Brianna spent as much time with them as possible. She passed the days taking notes on everything they did, filled up her diary with every thought she had, and got to know the men behind the mask, so to speak. She quickly learned she genuinely enjoyed their company. One night, the guys teased Brianna about her lack of security clearance and the need to blindfold her before she could visit their base.

"Poor Brianna, she had to wear a blindfold and didn't even get to have any fun in return for it. She's just not trustworthy, I guess," Shadow joked. "You know, she could be a highly trained spy and has us all fooled into believing she's really innocent."

Shadow leaned forward with his forearms resting on his thighs. He eyed her carefully and pretended he was seriously considering it. "Yeah, look at her shifty eyes. There's no doubt that she's a double agent. We've all been fooled, gentlemen. We should just give up now."

"I'm glad you've finally figured it out. It'll make your surrender much less painful," Bri stated. "For you." She brought her arms up, flexed her biceps, and leaned her head in to kiss her right one. "These guns are deadlier than any gun you own."

The guys all burst out laughing at her gestures. Brianna was most pleased to see that Bull had also joined in on the fun. She'd had the most trouble breaking through his tough exterior. After her talk with Rebel, the guys all agreed to answer questions about each other, and she'd been able to gather much more information since then. Except from Bull. He still didn't trust her and answered her questions with only the bare minimum of words.

She still had the original black cloth that was tied around her eyes from the first time she was brought to the base. "You know," she started. "I still have that first blindfold they used when they brought me out here. I'm keeping it. It's my promise to each of you that no matter what anyone does to me, I will never give you up. I'd never willingly allow anyone to hurt a single one of you. Even though you all have nicknames and I don't have one yet." She smiled.

The mood among the men suddenly became serious, but sincere. Bull was, surprisingly, the first one to speak.

"Well, Sunny, I, for one, appreciate that."

"Sunny?"

"Yeah, Sunny, short for Sunshine, because you always have such a sunny outlook on everything."

"Couldn't you come up with something scarier? Like Skull-crusher or something cool?"

"Nope. You're Sunny. No way around it." Bull grinned. She'd never seen his "sweet" smile before. It reminded her of a little boy's smile.

"Sunny" stuck among the group, and it fit her. She claimed she didn't like it, which made everyone call her that even more.

"You'll have to accept it, Sunny." Rebel smirked. "You're our little sister now, and we'll torture you mercilessly. But know this—no one else will. You're ours to protect now. We're your brothers." He motioned around the circle of men. They all nodded in agreement, except Reaper. The look of possession in his eyes spoke of something more.

Brianna fought back the tears of emotion that threatened to overtake her. She'd finally been accepted as part of the exclusive group. Even Bull looked at her as his little sister, and she cherished the feeling. "I've always wanted a brother. Now I have several."

"You have all of us," Shadow promised. "We're proud to be your brothers. We take care of our own."

Brianna felt the shift in the bond. She had a great love for her family and was all too happy to add this wonderful group of men to the mix.

Later that night after everyone else was asleep, Noah slipped out of his barracks and into Brianna's tent. He eased onto the uncomfortable cot with her and draped his arm over her, both protectively and possessively. Her body craved his warmth and his kisses. The way he nibbled along the back of her neck sent cold chills through her entire body. He held her all night as they slept, his hand splayed across her abdomen. Before dawn, she felt his reluctance to leave her bed before anyone else woke up.

Over the following week, Reaper made it a nightly ritual to find his way to her bed. Each night, Brianna found it increasingly difficult to resist the powerful urges he created in her. If anyone in his team knew what was happening between Reaper and Brianna, they never let on. She knew damn well they were aware. It was their job to know, and it wasn't like she could even hide her feelings for him during the day when they were all together. But at least they were good-natured enough toward her not to bring it up.

With every day that passed, Brianna fell in love with Reaper just a little more. In all the nights he snuck into her bed with her, he never once tried to go further than what her grandmother had called "heavy petting." She'd laughed at that term when her grandmother first used it.

Now, the petting was making her crazy. She couldn't take her eyes off Reaper when he was around and fantasized about him when he wasn't. Right or wrong, she had decided this definitely was not a one-night stand, and she was ready to take it to the next level. She would be leaving for home the following week, and she planned to make the most of her time with him while she could.

As she got ready for bed that night, she desperately hoped he wouldn't be called out for a mission. That would ruin all her plans. She washed her face and brushed her teeth as usual, then sprayed her body with her favorite perfume. The mixture of jasmine, rose, orchid and freesia was inherently feminine and unforgettable to the senses. There hadn't been a call to use it in this godforsaken place before now. She knew the sweat from the sweltering heat during the day would have rinsed it all off her anyway. But the colder desert night air would help keep it in place, at least until he joined her.

She climbed into her bed without her pajamas this time and waited for him to join her. Within an hour of lights-out, he opened the tent door silently and slid into bed next to her. She lay on her side, and he slipped his arm around her. He suddenly jerked his head up when his hand met her cool, bare skin.

"You're sure?" he whispered.

"I've never been more certain," she replied.

She turned her body into his, looked into his eyes, and watched the chocolate brown turn to black with passion and desire. She reached up and kissed him, softly at first, then ran her fingers through his short black hair.

She ran her tongue around the outline of his lips before seductively licking in the middle to urge him to open his mouth to her. When he did, a deep rumble rolled through his chest, and the kiss suddenly turned urgent and demanding.

Her hands never left his body, as she felt the muscles in his shoulders tense, then across his chest, down his stomach to the hem of his shirt. She started to slowly pull it up over his head when he grabbed it with one hand and flung it to the floor.

He rolled her onto her back, and he moved to cover her entire body with his. Through his jogging pants, she felt his erection pressed against her lower abdomen. She raked her fingernails down his back, moved her hands to his sides, and slid her fingers under the elastic waistband. He grabbed her hands and pushed them above her head, holding them both in one hand. She realized she must have had a puzzled look on her face when he gave her the sexiest half grin she'd ever seen. He whispered, "I plan on taking my time."

Noah rose up on his forearms, cupped her face in his hands, and paused to gaze deeply into her eyes. His eyes raked over her face, taking in the slight blush from the embarrassment he knew this intense intimacy caused in her.

Her lips were still swollen from their last kiss, and her breasts heaved as they rose and fell with her increased breathing. Reaper kept his eyes on hers as he dipped his mouth to hers again, licking, teasing, and pulling away. She tried to raise her head to capture his mouth again, and he pulled farther away, still watching. When she realized what he was doing, Brianna lowered her head back to the cot.

His kissed her cheek, to her jawline, and finally moved to her earlobe. His touch sent shivers through her entire body. He licked and sucked on her ear before finally pulling on it seductively with his teeth. Then he worked his way down her neck with openmouthed kisses as he licked and bit her skin. She tried to pull her hands loose to touch him, but his grip tightened just enough to keep her hands in place, and he continued his assault on all her senses.

She inhaled deeply to breathe in his musky, masculine scent and let out a long sigh. He continued moving lower on her body. She didn't even realize the moment when he freed her hands since his mouth had found the sensitive, hardened buds of her breasts. Noah licked and bit, teased and tempted her until she grabbed his head in her hands and pulled him back to her chest. She felt the rumble of his low chuckle reverberate through her. He started again, and her back arched in response to his touch as his hand found her other breast. Slowly, painfully slow, his mouth followed his hands as he tasted every inch of her.

Her hands seemed to have a mind of their own as they moved all across his body. She was in complete awe and appreciation of every muscle in his chest, shoulders, back, and arms. He moved lower down her torso, still kissing and licking her stomach. In hushed moans, she heard him whisper, "So beautiful."

His hands moved lower still. He cupped her heated mound possessively before he found the small nub of nerves that could send her soaring. His thumb ran over it slightly and instantly made her body beg for more and more. He watched her intently as he moved in small circles while applying more pressure.

Instinctively, her hips rose slightly to meet his touch. His fingers found her soft, wet center, moving one finger along the folds, just barely touching her where she so desperately wanted to feel him.

"Noah, please, now!"

But he didn't surrender to her request. He swirled his finger around her wet heat before finally pushing all the way in. Out. In. Out. His rhythm was such sweet torture.

"Baby, you're so wet for me."

"Noah…" His name was all she could mutter before his second finger found her wet desire and plunged in. He moved his hand faster, watched her expressions, admired how responsive her beautiful body was to his touch, and how it brought her closer and closer to climax. Then he suddenly stopped.

"Uh, no! Don't stop!" she cried.

He picked her legs up, bent her knees, and put them over his shoulders. Then she felt his hot, wet tongue pressed against her clit as his two fingers danced and played in her wetness again. He increased and decreased the pressure and rhythm at a maddening pace. He again brought her closer and closer to the edge and then mercilessly took it away. When he was satisfied she could take no more, his tongue and fingers again began to work their magic.

"Bri—look at me. Look at me," he commanded.

She opened her eyes and met his piercing gaze. She ran her fingers through his hair until she could no longer hold back the intense pressure built up inside her.

"Come for me, baby." Then he felt her inner walls tighten around his fingers, felt them shudder and quiver as she tumbled over the edge.

Noah reached for his wallet, pulled out a condom wrapper and was sheathed and back on top of her before she could even move. He placed his forearms on either side of her head, their faces only a fraction of an inch apart, and he pushed his long, hard length deep inside her. He felt her body mold around and accept him. With a sharp intake of breath, she arched her back and her hips rose to take him

"God, you're so tight. You feel so good," he moaned.

Their bodies, now joined as one, found the perfect rhythm as they performed this most intimate dance. He lowered his head to catch her moan in his mouth. He sucked on her bottom lip, playfully pulled on it with his teeth, then his tongue delved into her mouth again. She held on tight to his shoulders then moved her hands down to his back. Her fingernails dug into his skin as he brought her closer and closer to the edge again. He pushed up on his hands to drive deeper into her and find her sweet spot.

"Let go, Bri. Let me feel you."

"Come with me. I'm not going over without you."

He surged harder, felt her clench around him, felt the quiver of her sensitive flesh, and watched her face change as she tumbled over the edge of passion, and then he joined her. He let his arms go limp and just lay on her beautiful, sweat-soaked body for a moment before he pulled out of her. He heard her groan of disappointment and had to chuckle.

"I know exactly how you feel, baby."

He rolled onto his side, quickly discarding the condom. As Bri turned on her side, he molded his body to fit against hers. It was not normal for him to sleep completely naked, but neither of them would dare complain.

She was so completely sated, worn out and happy, she slipped into the deepest sleep she'd had since she'd arrived on the base. At some point during the night, he got up, dressed, and silently left her tent, because he was gone when she woke up at dawn.

She showered, dressed, and walked to the mess hall for breakfast. She was devastated to learn that his team was sent out on a mission and had left about an hour before. While she sat alone with her breakfast, she was lost deep in thought as she remembered the events of the night before. She relived every moment they'd spent together up until that point in her mind.

"Where'd you go?" Judge asked.

Brianna jumped, not realizing he'd sat down beside her while she was lost in her memories of Reaper. "Oh, sorry. Just thinking about the time I've spent here."

"That's right. You'll be going home soon, won't you?" Judge nodded.

"Yes," Brianna replied solemnly. "So, you went to school with Reaper, huh?"

"Yeah. He was an overachiever even back then. It was hard for the rest of us to even try to keep up with him. Smart, handsome, athletic. I don't know of anything the guy can't do."

"Sounds like he was pretty popular." Brianna smiled as she pictured the younger version of the man she'd fallen in love with in such a short time.

"He was more than popular. Everything came so easily to him. I guess that happens when you're born with a silver spoon in your mouth, though," Judge said sarcastically.

"Silver spoon?"

"You know, the kind that rich and influential families have? That's the kind of family he comes from. He always got whatever he wanted, from whoever he wanted, whenever he wanted."

Brianna felt very uncomfortable with the contempt Judge showed toward the man who was supposed to be his friend. "That may have been true when he was a kid, but he's worked hard to get where he is today."

Judge cut his blue-green eyes to her. "The only way to get ahead is to make your own way. Working hard doesn't result in getting ahead—blazing a new path does. A real man will go after what he wants and not let anything or anyone stand in his way."

As Judge finished his rant, Brianna's thoughts strayed to how he had been such a close friend to Noah. She knew Noah's sense of loyalty ran very deep, and that was one of the most endearing quali-ties about him, but she couldn't stop the uneasy feeling she always had around Judge. It was one of the reasons why she stayed so close to her brothers in Noah's squadron and didn't push the interview on Judge as much.

"My time in the Army will be up soon enough," Judge continued, more to himself than to her. "I'm already making exciting plans for my future."

"That's great," she replied noncommittally. She didn't usually engage Judge in conversation more than absolutely necessary.

"I've met a few influential people in DC, and I've already started paving the road to move to a high-level position in the Department of Defense," Judge boasted.

Brianna nodded and smiled politely. "That sounds great for you, Judge. I need to go work on my article while I have some time alone. I'll see you later."

He grunted in reply as Brianna scurried past him. Relieved to retreat to the privacy of her tent, she sat on her cot and worked on her article. One ear was always tuned to the sounds that surrounded her, though, as she waited for Noah to return.

She spent the next several days in an emotional haze as she watched for them to return and waited to hear any word of their mission. Nights brought dreams of Noah and their last night together. Each day brought another round of depression when he didn't return to her yet again. Her last day on assignment finally arrived, and she wasn't ready to leave. The men didn't return before her long flight back to Atlanta.

The military convoy arrived to escort her back to the airfield. She produced the same black cloth that was previously used, they blindfolded her, and she was put in the Humvee for the long ride. She didn't mind not being able to see so much on the way in, but now she wondered if she'd passed Noah along the way out. She needed just one last look, a wave goodbye, or any sign that he was still all right.

As she left that base, the thought that she did so without seeing him, talking to him, or touching him tore her heart out of her chest. She hated that she was forced to leave him behind when she wanted nothing more than to have one more day with him.

5

CHAPTER FIVE

The twenty-hour flight home was even more grueling for Brianna than the flight that delivered her to the secret location. Initially, her excitement over getting the story of a lifetime was enough to keep her occupied on the uncomfortable flight. Now, the thoughts of Noah dominated her mind, and the phantom feel of his lips on her skin drove her mad.

There was no time for closure, to say her goodbyes to her new friends, and to leave no words left unspoken. As it stood, she had no way to contact Noah, no method of communication with any of them, and no way to share her information with them. Purely out of desperation, she'd considered asking Judge to pass a note on to Noah, but she couldn't shake the feeling that he just couldn't be trusted.

She finally surrendered to the emotions that welled up inside her. Brianna opened her diary, her notes, and a new notebook to start crafting her article. If every scene insisted on playing on repeat in her mind, she decided she'd make the most of it. She spent the majority of the flight time deep in thought, developed writer's cramp, and thoroughly exhausted herself mentally before she finally completed the rough draft of her article.

After she put her things away, she shifted in the uncomfortable seat as much as possible and fell asleep for the remainder of the flight. Before she knew it, the plane was wheels-down and on approach to the airfield in the Atlanta area. Mixed feelings flooded her senses. She was elated to be home and see her family again. But she was also heartbroken as she thought about Noah and the other men.

My brothers, she thought sadly as she pictured each one. She reached into her bag and fingered the black cloth that served as her blindfold. *I'll make sure this article does you proud,* she vowed.

"Bri!" Missy screeched as she rushed to wrap her arms around her sister.

Brianna smiled and dropped her bags to free her hands. She pulled Missy closer to her. "I've missed you too, sis."

"That was the longest six weeks of my life," Missy complained. "Don't ever do that again."

Brianna chuckled, knowing that Missy was usually a little on the dramatic side. "I'm home now. You don't have to worry about me leaving again for a while."

"Are you planning another trip?" Missy asked, her smile fading and the worry clouding her eyes.

"Not right away," Brianna laughed. "But if I'm going to be a real correspondent, I'll have to travel to cover the stories as they come up."

"As long as any future assignment doesn't take as long as this one did," Missy conceded.

"Glad to have you home, baby girl." Evan wrapped his arms around Brianna, nudging Missy to the side. "Safe and sound."

"I've been in good hands, Daddy," Brianna assured him. "No one would dare mess with those guys."

"They have nothing on a mother intent on protecting her children," Diana declared as she pushed Evan aside to get to her daughter. "Never do that again."

If they only knew that I've been trying to figure out a way to get myself back over there, she thought.

Jessie and Ashley stepped up and waited for their turn to

welcome their older sister home. Evan picked up Brianna's bags and carried them to the car. Once they were all inside, Evan took a moment to appreciate having his family back together.

"Why don't we take our girls out to eat and then let Brianna get some rest?" Evan asked Diana.

"Sounds great to me," Diana agreed.

During their meal, Brianna filled her family in on the details of living on a ghost base, how the men worked together as a cohesive team, and how she became part of their close-knit group.

"Those hot men in uniform adopted you as their little sister?" Jessie asked, her mouth gaping open.

"They sure did." Brianna nodded, swallowing past the ball of emotion in her throat. "I have several very scary brothers now."

"I want to meet them," Missy said dreamily. "Reaper sounds exactly like my type. Think you can arrange to introduce me?"

Brianna's eyes snapped to Missy's at that comment. Her face instantly heated, her blood pressure spiked, and she was ready to tackle her sister for even suggesting it. When she saw the sparkle in Missy's eyes and the teasing grin on her face, she knew she'd just given Missy more information than she intended.

Missy's eyebrow slowly arched as she tilted her head to the side. She silently questioned Brianna, who quickly averted her gaze and refused to make direct eye contact with her again.

"They weren't allowed to give me their real names, so I definitely don't have any contact information for them. Sorry to disappoint you, Missy."

"That is very disappointing," Missy replied, her tone conveying her understanding of the situation.

Brianna finally gave in and looked at her. Missy gave her a small, reassuring smile. "But hey," Missy continued. "They're special ops guys, right? They'll find you."

That was Brianna's secret hope—that Noah would find her and they'd have the opportunity to be a couple. "I'll toast to that," Brianna replied as she raised her glass. The others joined her and lifted theirs. "To happy reunions."

Later, when Brianna crawled into her bed, her body seemed to melt into the soft sheets and plush mattress. The creature comforts of home would take some readjustment after the stark difference of the cot that had been her bed for the past six weeks. More than that, she'd grown dependent on Noah joining her, heating her body in every imaginable way, and cradling her after thoroughly loving her.

Now the bed felt cold and lonely without his thick body taking up most of the room. Tears slowly leaked from her eyes as she drifted off to sleep from sheer exhaustion. Her dreams were filled with visions of Noah—some were welcomed, and some filled her with dread.

Over the next several weeks, Brianna put the finishing touches on her article and submitted it to the *Atlanta Times Free Press* for publication. She waited on pins and needles as the editor took his time to review her writing, confirm fact checks, and make a decision on whether to run the article. By the time she finally received the call requesting a meeting to discuss it, she'd almost given up on it.

"Brianna, this is Les Vincent with the *Atlanta Times*. Can you come in this afternoon so we can discuss your article?"

"Yes, I'd love to," she replied, trying to sound outwardly confident. Inwardly, she was simultaneously screaming and feeling close to fainting.

After agreeing on a time to meet, she ran through the house in an excited frenzy. "Mom! Mom! Where are you?"

Diana stepped out of her home office, her brows drawn down in alarm and confusion. "In here, Brianna. What's wrong?"

"I just got the call from the editor. I'm going to meet with him today," Brianna blurted out.

"That's great, baby. Congratulations," Diana said as she clutched Brianna's arm. "I'm so excited for you."

"Thanks, Mom. I put a lot of work into that article, so I hope they don't change it too much."

"Don't borrow trouble, Bri. Go talk to him and see what he has to say before you start working yourself up," Diana chided her gently.

"You're right. Positive thoughts and all that jazz," Brianna replied.

~

"I'M BRIANNA TATE, AND I HAVE AN APPOINTMENT WITH LES Vincent." Brianna proudly introduced herself to the secretary.

"Just a moment." The older lady smiled as she checked the editor's schedule. "Here you are. If you'll have a seat, I'll let him know you're here."

After a few minutes, Brianna was led into his office. His desk was covered with stacks of paper in various heights, haphazardly strewn pens, and several bottles of water. The ultra-organized fanatic in her cringed as she took a seat across from him.

"So, you're Evan's daughter," he stated.

"Yes, I am. Do you know my dad?"

"No. I was given a directive from my boss, who was nicely asked by a golfing buddy, who knows someone who knows your dad, to read your piece," he replied dryly, his expression holding no humor.

His smile lit up his face as he continued. "And now I'm delighted that it all came down this way. To be honest, I never read unsolicited submissions from an unknown freelance writer. If I hadn't been forced to read it, I would've missed out on an excellent idea with an original focus on the sacrifices our servicemen and women make. You'll be thrilled to hear that DOD has approved your piece as-is. It looks like this story will be picked up and distributed nationally."

Brianna's blank expression and rigid posture made Les laugh. "Brianna, did you hear me?"

"Y-yes," she stammered. "I'm just speechless, literally."

His words swirled in her mind for a minute before she realized their full implication. "Did you say it's being picked up nationally?"

"Yes, I did indeed." Les smiled as he turned his chair to face her fully. "This is an amazing article, Brianna. You keep writing like this, you are going places."

As Les explained the next steps, Brianna's mind raced with possibilities. She wasn't afraid of hard work and making sacrifices to achieve her goals. She wanted to make a name for herself among the elite, the top of the top journalists. The more things seemed to fall into place, the more chaotic her life felt.

When she left for the unknown destination in a country half a world away, she faced her fears and stepped onto that plane with her own marching orders in hand. When she arrived at the base, not knowing a single person there, she quickly made friends with the men she wanted to introduce to the world. When she gave her body to Noah, she did it knowing she also gave him her heart.

Now she was stepping out into the spotlight, sharing their story with millions of people, and hoping that they found the same value in it that she did. Brianna tried to focus on Les as he talked animatedly about her future, but hopes that Noah would track her down through the trail of news coverage kept overtaking her thoughts.

"…you'll have to move to Miami," she vaguely heard Les state as he rambled on.

"Wait. What? Move to Miami?" she asked.

"Well, yeah. If you were just a freelance writer, you could live anywhere. But this is a staff position with the *Miami Herald*, so they'll want you on-site. Since both papers are owned by the same parent company, the editor in chief wants you to go there. Is that a problem?"

"No. It's not a problem at all." Brianna smiled.

Miami was where Noah called home when he wasn't off in a remote desert somewhere on assignment. She also remembered that Rebel mentioned he'd moved there not long ago to be closer to Noah. Hope that they'd be reunited grew inside her and became a new goal for her to reach.

Relaying the news to her family that night proved to be more difficult than she thought. She'd been home from her six-week stint in the desert for nearly three months, but Missy jokingly wouldn't let Brianna forget how she'd abandoned her. Brianna knew that Missy would honestly be upset that she planned to move away and start her own life.

"I have some great news," Brianna recited the lines as she'd rehearsed in the car on the way home.

"We want to hear all about it," Diana replied. "Brianna made me wait until everyone was here, so she only had to say it once." Diana laughed as she looked around the table at her family.

"I met with the editor of the *Atlanta Times* today, and he loved my article. In fact, he was so impressed with it, that he's making sure it gets picked up and distributed nationally," she began.

A round of congratulations and cheering ensued as they continued to pass the food around the table. As Brianna spooned the potatoes onto her plate, she casually added the punch line. "The editor in chief at the parent company told him to offer me a staff position…with the *Miami Herald*."

The silence in the room was only momentary before the shouting ensued.

"No, you just got home!"

"You're not moving that far away from home all alone."

"Can I have your room?"

"Everyone calm down. This is the deal. I'm grown, I've graduated college, and I'm ready to step out and make my own life. This is a phenomenal opportunity that is unheard of for a new, unproven journalist. That one idea, that one article, has moved mountains for me.

"The staff position isn't a glamorous job or anything, but it's what I want to do. I'll still have to prove myself, take some of the stories others don't want, but this can open so many other doors. In four weeks, I'm starting my new position as a staff writer in Miami."

Evan saw the same determined young woman he'd witnessed getting on the military transport plane sitting before him now. The will and desire to excel were ingrained in her very being. Not knowing how to give up, she pursued her goals with fervor and determination.

"I'm proud of you, Brianna," Evan replied warmly. "You'll do great in Miami."

Diana dabbed her eyes with her napkin and added her agreement. "Your father's right, Brianna. I'll miss you more than I can say, but I'm very proud of you, too."

"So, I get your room?" Ashley chimed in with a teasing grin.

"No, Ashley. I expect my room to become a shrine to my memory. You'll need to pay your respects to it daily," Brianna teased.

The following four weeks seemed to move all too fast for the Tate family. As Brianna made preparations to move, every step toward her new life took her further from the safety and security of her close-knit family. When she found an apartment online that appeared to fit her needs, Missy and Brianna made a quick weekend trip to tour it in person.

"All right, we're finally away from prying eyes and eavesdropping ears. Spill it," Missy demanded as they took their seats on the plane.

"What?" Brianna asked, momentarily confused.

"You know what. It's been nearly four months since you got back from that desert, and you haven't been on a single date. Every time I've asked about what happened, you've brushed me off. Now, spill it," Missy demanded.

With a huff, Brianna nodded. "Fine. Noah and I became pretty close while I was there, but he got called off base for a mission just hours before I came back home. He didn't make it back to the base before I left, so I never had a chance to say goodbye. Or anything else, for that matter.

"He mentioned that he's from the Miami area. It sounds crazy when I say it out loud, but I really hope that he finds me through my article."

"That would be an awesome story to tell your grandkids one day, Bri," Missy assured her. "If it's meant to be, it will be."

"I know I didn't know him that long. I barely even got his real name, but I just strongly feel he's the one for me," Brianna whispered, afraid to voice her beliefs too loudly.

"So you want to be close to the place he calls home, in case he decides to look for you." Missy nodded in agreement. "I have a good feeling about this. Even though I really don't want to lose my partner in crime."

"You'll just have to come visit me often." Brianna smiled.

Sweat glistened on their brows almost immediately after stepping outside the airport into the heat and humidity of Miami. The taxi delivered them to an attractive apartment complex. Each building consisted of five floors and had meticulously landscaped flower gardens. The buildings surrounded the gated pool area and gave the aura of a secret oasis.

Brianna and Missy exchanged excited glances as they rushed into the central office. An attractive older lady sat behind the desk, busily tending to typical office duties. When she heard the door chime, she looked up and smiled at the two young ladies entering.

"Hello, how can I help you?" she asked.

"I'm Brianna Tate. I called about the apartment that's open and scheduled time to tour the grounds in person."

"Yes, Brianna." She smiled. "I'm Wanda, and I remember talking to you. I'm so glad you were able to make it. Atlanta, right?"

"That's right." Brianna nodded. "Wanda, this is my sister, Missy."

"Hello," Wanda replied. "Are you moving in, too?"

"No, I wish," Missy laughed. "I'm just here for sisterly support."

"You just let me know if you change your mind." Wanda winked. "Come right this way, ladies. I'm the best tour guide you'll ever find."

Excitement, giddiness, fear of the unknown—Brianna's feelings ran the gamut of the spectrum. The one she felt most, however, was hope. She was so very hopeful that she'd reconnect with Noah.

She took her time to walk through the empty apartment to visualize how she'd arrange her furniture. Scenes of how her life would change flashed before her eyes. In every aspect, she saw and felt Noah with her. In the kitchen cooking together, in the living room watching TV together, and in the bedroom making love every day.

"I love it. I'll take it," Brianna gushed.

$$6$$

CHAPTER SIX

"Man, it's been a long damn day," Bull grumbled as the four men arrived back on base.

"So glad this one is over," Rebel agreed. "Being away from home gets harder the older I get."

"I've actually given this some serious thought," Reaper chimed in. "Before we were called out for this assignment, I looked into forming my own security firm. Since I haven't touched the trust fund my father set up for me, it'd be fairly easy to cover start-up costs."

"You're thinking of leaving the Army for good?" Bull asked.

"I am," Reaper confirmed. "Working for myself sounds better every day."

"Does one pretty little blonde have anything to do with that decision?" Shadow asked.

"I don't know what you're talking about, man," Reaper replied, his face stoic.

Shadow laughed heartily. "Of course not." He smiled. "I received an outside offer I've been considering too. Maybe I'll give Brianna a call when I get home. See if she wants to hook up."

Reaper rounded on Shadow, his eyes glowing with the intensity of a fire. "Don't even fucking think about it, Shadow. I don't care how big and bad you think you are, I will fuck you up."

The knowing smirk and laughter that shone in his eyes was the only answer Reaper needed to know he'd just been played. Of course, Shadow couldn't let their conversation end like that.

"To the trained ear, that would probably be an odd response for someone who's not interested in her," Shadow replied dryly.

"We're almost back to the base," Rebel chimed in. "I guess we'll see, huh?"

"Yeah, we'll see all right," Shadow laughed.

The Humvee rolled to a stop, and the four hulking men all exited at the same time. Even behind his sunglasses, Reaper knew his eyes gave him away when they searched for Brianna's tent first. His lips set in a thin line, he prepared to accept the razzing he knew his teammates would unleash on him.

"Go ahead. We'll wait here," Shadow encouraged.

He shook his head lightly, dropped his gear, and strolled over to Brianna's door. He rapped lightly on it to alert her to his presence before he swung the door open and stepped inside. He jerked his sunglasses off his face as he turned around and took in the barren furnishings.

She was gone.

He burst out of the door, almost taking it off the hinges with his force, and stomped across the way to the command tent.

"Where is Brianna Tate?" he barked out.

The private who'd carried her suitcase to her tent upon her arrival quickly stood at attention. "Her transport taking her back stateside has already left, sir."

Reaper stared the young man down for several seconds as he attempted to understand the words the private had just spoken. "I was told that transport didn't leave until twenty-three hundred hours."

"The flight plan had to be changed because of anticipated bad weather. She was taken to the airfield about two hours ago. That plane took off about an hour ago, sir," he explained.

Reaper gave him a single nod and stormed out of the tent.

When he reached the other men, he snatched his gear off the ground and trudged to his own barracks. In an uncharacteristic display of aggravation, he threw his gear onto the bed and began pacing in the tight area.

Rebel approached him first, and understanding dawned as he took in Reaper's demeanor.

"I missed her. The flight left early," Reaper said through gritted teeth. "Son of a bitch!"

"I've never seen you react this way over anyone, Reap. And I've known you a long time," Rebel replied. Reaper's eyes rose to meet his. Rebel nodded. "It's time."

"Yeah. I think you're right. It is time," Reaper agreed. "Our service contracts are coming back up for renewal over the next few weeks. I'll just take the honorable discharge and my walking papers back home with me."

"Steele Security, huh?" Rebel asked.

"Count me in," Bull said from the doorway.

Reaper nodded. "Shadow, you too?" he asked.

"I've decided to take another offer, Reap. But you know anytime you need me, all it takes is a phone call," Shadow replied.

"I have no doubt about that, Shadow," Reaper replied.

"She means this much to you?" Bull asked.

Reaper inhaled deeply, filled his chest, and lifted up to his full height. He looked Bull directly in the eye when he replied. "Damn straight, she does. I'm not leaving the Army for her, but she definitely helped me make my mind up."

"We're in," Rebel said, taking a step beside Bull. "Let's do this."

They left Reaper alone in the barracks and headed to the mess hall. Reaper allowed his memories to take over his thoughts as he absently unpacked his gear. Brianna's presence had brought a different kind of peace to him, one that he hadn't known he was missing until she was gone.

Now, simply knowing that she was on her way back home, thousands of miles away from him, was a depressing thought. His nights with her had made the barren desert a tolerable place. He'd looked forward to the time he spent with her and had even stopped dreading all of her questions.

The following day, Reaper approached his commanding officer and informed him of his intent to leave the Army. After an hour of unsuccessfully attempting to persuade him to stay, his CO finally relented and agreed to start the necessary paperwork. The weeks before his discharge seemed to drag by, each day seemingly taking longer than the last.

Patience had been drilled into Reaper's mind and personality through the countless hours of training and missions he'd been on over the years. In his line of work, he had to display an enormous amount of self-control to complete his assignments successfully. But this waiting on the edge of what could be a brand-new life with Brianna was close to maddening.

The day the transport left, taking Reaper home, the mixed feelings of leaving the only life he'd known since he left home at eighteen threatened to change his mind. The thoughts of a real life with Brianna pushed him forward. Knowing he'd have his own security company, and his brothers at his side, helped give him peace about his decision.

When he briefly stopped before he boarded the plane, Reaper took a good look at the area that had been his home and silently said goodbye. It was well past time for a new life to begin.

"It's fucking amazing how fast this business has grown," Rebel exclaimed. "You need to hire more men, Reap. We'll have to start turning business away if you don't."

"I'm working on it. I've lined up several interviews this week with some guys who have great potential. You two get to help me," Reaper replied as he looked at Rebel and Bull. "One guy is a tech support guru—we really need someone like him. All are former military, various branches."

"Let's put them through our normal process for interviews." Bull smirked.

"Uh, Bull? We actually want these guys to like us," Rebel laughed.

"Wrong kind of interview process, then." Bull smiled.

"Have you found her yet, Reap?" Rebel asked.

"I found her the day I got back, Rebel," Reaper replied as he continued working through the stack of paperwork on his desk. "You know I'm a planning man."

"Well, if you 'plan' much longer, you may lose your chance with her." Rebel shook his head.

"Not a chance. She lives here in Miami now. She's been working nonstop to prove herself, while I've been working nonstop to make this business successful. She'll be at the Rainstorm and Bead pub with her friends this weekend to celebrate her birthday," Reaper explained. "And so will I."

"How do you know that?" Bull asked.

"It's my job to know, Bull," Reaper replied with a sly smile. "I've done my recon on my subject."

"What a good stalker-soldier," Bull replied dryly.

Reaper looked up from his task and stared at Bull. He straightened his back and slightly narrowed his eyes as he considered his friend's response.

"You like her," Reaper finally replied, his smile uncharacteristically covering his face. "She got through that thick hide of yours."

"Shut up, man," Bull dodged as he shook his head.

"Holy shit, you actually care about her," Reaper said as he stood. "I don't believe it."

"Reaper, I'd hate to kick my boss's ass, but I'll do it if you don't quit this shit," Bull threatened.

Rebel, never one to let a taboo subject go without riling Bull as much as possible, had to voice his thoughts.

"You're right, Reap." He turned toward him and continued to poke at Bull. "Shit fire. How'd she do it, Bull? You thinking of stealing Reaper's woman or what?"

Bull stood quickly, his body set in his fighting stance. "Take it back, Rebel."

"I never thought I'd see the day," Rebel goaded him. "You, Reap?"

"Never."

"Both of you shitheads better back off right now," Bull threatened through his gritted teeth and clenched jaw. "You know I'd never do that to Reaper."

"Nah, man, that part I was just giving you shit over. But you do care about Brianna. She did get to you." Rebel laughed easily.

"I meant it when I said I'd be her brother and look out for her," Bull admitted. "She's different from most."

"I agree," Reaper said and smiled at his brother. "She is different from anyone else I've met. I'm glad you like her. You know the two of you and Shadow are the only family I claim."

"So, tell us about this party." Rebel grinned.

"I'll be glad to—after the interviews. The first candidate will be here soon. His name is Brad Sullivan, and he's the tech guru I mentioned," Reaper explained.

"How many interviews do we have this week?" Bull asked, trying to hide the groan in his tone.

"Ten," Reaper replied. "Two per day."

"I don't know which is worse—spreading them out or doing them all at once to get them over with," Rebel replied.

"I spread them out, so we're not sick of asking the same questions over and over by the end of the day. That would cause us to make rash decisions. Like Bull reminded us, these aren't exactly the type of interviews we have experience conducting," Reaper explained. "We need the best men in place as soon as possible."

"Something new come up, Reap?" Bull asked.

"We may have a government contract opening up to us if the stars align just right. Judge took a position in the Department of Defense and is trying to help get the contract approved. But since he's a new employee and this is a big deal, I don't know if it'll be approved," Reaper elaborated. "He also said he'd like to be a silent partner, offered money to help fund expenses."

"You don't need his money," Rebel replied, his brow furrowed into a V between his eyes. "You have plenty of family money. Why would he do that?"

"I thought it was strange too. Judge said he didn't realize I accepted the trust fund from my parents. He thought I'd entered the military because I was penniless," Reaper replied. "I had to explain the whole story of how it was set up in my name through my parents' lawyer when I was a kid. It was automatically mine, without accepting anything from them."

There were very few secrets in the tight-knit group, and the status of Reaper's family was well known. He and his father, Steve Steele, had a long history of butting heads, bouts of not speaking, and finally coming to blows before Reaper left home for good at eighteen.

In Reaper's eyes, Steve ruled his home with his iron fist and refused to consider any opinion that differed from his own. His take-charge attitude was overbearing and cast a suffocating shadow over the household. His rules were strictly enforced and doled out without preamble.

The visiting Army recruiter made an impression on the young boy. His senior year had consisted of visiting several colleges, taking the obligatory tours, and listening to countless hours of speeches extolling the values each would bring. But each had left him feeling as if something significant were missing, like the incomplete picture presented when pieces of the jigsaw puzzle were absent.

At first, listening to the recruiter explain the benefits of a military career was no different. It simply sounded like another pitch from a sleazy used car salesman. When the recruiter began listing the sacrifices a soldier had to make, the long days and nights on patrol, and the probability of leaving the comfort of his beloved country, he knew he'd finally found someone who was real. Someone who would be honest about what he'd face in his future. Someone who would tell him how hard and dangerous life can really be.

The scary truth was exactly what he needed to hear. It was what jarred him into action, into a decision, and into the direction of a life in the military. He'd still attend college—but as a cadet with a purpose. Eventually, he'd even have a family of his own—but with a distinctly different approach than his father. Rather than seeing the world with a spoiled rich boy stigma, he would see it through the lens of an experienced man.

Just before his high school graduation, young Noah approached his father, filled with excitement about his impending plans.

"Dad, I need to talk to you," he began his carefully constructed speech. "It's very important."

Steve's arms slowly lowered the newspaper, revealing the displeasure of being interrupted on his face. "This had better be good."

"I've made a decision about my future. My plans after high school."

"Go on," Steve said as he meticulously folded the paper. His tone conveyed that he knew he wouldn't like the direction this conversation would take. "Let's hear your master plan."

"I've decided to join the Army. I talked to the recruiter for a long time and basically mapped it all out. I'll still attend college, become an officer, and make a living doing what I love to do. My mind is made up, and I've already set a date for testing and swearing in."

"You what?" Steve asked. His voice was unusually low and threatening. He leaned forward in his chair, narrowed his eyes in anger, and balled his hands into fists at his sides. He was every bit as intimidating in this position as if he stood over Noah, yelling in his face.

"I've set the date—" Noah repeated and was promptly interrupted.

"I heard you!" Steve roared. "You will not go to that testing, and you will not swear in. No son of mine will give up a prestigious future to be some grunt, sleeping in the mud or a tent with a bunch of other grunts."

Steve stood and paced back and forth across the room. Noah's eyes drifted from Steve, who was still ranting and raving, to take in the opulence of his surroundings. *It figures,* Noah thought. *All he's worried about is what his friends will think. He isn't concerned about what I want.*

That thought summed up all of Noah's life within just a few words. It was that very realization that pushed him to keep his appointment, to excel on the tests, and to complete his swearing-in ceremony. Signing on the dotted line was a formality in his mind since his heart was already committed. The day after his graduation, he took his few prized possessions and left home.

He built a long, successful career in the Army. Taking extra classes each semester, he graduated early with his degree. His tenacity in everything he tried got him noticed by both his commanding officers and the men he led. He quickly climbed through the ranks, taking every training opportunity made available to him, and expanded his capabilities. He became the youngest Delta Force member, but that still didn't bring him the personal vindication he thought it would. His father's condescending rejection of him still rang loudly in his ears.

Today, he started to feel the pride in his accomplishments that had eluded him for far too long. All of his training, skills, dedication, and hard work were beginning to pay off. Merely months prior, he started his own security firm and was already well in the black. Word of mouth had already spread quickly about his firm's abilities, making them the first choice for many high-profile clients.

Hiring several more employees would allow him to take the more complicated contracts that he'd recently received. As he worked through the scores of paperwork on his desk, his thoughts kept straying back to Brianna. The feel of her skin against his during the hot desert nights lingered in his mind even now. The sweetness of her breath, the sensual sounds she made, and the way her body felt in his hands kept him awake at night.

He would never get enough of her.

By the weekend, his plan to persuade, entice, and pursue her would be well in play.

"Reap," Rebel called to him and interrupted his thoughts. "Brad's here."

"Good. Let's get started."

Reaper moved with a new determination as he greeted Brad and ushered him into his office. After brief introductions, the trio started the interview process and professionally grilled the applicant on his skills and experience. By the end of it, all three had already made their decision and silently communicated it.

"Brad, when can you start?" Reaper asked with a smile.

"As soon as you give me the word. I'm working a temporary assignment right now, but my manager knows I'm looking for a permanent position," Brad answered.

"Next Monday, one week from today? Is that enough notice?" Reaper asked.

"That's perfect. I'm proud to be part of this agency. It's become very popular, very quickly, in the serious security circles," Brad extolled. "That's exactly the type of firm I want to be part of."

"I appreciate that, Brad. We work hard and take our responsibilities seriously here. I have no doubt you will too. Glad to have you on board," Reaper said, shaking his hand.

After Brad left, Rebel turned to the other two men and commented, "One down. Only nine more to go."

7

CHAPTER SEVEN

"We deserve to go on a huge bender after the week we've had," Bull declared as they stepped out of the office of Steele Security. "I'd rather run point for a month than sit through one more interview. Next person hired is an office manager, Reaper."

"You're not kidding." Reaper shook his head. "I love having this business, but interviewing has to be the worst job ever."

"Here's the Rainstorm and Bead pub. Thank God," Rebel exhaled. "Let's go have a beer or a maybe a keg."

They made a slow loop around the perimeter of the room to scan their surroundings. The trio stayed on duty even when they were off the clock. As Reaper approached the bar, he ordered three beers and let his eyes settle on Brianna.

She stood beside a tall table covered in presents, beer bottles, and a birthday cake in the middle. Several of her girlfriends surrounded her, and one placed a pointy happy birthday hat on her head. Reaper's hand froze midair as he raised his bottle to his lips. Brianna laughed heartily at the ridiculous hat but wore it with pride.

She was even more beautiful than she appeared in his dreams. Her long blond hair had lighter blond streaks as if the sun had picked specific areas to place light kisses. Her skin glowed from her Miami suntan, and her warm smile lit up her gorgeous face. If he'd had any doubts about finding her, they quickly melted away when he realized he couldn't take his eyes off her.

The thought of another man taking his place with her was enough to drive him into a blind rage. The knowledge that he'd never felt that way about anyone before convinced him to take a chance. Seeing her again solidified his feelings.

Brianna moved to the front of the table and began to open her birthday presents. He seized the perfect moment as he quickly stole up behind her, wrapped his arms around her waist, and murmured into her ear.

"Hello, Brianna. Have you missed me?"

She jumped in surprise and quickly whirled around to face him, ready to tear into the idiot who had dared to touch her. The shock of seeing him rendered her speechless for a few seconds as she openly stared at him. Then her jaw dropped open wide as the realization that he was real sank in.

"Noah!" she squealed as she automatically jumped into his arms. Her heart raced, and she couldn't contain the smile that was now permanently affixed to her face.

Of all the people she expected to see at her birthday party, Noah Steele wasn't one of them. Inwardly, she had fantasized about this moment so many times that she almost thought her daydream had taken over. But now, holding him close to her, she realized no fantasy could ever compete with the real man.

Noah effortlessly lifted her off the floor, further crushed her to him, and embraced her in the enormous bear hug that epitomized his size.

"Oh my God! I can't believe it's really you!" she whispered to him. "Are you actually here with me right now?"

"I'm definitely here, baby," he murmured.

Brianna's girlfriends were struck with the same speechless reaction as they watched the scene play out in front of them. Their eyes roamed from one man to the next, taking in the exquisite physiques and rippling muscles, all the while their mouths continued to gape open.

Reaper released Brianna, allowing her to slowly slide down his body, keeping their contact in place for as long as possible. Their eyes locked as Reaper's hand rose to cup her cheek. An uneasy throat-clearing caught her attention and reminded her they weren't alone.

Turning to their audience, Brianna ruefully explained. "Remember the guy in the Army I told you about? Reaper? This is him!"

Brianna quickly made a round of introductions, and the group rearranged tables and chairs so they could all sit together. Reaper took his seat next to Brianna, wrapped his arm possessively around her chair, and felt the puzzle pieces of his life were falling into place. The gorgeous blonde who had stolen his heart was at his side, his business was growing by leaps and bounds—almost faster than he could keep up with—and he was happier than he'd been in a very long time.

Brianna animatedly talked with her friends, regaling them with the story of how she and Reaper first met. As she finished her story, she turned toward him and drew in a ragged breath when she recognized his provocative expression.

"What's that smile for?" she asked breathily.

"It's for you," he replied smoothly.

The pub lights dimmed as the familiar sensual bass chords of "Love Bites" reverberated through the room.

"They're playing our song." The caress of Reaper's sensual tone completely captivated her, pulling her to him without conscious thought. Before she knew it, her hand was in his as he led her to the dance floor.

He wrapped his arms around her waist and pulled her body to his. She instinctively wrapped her arms around his neck. When he dipped his head to her ear, his deep voice sent cold chills cascading over her skin. "You have no idea how many times I've thought about having you in my arms again."

His hands slowly stroked up and down her ribs, his fingers

flowed effortlessly over her shirt but burned straight through to her skin and left her with his unique brand. With each languid movement, her breaths became heavier and faster, her chest heaved with the exertion of restraining herself. Any rational thought about taking their relationship slowly this time quickly evaporated, exactly like the steam emanating from her overheated body.

"You're even sexier than I remember," he continued. "More than I can resist."

His lips hovered barely above the skin on her neck. He threaded his fingers through her hair, lightly grasped the silky strands, and gently tilted her head to the side. Placing wet, sensual kisses along the sensitive skin on her neck, from her ear to the dip at her collarbone, Noah continued his meticulous reacquaintance with her body.

With each word and touch, Brianna became more pliant against him. She molded her body to fit his, and they continued to sway to the music as he worked his way back up her neck. When he reached her ear, he increased her growing discomfort with his words. "By the time we step foot outside this pub, you'll be mine. If you have any objections to that, now is the time to tell me."

Before she could respond, Noah's lips found hers. A small taste quickly became an overwhelming need to consume her. Her unique flavor was the only aphrodisiac he needed. The velvety smooth brush of her tongue against his fueled his desire. She moaned softly into his mouth, so full of passion and intense need that it overflowed from her involuntarily.

"So you agree?" He smirked as he broke the kiss.

"I wholeheartedly agree," she panted as she tried to catch her breath. "As if there were ever any question about it."

"There wasn't for me," he admitted with a sexy wink. "Just had to make sure you were convinced."

"It certainly took you long enough," she challenged.

He slowly quirked one brow up, a glow of amusement lighting up his eyes. "Are you trying to say I'm slow on my game?"

She shrugged one shoulder and cut her eyes to the left as she slightly pursed her lips. "If the shoe fits and all."

"Some things are worth the extra time. Slow, deliberate movements heighten the senses. Intense, precise drives at the right time are deeply satisfying."

Keeping his voice even, his pace slow, and his eyes locked on hers, he completed his mission with a slow stroke down the front of her neck. "I'd much rather take all night, so there's no doubt about my skills.

"Honestly, you should already know that I take my recon missions very seriously," he added with a straight face.

Her reply was a groan of frustration followed by dropping her forehead to his chest. She shook her head from side to side but had to laugh at herself when she felt his chuckle rumble through him. "You'll pay for that later."

"I'll hold you to that."

Raising her eyes to his, she smirked at him. "Fell right into your trap, didn't I?"

His full-on smile had always caused the breath to seize in her chest. His straight white teeth shone against his naturally tanned skin. The crinkle around his eyes was kissable, as were his plump, sexy lips. Putting the whole man together in one package was lethal to the female population.

"Yes, you did. Now that I've caught you, I won't ever let you go, Bri." He spoke sincerely.

Hearing the words from Noah gave Brianna the courage, and the extra push, she needed to confess her own feelings. "You've had me since the moment I met you in the desert, Noah. I don't want to be let go."

The uncharacteristic display of shock on Noah's face momentarily knocked Brianna off-kilter. When he realized she'd misread his reaction, he cupped her face with his hands and poured his love into his kiss.

"Are you saying you've waited for me? All this time?" he asked, his lips brushing against hers from the closeness.

The warmth of his hands on her face seeped through her skin, warming her to the core. Nodding slowly, she silently confirmed his question. Shock turned to relief as he captured her mouth with his again. Overcoming obstacles had become a way of life for him, but this was one hurdle he'd never expected to clear.

A pure, unconditional love that was meant for only him had previously been just out of reach. He'd never felt it from his own family. He had accepted that if his parents, who were supposed to love him without stipulations, couldn't manage it, then no one could. But in the most unlikely place on earth, he'd found the very thing that had evaded him his entire life.

The slow song had ended, but neither attempted to move from the crowded dance floor. As strangers dispersed all around them, oblivious to the monumental moment that just passed between them, Noah's focus was solely on Brianna. Whether it was too soon was up for debate, but he knew he wanted Brianna and no one else. His heart was linked to hers, their fates were intertwined, and the profound connection was mutual.

"Let's get a drink," he suggested. "Sit down and talk for a while."

"Okay," she agreed.

She placed her hand in his upturned palm as they walked back to their table. When he wrapped his hand around hers, she felt cherished and protected. She'd waited for him because she couldn't picture herself with anyone else. She wasn't naïve, she didn't have a schoolgirl crush, and she didn't try to convince herself that he'd waited for her.

She just knew herself and what she wanted. She also knew no one else could ever measure up when compared to Noah.

After she'd moved to Miami, her new friends had encouraged her to go out with other guys and not spend her time waiting for Noah. They argued that she didn't know what the future held. They contended it was pointless to remain loyal when he wasn't even aware of her sacrifice.

Remaining true to herself and her feelings, despite what others said, had never felt so good.

They took their seats, and Noah ordered another round before turning his attention back to Brianna. "It seems I only have one speed with you."

"I know exactly what you mean."

"It's a good thing we're on the same page because I know how to make you disappear until you give in to my demands," he jokingly threatened before taking a drink.

"You make that sound very enticing," Brianna teased as she watched his brown eyes darken to black from desire.

"Come home with me tonight, and I'll show you," he promised as he slowly lowered his beer bottle.

"But would you still respect me in the morning?" she asked, partly joking but also part serious.

Understanding dawned in Noah's eyes, and he leaned in to give her a comforting kiss. "Nothing would make me not respect you, Brianna. If you need time to get to know me again first, I'll gladly give you whatever time you need."

"I can't wait to learn everything there is to know about the new Noah Steele," she replied earnestly.

"Let's get out of here," Noah suggested.

"Thought you'd never ask," Brianna laughed.

Rebel watched them both stand, and his knowing smirk made Brianna giggle.

"Something to say, Rebel?" she asked.

"Nothing I haven't already said to my boy, Reaper." Rebel grinned.

"Yeah, yeah, shut up, man," Noah chuckled. "We're heading out. You kids get home before curfew tonight."

"Yes, Dad," Bull deadpanned before taking a swig from his longneck bottle.

"Don't do anything we wouldn't do," Rebel added.

"Should be an interesting night in that case," Noah shot back.

As they walked hand in hand toward the door, they could still hear Bull's and Rebel's laughter carrying over the crowd. "I'm glad the guys came with you tonight. I've missed my brothers," Brianna admitted. "But where's Shadow?"

"He took another assignment," Noah replied, intentionally leaving his answer vague.

"I'm glad you didn't take another one," Brianna replied. "I'm thrilled that you're here. When did you get back home?"

"A few months ago. I've spent that entire time getting my company up and running. Business has taken off faster than I could've hoped for, and I'm so thankful," Noah explained as they walked across the parking lot.

"What company?" she asked excitedly.

"Steele Security," he replied humbly.

"I've heard of your company. You really have been busy. My editor assigned me to a piece in the lifestyle section of the paper. I don't normally report on that type of story, but he asked me to help out in a jam. Anyway, that name kept coming up when the other reporters talked about a huge event coming up soon," Brianna replied. "That's so impressive, honestly. You're already the talk of the town."

Noah's half smile and a nonchalant shrug of one shoulder conveyed exactly what he thought about the notoriety. "We're lucky to have been selected for several excellent contracts, especially for a start-up company."

"It sounds like more than luck to me," Brianna bragged on Noah. "It sounds like the secret is out about how phenomenal you are at your job."

"We'll see," Noah replied. "Enough about me. Let's talk about you."

"Why do I have the feeling you already know all there is to know about me?"

"Fair enough." Noah nodded. "I know you work at the *Miami Herald*, you take the dangerous assignments the others will hardly touch, and you're great at it."

"And?"

"And…I knew you'd be here tonight. You're the only reason I came here." He inclined his head toward the pub. "There's one thing I don't know, though."

"What?" she asked. She was still trying to catch her breath from his admission.

"Did you drive here?" he smiled.

"No, I took a taxi, so I didn't have to worry about driving."

"Good. I'll give you a ride to your apartment," he offered. As he clicked the unlock button on his key fob, the lights on his full-size SUV flashed. He opened her door, helped her into the vehicle, and stole a kiss before he moved around to his side.

"Wait. You know where I live?" Brianna asked as Noah climbed into the driver's seat. "You said apartment."

"The shocked look on your face is so cute," he laughed. "Yes, I know where you live. I'm pretty good at my job, Brianna."

He took the long route to her apartment to keep her for as long as he could. Noah then walked her to the door of her apartment. He took the keys from her hand, unlocked the door, and stepped inside first. "Wait right here."

"Why?" she asked, clearly confused.

"I need to check the apartment before I leave. Just to make sure it's safe for you," he explained.

"Noah, I walk in here alone every day." Brianna shook her head.

"That was before."

"Before what?"

Turning to look her in the eye, he replied, "Before me."

He completed his thorough search of her apartment and returned to where she waited just inside the front door.

"Satisfied that no bad men are hiding in the closets? And that there are no pictures of other men in my bedroom?" Brianna asked pointedly.

"I am now." Noah grinned mischievously.

"Yeah, you're trouble all right," Brianna retorted. "But since I'm already attached to you, I guess I'll still keep you around."

"Damn straight, you will. There's no way you'll ever get rid of me."

He wrapped his arms around her waist and pulled her to him. As he kissed her, his tongue lightly grazed the part in her lips until she opened to give him full access. He moved his hands to her face and cupped her cheeks as he tilted her head to deepen the kiss. He pushed her backward with his body until the wall was at her back.

He slid his hands down her arms until he reached her hands. He grasped them in his, pulled them above her head, and held them in place with one of his hands. The other hand trailed down her shirt, reached the hem, and moved underneath the thin material. When his fingertips found the soft skin of her stomach, she moaned softly.

He pulled away from the kiss, but his fingertips continued to draw slow figure eights on her bare skin as he gazed deeply into her eyes. "You have no idea how hard it's been to stay away from you these last several months. I had to establish my business before I could approach you, to build something for our future. But you've been on my mind every damn day and night."

"Since we're confessing our secrets, I guess I should tell you that I jumped at this job, and the opportunity to move here, because of you. I hoped you'd find me through my articles and realize that I've been in Miami waiting for you," Brianna whispered. "Because you've been on my mind every day and night, too."

The inferno that burned in Noah's eyes revealed the struggle he faced to restrain himself. He placed a soft, chaste kiss on her lips, ran his thumb across them, and let his eyes follow the trail. "If I don't leave now, I won't ever leave. Goodnight, my princess."

The bass timbre of his voice washed his whispers straight through her. She inhaled sharply, her eyes widened, her mouth parted, and the rise and fall of her chest quickened. The ache deep inside her, which spoke of her need for him, increased exponentially as she watched him back away from her toward the door. When his hand grasped the doorknob, she opened her mouth to speak, but he slowly shook his head.

"Tomorrow. Sleep well, princess." With that, Noah slipped out the door, making sure to lock it as he left.

She stood motionless and stared at the door for a full minute after he left. Brianna then finally found her voice. Exasperation and frustration filled her as the scene between them replayed in her mind.

"How the hell am I supposed to sleep now?"

8

CHAPTER EIGHT

Early the next morning, a knock on Brianna's door woke her. She padded to the door in her bare feet, pajama shorts, and a tank top, and peered through the peephole.

"I know you're looking at me, princess. Open the door," Noah called from the other side.

She quickly glanced in the mirror and ran her fingers through her bed hair in a hurried attempt to tame it. "Just a minute," she called.

Laughing, Noah replied, "I know what you look like when you wake up, Brianna. Let me in."

She slowly opened the door and stepped back to give him room to enter. "What are you doing here so early? The sun isn't even up yet."

"I missed you." He shrugged. "Come on." He took her hand as he led her to the bedroom. He shed his clothes down to his boxer briefs before he climbed into her bed. He lay on his side and patted the mattress beside him. "Your spot is getting cold."

She shook her head but smiled before she crawled back into the bed and took her place beside Noah. His arm draped over her from behind, and he pulled her to him, her back to his front. When they were comfortably positioned and fully relaxed, Brianna murmured to him, "I've missed this so much. I've missed you so much."

"So have I, princess. I've been awake all night thinking about how I used to sneak into your tent and crawl into your bed at night. I couldn't get this bed out of my mind, how you were all alone in it. I fought the urge to show up here for as long as I could," he whispered to her.

"Is there really any reason we should fight it anymore, Noah?" Brianna asked tentatively.

"You mean, do I think we're moving too fast?"

"Yes, that's exactly what I mean."

"For some people, it would be way too fast. But it's not for you and me. We obviously both know what we want. Fortunately, that just happens to be each other.

"If there's one thing I've learned in my line of work, it's that we don't have a promise to tomorrow. I don't want to regret not being with you every day. Just because someone, whose opinion doesn't even matter, thinks we should take things slower," Noah stated adamantly.

She turned over to face him and lovingly stroked his cheek. She reveled in the feel of his morning stubble on her skin. "I don't want to take it slowly either, Noah. If anything were to happen to one of us, I'd want you to know exactly how I feel. I'd want you to know why I waited for you to find me, to come home to me."

"Why?" Noah asked. "Tell me why, Brianna."

"Because I love you. I fell in love with you in that desert almost a year ago, and I'm still in love with you today. I'll never stop loving you," she promised.

"I am so completely in love with you, princess."

He rolled her onto her back and positioned his body above hers, with his weight resting on his forearms. As he dipped his face to hers, he covered her mouth with his and instantly brought her entire body to life at once. As he lowered his hips to meet hers, he surged upward and glided across her clit. He groaned when her fingernails dug into his flesh.

Brianna quickly pulled his shirt over his head and ran her hands over his chest and stomach. She lifted her back up off the bed as she placed open-mouth kisses on his bare skin and then trailed her tongue across his chest.

"Are you sure about this?" Noah asked, suddenly serious. "I won't be able to stop if you keep doing that."

"I'm positive, Noah. I have no doubts at all."

He stared intently into her eyes as he looked for any signs of fear or hesitation. Her eyes only spoke to him about the love she felt. It swirled in her cobalt-blue pools, lured him in, and held him as a willing prisoner.

"I want nothing more right now than to give you the things I couldn't give you in that tent. It's about to get loud in here. Hope your neighbors don't mind," he boasted.

He slid his hand down and quickly pulled her tank top over her head. As he slid his body down hers, he captured the hardened peak of her breast in his mouth. While he licked, sucked, and lightly bit it, he lavished attention on the other one with his fingers. He rolled one nipple between his thumb and middle finger then he squeezed it while he bit the other. She writhed beneath him, her fingers ran through his hair, and her moans of pleasure filled the room.

He slid farther down her body, and his mouth continued to work its magic against her skin. When he reached her boy-shorts pajamas, he hooked his fingers into the fabric at her hips and slid them off of her. He took his place between her thighs, his warm tongue circled, his lips sucked, and his teeth grazed her repeatedly until she utterly came apart.

Her screams of ecstasy and heavy breathing were only masked by her demand. "Oh my God, Noah. That was incredible. I can't wait any longer—I need to feel you now."

"Your wish is my command, princess." He smirked and shed his clothes. Within seconds, he was completely naked, sheathed, and restraining himself from pushing deep into her. "I had to let you leave before, even though I didn't want to. As of now, you are mine, and I won't let you go again," he asserted.

"You'll never have to let me go, Noah," she promised.

He leaned his head down to capture her lips again. As his

tongue swirled around hers, he surged forward and drove into her as her nails once again found his bare skin. He caught her moans in his mouth as he pushed forward, arched his back, and surged into her over and over. He felt her inner muscles grip him like erotic velvet fingers. He knew she was close to tumbling over the edge.

He intentionally changed his pace, slowing and breaking their kiss. "You owe me some screams," he murmured in her ear. "I'm collecting them right now."

He hooked his arms behind her knees as he continued his initial barrage on her senses. The intense buildup of pleasure started low in her belly. Her inner muscles gripped and stroked him with each movement until the dam erupted and she screamed out his name.

"Oh my God, Noah!"

"Mmm, I love that sound. That's one."

"You're counting?"

"I'm definitely counting." He smirked before he began moving again. "The second one is coming up very soon."

An hour later, Brianna lay sprawled across the bed, breathing heavily and trying to slow her heart again after the intense physical exertion.

"The number was four, in case you lost count," he boasted.

Brianna's head rested on his chest, her arm draped across his stomach, and her leg wrapped around his. She giggled at his announcement before replying. "Yeah, I was there. I remember. Four is a great number."

"It's okay. I must be more tired than I thought," Noah teased.

"Well, I suppose you need to rest up, then," she challenged. "If that wasn't your best, I'm afraid you have more proving to do."

"You know, one of these days, that smart mouth of yours will get you into trouble," Noah laughed as he pulled her closer to him. "Good thing I'll be there to protect you."

Brianna traced the lines, bumps, and ridges of his abdominal muscles with her fingertips. His body was pure perfection after hours of intense exercise. "I know you're the best at what you do, Noah. But I've always taken pride in my independence and my ability to take care of myself. I don't really need you to protect me."

"Humor me," he replied as his fingers lovingly stroked the smooth skin on her back.

"This is going to be one of those sore spots in our relationship, isn't it?"

"Sounds like it," he replied. "You think you can handle every situation, and I want to handle every situation."

"Compromise?" she asked.

"What are you proposing?"

"If I feel like I'm getting in over my head, I'll ask you for protection," she offered.

"And if I think you're getting in over your head before you realize it?" he asked.

"Tell me. Talk to me about it. But don't try to take away my right to make decisions for myself. It's important to me," she explained.

"It's important to me for you to be safe," he explained patiently. "I understand there will usually be an element of danger in the stories you get, but you have to be smart about it. Don't walk into a situation blind. Don't think you can talk your way out of every situation. The bad guys don't work like that, baby."

"How about I keep you on speed dial, then?" she kidded.

"I'd better be on speed dial regardless. But if you're going into something dangerous, I'll be beside you," he clarified.

"Agree to disagree." She shrugged.

"Disagree all you want. As long as I'm beside you."

She shook her head as she muttered under her breath, "Stubborn man."

Noah's answering whisper made her laugh. "Stubborn woman."

Over the next several months, Noah and Brianna barely left each other's side. She joined him at Steele Security as frequently as her position allowed. She learned the business from the inside out and helped to set up the office routines efficiently. Gaining insider knowledge of how security teams were set up, how they communicated, and where their vulnerable spots were located gave her a new perspective for her own protection.

When Brianna ventured into the seedier parts of the city on a tip for a new story lead, Noah acted as her personal sentinel. He stood guard and dared anyone to make the wrong move. Pride swelled in Noah's chest every time he watched her in action.

She was a natural at making people comfortable with talking to her, giving her their innermost secrets, and willingly giving up information that could get them killed. She drew them in with her kindness, comforted them with the assurance they were doing the right thing, and encouraged them with her belief in them.

He stayed just far enough away to allow her space to talk to her subject, but close enough to intervene if necessary. She still maintained the innocence of someone who hadn't experienced the dregs of humanity—the false belief that it would always happen to someone else. Noah's line of work had proved the opposite to him. Anyone would screw others over with the right motivation.

"So, now that I know enough about Steele Security that I could be one of your agents, does that mean I can go on my assignments without you?" Brianna asked one evening.

"Nope," Noah replied casually.

"Wow. Thanks for the talk, Noah."

He leaned forward in his chair, placed his elbows on his knees, and locked his eyes on hers. With her rapt attention on him, he rephrased his original answer. "No, Brianna, that does not mean you can go without me. You know what we do, but you haven't been trained as we have. You're still way too trusting of others—people who aren't known for being model citizens."

"You don't think I could take you?"

Noah laughed heartily. "No, you can't take me. You're nowhere close to being able to take me down."

"Let's try it," she suggested.

"By all means," he said as he stood. "I'll even stand still and let you do your worst. Or best."

"Really? I can try?"

"Yes. Come at me."

Brianna stood and let her eyes roam around the large living room. She allowed time for her gaze to settle on specific areas of the room but didn't look directly at Noah. She tried to remain aloof and casual as she planned her attack. Suddenly, she burst forward, wrapped her arms around his waist, and attempted to tackle him to the ground.

Leaned forward, with her weight pushing down through her thighs, calves, and feet, she pushed with all her might. The wall of muscle wouldn't budge an inch. That is until he bent slightly at the waist, wrapped his arms around her waist, and effortlessly lifted her off the ground—and held her upside down.

He walked around the room with her in his arms, and she continued to flail, curse, and attempt to kick her way out of the predicament. To no avail. He carefully placed her on the couch before he covered her body with his, pinned her down, and prevented her from making the slightest movement.

With his face hovered just above hers, he chided her calmly. "This is why you need me with you. If any other man did this to you, I'd have to kill him, dump the body in a vat of acid, and throw it overboard into the ocean."

"You only won this round because I wasn't expecting to be picked up."

"Exactly my point. You have to be prepared for anything out there. I'm not trying to control you, Brianna. All I want is to keep you safe and sound."

"I understand."

Noah narrowed his eyes at her, knowing that she didn't actually agree with him. A knock at his door momentarily drew his attention away from the conversation. As he rose from the couch, he cut his eyes back to her. "Don't think this conversation is over yet."

"Wouldn't dream of it." She smiled sweetly.

He shook his head, ran his hand through his hair, and muttered something under his breath as he walked away.

"What was that? I couldn't hear you."

"You weren't meant to," he replied dryly.

He couldn't help but smile when he heard her laugh in response. Their relationship progressed so smoothly, so naturally that he didn't question whether they were meant for each other. It had become a given. They alternated staying at each other's places, and that

hadn't been a burden at all, especially when he infinitely appreci-
ated the company.

Before he reached the door, he checked the security camera to
see who their uninvited visitor was. When he saw his old friend at
the door, his strides lengthened, and he quickly swung the door
open.

"Richard! So good to see you, brother," he said, giving his friend
a brief, manly hug.

"You, too, man. Sorry to just drop in on you like this," Richard
replied.

"You're always welcome here. Come on in," Noah said as he
stepped aside to give him room to enter.

"Man, this is a nice house," Richard said, astonishment lacing
his voice. "Steele Security must be doing very well."

"We are doing very well, actually. Growing more every day,"
Noah beamed.

"That's great. I'm proud of you. I actually have some great news
for you," Richard began. "I've moved into a better position and can
help influence decisions on escorts to foreign countries. I'd like to
hire Steele Security. We'll have to sign a new contract for each
escort, but it pays well."

"That's awesome news, Richard. Congratulations on your
promotion, and thanks for your confidence in us. You know we
won't let you down."

"I have no doubt about that, Reaper," Richard replied.

Brianna heard voices in the foyer, stepped out of the den, and
moved toward the conversation. When she reached the doorway to
the entrance, Richard turned and eyed her for a moment.

"Brianna. I didn't expect to find you here," he said, somewhat
stunned.

"Hello, Judge," Brianna replied. The discomfort she'd felt
around him in the desert returned to her full force, though she still
couldn't identify what drove it. "How've you been?"

"I've been great, Brianna. Never better," Richard sneered.
"You?"

"Same," she replied. "Never better."

"I don't think you two have ever officially been introduced—not with full names anyway," Noah said, looking between them both. "Brianna Tate, Richard Hollingsworth."

"Richard, it's nice to meet you finally," Brianna laughed.

"Likewise, Brianna," Richard replied. Turning to Noah, he continued. "Do you have time to finish the conversation about investing in your company?"

"Sure, come on into my office, Richard." Noah gestured with his arm. To Brianna, he added, "Babe, it won't take too long,"

"Don't worry about me," she replied as she lifted up on her tiptoes to kiss him. "I have plenty of work to do to keep me busy."

The two men walked into the office and closed the door behind them. Taking a seat, Richard gave Noah his sly smile. "So, things are pretty hot and heavy between you and Brianna, huh? Are you already living together?"

Noah knew there would be scoffers and naysayers, so he had prepared his answers to the intrusive questions ahead of time. "We spend a lot of time together, but we each still have our own place."

"Isn't it a bit too soon for all this lovey-dovey shit? Most men I know wouldn't so willingly tie themselves down to one woman."

"We obviously don't know the same men, then," Noah replied, intentionally keeping his tone in check. "We've been together for just a few months shy of a year. But we've been alternating staying at each other's places for the majority of that time. A real man wouldn't be afraid to admit when he's in love, or care about what others think."

"Touché. I've never been in love myself, so I wouldn't know. Anyway, if you're happy, that's all that matters," Richard conceded, attempting to appease Noah. "Now, let's talk about why I came here. I'd like to invest in your company, only acting as a silent partner."

"I have a few questions about that." Noah steepled his hands. "First, why would you want to do that when you're in DC?"

"I bought a house here, and I travel back and forth on the weekends. I work in DC, but Miami is my home," Richard explained calmly.

"Second question. Wouldn't that be a conflict of interest since you have influence over the contracts?"

"Technically, I don't influence the contracts. The head of the department that executes the contracts is a good friend of mine, and he trusts my judgment," Richard shrugged. "It's best for everyone when we have escorts we can trust. Plus, you already have the highest level of security clearance there is, so that's one less hassle."

"Third question. What do you mean by 'silent partner,' exactly?" Noah asked.

"Only that I put up part of the operating money and you guarantee my contracts always come first. I'll give you plenty of notice, but I can't wait if the reigning queen of Hollywood comes to Miami and wants to hire you."

"You realize I don't need your money to operate my company, right?"

"I do. It's more like insurance that someone will always be available to cover our people. My name doesn't even have to be on any of your legal documents," Richard offered.

"I'll hold your money in escrow in the event I have to hire extra help unexpectedly. But I don't foresee a problem with being able to accommodate DOD's needs," Noah agreed.

Richard stood, extended his hand to Noah, and as they shook hands to seal the deal, he smiled widely. "Glad to be in business with you, Steele Security. This will definitely be a very lucrative business."

"Thank you for choosing Steele Security for your safety needs." Noah finished with a smile and a firm, final handshake.

9

CHAPTER NINE

"What was that about?" Brianna asked as Richard left without saying goodbye.

"He wants to be a silent partner in my business," Noah replied, absently rubbing his chin.

"Silent? Why?" Brianna asked.

"He said so he'll get first dibs on the escort contracts. He recommended us to his buddy in the DOD, so he wants to make sure we always have coverage for them."

"I really don't understand the loyalty you have toward Richard," Brianna blurted out.

Noah's head jerked sideways to look at her. His brows furrowed into a V, his eyes narrowed, and his mouth hung open. "He's been a friend since high school and has had my back since I first met him. Why would you say that?"

"He just gives me a really uncomfortable feeling, and you know I don't get that vibe often. I don't trust him."

"Well, I do, and I think I know him a lot better than you do."

Brianna nodded as she agreed only with his latter statement, but she wanted to drop the subject before they had their first fight over nothing more than her intuition. Her gut screamed that there was more to the story with Richard than he let on. Noah was loyal to a fault, and she feared that unyielding loyalty would end up harming him one day. If it didn't come from Richard, then it would happen with someone else whom he trusted without question. The code Reaper lived by didn't always apply in the world Noah now lived in.

"So, are you still hiring more men?" Brianna asked as she abruptly changed the subject.

"Yes, I'm building up my empire," Noah joked. "There are more requests for proposals in my inbox, and several more arrive each day. It's amazing how many people need security consultants for their homes and businesses, and how many traveling celebrities need extra security to go out in public."

"I think I may need extra security this Saturday night," Brianna admitted. "Can you spare anyone for me?"

"Where are you going Saturday night?" Noah asked as concern overtook his features. For Brianna to willingly ask for an escort, there had to be real danger involved.

"There was a tip called into the police, but they don't have the manpower to investigate. He called the paper and asked for someone there to investigate it instead. It sounds like it could be a significant story if it pans out. I have to go into northwest Miami to meet with my source," Brianna explained.

"Northwest Miami? At night?" Noah stared at her like she'd lost her mind.

"Hopefully I'll have back up."

"Today is Monday. Your meeting is being planned several days in advance. That gives anyone who wants to do you harm plenty of time to plan an attack. Why does this meeting have to wait so long to take place?"

"Because that's when my informant is off work and can talk to me," she explained.

"You're definitely not going alone. I'll call Bull and see if he's available to come with us."

"Oh, good, security in stereo," she joked. "I'll not only have the two of you in my ears, but you'll make outrageous demands and scare my source into permanent hiding."

"Bri?"

"Yeah?"

"You should run now."

She squealed with amusement as she ran through the house, toward the sweeping staircase. Just as she reached the bottom step, she suddenly flew through the air and landed on a very thick, muscular shoulder. Noah's arm wrapped around her and held her securely in place as he took the stairs two at a time. When he reached the landing at the top, he swatted her ass playfully. "Be still. You're squirming."

"Because you're carrying me over your shoulder!" she exclaimed with laughter.

"We're almost to the bedroom. It's time for you to put that sassy mouth to better use than talking," Noah replied suggestively.

"My personal Neanderthal man. What more could a girl ask for?" Brianna mocked.

"Yeah, you're way overdue for an attitude adjustment." Noah jokingly threatened her as he deposited her onto the bed.

"Well, come adjust my attitude for me, big guy," she cooed seductively.

"If you insist," Noah replied as one side of his mouth rose in his sexy, cocky grin. "I'm more than happy to oblige."

Noah and Brianna filled the rest of the week with the usual routine—completing RFPs for new contracts, researching information for her upcoming blockbuster story, alternating spending the night at his enormous house and her small apartment, and making love until exhaustion overtook them.

Saturday night, Bull arrived early for the rendezvous in one of the more dangerous neighborhoods of the northwest Miami area. Brianna used her most persuasive techniques on Noah to get him to relax about the meeting. While he loved her attempts, he refused to budge an inch when it came to ensuring her safety.

"Hey, Sunny," Bull said as he walked in. "Are you ready for your meeting tonight?"

"Hey, Bull," she replied, hugging his neck. "I am more than

ready. Noah shouldn't have asked you to come along, though. He's overreacting."

"Have you ever been to that neighborhood before?" Bull asked.

"No, but it can't be any worse than the others I've been in."

"Yes, it can. You'll see, and you'll probably wish we had an army with us," Bull chuckled. "Just stick close to Reaper. He won't let anything happen to you."

"Where will you be?"

"I'll be around. Close enough to help but not where anyone will see me," Bull replied.

"This just seems like overkill to me."

"It may be, but I'm not taking any chances with my only little sister." Bull smiled.

"You know that I can't resist when you say that, Bull," she playfully admonished him. He shrugged and laughed in reply, telling her that he knew exactly what he was doing.

Bull gave her a quick kiss on the cheek and continued walking until he found Noah in his office. "Hey, Reap. You ready for tonight?"

"Yeah, I've had a couple of guys checking out things in that apartment building today. We're not walking in there blind," he replied.

"Let's see what you got."

Noah handed Bull several pictures of the area, building, and apartment layouts. He also had a full background check on the informant with the help of an old friend.

"So, we're meeting a Mr. Ammar Wasem tonight. Originally from a small village in Syria, close to the Iraqi border. Moved to the US eight years ago. Married, two young kids, and has maintained steady employment. No arrest, no blips on the radar for anything, not even speeding. Either he's legit, or he has the perfect cover for a sleeper cell member," Bull solemnly concluded.

"Either we're walking into a trap, or he really does have information about a big story for Brianna. At this point, I'm not sure which would be worse," Noah replied, clearly agitated.

Noah stepped into the doorway and called down the hall. "Brianna, can you come here for a minute, babe?"

A couple of minutes later, Brianna entered Noah's office and took a seat across the desk from him. "You rang?" She twirled her hair around her finger and gave him a playful smile.

"I did." He grinned in reply. "Tell me about this tip your source called into the police and then to your paper."

"He said there are American gunrunners in his former village, setting up a black market to sell guns to the rebels in the area. If they're successful, he said the rebels would slaughter anyone who defies them. His brother still lives there," she explained.

"Did he say who they think is behind this?" Bull asked.

"Not exactly. He alluded to the US military, but then he also said businessmen were involved. He wouldn't talk on the phone for very long since it isn't secure. He sounded terrified."

"What floor is he on?" Noah asked Bull.

"Third floor. I've already staked out my lookout spot. You'll both be well covered," Bull replied.

"You went to his apartment?" Brianna asked. "What if he saw you and got scared off?"

"I'm only seen when I want someone to see me, Sunny," Bull replied. "Since I didn't want to be seen, no one saw me."

"You know, Bull," Brianna spoke, trying to hide the smile in her voice. "I'm having a hard time deciding if I liked you better when you didn't talk to me, or now when you talk too much."

"Brianna," Bull replied, failing to hide his humor. "You'll pay for that when Reaper isn't around to protect you from me."

"If I didn't know you both better, I'd swear you were brother and sister from how you pick at each other." Noah shook his head in mock reprimand.

"She usually starts it," Bull said defensively.

"Spoken like a true big brother," Brianna retorted.

Later that evening, Noah, Brianna, and Bull left for Brianna's meeting. While the nervous energy caused Brianna's leg to jump, Noah remained calm and relaxed as his eyes assessed every aspect of their surroundings. Bull was in a separate vehicle, but he stayed back to help watch for any tails on Noah and Brianna. Even though Noah was highly skilled at identifying a tail, he'd never take chances on safety where Brianna was concerned.

Once they reached the neighborhood in northwest Miami, Brianna instinctively slid her hand over to grasp Noah's. His squeeze helped to calm her fraying nerves but didn't wholly alleviate them.

"I'm so glad you and Bull are with me tonight, Noah."

Without blatantly gawking at the surroundings, she panned the area with her eyes to take in the neighborhood. The dilapidated buildings were covered in graffiti, some with gang tags, some simply with insults hurled at anyone reading them. The bars on the windows and doors told her everything she needed to know about the crime rate of the area. The groups of people huddled at different spots along the streets slowly turned their heads and watched the sleek black SUV roll by them with blatant suspicion.

"So you don't want to go in alone?" he asked teasingly as he parked the car.

"No, I actually don't want to go in at all right now," she replied. "But if this story is real, I have to cover it, so I need to get over my irrational fears."

"Fear isn't always irrational, Bri. You have to control it—don't let it control you. But it's healthy to have fear because it keeps you on your toes, alerts you when something's not right, and can help save your life."

"Control it. Got it." She took a deep breath and looked at Noah. "Ready to go in?"

Noah checked the area around the car again and nodded. "Let's go."

Once she was out of the car, Brianna rushed to Noah's side, heeding Bull's advice to stick close. Noah wrapped his arm around her protectively and pulled her slightly in front of him. His right hand slid to the gun holster hidden at his side and quickly unsnapped it.

"Let's take the stairs," Noah said as he pushed the door open.

He quickly checked the stairwell and found it empty. They hurriedly took the stairs to the third floor. Noah covered each entry point as they passed and they worked their way to apartment 3F. Brianna stood in front of the door, took another calming breath, and knocked.

The clinking and clanking of internal locks and chains being turned and removed filled the air. The door opened a couple of inches as an eyeball filled the dark space. Noah had his back against the wall, his hand on his gun, and was ready to pounce at the first sign of trouble.

"Who are you?" the thickly accented voice of a female asked.

"I'm Brianna Tate. I'm here to talk to Ammar Wasem. He called me at the *Miami Herald*."

"Shatha, let her in," a male voice commanded from inside the apartment.

The young lady stepped back and opened the door wider to allow them to enter. When Noah stepped around to follow Brianna, Shatha's eyes grew wide as her bottom jaw dropped open. She started to protest when Brianna spoke.

"This is my bodyguard. He goes where I go. He won't interfere."

"He can wait in the kitchen," Ammar replied. "We will talk in the living room."

Shatha showed Noah to the kitchen and offered him food and drinks. He politely declined as he took a seat with a perfect line of sight to Brianna. He couldn't hear the hushed conversation from where he sat, but anyone after Brianna would have to get past him first.

When Brianna took her seat across from Ammar, she pulled her notebook and pen out of her bag to prepare for her interview. The voice-activated recorder rested on the coffee table and waited for the cue that it was time to begin.

"To recap our previous conversation, you said your brother still lives in your home village of Balikh. You believe that someone in the US military, possibly with business connections, is selling weapons to hostile rebels in the area. Is that correct?" she asked.

"That is correct. The man behind it is an American, and he is working with some evil men in Balikh. They are setting up an elaborate front to hide their sins," Ammar replied. "The blood on their hands will be great if they're not stopped in time."

"Do you have any proof of this accusation? Any names of those involved?"

"I only have the word of my brother. That is proof enough for me. He read your article on the soldiers you joined in the desert, Miss Tate. He was very impressed with how you covered it. That's why I called your paper.

"We hoped you would take this story, find out who this American is that's behind it, and stop him. It would be easier, and faster, to stop this one man than to stop many in my country. Many who are abandoning their true faith and resorting to becoming terrorists."

"I can tell you're very passionate about this subject," Brianna acknowledged. "The rebels' actions seem to be speaking for an entire ethnic group of people, don't they?"

"Yes, that's part of their plan. If a group this large is divided and fighting against each other, it makes it harder for anyone on the outside to distinguish the good guys from the bad guys. By the time you figure it out, it's too late, and the damage has already been done," he explained sadly.

"How does your brother have this information?"

"It's part of his job. He knows the inherent danger in coming forward and giving out this information. But saying nothing could result in the death of tens of thousands of people. Neither of us can live with that on our conscience."

"What is the information he has?"

"He works in customs for our country. He received a request for fast-track approval of an incoming shipment. When he looked into it further, he discovered more and more information.

"The individual pieces of the puzzle look benign, but you'll see the full picture of the cancer that's taking over Syria when you put all their pieces together. I will tell you what I can tonight, but my brother is the one who wants to speak with you," Ammar finished.

The more Ammar told Brianna about his homeland, the American, and the black-market arms dealers, the more spectacular the story sounded. Even the most unbelievable parts of the story became plausible as she felt his anguish through his words.

At the end of the interview, she thanked him for his time and hospitality. "Ammar, what you and your brother are doing is very brave. Even though you're worried about the safety of your brother and your own family, I guarantee your names won't be used or given out by me."

"Miss Tate, if you can help stop this travesty, all the worry and danger will be worth it. There's so much at stake, it's hard to pick just one or two things to focus on," Ammar replied sadly.

"I'll be back in touch soon. Please give your brother my number," she said, handing him her card. "I'm very interested in talking to him and helping to stop this from happening."

As soon as Noah and Brianna were seated back in the vehicle, Noah's phone began ringing. He transferred the call to the Bluetooth connection, and Bull's voice came across the speakers.

"Drop this story now, Brianna. Please," he pleaded.

The sincerity and concern in his voice shook Brianna. "What? Why would you say that?"

"I heard the whole conversation. If it's true, it's too dangerous for you to get mixed up in it. This operation should be a joint task force between the CIA, NSA, and the FBI—at least. You are not trained for this, Bri. You'll end up getting killed. Please don't," Bull implored her.

"Bull, you're overreacting. I'm just investigating this and getting the facts. I'm not going to apprehend them myself. I'll dig and find out who's behind it, then turn the evidence over to the authorities. I'll have the complete story out of it, then," Brianna consoled.

"Reaper, call me when you can," Bull stated flatly before disconnecting.

Brianna felt her heart drop to her feet at Bull's abrupt disconnection. She'd seen him go from burning hot to freezing cold in zero-point-two seconds with others before, but never with her. Their sibling bond had emerged in the desert and had become much stronger in the time she'd reconnected with Noah. To be shut out so heartlessly stung her to the core.

"What did he say, Brianna?" Noah cut his eyes at her.

Brianna knew deep down that it wasn't in Bull's nature to overreact to anything. She swallowed the pain rising from her chest and recounted the entire conversation for Noah. He drove wordlessly and listened intently to every word all the way back to his house.

As he pulled into his garage, Noah turned off the ignition but didn't move to exit the car. His eyes swung up to meet Brianna's. His approach with Brianna was softer than Bull's but packed no less punch.

"I can't lose you, Brianna. What we have, I've never had with anyone before. Without you, I'm only a shell of a man—completely hollow inside. Not really living, not really dying. The love I have for you could never be given to anyone else."

"You'll never lose me, Noah." She crawled over the center console to sit in his lap. She stroked his face as she spoke. "I waited for you, and I would've kept waiting if you hadn't come home when you did.

"After meeting you, spending time with you, and falling so deeply in love with you, I knew there'd never be another man in my life. We both knew that our jobs would have some danger factor to them when we started this. Don't ask me to change."

"Don't make me live through losing you," he said grimly.

Before she could answer, he wrapped his arms around her and crushed her to him. "I love you in ways I've never loved anyone. I depend on you in ways I've never depended on another. You're as much as part of me as I am, Bri."

He lifted her in his arms, slid out of the vehicle, and carried Brianna the entire way to their bedroom. He poured all the words he couldn't verbalize into their lovemaking as he spoke to her wordlessly.

You own my heart.
All of my love is yours.
Stay with me forever.

10

CHAPTER TEN

The courier dropped off a large envelope at Noah's house that had originally been delivered to the *Miami Herald* office. Brianna held it in her hands, felt the weight of the documents inside as they magnified and multiplied in her heart. Her source from the remote desert village found a way to get the copied documents to her so she could begin researching before meeting him in person.

She placed the unopened envelope on her desk and stared at it as if she could bore a hole in it from her gaze alone. She remembered their conversation from several weeks before, and she still felt the urgency and fear in the man's voice.

"Miss Tate," he began tentatively, his accent thick and difficult to understand over the phone. "You are a reporter, yes?"

"Yes, I'm the journalist, Brianna Tate. Who is this?" she asked, her journalistic senses tingling with a premonition that this could be exactly what she needed for a breakthrough story.

"You spoke with my brother a few weeks ago. I found your name on a story you wrote about the American military presence in the Middle East. I've stumbled upon proof that rebels are planning to buy American guns. These rebels will raid my village and kill my people. I'm asking for your help to stop this travesty."

"How did you stumble upon this proof? Who do you believe is supplying the rebels with guns? Where are you from? I'm going to need more information to go on than this," she pushed. She knew she had to verify that what this man said matched the information Ammar had given her.

"I have several documents that I found and copied. They're the shipping manifests, and I can get the separate corresponding receipt log that matches, shipment for shipment. A military transport plane has been scheduled to deliver them. Someone high up must be involved, approving the shipments.

"You'll have to come here to get the receipt log in person, though. I can't risk copying and mailing it, in case the mail is intercepted," he whispered. "I would be found out instantly as I'm the only one who catalogues the shipments."

Brianna convinced him to share all of his pertinent personal information with her. Before she hung up, she had his name, exact location, and a time and place to meet. He promised to mail the copied shipping manifest documents to her. If she agreed that there was a story worth pursuing after reviewing the documents, she would then travel halfway around the world to meet with him in person.

She ripped open the cardboard envelope and quickly removed the paperwork inside to begin scouring the information. She immediately recognized the logo at the top of every manifest, and she suddenly wrapped her arms around her midsection, doubled over, and fought the intense nausea that washed over her. Her hands shook, her heart raced, and her thoughts whipped through her mind in a blur. Two words stood out like neon signs in the pitch-black night.

Steele Security.

"No, I refuse to believe Noah plays any part in this. He wouldn't do this." Brianna talked to herself as she paced back and forth.

Over the following several weeks, she spent every waking hour researching the dates and information shown on the invoices. As she pored over the documents, she found several suspicious transactions and traced offshore bank account numbers. Each new revelation brought her back to the same conclusion.

There was definitely a ringleader arranging the illegal weapon shipments. But the identity of that one person wasn't obvious. The documentation to support the armed escorts by Steele Security was all in place, all official, and all pointed to Noah Steele as the man behind the front.

The strain of all the evidence she'd found weighed heavily on Brianna's heart and mind. On the one hand, if she believed what she'd found was true, then she had to believe the worst about the man she loved more than anything in the world. She would have to face the fact that she really didn't know the man she practically lived with, gave her love to, and shared her bed with, at all. She'd have to admit to herself that she'd made an egregious mistake in trusting him with her life.

On the other hand, if she chose to ignore it, and the data were actually true, she'd be just as guilty as he was. If she let blind faith take over instead of the cold, hard facts she'd grown accustomed to, she would go against everything she ever believed in. When this story broke wide open, and it definitely would, her own reputation would be scrutinized every bit as harshly as Noah's would.

Either way, she couldn't find a solution to this situation that didn't result in losing something she didn't think she could live without. From her viewpoint, she would lose Noah, her career, or both at the same time. Her career choice provided her with access to people and documents that she wouldn't have been able to reach otherwise. She realized that what she was actually searching for was the proof that Noah was innocent.

Over those same weeks of research, she approached Noah with various questions about his line of work. After having spent so much time around a nosy, inquisitive reporter, Noah stopped questioning why she sometimes needed very specific information.

"Noah." Brianna approached him. "I have a few questions about your government contracts for security transports."

"Shoot," he replied, leaning back from his desk and giving her his full attention.

"Do you provide armed escorts for materials or weapons shipments?"

"No, we only provide armed escorts for people. Mainly officials who are traveling to highly volatile areas," he replied.

"So, your guys wouldn't be on the plane unless a person needed protection?"

"That's right," Noah confirmed.

"Why wouldn't the military just send an armed squad with them?"

"They don't always have the extra manpower to spare. Troops are stationed everywhere, and each person has a specific job to do. They can't just drop that job because one of the suits decides he needs to be in the Middle East or Africa," Noah elaborated.

"Who has the authority to set up a transport contract?" Brianna asked, trying to keep her voice calm and her breathing even as she waited.

"Well, the senior director of the Department of Defense has to sign the contract with us," Noah explained. Brianna held her breath. "But Richard is my liaison with the DOD. He has the contracts drawn up, signed, and executed."

Brianna gasped, her eyes grew wide, and her mouth gaped open. Noah's eyes narrowed at her uncharacteristic response, his head tilted to the left, and his arms slowly crossed over his body.

Richard Hollingsworth.

The man who was also known as Judge.

Richard had been coming much more frequently over the past few months. Having a house in Miami was the perfect excuse for him to show up with a contract for Noah to sign rather than sending it over the secure email system DOD used. The missing pieces of the maddening puzzle began to become clearer to Brianna. She had no proof of it, but her gut instinct told her she was on the right path.

"I just realized I forgot about a meeting. I-I'd better go," Brianna stammered.

Noah's face became unreadable. She knew he was onto her lie. Not only was her response openly obvious, Noah had been trained in all manners of reading people's expressions, so he could see straight through her ruse. She'd worked hard to keep her features schooled when she'd planned surprises for him in the past. She wanted to kick herself now because she knew she'd failed miserably during a time when she desperately needed her emotions to remain neutral.

All of her digging, researching, and questioning others had revealed more lies, more disturbing revelations, and a story that was bigger than she could handle. She couldn't break this story and expect no repercussions. Bull's dire warning when she first took this story replayed in her mind, telling her she wasn't trained for this and she'd end up hurt.

What scared her most was what would happen to Noah and his business. She knew she had been acting differently toward him since her investigation trail implicated Noah. Intense levels of worry and stress over what she should do and what she should believe had changed her, made her doubt everything she thought she knew, and kept her awake at night.

A week later, she tried to approach the subject again by asking Noah different questions. This time, she focused more on Richard specifically, rather than the business aspect of it.

"How long have you known Richard?" she asked.

"Not sure exactly, since before high school. Why do you ask?" Noah eyed her suspiciously.

"What was he like in school?" she asked.

"A lot like he is now. Hard for most people to get along with. He had a few close friends but kept his circle small. His family had money, and he liked to flaunt it a little too much. He also had a reputation for using girls and dumping them," Noah said as he tilted his head and cut his eyes at Brianna.

"Why did he decide to join the military?"

He crossed his arms over his chest as it expanded with his extra deep breath. "For the same reason I did. *To piss his father off.* Why are you asking so many questions about Richard all of a sudden?"

"I never interviewed him when we were in the Middle East. Just tying up some loose ends," she lied.

"I don't think so, Brianna." Noah slowly shook his head. "That was too long ago, and your article about that has long since been out of circulation. Want to try again?"

Sighing, Brianna had to admit she didn't have a reason to ask questions about Noah's friend that she could give him. Their relationship became more strained from Brianna's suspicions about Noah's involvement, and from Noah's suspicions about Brianna and Richard. She had always tried to remain unbiased in her reporting, always giving both sides of the story and not slanting the facts to weigh heavier to one side. But with this story, she reluctantly conceded she was desperately searching for any proof that Noah was completely innocent.

"It's complicated, Noah," she dodged.

"Complicated?" His voice rose as his brows furrowed. "What *exactly* is complicated between you and Richard?"

"You know how some of your work is classified and you can't tell me about it? How all of the missions you were on are still classified and you won't trust me with any information about them? But I don't push you for it because I know you have good reasons for not telling me. I need that same respect from you right now," Brianna insisted.

He leaned back in his chair and continuously assessed her every reaction. Reaper narrowed his eyes in anger as he spoke. "*Classified information* and *hidden information* are two very different things."

"Sometimes they're one and the same. Aren't they?" she replied sadly.

"It would seem so."

Brianna left Noah's office more hurt and confused than when she'd entered it. She still had no concrete proof to clear Noah's name, but she knew in her heart that he'd never be part of an illegal scheme. Especially not one that involved smuggling guns to rebels in third world countries. What kept her from involving the authorities was that they wouldn't care what her heart told her. On paper, Noah looked guilty as hell.

Richard had knowingly involved his longtime friend in his illegal scheme, but he'd set everything up so only Noah would be blamed. Richard's name wasn't actually on any of the paperwork, Brianna was positive of that. He had made sure all the official names and seals were in place.

Since he wasn't a senior director, he wasn't authorized to

arrange security details for anyone. She concluded that Richard must have forged the senior director's signature on the contracts he arranged with Steele Security, allowing the DOD to pay the bills for transporting his weapons. She deduced that the man who was being escorted must be in on the operation, too. She still had to find rock-solid proof that Noah wasn't involved in any of the illegal business occurring.

But how? she asked herself.

Over the following week, Brianna and Noah avoided each other as much as possible. The unintentional silent treatment ate away at the thin sheet of trust they were both treading on. Noah spent more time in his office, while Brianna spent her time tracking down every possible bit of information she could find. One contact directed her to another, until she reached the desk of someone in the DOD who could answer her questions about government contracts.

"George Dant," he answered.

"Hi, this is Brianna Tate with the *Miami Herald*," she introduced herself for the twelfth time that morning. "I'm trying to find some information about a private contractor the DOD uses to escort officials and dignitaries to hostile countries. Can you help me?"

"Sure, that's an easy one. We don't have any such contractor. Government officials traveling to hot zones are only escorted by US military convoys. No private contractors can be used due to security clearance requirements," he explained. "No one outside the military and a few governmental agencies are eligible for the level needed."

"I wasn't aware of that stipulation," Brianna stammered. "Are there any situations where a privately contracted security firm would be used on a military transport plane? Especially one that had the security clearance from prior military service?"

"I suppose it's possible, though I can't think of any off the top of my head. Usually when we contract, we don't provide their transportation too. The contract would be for the whole package."

"This is very helpful. Thank you so much, George," she replied glumly.

"Anytime."

Hanging up, she glanced at her clock and realized that time was quickly slipping away from her. The tension in the air still hung thick, and their once-happy home had become oppressive. With her flight to meet with her informant approaching later that night, she decided she had to clear the air with Noah.

She'd tell him everything and allow him to help her set the record straight. She realized that was the path she should've taken from the outset, and she considered how she'd approach the subject with him. This was more his expertise anyway. This story was much bigger than she'd anticipated, and too much was at stake to make a mistake now.

When she entered his office, she kept her voice calm and even but awkwardly shifted from foot to foot as she stood in the doorway.

"Noah, can we please talk about what's really going on?"

Her voice was quiet, and for the first time since he met Brianna, she seemed almost afraid to ask him a question. He watched carefully as her eyes moved around the room, not settling on any one thing for too long. The sadness in her eyes was obvious, and he didn't know how to respond.

He mused, *Yes, Brianna, what exactly is going on?*

He'd definitely sensed a change in their relationship over the past few weeks. He had never considered it to be calm by any stretch of the imagination. She was a headstrong investigative reporter who pursued every aspect of her life with the same determination she displayed for a really interesting lead. He was a former Delta Force operative who was every bit as headstrong and determined, if not more.

He knew when he met her that she was very ambitious. She wouldn't get the good stories by sitting on the sidelines, or being afraid to ask the tough questions. She had never backed down from a good debate, especially with him. But for the last several weeks, there had been a different air between them.

"Now is not a good time, Bri," he stated flatly. "I'm very busy."

He couldn't bring himself to look her in the eye, and he felt like a coward for it. So he continued diligently studying the paper in front of him instead. He didn't actually see one damn thing that was on the page. All he knew was that if this conversation played out how he thought it would, his world would come crashing down around him.

Facing down enemies with a fully automatic machine gun aimed squarely at his head was nowhere near as daunting as facing what he believed to be the case here. She'd become withdrawn, secretive, and intentionally created distance between them. She'd quietly creep into their bedroom at night, long after he'd gone to bed. She had stopped waking him to make love after she had a late night of researching and writing. All the signs were there, pointing to the one conclusion he wasn't ready to accept. She was preparing to leave him but hadn't decided how to tell him yet.

The thought of losing her shut him down mentally. Living without her touch shut him down emotionally. At least with a tangible enemy, he could form an effective plan of attack and protect what was his. With this, he had no plan of attack. He had no recourse. All he had was a vision of life without the one person who'd given him hope of having a happy family life.

She cleared her throat nervously, and she couldn't hide the disappointment and sadness in her voice. "Okay, Noah. I didn't mean to bother you at work. We just really need to talk. But I understand you're too busy for me."

"Yeah, lots to do. We can talk later, okay?"

He still wouldn't look her in the eye. He mentally berated himself for how he refused to deal with the situation. She stood before him, asking for his time and attention, but he was too troubled to give her what she needed. His inner voice was sorely irritated with him. *"Pussy—man up, and look at her!"*

She lingered in front of his desk for a few seconds longer and inhaled, as if she were about to say something else, but instead, she turned and slowly walked away. He allowed himself to look up at that moment and watch her leave. He noticed how her toned, athletic body moved. She had the muscle-toned body of the true yoga fanatic and long-distance runner he knew she was. He noticed how her long, straight blond hair glittered under the lights, even under the unforgiving fluorescents.

But one thing was definitely different in her stance. She had always held her head high and her shoulders back, as if she were ready to take on anything and anyone. Now, as she left his office, he noticed she looked at the ground, and her shoulders almost slumped as if she had the weight of the world on them.

He jumped to his feet, and his chair flew backward as he rounded his desk. Reading her had always been second nature to him, so he hadn't understood why he wasn't able to read her over the past few weeks. Seeing her with fresh eyes brought it all into perspective for him. He'd been trying to interpret her actions through his own feelings, instead of identifying her feelings, her actions, and her intentions.

The abnormal sorrow and defeat displayed in her posture snapped him out of his funk. Taking the steps two at a time, he reached the top of the landing just as she unzipped the suitcase lying on their bed. She robotically moved from the dresser to the suitcase, absently folding and placing items inside. Every few seconds, she wiped at her eyes, and his heart squeezed in his chest each time.

"Are we going somewhere?" he asked as he watched her quickly dry her eyes before turning to face him.

"I have to go to Turkey and meet with my source. I reminded you last week."

"That's today?" he asked disappointedly.

"Yes, I'm leaving tonight." Her voice cracked, and she quickly turned away from him. "I'll be back in a week."

"I hope you find what you're looking for," he offered.

His hands ached to touch her. His fingers craved the touch of her skin. His lips hungered for the taste of hers. But he wanted her to be the one to initiate it, to fortify that he was still in her heart.

"So do I. You have no idea how much," she replied solemnly. "I'm going to take a nap before I have to leave for the airport. I have a feeling this will be a painful flight." She crawled into their king-size bed, pulled the covers up to her chin, and closed her eyes.

Forlorn, Noah simply nodded and left Brianna alone in their bed. As he entered his office, his cell phone lying on his desk was ringing.

"Steele," he answered.

"Our client and her entourage are arriving today instead of tomorrow." Rebel's tone relayed his annoyance. "We need to get to the airport to pick them up, but we need to do a security sweep of the hotel first."

One of the many new pop music sensations was performing at an outdoor concert in Miami Beach over the weekend. This particular singer was notorious for being the ultimate diva, showing up unscheduled, and expecting others to immediately accommodate her schedule without regard to theirs.

Noah muttered a curse under his breath. "Fuck. What perfect timing."

"Yeah, no shit, man. I had plans tonight," Rebel complained. "But what are you going to do, right?"

"Right. Give me ten, and I'll be on my way to pick you up."

He hung up with Rebel and jogged back up the stairs to Brianna. He found her sleeping soundly, so he leaned over her and kissed her softly on the cheek.

"I love you, Brianna. Always," he whispered.

He quickly changed into his work clothes in the walk-in closet, and he left before she stirred. His sixth sense of dread wouldn't leave him, though. Like a black cloud hovering just over his head, the sense of trouble brewing continued to grow in his mind.

Something very bad was about to happen. He would bet money on it.

11

CHAPTER ELEVEN

Her arrival in Turkey was no easier on her than her departure from Miami had been. Brianna missed Noah more with every second ticking away on the clock. The painfully long flight left her with way too much time to herself, time to think about everything that had happened, and time to realize what was most important in her life: Noah "Reaper" Steele.

He was the man of her dreams, the one she'd waited for when she couldn't even contact him, and the one to whom she wanted to spend her life giving all her love. She mentally berated herself for not treating that love as a precious gift over the past several weeks.

As she distractedly exited the plane, her plan was simple. Find proof that would exonerate Noah and get back home as soon as possible. She decided she didn't care what the evidence pointed to, how many flashing neon arrows pointed at Noah, or if she had to sacrifice her job to protect him.

After a few clicks on her cell phone, she held her breath as the ringing began. The urge hit her suddenly and urgently. She had to talk to Noah, she had to apologize for the distance she'd created, and she had to admit to being in over her head.

He should've been on this trip with her. One of the few fights they'd had was over her blatant disregard for her safety, in Noah's words. Since she was young and wanted to keep her independence, she'd initially mistaken his input as an attempt to control her. The last thing she wanted was to feel as if she had to ask for permission. Now, as she looked at the unfamiliar, unfriendly faces in the airport, she realized she couldn't have been more wrong.

Noah was merely concerned about the woman he loved. He knew the dangers that were in the world all too well, and he wanted to protect her from harm. She groaned out loud in frustration with herself. "This is his job. This is what he does for a living. I am so stupid," she chastised herself.

Noah's voice filled her ear as his voice mail greeting urged her to leave a message. She listened to the smooth, bass timbre of his voice, and it quieted her nerves, helped her to refocus on her own mission.

"Noah, this is Brianna. I'm sure you're busy with your new client, but I just wanted to say a couple of things. I'd rather tell you than your voice mail. But just in case I miss you later, here goes.

"I love you more than anything or anyone in the world. It was stupid of me to come here without you, and I'm genuinely sorry about that. I wish you were here with me. I'm sorry I've acted so weirdly the last few weeks. I'll tell you everything that I've found while investigating this story. I know I should've told you before I left, but I literally just realized how stupid I am while standing in this airport.

"I'm going to see this through, and then I'm coming home to you. I love you, Noah."

Just as Brianna slipped her phone into her pocket, her suitcase appeared on the carousel in baggage claim. Once she secured her rental car, she realized how tired she was. The days and weeks of stress and turmoil had finally caught up with her. She was more than ready to reach her room and stretch out on the bed.

"Hi, I'm Brianna Tate," she said as she approached the front desk of the hotel. "I'm checking in."

"Welcome, Miss Tate," the young man behind the counter

replied. "Welcome to Turkey. Your room is ready. Do you need help with your luggage?"

"No, thank you. I can manage," Brianna answered, taking her room key.

She was infinitely grateful that her meeting with Ammar's brother, Deron, wasn't until the following day. Besides Noah, all she could think about was taking a long, hot shower, followed by ordering room service, before she allowed the bed to swallow her whole.

Checking her phone for a call or text from Noah became a new obsession. She looked at the touchscreen repeatedly on her way up to her room, once she unpacked, before and after her shower, and countless times while she ate her meal. Before she slipped off to sleep, she whispered a small prayer.

"Please don't let me be too late to save us."

The next morning, Brianna dressed and checked the map one last time for the precise location where she'd meet Deron. Watching Noah over the past several months of working with him taught her to scout her surroundings ahead of time whenever possible. Check for the ways out, look for vulnerable areas, and identify the most likely hiding spots for unwelcome party crashers were all at the top of her to-do list.

The locale of the meeting was over an hour away from where her hotel was located. The time she spent driving alone through the desolate land made her extremely nervous. The paved road eventually changed to rock and sand. The city landscape disappeared in her rearview mirror, replaced by flat, barren views. Mountains made of solid rock stood tall in the distance where the road curved and winded in the canyons.

Nights of lying comfortably in Noah's arms as he recounted the missions he could talk about immediately sprang to mind. He always stressed the importance of having the high ground in a firefight. Being caught in the lower section of the canyon almost always meant sure death. Her rash, foolish decisions now mocked her, asking if her independence was such a great idea after all.

The hard-packed dirt road took her past a small village.

Rectangular, flat-roofed homes made of uncolored brick and stone were placed side by side. Children played close to the unpaved road, so she slowed her speed in the event they bolted out in front of her. The hard stares from the villagers who stopped their daily chores and watched her as she drove past stole her breath.

She finally reached her destination, where she found an old, deserted village with very few structures left fully intact. She parked her rental car in an alcove, hidden by a sizable protruding boulder before she stealthily moved around the buildings to conduct a sweep of the area. Most of the roofs had long since caved in, leaving the walls standing as lone testaments to time's harshness.

She entered the building where she'd meet Deron and checked the view from each window. She had some measure of relief when she found nothing conspicuously alarming. She moved from room to room and located the doors in the back of the house that would be difficult to monitor. She moved broken pieces of brick and rock to use to block the doors from inside the house. With only one accessible entrance, she wouldn't have to be overly concerned about someone slipping in undetected.

When she moved to the adjacent building, she found a room that gave her the best viewpoint and multiple ways of escape. She'd already planned her route by foot to her car and had nothing but time now. As she made her seat as comfortable as possible, she wiped the sweat from her brow.

"How can people stand this heat all the time? This is awful," she said aloud. She took a swig of her water from the canteen and relished the feel of the cold liquid.

She pulled her phone from her pocket and checked for anything from Noah once again. She wasn't surprised to see "No Service" in the top left corner of her cell. She made a mental note to add "not buying a satellite phone" to her list of stupid decisions she'd made recently.

She wouldn't know if he'd called or texted until she was back in a cell service area. He'd be waiting to hear from her, wondering where she was, and if she was safe. "If I haven't already damaged our relationship, leaving him in the dark while I'm halfway around the world will surely do it," she whispered solemnly.

Hot, frustrated tears slowly rolled over her cheeks as she relived every moment with Noah that she could recall. She inhaled a deep, calming breath, and she focused on the positives. Noah was a good man, and he had a very caring side not many got to see. She was a fortunate recipient of that side of him, and she would beg his forgiveness for the distance she'd created between them if she had to.

"I'm really not usually so morbid," she cried. She wiped her tears away and retrieved her pen and paper. She wrote down her questions for Deron so she wouldn't forget the points she needed clarification on. "Anything to distract me from why this feels like the end all of a sudden."

In truth, that feeling started before she left Miami. All of the evidence she'd collected, including the foreign bank account numbers, was hidden inside the spare bedroom in Noah's house. She'd discovered the place by accident one day. The wood floor plank was loose, loudly creaking when she stepped on it. She carefully pried it up and found the perfect hiding spot for small items. Initially, she'd planned to hide one of Noah's Christmas presents in there. Before she left for the airport, she'd made a last-minute decision to drop the flash drive with her research saved on it into that little hole in the floor.

That decision seemed to solidify in her mind that things would not go well for her in Turkey. She'd learned to trust her gut instincts in extreme circumstances, and it hadn't led her astray so far. She silently prayed it was just her hypersensitivity to the subject matter that made it feel different on this trip.

An hour later, she heard a car pull up, the engine cut off, and a door open and close. Slowly stretching her upper body and craning her neck to peer out the window, she saw a man who very closely resembled Ammar looking around nervously. He appeared to be alone and checking to ensure no one had followed him.

When he stepped inside the building, Brianna grabbed her backpack and quickly moved to follow him. If he tried to remove the barricades she'd constructed, she reasoned she'd leave immediately without even looking back.

When she entered the abandoned house, she found Deron sitting at a makeshift table, which was simply a square, weathered piece of wood on top of an old barrel. It worked, as far as functionality went, so she took a seat on the other pile of flat rocks across from him.

"Brianna, I presume?" he asked. His accent was just as thick in person as it was on the phone.

She gave him a single nod in reply. "Ammar?" she asked, purposely mixing up their names.

He smiled. "Deron. Ammar is my brother you met in Miami. At his apartment."

"Deron, it's nice to meet you. I had to make sure you were the man who's supposed to be here," she explained.

"Understandable. You've traveled a long way, to a country with beliefs and customs very different from your country. I would not have allowed my wife to make such a trip," he replied.

The condescension in his voice was cleverly disguised under a thin veil of concern, but she knew it was there nonetheless. She smiled knowingly as she removed her pen and notebook to get to the reason why she was there.

"I assume you brought the papers with you?" she asked pointedly.

Deron reached under the table to retrieve the papers from his briefcase and slid them over to her. "Everything is there. You must be certain not to bring attention to those when you leave here. Mix them up and hide them in your other papers. If those are seen, my entire family will be killed."

"I'll be extra careful with them, Deron. Do you have any names of the Americans involved? Anything that would help me identify them?" she asked.

His black eyes hardened as he assessed her and looked for something to latch on to and put his trust in her. She could feel it in how his eyes implored hers. He wanted to trust her to help him but feared she'd use the information carelessly and put his family in jeopardy.

"It's the best way I can help you. I can get to the right people, but I need the right information to give them. I'd never give your name or anything that would implicate you. With these papers, I can match the shipping manifests and the money paid to the Americans behind it. But I need the names to keep from using these catalog copies, so I know where to start," she clarified.

"Take this picture with you. This is the man who keeps making trips here, meeting with the rebels, and arranging the shipments," Deron said as he slid a four-by-six snapshot to Brianna.

When she picked up the picture, she gasped loudly. Unable to catch her breath, she feared she'd hyperventilate and pass out in front of Deron. He immediately realized she knew the man in the picture, and his demeanor completely changed.

"I've made a mistake coming here. I must go," Deron snapped as he stood quickly.

"No, you didn't make a mistake," Brianna finally assured him. "I know this man, and part of me suspected him, but I wasn't one hundred percent sure until I saw this picture. It's both good news and bad news for me. I won't do anything to jeopardize your family, though. I give you my word."

"Thank you—" Deron started to speak.

The sound of cars approaching on the dirt road caught their attention. The hairs on Brianna's neck stood at full alert, her heart raced, and her chest heaved with rapid breaths.

"Who did you tell about this meeting?" he demanded. "Who knows?"

"Only my boyfriend, but he's still in Miami, and he didn't know exactly where we'd be. Who did you tell?" she asked as panic threatened to overtake her.

"I only told my brother. He would never turn me in," Deron spat out at her.

"We need to get out of here right now. That car is headed in our direction," Brianna said as she quickly stuffed the papers into her backpack. "Get out of here, Deron," she commanded.

She moved along her preplanned route. She rounded the corner to her car just as the two other cars slid to a halt inside the abandoned village. Deron had immediately jumped into his car and moved it out of sight a split second before the others arrived. She didn't see him on the road, however, so she assumed he'd found a place to hide and wait them out. More likely, he counted on her to be a diversion, to draw the men to her car, and give him the opportunity to reach his family safely.

If she started the ignition, the sound of the motor would undoubtedly draw attention to her location. Then she would have a matter of seconds to take off, but they'd quickly find her on the only road around for miles. Her natural curiosity got the best of her, so she climbed the rock wall to see whom she was up against. As she reached the top, she flattened her body against the sand and dirt ground to avoid being seen. Her eyes landed on a remarkably familiar figure. When he turned to face her as he looked around the village, she recognized the man who stood in front of her, without a doubt.

Richard Hollingsworth himself.

"Let's go. No one is here. There's another abandoned village about fifteen kilometers from here," one of the men called out.

Richard remained still for several seconds longer, and Brianna held her breath. She silently willed him to leave so she could make a clean getaway. Brianna didn't move a muscle until Richard got back in the car. When they were well down the road, headed in the opposite direction she needed to go, she hurried to her car.

Her hands shook uncontrollably as she tried to insert the key into the ignition switch. The adrenaline dump to her system wreaked havoc on the control of her motor skills. With the key finally in place, she rolled down the window and listened for any sounds before starting the engine. She put the car in drive, got back on the main road, and didn't take her foot off the gas until she reached her hotel.

She rushed inside the hotel, reached her room, and bolted the door. As she paced back and forth, she glanced at the time. It was very late in Miami, but Noah would want her to call, especially if he knew how dangerous the situation had become.

"What can he do to help me from Miami, though?" she asked herself.

She powered up her laptop and immediately checked for the next available flight home. "The sooner, the better," she muttered as she waited for the flight times to load.

She booked the first available flight back to Miami, eight hours away. She completed the online check-in to ensure her seat was reserved and began rushing around the room, haphazardly throwing her belongings into her suitcase. She carefully tucked the new evidence, including the picture, underneath the lining inside her purse. If anyone manually searched it, only a small hole would show in the lining. Her purse contained enough other papers and personal items to camouflage the new ones.

Now, all she had to do was get to the airport without being seen by Richard. Then she'd be home free, back in Noah's arms and completely protected. That was the only place she ever really wanted to be again.

As she entered the elevator, she hit the button for the lobby repeatedly. The doors seemed to close even more slowly, purposely taunting her. She quickened her pace once she reached the entry area. She'd already opted for the quick check-out, so she was able to go straight to her rental car and not look back.

As she turned the corner from the lobby toward the door to the parking garage, she smacked into Richard's chest and bounced off of him. The shock both of their faces wore was apparent, but Brianna knew hers also held a trace of guilt. Guilt that she knew the truth about him. Guilt that she'd spied on him. Guilt that she had a picture of him meeting with the radical leader of the rebel forces in her purse. Guilt that she would share all this information with Noah, and then Noah would help her take Richard down.

The irony that he would soon be judged himself hit her.

"Brianna, what are you doing here in Turkey?" Richard asked. His eyes lit with understanding while he waited for her to concoct a lie.

She chose to tell the partial truth instead. "I was sent here by my paper to follow a story lead. It didn't pan out, though. Made the trip for nothing, after all."

"That's too bad. I'll bet you thought you were so close to landing the story of a lifetime, too."

"Not really. Everyone has a different definition of what the story of a lifetime is. My definition would be my life with Noah," she replied as she lifted her chin in defiance. "I'm running late, so I'd better get going. By the way, why are you here?"

"I had a meeting with some local officials on behalf of my boss. Trying to improve relations."

"That sounds very interesting." Brianna smiled. *And that's not the responsibility of the DOD, Richard.* "Have a safe trip back home. I'm sure I'll see you again soon."

"Yes, indeed. Have a good flight." Richard smirked.

12

CHAPTER TWELVE

"How long will she be here?" Rebel asked.

"They're supposed to leave immediately after the concert," Noah replied.

"I'll believe it when I see it," Bull replied.

The hidden microphones and almost invisible earpieces kept the men in constant contact while they were nearby. Staying on top of the pop star diva's every movement had proven to be more of a challenge for the team than they'd thought. A change of plans at the last minute was usually the last resort for a security team, but it was the way Kristen Garrett operated from minute to minute.

"No matter when it is, it's not soon enough," Noah muttered under his breath.

"I heard that, man," Rebel agreed. "She's driving me crazy."

"After we get national recognition for this job, I say we hire more men to babysit. We can manage the men," Bull suggested.

"Hell yeah," Noah replied and kept his voice low. "I completely agree."

"Miss Garrett, it's time to leave for your show," Noah prompted her.

"Okay," she giggled. "I'm ready to go. It's a sold-out show, you know. Even if I'm late, they'll wait for me. It's not like they can start without me."

"No, they're not likely to start without you," Noah agreed. "But the later we wait, the more congested Miami traffic will be. Fans can get irate if they have to wait too long."

"You're probably right," she answered with a dismissive sigh.

"Miss Garrett is coming out. Is everything clear?" Noah asked.

"All clear," Rebel and Bull each replied back.

"We're clear to go." Noah smiled as he opened the door for her.

Once she was outside the safety of her hotel room, the hulking men surrounded her tiny frame and almost completely shielded her from the nosy onlookers. Her heels clicked and her gum popped as they walked through the hotel and out to her waiting limousine.

Bull and Rebel followed behind in a separate vehicle, occasionally chatting in Noah's ear while he wasn't able to reply. The distraction at least made the ride more entertaining than listening to Kristen's phone calls. When Noah delivered her on time to the backstage door, her tour manager and the arena security team met them to take over.

"You'll be well compensated for the extra time and attention our visit required of you. I'm impressed with your work, and I'm not impressed often. You'll be hearing from others in this industry very soon." The manager smiled as he shook hands with Noah.

"Thank you. I appreciate the referrals. Give me a call if you ever need our assistance again in the future," Noah replied.

He climbed into the truck with Bull and Rebel and then heaved a deep sigh of relief. "Thank God that's over. I don't think I could take one more minute of Miss Pop Star's gum-popping."

"No shit, man. I heard that popping in my earpiece and thought I'd go mad. I don't know how you stood it when you were sitting right beside her," Bull replied.

"Well, I did have you two chattering in my ear," Noah laughed. "Take me home. I'm ready to relax and have a beer. Brianna left me a message yesterday, but I haven't even been able to listen to it yet. I couldn't get away from Miss Garrett long enough to take a personal call."

"Guess Bri made it to Turkey all right," Rebel chimed in.

"Yeah, seems so. That's probably what the message says anyway. I'm starving, I'm tired, and I never want to hear pop music again as long as I live," Noah laughed. "That management idea is the best idea I've ever heard, Bull."

"Let's make it happen," he exclaimed.

"Her manager said he'll refer us to others in the industry. If we start getting a lot of high-profile people and contracts, this business will grow even faster. Exciting times."

Noah's thoughts immediately drifted to Brianna. In his mental picture of the future, he'd always been able to clearly see her beside him. They'd build a life together, have a family, and grow old side by side. Whatever troubles one faced, the other would be there to help.

The uncertainty of their relationship made that picture less clear to him now. His love for her hadn't changed or diminished, but something between them was off. He couldn't wait to listen to the voice mail, even if it was just her confirming she'd made it safely. He hoped that by hearing her voice and the tone of it would give him some clue of where her mind was.

After Bull and Rebel dropped him off, he showered and then checked the time on his watch as he finished toweling off. Turkey was eight hours ahead of Miami, making it just after seven in the morning there. Brianna's meeting was at nine, so Noah knew he wouldn't be able to reach her until later in the day.

She'd spend her early morning making the necessary preparations to meet with the stranger. Then she'd take her time asking questions, extracting every bit of information she could obtain, before settling down with all of her notes and penning the next Pulitzer Prize-winning article. With a full day ahead of her and a long day behind him, Noah climbed into bed and turned on the TV, fully intent on watching the news, then he would listen to Brianna's voice before he went to sleep.

When he opened his eyes, the sun streamed through his bedroom windows, the TV was still on, and he hadn't moved a muscle all night. He sat up in bed, cursed under his breath, and swung his feet over the side. He rubbed his eyes and reached for his cell phone, but it wasn't in its usual place.

Noah quickly stood, walked briskly to the bathroom, and found it on the vanity counter where he'd left it the night before. There were six missed calls from Brianna, all spaced several minutes apart. The times indicated that she was urgently trying to reach him as he slept.

"Shit, shit, shit," he repeatedly yelled as he scrolled through the times of her calls. "Please be okay." He prayed aloud as he tried calling her.

With each call, it went straight to voice mail. No ringing. No waiting for Brianna to pick up. Only her voice instructing the caller to leave a message and she'd call back as soon as she was able. He stomped through the house in frustration, threw on his clothes, and tried her cell again with no luck.

As he brought it back up to hit redial again, his phone rang in his hand. A strange, foreign number flashed on the caller identification, and he immediately felt hope that Brianna was calling from a local telephone. Maybe something had happened to her cell phone. Perhaps the battery had died, she'd lost it, or it had been destroyed. No matter, she was calling to tell him she was okay.

"Brianna?" he asked, panic lacing his voice as he answered.

"Is this Mr. Noah Steele?" the polite voice asked.

"Yes. Who is this?"

"This is US Ambassador Elliott's office in Istanbul, Turkey. I'm afraid I have some terrible news. My apologies for delivering such news over the phone, but I need to inform you that Miss Brianna Tate's plane experienced a mechanical malfunction during takeoff tonight. I'm very sorry, Mr. Steele, but there were no survivors," she explained.

"What?" Noah asked, confused. "What are you saying? I don't understand. Her flight isn't scheduled until tomorrow."

"The airline shows she changed her flight and checked in for the flight to Miami tonight. I'm very sorry, Mr. Steele. The officials are still at the scene, but the damage was far too extensive for any survivors. All three hundred thirty-seven passengers, plus the crew, are presumed dead," she replied. "You were listed as her emergency contact on her airline profile. I'm very sorry, Mr. Steele."

Noah dropped the phone and stared at it as if it had bitten him. The rapid rise and fall of his chest mirrored his fast breathing. His heart pounded in his chest, beating fiercely against his rib cage. The blood surged through his veins, swishing through his ears and drowning out any other sound.

His knees simultaneously buckled as his guttural cry echoed throughout his large home. "No!" He bent at the waist and let his forehead drop to the floor as his fists pounded it relentlessly. He chanted a mixture of painful pleas and sobs over and over. "Please, God, no. Don't take her from me. Bring her back home to me.

"Brianna," he whispered as tears continued to stream down his face. "I don't want to do this without you. I love you, baby. So fucking much."

He fell over to lie on his side and remained on the floor in shock. The ominous feeling he had before she left for this trip just made it harder for him to accept. He'd been warned, yet he let her go alone anyway. There was nothing he wouldn't give just to hear from her again.

"The voice mail," he said aloud. "Maybe there's another explanation. Please, God, let there be another explanation."

He scrambled to his phone and played the voice mail on his speaker. When her sweet voice spoke to him, the tears and heartache returned full force,

"I love you more than anything or anyone in the world. It was stupid of me to come here without you, and I'm genuinely sorry about that. I wish you were here with me. I'm sorry I've acted so weirdly the last few weeks. I'll tell you everything that I've found while investigating this story. I know I should've told you before I left, but I literally just realized how stupid I am while standing in this airport.

"I'm going to see this through, and then I'm coming home to you. I love you, Noah."

He rewound the message and played it repeatedly for an hour.

I'm coming home to you.

I'm coming home to you.

I'm coming home to you.

"Come home to me, Brianna! Come home to me now!" he shouted.

How do I let go of the one person I love more than life itself?

How do I carry on like I give a fuck about anything else?

How do I get past this pain that's worse than a white-hot knife cutting my heart out of my chest?

The questions and doubts assaulted Noah's thoughts and bombarded him with more pain than he'd ever thought a man could survive. If she were really dead, if he would never really hold her in his arms again, all he wanted to do was join her. His life, his business, and his will to live had been tied up in his love for her.

He'd become one of those weak men he pitied. The ones who shriveled up and lost their will to live when their woman left them. The ones he'd previously judged and found severely lacking in balls and testosterone. Now he fully understood what they'd experienced and what brought them to their knees.

The kind of love he had with Brianna was a once-in-a-lifetime type of love. Any other person, any other feeling, would fail woefully in comparison to Brianna. He sat up, his back against the wall and his head in his hands, and tried to will his body to give up. He tried to will his mind to let go. He just wanted to slip into oblivion and be happy again, because he couldn't imagine happiness ever returning to him in a world where Brianna wouldn't ever come home to him.

Rebel and Bull were suddenly at his side, asking questions and demanding answers he couldn't give voice to. He couldn't bring himself to say the words out loud and make them come true.

"Reaper, what's wrong with you? What happened?" Rebel asked.

"Come on, man. Help us out here. What's going on?" Bull added.

For a moment, Noah irrationally considered if he didn't say it, if he believed with everything he was that she wasn't really dead, she'd come back to him. But he'd seen too much death to think that. He was grasping at any shred of hope he could find, but there was none there.

"Brianna's plane crashed. She's dead," he finally replied. He hung his head, his chin to his chest, and the sobs racked his body again. "She's gone. She's never coming back."

The finality of his words hit Bull like a sledgehammer to the chest. He fell to his knees beside Noah, panting heavily, and fighting the tears that filled his eyes. "What?" he whispered, praying he'd somehow heard wrong.

Rebel sat down hard beside Noah, his back also against the wall as he stared blankly at the other wall. Tears slid down his face as he slowly shook his head from side to side. "No. That can't be right. They're wrong."

"I wish they were. The airline has her checked in for the flight. All three hundred plus passengers are dead. No survivors," Noah replied glumly. "I don't know what to do. What am I supposed to do?"

Neither answered his rhetorical question because they didn't have an answer. For the first time they could remember since being a team, they didn't have a plan of action. They didn't have a Plan B in case something went wrong. There was no fail-safe. Their tightrope didn't have a net to catch them, and they were all free-falling, hurtling toward the ground together.

A crash and burn was imminent and unavoidable. The casualties would be considerable. The devastation would be complete. But the worst was still yet to come.

"Reaper, I'm sorry to bring this up now. But has anyone called her family?" Rebel asked, fruitlessly wiping his tears.

"Fuck," he replied. "I don't know. I haven't even thought of that. I haven't thought of anything else."

"They need to be called, Reap. They deserve to know, too," Rebel added. "They love her, and they love you."

Noah nodded but just stared at his phone. "How do I tell them that—" His voice broke, and it took all the strength he could muster to swallow the sob that clogged his throat. "How am I supposed to tell them that their daughter is dead? That I didn't protect her? They'll hate me, and I deserve it."

"They won't hate you, and you don't deserve it. Give them more credit than that," Rebel urged. "As much as it hurts, they know Brianna is a grown woman and makes her own decisions."

Noah nodded and picked up his phone. He reluctantly dialed Evan's number as he prepared to hear her parents endure the barrage of emotions he was still battling through himself. When Evan answered the phone, Noah cringed at his jovial voice.

"Good morning, Noah," Evan answered. "Diana and I were just talking about you. We'd love to see our kids again soon. How are you?"

Evan and Diana had visited Miami for a long weekend, and Noah had insisted they stay at his house. Their time together that weekend was a mixture of work and business since the Tate family owned a chain of luxury hotels. Evan was considering an expansion and had appointments to look at properties in the South Beach area.

Evan and Diana adopted Noah as their own son that weekend. Brianna's weekly calls to her parents lengthened since they also expected an update from their new son. Noah's estrangement from his family had been difficult for him in so many ways. He missed his parents and his siblings, but the nature of their relationship couldn't be helped. When Evan and Diana welcomed him into their lives with open arms, showed him the parental love he'd missed, and loved him for who he was, he believed he could finally be part of a family.

For the first time, he also looked forward to having a family of his own. With Brianna. Now he had to tell her parents that one of their worst nightmares had come true.

"Evan, I really wish you and Diana were here. There's something I have to tell you," Noah began.

"What's wrong, son?" Evan asked, dread filling his voice.

"It's Brianna." Noah coughed, masking his sob. "Her plane… there were no survivors. I'm so sorry. I'm so sorry I wasn't there to save her."

Silence filled the line, and Noah pictured Evan trying to assimilate the bombshell that had just been dropped on him. He understood how Evan felt since he was utterly devastated by the news.

"What? I don't understand. Where? When?" Evan stammered.

"She was in Turkey, following up on a lead for a big story," Noah explained. "She was supposed to fly home tomorrow, but the embassy called and said she changed her flight to come home early. They didn't have very many details."

Evan's sobs tore through his body, filtered through the phone, and poured into Noah's broken heart. "Was it the same accident they've shown on the news?"

"I don't know, Evan," Noah replied, wiping his face again. "I haven't had the TV on at all."

"Noah, I have to go tell Diana," Evan stated solemnly. "Then I'll have the pilot ready the jet, and we can make the arrangements together. If you don't mind, I'm sure Diana would agree that we'd prefer to stay with you."

"Of course. Of course, you can stay with me," Noah replied. "As long as you want."

"We'll see you soon, son. We love you."

"Love you both," Noah responded. "I'm so sorry, Evan."

"Brianna loved you more than anything, Noah. She told me all the time how wonderful you were to her. You have nothing to be sorry for, son," Evan assured him. "That was not your fault or even in your control."

When he disconnected the call, Noah stumbled downstairs to the den, with Bull and Rebel close on his heels, to turn on the TV. He flipped the channel to the news and saw the footage replayed on a loop in the small picture window beside the anchorman's head.

"In case you're just tuning in, the top story of the day is the apparent plane explosion immediately after takeoff from an airport in Turkey. From the footage shot by onlookers with their cell phones, it's clear that no one could have survived that blast.

"Relatively small pieces of the plane have been found up to one hundred miles from the point of the explosion. No one has claimed responsibility for this act. At this time, it's unknown if there was some sort of issue with the plane itself or if this was the work of a terrorist group. We'll update you as soon as we know more."

Noah, Rebel, and Bull silently watched the scene repeatedly play on the flat screen until Rebel took the remote and turned it off. Noah didn't even notice it was no longer playing. The images were burned into his mind, and now he'd relive them every day of his life. He watched Brianna's last few minutes of life, he questioned if she had any idea of what happened, and the knowledge that he'd never see her again had killed his newfound zest for life.

"What did Evan say?" Bull asked.

Noah gave them a recap of the conversation. "He said it wasn't my fault," Noah added thoughtfully. "Evan doesn't blame me."

"They're good people, Reap. None of Bri's family will blame you. They know you love her more than anything. Hell, you hunted her down after only knowing her for six weeks. There's no doubt you're crazy about her," Bull replied.

Several hours later, Noah still sat in the same spot where he watched the raw footage of the exploding plane. He vacillated between extreme pain, complete numbness, and bitter anger as he attempted to deal with the effects of his loss. Bull and Rebel left earlier after Noah insisted he wanted to be alone.

The chimes of the doorbell evoked little more than a head turn in the general direction of the front door. After about a minute, someone pounded on the door, and then a voice called his name. He immediately recognized the voice, sprang from the couch, and sprinted toward the front door.

13

CHAPTER THIRTEEN

When he jerked it open, he found Evan, Diana, Missy, Jessie, and Ashley at his doorstep. All of their eyes were swollen and bloodshot red, but they were also apparently grateful to see him. The family surrounded him as arms wrapped wherever they could latch on to someone else. Sniffles, loud sobs, and muffled cries filled the entryway.

Evan was the first to release his hold on Noah, causing a chain reaction from all the women. As each person wiped their eyes, Noah took in his new family. Through better or worse, the special bond would remain between them.

"Come in," Noah spoke. "My home is your home."

"How are you holding up, son?" Diana asked as she sniffled and wiped her eyes.

"Me?" Noah asked incredulously. "How are you holding up?"

"I'm not really," she replied honestly. "But I worry about all of my kids, Noah. Now answer me."

He drew her into his arms and kissed the top of her head. "I'm not holding up either," he whispered. "I want to wake up from this horrible dream and have her here with me."

"So do I, Noah," Diana cried into his shirt. "So very much."

When everyone regrouped after putting their luggage in their temporary bedrooms, Evan raised the question that haunted everyone's mind.

"I don't know how to handle this," he started. "This isn't something I've ever really prepared for. On the one hand, I feel like I'm giving up all hope by saying this. On the other, I feel like I'm honoring my daughter by saying it. I can't win."

Evan dragged his hand over his face, scraping against the stubble that had grown throughout the day. He looked tired and drained of all emotion, but Noah knew it simmered just under the surface. The right or wrong word would set it off again. He knew because that's how he felt, too.

"There is no right or wrong thing in this situation Daddy," Missy soothed. "We've never been in this spot before, and we'll always second-guess everything we do. But I know you, and I know whatever it is, you're doing it with the best of intentions."

"Thank you, baby girl," Evan replied as his eyes misted. "I'd like to have a funeral for Brianna. From the news report, there's no chance that anyone survived. To honor her, to celebrate her life, and to give the family the closure we need, I think we should go forward with the funeral."

Diana's tears streamed over her cheeks, like small rivers with no end. She nodded her agreement, but she was unable to verbalize anything. Evan looked at his daughters, his eyes questioned them, and they each nodded their agreement.

"Noah." Evan turned to face his son. "I know the bond between a man and the love of his life. Just as I know the bond between a father and his daughter. This is your decision, too. You're every bit a part of this family as much as Brianna is."

Noah lifted his eyes to meet Evan's. The bond between the two men was now sealed in death, the death of one they both loved. "You don't know how much that means to me. How much all of you mean to me," he continued as he looked at each face.

"This is the worst thing I've ever been through. I think the funeral will be even worse, but paying our respects to Brianna will help us to start to heal. Just one day of living in limbo has been hell," he replied. He wanted to console the others, make them believe that healing was possible, but he didn't believe one word of it. Inside, he knew he'd never recover from this blow.

"We all agree, then?" Evan asked.

Everyone replied with a low, mumbled "yes," and Evan stood. "We can make the decisions of how and where tomorrow. There's no reason to rush. For the rest of today and tonight, I think we need time together to remember her, share stories, and try to help each other with the grief."

"It just doesn't feel real. None of this feels real. I'd swear I was in a dream," Missy said aloud.

"I agree," Jessie chimed in. "I expect her to text me any second now to ask about my day."

"Has anyone tried calling her cell?" Ashley asked.

"Yes," Noah replied. "I have. Repeatedly. It goes straight to voice mail."

A quick rap on the door drew Noah's attention just as it opened. Rebel and Bull walked in, their demeanor matching the somber mood inside. Their long, sad faces and red-rimmed eyes showed Brianna's brothers had struggled with the news on their own as long as they could stand.

"Bull came over to my place," Rebel started. "Neither of us knows what to do. I can't think straight for shit. All I know is we need to be here."

"She's our little sister," Bull added. "We love her, too."

"I know you do. She loves you both, too," Noah replied. "You're always welcome here. We were just discussing our next steps. Have a seat, guys."

"She does love you both," Missy replied. "She talks about all her 'Steele men' all the time."

Bull fought back the unexpected emotions that rose inside him. His sense of duty and honor were the attributes that defined him, and he'd failed her. He promised to protect her, and in his mind, he'd failed.

Rebel gave Missy a small smile as he pictured Brianna sharing her pet name for them, but it quickly disappeared when the vise squeezed his heart again. The beautiful, petite blonde who'd worked her way into their close-knit group, into their lives, and into their hearts would never come home again.

"What next steps?" Rebel asked Noah as he sat and attempted to rein his feelings back in.

Noah swallowed the heart-sized lump in his throat before answering. "Brianna's funeral. Her memorial service."

"Already?" Bull blurted out before he even realized he'd said it. "Sorry, I just hoped we'd get better news, someone made a mistake, that she's okay. It just feels too soon."

"We understand, Bull," Evan assured him. "Diana and I have talked about this since the minute Noah called. I've done everything I know to do. We called the embassy, I called in favors from friends, and they called in favors from other friends.

"Maybe I shouldn't admit this, but a friend checked her passport, her credit cards, and her cell phone. None have been used anywhere since the explosion. He's still monitoring them, but since I haven't heard from him, I know he hasn't found anything," Evan explained sadly.

"I'm sorry. I didn't mean to add more stress on you with my outburst," Bull apologized.

"No need for apologies here. We'll all go through a wide range of emotions for a long time to come," Diana replied. "Crying one minute, fighting mad the next."

For the rest of the evening and late into the night, Noah's family told their fondest stories of Brianna. Some were funny, some were touching, but all were the exact personifications of Brianna herself. Her strength, determination, and drive to excel were accented by her humor, her desire to help people, and the way she freely gave her love to her family and friends.

When exhaustion kicked in and eyes involuntarily closed, Noah insisted the group should retreat to their rooms and get a good night's sleep. He'd already decided he couldn't sleep in the bed he shared with Brianna. It was just too big, too cold, and too lonely. The nights he slept alone while she traveled for work were different. He still smelled her scent on her pillow and felt her presence beside him. Knowing she wouldn't be back, he didn't think he could handle those kinds of ghosts.

Stretched out on the couch with his arm slung over his eyes, Noah tried to relax and allow his mind to fall into a deep sleep. One where he could be with Brianna again in his dreams. After what felt like an eternity of waiting for sleep to overcome him, Noah was still wide awake. He turned on his side to try a different position, but that didn't work either.

Reluctantly, he rose and robotically walked the long path to their bedroom. His feet carried him closer and closer to the very place he'd tried to avoid. He crawled onto the bed and placed his head on the pillow. The tiny wisp of air from his movement released Brianna's perfume, and it immediately surrounded him.

Turning his face to the pillow, he inhaled deeply to savor her scent. Visions of her smiling and laughing instantly filled his mind. Her arms reached for him and sensually pulled him toward her. Her lips moved over his, and the sounds she made as he made love to her filled his ears. Love reserved only for him shone in her eyes as she mouthed, "I love you."

Noah hugged the pillow tightly to him as his heart shattered into a million jagged pieces, never to be put back together again. But that was where he felt her the most. That was where he could be with her still, even if it were only imaginary. Even if it was only for a short time. Enveloped by the scents, sights, and sounds of her in their bed, Noah finally drifted off to sleep.

With the bright morning sun lighting his bedroom, Noah stirred and stretched in the bed before extending his arm to pull Brianna to him. When his hand met the empty, cold sheets on her side, he opened his eyes and raised his head.

"Brianna?" he called out.

Then all the events of yesterday came crashing into him all at once.

He wished he could go back to sleep and continue his dream. He was with Brianna, and they were planning their wedding. All he cared about was planning their honeymoon, but she playfully scolded him on the importance of having the actual ceremony before they left for their honeymoon.

He was happy again in his dream. Brianna was happy—and alive. She was warm, loving, and full of life. Now that he was awake, the profound sadness returned, but now it wasn't muted by numbness and shock. The pain was excruciating and overwhelming. It threatened to steal his breath and laugh at him as he suffocated under the weight of it.

His sense of duty and responsibility to his friends and family pushed him to get up and shower. When he descended the stairs, he heard quiet voices coming from the kitchen. As he approached, he found Evan and Diana huddled together over a cup of coffee at the table.

Evan's arm was wrapped around Diana's shoulders as her sobs caused her body to shake violently. Noah knew he couldn't take their pain away when he could barely deal with his own grief. He stood behind them, bent over, and wrapped his arms around both of their shoulders.

After several minutes, Diana wiped her face and calmed her cries. "It just hit me hard again this morning," she explained apologetically. "My emotions are all over the place, and I can't seem to focus on any one thing."

"You don't have to apologize to me, Diana," Noah assured her. "I'm in the same place you are. No matter how strong I've been in the past, this has shown me that I'm pretty damn weak."

"You're too hard on yourself, Noah," Evan replied. "This has knocked the wind out of all of our sails."

"Evan and I have been talking about Brianna's memorial service. What do you think we should do?" Diana asked Noah.

"She loved the beach and the ocean. Anything to do with the water," Noah said.

"We could rent a boat and take it far offshore, way out where it's deep. For her memorial service, we can write down our favorite memories, seal them in a bottle, and throw the bottle overboard," Diana offered. "Do you think she would've liked that?"

"I think she would've loved it," Noah replied warmly. "It's unique, just like her."

"Have you noticed that we all refer to her in both present and past tense?" Diana stared off into the distance, her eyes unfocused, and her voice soft as she asked.

"I have noticed," Noah replied. "When I feel like she's here with me, I use the present tense. When I feel alone, I use past tense. It's not conscious, but it's definitely real."

"I agree," Diana replied.

"If we're set on the boat and bottle, I'll start making some calls. I have to do something," Evan stressed. "I feel so useless, and I just need to stay busy."

"Everyone deals with this differently, Evan. I've pretty much shut down. It hurts less to feel nothing than to feel everything," Noah confessed. "When I let my guard down, it hits me full force. I haven't found the best way to deal with it yet."

"I can't stop feeling everything," Diana replied. "I wish I could be numb. It would probably be a nice reprieve."

Evan stood, kissed his wife on the cheek, and walked toward the kitchen door. "I'll start calling around for boat charters while you shower, honey."

Diana rinsed out their coffee cups in the sink before going to wake her daughters to tell them the plans. Noah recognized the lost, wounded look in her eyes. It was the same one he saw looking back at him in his reflection.

Two hours later, everyone had showered and dressed. Rebel and Bull sat on the couch with Diana as they waited for Evan to finish his phone conversation. Missy, Jessie, and Ashley huddled together on the love seat, while Noah sat in his recliner, lost in thought. Evan's voice brought him back to the present.

"I've charted a yacht to take us out tomorrow. We'll leave early tomorrow morning and spend the day out on the water. We're all under so much stress and grief. I think we all need the day away from everything else. Away from the news, away from the ghosts that haunt us, and out where Brianna would've loved to be," Evan stated.

"The yacht is large enough to give us enough space to say our own goodbyes but small enough that we can also spend quality time together. It's extravagant, but my baby girl deserves the best." His voice broke, and the emotions he'd held at bay rushed to the surface.

"It sounds beautiful, Evan," Noah complimented him. "Brianna would love the gesture."

"Jessie, Ashley, and I are going shopping at the craft store. We want to pick out the bottles if that's okay. We may need more than one to hold all of our best memories," Missy added.

"That sounds perfect, sweetheart," Diana replied. "Thank you, girls. We know this is very hard for you, too."

The girls surrounded their mother, hugged her, and kissed her before they left together. Evan retrieved his laptop to show the others the yacht he'd secured. The gesture, in Brianna's honor, was important to him. Every aspect of it had to be of the highest caliber to serve the memory of his beloved daughter.

"Noah, what can we do for you?" Rebel asked.

Shaking his head, Noah gave his friend a sincere look of appreciation. "Nothing. You and Bull being here is enough."

"This is where we belong," Bull replied. "This is our family now, too."

Diana cooked for the group and insisted that everyone sit at the table together to eat. Noah did as she asked regardless of how hard it was for him to swallow any food. This was her contribution to help others, and it made her feel good to be able to care for them. He would allow her that small measure of comfort.

Several hours later, Missy, Jessie, and Ashley returned from their shopping trip with their arms full of bags from various stores. Missy put her bags down and rummaged through them until she found a specific item.

"I found this bottle to hold the memories," she said as she held it up. "It's elegant, and I think Brianna would like it." The tall, glass bottle had a light green tint, a wide mouth, and a thick cork stopper. The words "Love Lives" adorned the front in raised glass letters.

"It looks big enough to hold everyone's papers," Diana replied.

"I think so too," Missy replied. "All of our memories should be together, in one bottle, and sealed with our love. That's the only way it feels right to me."

"We also picked up some flowers to make arrangements, candles, and picture frames. We wanted to put different pictures and snapshots of Brianna around the yacht. I can also make a DVD with her favorite song playing in the background," Jessie explained.

With all the arrangements made, the entire clan found tasks to complete that kept them busy throughout the rest of the day. Mentally drained at the end of the day, Bull and Rebel left, and the rest retreated to the solitude of their rooms for the night. They never admitted it aloud, but the dread of what the next day held weighed heavily on their shoulders.

The next morning, everyone dressed and somberly drove to the marina. Evan checked them in, and they were escorted to the yacht. They took their seats inside the cabin as Missy passed out the strips of aged parchment paper and pens.

"Start writing down your favorite memories of Brianna. Roll up the strip of paper and put it in the bottle. Once it's full, we'll seal the cork stopper in it and toss it overboard," Missy explained tearfully.

She'd put a layer of small stones in the bottom, covered by sand, to help weigh it down. Once the memories were tossed into the ocean, the bottle would sink to the bottom and find Brianna's final resting place.

One by one, the memories filled up the glass bottle until there was no more room. Noah picked up the bottle and sealed it with the natural cork stopper. He eyed the bottle carefully as he thought about all of the memories contained inside. All of the memories would remain with him since they talked about each one as they dropped them into the bottle.

The crew took the flower arrangements and placed them strategically along the stern of the yacht. Beautiful bouquets of large white, yellow, pink, red, and orange lilies, paired with a multitude of candles, adorned the outside seating section. Noah felt the yacht progressively slowing until they came to a complete stop. The waves continued to rock the boat gently as Missy, Jessie, and Ashley lit the candles.

Noah walked to the edge of the boat, held up the bottle of memories, and prepared to give his eulogy.

"Brianna, you are the love of my life, and you will always live in my heart. Not one day will go by that I don't think of you, miss you, and wish you were at my side. After loving you, no one could possibly take your place in my life or my heart. This isn't goodbye, my love. This is until I see you again…until we can be together again. I love you, baby," Noah concluded and passed the bottle to Diana.

"My baby girl. It seems like yesterday when you were born. You grew up so fast and went out into the world. You were never afraid, though. You were the bravest person I know. My world is a little darker now without your smile and your beautiful personality to brighten it. You'll forever be loved," Diana finished and handed the bottle to Evan.

Evan held the bottle in his hand, his knuckles white from his tight grip. "Daddy's little girl. That's what you always were, Brianna. You had me wrapped around your finger from the first second I held you. I just never imagined I'd have to bear losing you first. If I could trade places with you, I'd do it in a heartbeat. I miss your voice so much, your bubbly personality, your gorgeous smile, your infectious laugh. I'll never be whole again without you. I love you. Always," Evan choked out.

Evan handed the bottle back to Noah. "Will you do the honors, Noah? I think it's fitting since Brianna gave her heart to you and wanted to spend her life with you."

Noah took the bottle and stared at it again. His private message to Brianna was like an unspoken prayer in his mind, but he knew she heard him. Rearing back, he threw the bottle into the deep, blue ocean and watched as it sank.

"I'll never say goodbye, baby," he whispered.

14

CHAPTER FOURTEEN

Current Day

Noah stared in amazement at his old friend Richard, whom he had thought was dead. He couldn't believe the man stood before him now, alive and well. He'd attended Richard's memorial service, had grieved his friend's passing, and visited his grave once a year to pay his respects. According to the news reports, an anti-American terrorist group with a known affiliation with the Islamic Jihadist Union had held his friend hostage all this time.

Smaller fractions of the union were located all through the Middle East and northern Africa. Noah knew Richard frequently traveled to those areas for business, but he'd never guessed that his friend was in trouble, needed his help, and waited for someone to rescue him.

Noah's guilt ate away at him. He had been living in the comfort and safety of home while his friend fought for his life every day. The shame of leaving a brother behind was overwhelming.

Noah hugged his longtime friend and patted him on the back. "Richard, I still can't believe you've been alive and held captive all this time. After Brianna's memorial service, I received word that you were also on that plane. I can't tell you how much that shook me up."

"Everything is still surreal to me. I imagine it is for everyone else too. I'm still trying to get my bearings," Richard replied.

"I have to ask this because not knowing has killed me for three years. How is it you and Brianna were both in Turkey at the same time? Did you see her?" Noah asked.

"Yes, I did see her once, and it surprised the hell out of me. She was leaving the hotel as I entered. I asked her what she was doing there, and she said she was chasing a lead that didn't pan out. She had her suitcase with her and was in a hurry to get to the airport," Richard answered.

"Then what happened?" Noah pushed. He knew he was a terrible friend, pushing for information about Brianna when Richard had just been set free, but that didn't stop him.

"My meetings with the local leaders were over, and I was ready to get home myself," Richard explained. "I realized if Brianna was headed to the airport, there had to be a flight leaving soon. I called the airline and changed my flight.

"On the way to the airport, my car was hijacked, and I was taken hostage. I'd been seen negotiating with the established leaders, and the rebels didn't appreciate my involvement. They tried to use me as leverage. If anything happened to me, the people wouldn't receive any assistance from DOD."

"How did you manage to get away?" Noah asked.

"One of the women who brought my food helped me," Richard lied. "She felt sorry for me, and for her involvement in it. We arranged for me to 'overpower' her and escape. I only hope that they believed she couldn't fight back. It's awful to even think that she paid the ultimate price just for helping me."

Richard was so sincere and so convincing that even he almost believed his story was true. Almost.

Richard felt Noah's dark, piercing eyes assessing him. He knew Noah imagined the scenario playing out in his mind as he examined every detail, looked for gaps, and pieced together the news coverage that explained his sudden return. If Noah had to die because he'd figured it all out too soon, so be it. He was just another casualty of war—or of money. *Take your pick,* Richard thought to himself.

Richard knew Noah would find a hole in his story eventually. But he planned to have already recovered precisely what he needed and be long gone again by then. Noah had always been too intelligent for his own good in Richard's mind. The two men had been Airborne Rangers and later part of the elite Delta Force together, so they were both very skilled in terrorism and counterterrorism measures.

"I'd stayed away from the news when that happened because I couldn't watch that footage of the plane exploding one more time. It was a few days later when I learned you were presumed to be on that plane too.

"I pushed hard on a lot of people to get clearance to get to the site of the explosion, but it was closed to any nonessential personnel due to the terrorist threat. I should have pushed harder. I should have looked for you," Noah insisted vehemently.

"No way," Richard shook his head. "There was no way you could've known. Even if you had somehow made it out of the States, you would've been taken as a hostage or even killed."

Noah's face became hard as he said, "We never leave a man behind. *De oppresso liber.*"

What was that quick flicker in Richard's eye? Guilt? Noah's suspicions immediately reared, and his internal radar flashed red lights. The look in Richard's eyes was gone as quickly as it came, so Noah didn't push it. Pushing the thoughts aside, he internally chided himself for doubting Richard. The man had probably endured terrible things that he couldn't discuss yet.

Richard responded, "Liberate the oppressed. And I am liberated, so let's celebrate."

Noah's thoughts kept circling back to one question. What about Bri?

"I have to ask you one more thing, Richard." Noah hesitated for a moment, not sure if he wanted the answer or not, then pushed ahead. "Was Brianna taken hostage with you? Or was she on that plane?"

Richard knew this question would come sooner or later. Letting out a deep breath, he replied, "No, Noah, she wasn't with me. I'm sorry, man."

Noah nodded, never lowering his eyes from Richard's. "At least you're home safe."

Noah and Richard easily engaged in a light banter over the next hour. Noah relayed some of the more memorable stories Richard had missed. Noah felt like a part of himself had been restored in getting his friend back, but another part of his heart felt like it had been ripped in half again.

When the news first broke of Richard, Noah had held on to some hope that Brianna would emerge alive, too. But when Richard confirmed she wasn't with him, he knew she had been on that fateful flight, and he felt like he had lost her all over again.

Noah found it challenging to keep his mind on the conversation at times, even though he was glad to be with his old friend again. His mind returned to thoughts of Brianna and how tense their relationship had become those last few weeks they were together. If only he had one more chance with her.

The conversation lagged, and Noah finally said, "I'm going to go now and let you get some rest. You probably have people coming out of the woodwork to talk to you. I'm just glad you're home, man."

Noah felt guilty for the fleeting wish that Brianna had returned instead of Richard...or even with Richard. He was glad for his friend, but something felt off about the circumstances. There were no reports of any demands for his release. The US government didn't negotiate with terrorists, so that wasn't an option either. Something didn't add up in the way that Richard suddenly appeared on the scene, in Miami, and seemingly unscathed.

You sound like a conspiracy theorist now, Reaper. He shook off his suspicious thoughts and chalked it up to the fact that the press hadn't been given a lot of information yet. More would come to light after the government officials decided what unclassified information could be released. His military career had taught him all too well how certain top-secret details would never become declassified.

Climbing into his truck, he pulled out his cell phone and punched in his friend's number. He recounted his visit with Richard to Bull. They ended the call, and Bull promised to relay the information to Rebel.

~

RICHARD CLOSED THE DOOR AFTER NOAH LEFT AND SMILED AT HIS cleverness. So far, so good, he thought smugly. He believed Noah was so shocked to see him that he didn't doubt his concocted story at all. Not yet anyway.

"Now," Richard voiced aloud. "It's time to get my business back up and running."

Richard picked up the phone and dialed. "Remember me, old friend? It's time for me to come back to work. I'll need your help in getting started, and I'll definitely make it worth your while."

The voice on the other end hesitated before he answered. "Richard. Saw your picture in the paper. What can I do for you?"

"Meet me tomorrow night. We need to talk, in person," Richard demanded.

"Let me know where and what time. I'll be there," the man replied.

"One of my men will contact you tomorrow. Looking forward to it."

Richard fisted his hands as he paced in the hotel suite. Angrily, he stalked back and forth across the room, spitting out his thoughts to himself.

"That stupid little bitch. She thought she could beat me. Three years, I've had to lie low, and now I'm going to make her pay for it. Slowly and painfully."

He had a very lucrative business set up before Brianna somehow got ahold of incriminating information against him. She went deep into hiding and took that information with her. Until he got it back, his life was on the line. Technically, he had always been in danger due to the type of people with which he conducted business, but he could handle them. As long as he obtained the goods they needed, there was nothing to worry about.

But Brianna had been on a mission to tell his story, and nothing had swayed her from that. Richard had waited three years for her to show back up at Noah's door. His life and plans had been put on hold while he looked for her. If he'd reappeared before he found her, she would've annihilated him. He thought he had made sure his tracks were covered, but somehow, Brianna found out. He wouldn't make the same mistake again.

When his hired man, Bosco, called to say he'd found Brianna, Richard was elated for the first time in three years. She hadn't left the safety of her hiding place on her own, but he knew that his picture on the front page of every newspaper and internet post would jar her into action. He wagered it all on his assumption that she'd be more worried about Noah's safety than her own. For Noah, she'd let her guard down, and Richard would make sure she disappeared permanently this time.

Richard had recently received word that a dirty CIA agent wanted to make a small fortune in weapons trafficking. The agent turned out to be an old acquaintance from his military days. He planned to use his friend to build up his business again, and more importantly, keep his customers from cutting off his head. His CIA friend would have the right connections to get the specific weapons he needed for this shipment.

Richard made a few more calls to his former friends and business partners. The majority of the men he used as his security team had less than stellar backgrounds, but that type fit his plan perfectly. Someone less educated, less cunning, and with a criminal history made a great fall guy in the event something went wrong. Still, he'd be meticulous in how he set up any business meetings.

Several hours later, darkness fell in Boulder, and Bosco watched lights flicker through the windows along the row of townhouses from his spot in the tree. All of the houses, that is, except Brianna's house. He climbed down from his perch and silently moved across the yards and the street. He walked along the wall at the side of her townhouse to the back sliding glass door. He pulled on the door, and it slid open without a fight.

Bosco called Richard after he searched her townhouse. "She's gone. Yeah, I checked the house. She must have gone out the back. Clever little minx, huh? I'm on the next flight to Miami. Be there in a few hours."

Richard was extremely pleased with himself. He had secured several new contacts, talked business without anyone even knowing, and made a few new deals. His covert venture would be back in full swing soon. It was so much easier to be the bad guy when he looked and acted like the good guy. No one watched his every move when they viewed him as part of the world's elite class.

He was back in his element now, instead of hiding in some dirty third world country. *Damn, the last three years have been hell,* he thought glumly. His last shipment before going into hiding was interrupted, and the buyers were not happy. It was a good thing he had built a long relationship with them and convinced them he could help them in the future. In the meantime, he helped them develop their own supply networks and stayed alive.

His buyers helped him get back into the US because they learned of a new weapon under development, and they wanted it. Richard's DOD job and all his contacts would help him get it. He'd make enough money off this one shipment to retire to his own private island, but he knew he wouldn't stop there. He had some favors to pay back first, though.

It wouldn't be long before Brianna showed up, and he could tie up all the loose ends. He arranged for his face to be plastered across every major newspaper, but he already knew where she was hiding. He had plans for Brianna and Noah.

Noah had served his purpose. *Too bad he started thinking with his dick over that stupid little bitch,* Richard mused smugly.

NOAH DROVE TO HIS STEELE SECURITY OFFICE IN DOWNTOWN Miami. It was a Saturday afternoon, meaning he could've gone home instead of to work. His men were fully capable of planning and coordinating security for the foreign dignitary reception at the Miami Premiere Banquet Hall later that night. He honestly didn't want to go home yet.

The night Noah and Brianna reconnected in the Rainstorm and Bead pub replayed in his mind as he drove. He could see her across the bar, laughing and having fun with her girlfriends on her birthday. He could smell her perfume and feel her touch. The electricity between them hadn't diminished in any way.

When he'd found her, she worked for the *Miami Herald* and frequently traveled for her investigative stories. His new security business was growing by leaps and bounds and occasionally called for him to travel. Regardless of their time demands, they always made time for each other. They stayed up all night and talked for hours on end about everything and anything.

He fell in love with her in every way during their time together. Her love of life and her determination to live each day to the fullest were contagious. She loved to laugh and found humor in most anything. She didn't let daily aggravations and frustrations get her down. She always looked on the bright side and was somewhat naïve to how dangerous the world could be. He had seen the evil firsthand, but she helped balance him with the good that was still in the world.

When she caught wind of a big story that she was both excited and anxious about, she couldn't wait to dive in headfirst. As she investigated and gathered information from various sources, she talked with Noah less and less about it. Whatever it was she found, it had rocked her foundation, changed her, and altered their relationship. She became more reserved, nervous, and he was convinced she looked at him differently. He tried to talk to her about it several times, but he didn't get the answers he needed.

He knew he could push and get the answers he wanted. He was trained to interrogate suspects in numerous ways, and he was good at it, but he drew the line at using those tactics on the woman he loved. If she wasn't ready to talk about it, there was a reason, and he knew he needed to give her space.

Their last conversation continued to haunt him three years later. Brianna had approached him in his office and asked if they could talk about what was going on. He wanted to hear it, get it out in the open, and fix whatever had gone wrong between them. But losing the only woman he'd ever loved was the only thing that frightened him.

He replied that he was too busy at the moment, stating that they'd talk about it later. But his "later" never came.

"If only I'd known that would be the last time I ever saw you." Noah shook the memory from his mind.

He would forever regret how poorly he handled that conversation, the last one he had with her. He still didn't know what she'd found that had changed her so drastically over those last few weeks together. Those unanswered questions were challenging to live with after the fact. His feelings for her didn't change, still hadn't changed, but the regret of not fighting tooth and nail for her, for them, was palpable.

"They say you never know what you have until you lose it. I knew what I had, but I realized too late that I didn't do enough to keep it," he stated aloud.

Brianna was still as much a part of him today as she was on the day he found her again over four years before. It had been three years since she died, and he still thought about her every single day. Noah didn't date for a full year after Brianna's death. He just couldn't bring himself even remotely to care about another woman. He had occasional dates over the past two years, but nothing serious.

Walking into his office, he decided he had to get his mind on work and off of Brianna. The reception planned for later that night was both a blessing and a curse. On the plus side, his firm had been hired to provide additional security for the major international event. His firm worked with the local Miami police department and with various other federal organizations to coordinate coverage. His business was doing very well and had gained significant accolades from influential people in the world. The coverage from tonight would only further that, and then he would focus on opening more security firms in other major cities, employing more former military men in a position that suited their training and discipline.

The downside was he wasn't actually working the event. While he always considered himself to be on duty, his date for the evening didn't. He wasn't looking forward to spending the evening with this particular acquaintance. Alexa Bishop was part of the Miami elite club, and her wealthy family made significant contributions to political campaigns.

The woman was utterly ruthless when it came to business, but her elegant good looks and instant charm fooled many people in the boardroom. They never guessed that she was the biggest shark in the water. She knew what she wanted, and she was accustomed to getting it.

Alexa had made it clear, on more than one occasion, that what she wanted was a commitment and a ring from Noah. He had made it abundantly clear to her that scenario would never happen. He frequently encouraged her to find someone else and get married, because that life was not in the stars for him. She always sidestepped the conversation and acted as though she hadn't heard him.

He wasn't playing hard to get, and deep down, he thought Alexa knew he told her the truth. But for now, they continued to use each other and take what they needed, whether that was an occasional escort to a high-society function or for sex.

Alexa's father, William Bishop, built his business in exporting and shipping goods to other countries. Through his business dealings, he became very familiar with numerous foreign dignitaries, ambassadors, business leaders, and other officials at all levels of the US government. William would rub elbows with all the right people at the event tonight, who could grease the wheels at the shipping ports, speed up the red tape of customs, and make him even wealthier than he already was.

Noah opened his email to double-check any last-minute security changes that were required for the evening's event. He found an updated attendee list that added Richard Hollingsworth to the party.

15

CHAPTER FIFTEEN

The unsettling feeling of being watched wouldn't go away. So as Brianna's new identification said, "Leslie Solomon" made airline reservations for a flight leaving from Denver early that afternoon. At the beginning of her three years of WITSEC living, she had purchased an older car and parked it in a storage unit that was just over a mile from her current house.

One thing about her townhouse she was grateful for was how the backyards were arranged. Around each yard stood an eight-foot-tall wooden privacy fence with a built-in gate that led to the next yard. Another gate was positioned along the back line of fencing that led to the neighborhood directly behind the townhouses.

Her neighbor to the right of her townhouse was close to her age and had small kids. They talked at least once a week and had left their adjoining gate unlocked in case the kids' toys ended up in the wrong backyard. She knew it wasn't safe to leave through the front door, so she eased out the back sliding glass door, through the gate to her neighbor's yard, and then on to the back gate.

With her current disguise, no one watching would realize she didn't belong to that yard as she walked through the back gate. She was nothing more than a woman visiting for a neighborly chat. She continued walking through the bordering neighborhood and on to her hidden second car.

Inside the Denver airport, she checked in for her flight and walked to the line for security. She knew there were cameras all through the airport, especially at the security checkpoint, so she kept her head down as much as possible while waiting in line, without appearing suspicious. As she neared the TSA agent checking identification and boarding passes, a moment of panic hit her when she realized it had been three years since the Leslie Solomon license had been made.

Drastic changes in appearance raised too many questions in an airport. She handed her license and boarding pass to him and held her breath. He looked at the picture on the license, then at her, then back at the photo, then back at her. He finally made a few marks on her boarding pass and handed it, along with her license, back to her. He eyed her somewhat suspiciously, but when she said with her Southern twang, "Thank you so much," his look softened. He smiled and said, "Have a good flight," before turning to the next person in line.

She made it through the checkpoint without incident and walked to her gate to wait for her flight to Miami. She was sure that her Kristina Miller alias had been compromised, but she wasn't sure if Leslie Solomon had been or not. Until she knew for sure, she had to be extra careful when she arrived in Miami. The newspaper article said Richard Hollingsworth was in Miami, so she knew it wasn't him watching her. But then, she knew he wouldn't do it himself. No, she thought, he would be in Miami…with Noah.

With her thought, she let out an exaggerated and exasperated sigh. She'd have to think this through carefully. There were specific tasks she had to see to herself and plans she had to lay out carefully until this fiasco was over, one way or another. She never felt completely safe in trusting Marshal Stevens. Something about the man just didn't seem right from the beginning, and his lack of surprise over the recent turn of events solidified her resolve.

She heard the airline attendant announce over the intercom that her flight had started to board. Brianna collected her purse, stood with her boarding pass in hand, and waited for her zone to board. As she walked down the jetway, she wasn't sure if she was walking to or from hell, but she had a sneaking suspicion this would be the hardest trip to Miami she would ever make.

She settled into her seat, buckled her seat belt, and listened as the flight attendant reviewed the safety information on the TV screen in front of her. When the plane began to move, she leaned her head back against the seat, closed her eyes, and let her mind rest. She'd been running on an adrenaline-high for several hours now and was beginning to crash. She knew she was safe for at least the next four hours.

She reasoned that even if her current alias had been compromised, no one would try anything on a plane full of people. Once she landed in Miami, she would find a small hotel, pay with cash, and stay out of sight. If anyone recognized her as Brianna Tate, whatever name she used wouldn't save her anyway.

With her head resting on the back of the seat, Brianna closed her eyes as the plane lifted off. Living as someone else for the past three years had exhausted her to the bone. She figured if someone had been watching her townhouse, she had a few hours before he realized she was gone. It was still daylight, and the rain should've started by now. Nothing would appear out of place until later when the darkness inside her home would be evident. Hopefully, she would be settled into some out of the way motel in Miami before then.

She was returning to Miami as Leslie Solomon, but she wished like hell she could just be Brianna Tate and be done with this whole fiasco. She had missed her three sisters and her parents, more than she could bear at times. She had missed so much of their lives. Questions about them taunted her mind. Were any of her sisters married yet? Was she an aunt?

She thought of her mom and dad so often, she could almost see them standing before her. She worried about their health and the strain losing her had put on them. Most of all, she missed laughing with her family, regaling stories of each other during family dinners, and just spending time with them.

Her dad had been such an instrumental part of her getting her first big job after college. Her parents took a chance on real estate development at the most opportune moment. After they made their first small fortune, they decided to expand into high-rise executive offices, and they eventually established their luxury hotel chain across the Eastern US.

Neither of her parents was thrilled with her career choice since they both apparently wanted her to choose a career in business and manage their hotels. But being cooped up in an office every day was never in her plans.

Then there was Noah. She couldn't even articulate how much she still missed him every day. She dreamed of him so often that she expected to conjure him by sheer will. She never had the chance to finish that conversation with him the last day she saw him. It tore her heart out to think that would be the last time they ever talked.

As she drifted off to sleep with the gentle rocking of the plane, her unconscious mind took over and replayed the entire scene in her dreams of when she first met Noah. She woke from her nap full of regret and sadness. As the flight attendant gave instructions for landing, Brianna shifted in her seat and focused on her plans and what she needed to accomplish.

The Miami heat hit her like a brick wall when she stepped out of the airport. Three years away from the excessive heat and humidity felt like an eternity now. She hailed a taxi and gave an address that she knew was a few blocks from Noah's neighborhood. She checked her surroundings but didn't see anyone who appeared to be following her. Regardless, she refused to take any chances.

Once the taxi dropped her off, she walked for about an hour, crossed streets, doubled back, and changed her route several times. Convinced she was not being watched, she found a small, clean hotel and paid cash for her room for two nights. She also ordered the maids to stay away. She removed her pair of miniature binoculars, stowed her backpack in the closet, and started her walk through the affluent subdivision toward Noah's house.

Noah's house was actually more like an estate, set behind a stone and stucco wall that stood six feet tall, complete with a state-of-the-art security system. The wrought-iron gate across the cobblestone driveway was automatic and opened by keypad entry or a remote inside his vehicle. Once inside the house, the alarm had to be disabled within twenty seconds, or the alarm would sound and automatically notify the police.

There were several trees on his property, but she could see the circular drive where it curved at the front door. She found a hiding place and waited as she watched the area. She lifted her binoculars and carefully watched as five black SUVs pulled into the drive, punched in the key code, and drove through the gate. One man after another exited the vehicles. The entire security team was dressed in tuxedos, and all had security earpieces in place.

When Noah walked to the waiting limousine and climbed into the back, her breath seized in her chest, and her heart pounded. He was dressed to the nines in his tuxedo and looked even better than she had remembered. She remained motionless in her hiding place as the vehicles exited his property.

Once they were out of sight, she slid the binoculars into her pocket and casually strolled down the sidewalk. She approached a small café and overheard a patron seated at a sidewalk table mention the streets around the banquet hall were closed. The dining couple complained that all the visiting government officials received special attention and made it difficult for the residents to maneuver around the barricades. She immediately decided a change of plans was in order.

Noah and his entourage arrived at the Premiere Banquet Hall for the gala. The hall was immaculately decorated to welcome most of the foreign dignitaries and business leaders of modern civilization. Noah was dressed in his Armani tuxedo and Alexa, his date for the evening, glittered in her formfitting white ball gown on his arm. But his primary concern was always security.

He had dozens of fully capable men stationed throughout the building. Some appeared to be guests, and others were visible security personnel. He walked through the crowd with Alexa, stopped every few feet as she attempted to introduce him to new people, and mingled with the partygoers.

Brianna headed directly to the banquet hall when she figured out that was where Noah would be. She knew she could have—should have—taken that time to get into his house. He'd be preoccupied with the security detail, and the police would be preoccupied with directing traffic and avoiding international incidents. She also knew Richard would be there, but her overwhelming desire to see Noah again won out over her common sense.

She worked her way around to a back entrance, picked up a box off the delivery truck, and followed the others into the serving area. There were several complete black server outfits in various sizes hanging on a rack for the contracted servers. She grabbed a dress and shoes in her sizes and ducked into a storage room to quickly change clothes.

When she emerged fully dressed, she picked up a tray of hors d'oeuvres and exited the kitchen into the main event. She worked her way through the multitudes of people and offered small plates of elegant finger foods. Even with her disguise in place, she was still careful to keep her face turned away from anyone who potentially could recognize her.

Brianna's eyes locked on to Noah and his date. She immediately hated how they looked so happy together as they mingled with the world's elite. Alexa was flawless in this type of setting, and she knew it. She had her arm draped over Noah's arm to keep him close to her. She occasionally splayed her perfectly manicured fingers across Noah's chest as she carried on a conversation with others.

It tore Brianna's heart out to see him with someone else. He looked so happy with another woman on his arm, at his side. She never expected him to live alone for the rest of his life, but it still shredded her heart to witness it firsthand.

A familiar voice caught her attention and pulled her gaze away from Noah. Richard. She was careful to approach him from behind. She tried to eavesdrop on his conversations while keeping her back to him. She overheard him telling another guest where he was staying while in Miami and how he enjoyed the exclusivity of that luxury hotel.

Then she turned and saw Noah looking directly at her, and her heart stopped beating in her chest.

"Noah, this is Ambassador Bachar of Turkey," Alexa purred and poured on the charm. Noah had smiled, nodded, and started to introduce himself when he caught a glimpse of someone who looked vaguely familiar.

He walked a few steps away from Alexa and heard her make excuses for him "always working." He kept moving through the crowd as he tried to locate the woman he had just seen. She was dressed as one of the servers, but there was something about her he instinctively recognized.

When a large group moved directly in front of her, blocking Noah's line of sight, she turned and quickly fled to the kitchen. There were several hallways behind the kitchen used only for wait-staff and deliveries. If she could make it to the hall before Noah found her in the kitchen, she could get away. She walked as fast as she could without drawing attention to herself. She was almost to the door when she heard that familiar deep, male voice call out to her. "Hey, wait a second!"

The kitchen staff was buzzing about, keeping the food and drinks flowing, and preparing the main course meal for the hundreds of people in attendance. She glanced over her shoulder to see Noah standing in the doorway at the other end of the massive industrial-sized kitchen, with two large cooks blocking his way as they tried to exit the kitchen with the first course.

She snapped her head back around and kept walking through the door. When she was safely in the hallway, she grabbed her stashed belongings and ran as hard as she could in heels. Once out of the building, she slowed to a casual walking pace, hopped in a taxi waiting nearby, and went straight back to her hotel room.

That was way too close, she thought.

After that near heart attack, Brianna was angry with herself for almost getting caught. *So stupid! Stupid! Stupid! Stupid!* She silently admonished herself for giving in to her curiosity and desire to see Noah again.

She opened her suitcase and pulled on her black yoga pants and a black tank top. She put a black, long-sleeve turtleneck shirt, the black spandex gloves, and a ski mask in her purse. She couldn't wear them just yet. Even at night, Miami in May was nowhere near cool enough to wear any of that type of clothing.

She sat alone in her barren motel room and waited until it was late enough that most people would be tucked away in their homes. Accustomed to planning every detail, she went over the steps she'd need to take to get into Noah's house. Watching the alarm code key through the binoculars earlier had been a stroke of luck.

Seeing Noah with another woman on his arm was excruciating. Brianna only hoped she could get in and out of his house undetected with the proof that would tie Richard to everything. Noah had obviously moved on without her, and she saw no reason to disrupt his life. She could return to Atlanta, to her family, and he'd never have to know.

The streets quieted, traffic was sparse, and most lights were off in the surrounding houses. Brianna set out on foot on her original route to Noah's house. Once she reached his street, she kept to the shadows until she reached Noah's estate. Brianna stopped behind a tree, put on the long-sleeve shirt, ski mask, and gloves, and hid her purse. She crouched down and moved along the concrete and stucco fence to the backyard.

Noah had a walk-through gate on the back of the property that would be much less conspicuous than walking up to the front gate that spanned his entire driveway. The back gate had the same keypad entry as the front one, and she crossed her fingers that she correctly read the code she'd seen used earlier.

She stayed low to keep out of the view of the cameras positioned strategically around the property. Once she reached the gate, she waited for the camera to start its movement toward the opposite direction. Then she stepped up to the keypad and entered the set of four numbers. The red light blinked. Two more tries before the alarm was tripped. She took a deep breath and held it while she entered the numbers again. She breathed a huge sigh of relief when the green light blinked, and the gate popped open.

She closed the gate behind her and stealthily approached the back door of the house. She was on the grounds, but she still needed to avoid any motion sensor lights or nosy neighbors that watched the front of the house. She pulled the tools to pick the lock out of her bra and quickly had the door open. The alarm beeped as she rushed to it. She keyed in the code to reset it before the alarm sounded.

She turned to walk away and suddenly had a second thought. On the off chance that any of his men came to the house that night, they would know someone was there if the alarm wasn't set.

A security firm owner with an elite military background who forgot to set his alarm before he left? Um, no, not happening, she thought sardonically.

She quickly reset the alarm and silently made her way to the front of the house, up the curved marble staircase to the second floor. The landing at the top of the stairs overlooked the entryway of the front door. Directly behind the landing was a long hallway with the master bedroom at the end. Brianna moved silently down the hall to one of the guest bedrooms.

16

CHAPTER SIXTEEN

*N*o way. *It couldn't have been.* Noah repeated that mantra in his head for the rest of the night. She moved like Brianna. Her hair was the wrong color, but he smelled her scent. He caught it as he followed her through the crowd and into the kitchen. He could trace that scent anywhere. It had stayed with him and tortured his mind and senses long after Brianna died.

He couldn't get into the kitchen to follow her out the back door. The kitchen manager was furious with him for delaying the first course for even a couple of minutes. He decided to wait for her to come back out to help serve, then he would look at her up close. But she never reappeared. His tolerance for this setting grew thin. His date made it clear she wasn't happy with his behavior, but damned if he cared. Alexa was the last person on his mind tonight.

He somehow managed to make it through all four courses and stood outside the building waiting for his limousine to pull up. Alexa smiled and kissed the air at everyone's cheek that passed. She said her goodbyes and had a few "let's do lunch next week" conversations. It took every bit of Noah's strength to keep from just walking home and leaving her standing on the sidewalk, alone.

Finally, he thought. The limousine arrived, and he took Alexa's elbow and guided her into the back seat. He gave the driver Alexa's address and rolled up the divider window. "So, I guess we're staying at my house again tonight," she said with a sigh of aggravation.

Alexa assumed he would spend the night with her. She had often complained they always went to her place and never his, not even once. He couldn't tell her that he couldn't share his bed with her. Not the bed he had shared with Brianna. Not the bed where her essence still slept with him every night.

She turned to him, caressed the side of his face, and moved closer to him. He knew what was on her mind. "Not tonight, Alexa," he stated with finality. "You're going to your house, and I'm going to mine tonight."

She stayed mad at him for the rest of the ride, but Noah didn't care. He just wanted to go home, alone. His ghosts were back. After he dropped Alexa off at her house, he couldn't get Brianna off his mind. She was never really far from his thoughts, but some days were worse than others. Today was one of those worse days.

After her plane exploded, Noah tried to backtrack the limited information she'd shared but came up with dead ends. He went through all her notes that were left behind, trying to find any scribbling that was remotely related to her trip to Turkey but turned up with zilch.

His current thoughts were interrupted when he felt the limousine slow down, and he realized they were pulling in his driveway. His homecoming was to a dark house. *Perfect,* he thought. *Matches my mood.*

Noah's limo dropped him off at his front door and then drove off. He walked to the front door with his head down, looking at his feet as he walked. After he unlocked the door, he moved to the keypad to turn off the house alarm and went straight to his office. He wanted to look at the list of servers again to try to narrow down which one had disappeared. After he saw his ghost, he made it a point to memorize every woman's name tag. The name of the one who gave him the slip had to be there.

His home office was on the first floor and in the back corner of the house. He wanted it away from the kitchen, entry, and bedrooms to keep the distractions to a minimum, but on the main level for a quick exit strategy. His security system cameras transmitted back to a recorder in his office, and he could watch the cameras in real-time on a flat screen TV mounted on the wall.

He sat at his desk and huffed as he went through the names on the list of servers at the banquet hall. He located the missing name, but her picture showed she was a tall, thin Hispanic woman. Definitely not the woman he saw that night. They had a security breach on his watch, and he had no idea what that even meant yet.

He picked up the remote for the TV and did a double take at what he saw on the internal security camera. Someone was in his house. On the second floor. At that very moment.

Not that he needed backup, but with the security breach at an international gathering earlier tonight, he didn't want to take any chances. He called Bull and relayed what he knew as he watched the dark figure walk down the hallway toward his bedroom. It then quickly turned right into a guest bedroom.

Bull said he would call Rebel, and they would be at his house within three minutes. Noah hung up, took off his tuxedo jacket, and started climbing the curved staircase.

His Glock .40 was drawn and held down at his leg. He wouldn't use lethal force in his house unless he had no other choice. He'd rather take the son of a bitch alive and make sure he paid for breaking in to the wrong home. He heard a creak in the wood floor and froze on the landing at the top of the stairs.

With his back against the wall, he waited to turn the corner of the wall to enter the hallway. Just as he started to turn, he heard a noise on the first floor. He had watched the cameras and was positive there was only one person in the house with him.

He went down the back stairs, Noah guessed.

He ran back down the stairs, around the corner, and into the den that was at the back of the house. Just as he reached the room, he saw a black-cloaked figure crouched down beside his leather sofa. The intruder hadn't seen him yet.

He was trained to move silently in the night, but this person was apparently less adept at it. As the intruder made a move toward the back door, Noah rammed into him. Noah heard an "oomph" when he knocked the breath out of the other guy before he fell to the ground.

Brianna didn't hear Noah come in, and she certainly didn't hear him come up behind her. *Damn, that hurts,* she thought as she struggled to right herself. Unable to take in a breath, she staggered to her feet and clumsily ran toward a row of glass patio doors. The room was full of oversized furniture—the couch, love seat, end tables, and coffee tables.

She had a straight line to the doors, but Noah had to run around his furniture. As big and quick as he was, he wasn't fast enough to get to her before she was out the door and running across the yard. It also helped that he was still wearing his tuxedo shoes and he didn't have good traction in the grass.

She made it to the wall and used a lawn ornament as a stepping stool to jump on top of the fence and scale over it. She ran until she reached her hiding spot where she gathered her purse. She took off the mask, shirt, and gloves, stuffed them into her bag, and then nonchalantly walked down the sidewalk.

"Where'd he go? Where is he?" Noah yelled, severely pissed by that point. Bull had pulled up just as the intruder jumped over the fence. Noah ran to the gate, punched in the numbers, and impatiently waited for it to open wide enough for him to get through it. He jumped into the SUV with Bull and yelled, "Go! Go!" Next, he only had to find the son of a bitch and secure him until the police got there.

Bull slowed down when he reached the intersection, and they scanned the few people milling about for anyone who fit the description. There were very few men on the street, and none of them had the right build. Noah kept looking down the road; his eyes scanned each person and mentally calculated if he or she could be the one. Then he saw her, with the short black hair, lean, muscular body, black pants, and a black tank top. There was also something black that protruded from her bag.

Noah yelled, "Her! Right there in the black! Don't let her get away!"

Bull punched the gas, and the tires screeched. She turned and looked in their direction, and Noah immediately recognized her as the woman at the banquet earlier. Bull relayed their location and situation to Rebel, who had also called in a couple extra guys. No way was anyone getting the best of him two times in one night.

When she heard screeching tires behind her, she took off in a sprint.

Oh shit, she screamed in her mind.

Brianna immediately realized she'd been made. As she turned the corner at the end of the block, she took off running in a dead heat. Her fear and adrenaline pushed her harder and harder. The sound of SUVs closing in on her drove her to a near panic attack.

She turned a sharp left and ran across a vacant lot. The SUVs had already passed the street where they could've turned, and the next street up was a one-way street in the wrong direction. She kept running until she came to a dark parking garage. She needed a break to catch her breath, so she ran inside and hid between two cars. The garage required a key card to enter and had orange and white wooden arms to prevent unauthorized entry.

The sound of wood splitting and splintering told her the arms were of very little use in this situation. The men were too determined to find her. She stayed crouched down and moved between the cars as she worked her way to the exit. She didn't know where she would go next, but she knew she was a sitting duck in this garage.

She stayed down until she didn't hear the vehicles any longer, and then she made a run for it. As quickly as she darted out from between the cars, the SUVs descended on her from every direction and boxed her in with the concrete wall behind her.

Several large men stepped out of the SUVs, guns drawn, yelling at her to put her hands up. She raised her hands above her head and watched as Noah exited the SUV directly in front of her. She tried to resist openly staring at him and only allowed her eyes to glance up at him fleetingly. She was still in her costume, with her wig, colored contact lenses, and thick eyeliner to change the shape of her eyes, but she knew she'd be found out in a split second.

As Noah stepped out of the vehicle, his eyes lasered in on the woman who dared to break in to his house. He reverted to his years of training to keep his anger under control with her. He took a step toward her and momentarily froze in his tracks. The way her body moved and the way she carried herself reminded him so much of Brianna.

She's thinner than Brianna, he thought. *Her hair is all wrong, and so is her eye color. But I see Brianna when I look at her.*

Just the thought of someone else reminding him of Brianna pissed him off. He was infuriated because a common criminal caused him even to compare her to his Brianna. He sauntered toward her and never took his eyes off hers, his anger rolling off him in waves.

Brianna knew he didn't recognize her yet, but she knew the expression on his face all too well. He smiled, but it wasn't his friendly smile at all. There was no humor in his eyes. For the first time since she met him all those years ago, she was afraid of him.

"I have a few questions to ask you. And you will answer them. You will give me all the information I want, or you will be sorry. We understand each other." He didn't ask a question. He made a statement, and it was not up for debate.

Noah glared at the lady in black who refused to look up at him. If she thought not making eye contact with him while he spoke was a sign of submission that would make him go easy on her, she was dead wrong. She didn't move a muscle. He wasn't even sure she was breathing.

Definitely scared. Definitely an amateur, Noah thought.

"You were at the banquet tonight."

Even though he didn't state it as a question, she knew he expected confirmation.

The large men with him moved toward her. She couldn't turn her head to look, but she was sure the biggest one of them stepped directly behind her. She couldn't see him, but she felt the power emanating from him. She kept her eyes trained on the floor and watched as Noah's feet approached her.

When his feet stopped, she chanced a glance up at him. He

narrowed his eyes slightly at her and tilted his head to the side. From the look he shot her, he was very pissed that he hadn't received a response from her yet, but there was a hint of recognition in his eyes. She knew he'd figure it out at any second. She quickly lowered her eyes, tilted her head, and allowed the short hair from her wig to partially cover her face.

"And then you were in my house." This time, he bit the words out, anger lacing each syllable. "Now, I want to know why."

He stood so close to her that she could smell his cologne. She felt the scrutiny of his eyes as he assessed her. She knew he read her body language, read her eyes, and looked for information to use against her. She knew she probably gave him more than he needed. She didn't have a backup plan in the event she was caught, so her mind raced to come up with one at the last minute.

She quickly considered her choices.

If I speak, he will recognize my voice.

If I don't speak, I don't know what he will do with me.

If he calls the cops, then what do I do?

Is there any chance in hell I can run and get away from all these guys?

The questions flew through her mind in all of about one second, but she felt like she had been standing there, tongue-tied, for hours. She realized too late that she'd taken her eyes off the floor and had looked at the exit. That told him exactly what she thought about.

She realized her mistake, and her eyes flew back to Noah. She saw the slight nod of his head toward the giant that stood behind her and instantly knew that she was busted. Before she could move, the man behind her grabbed her upper arms, and Noah moved in on her. He then stood directly in her face.

Mmmm…he smells so good.

Stop that! Focus!

Brianna suppressed a groan. If she wasn't careful, her inner dialogue could be the death of her.

Noah grabbed her wrists in his massive hands, dug his fingers into her flesh, and squeezed as he pulled them down to put a pair of zip-tie cuffs on her.

"Oww! Damn it!" She scowled at the sudden pain in her wrists.

Noah stopped and looked at her, really looked at her, as if he were just seeing her for the first time. As if he'd just seen a ghost.

"What the hell?" He looked hard into her eyes, took a step back, as his hand flew to his face. He raked his hand across the stubble forming on his jaw and then bent to look more closely at her face.

"Bri-Brianna?"

Noah, Bull, and Rebel all looked as if they had seen a ghost. They all stood still and just gawked at her. She knew the very second they finally saw past her disguise. Noah's ordinarily unreadable face displayed his wide variety of emotion. It ranged from complete surprise and shock, to elation, and then to anger.

He was really, really angry.

Well, hell, here it comes, Brianna thought.

He paced back and forth in the garage as he tried to burn off the extra energy from his sudden adrenaline dump. His body temperature spiked from his intense fury. When he first realized she actually was Brianna, he thought his prayers had finally been answered. But when he realized that she was alive, had been at the gala, and then in his house, he knew he had been played the fool. The Brianna he loved became a figment of his imagination, replaced by the liar who'd put him through hell.

He vowed to himself to break her, just as she'd broken him.

"I understand now. Did you miss me, Bri? You crashed the party at the banquet. Then you broke in to my house." His voice trailed off, but the anger was definitely still there, and his words dripped with sarcasm.

Brianna looked from Noah to Bull. His narrowed eyes and the blatant glare in his gaze told her any trust she had previously earned from him was completely gone. And that fact really hurt.

"No, on second thought, missing me couldn't be why you're here now. Because you let me believe you died three years ago. Clearly, you're not dead. So, no, you didn't miss me," Noah continued.

Brianna looked at Rebel and tried to get a read on him, but his face was expressionless. His face was like stone, except for the muscle that twitched ever so slightly in his jaw from clenching his teeth so hard. That wasn't a good sign either.

Noah continued. "So, baby, what exactly did you steal from my house?"

Steal from him? He thinks I broke in to take his things? Brianna's mind raced.

Brianna tried to comprehend his question, but she could only shake her head. The man behind her still held on to her shoulders so that she couldn't run. But at that moment, she knew he was probably the only thing that prevented her knees from buckling under her.

One side of Noah's mouth curved into a half grin, but she knew he found nothing funny about this situation. He took a few steps closer to her, and she instinctively tried to back up, but realized the man behind her was as hard as a concrete wall and just as immovable. Noah took another step closer so that they then stood toe-to-toe. Noah towered over her in front, and the concrete mountain of a man towered over her from behind.

In a flash, Noah raised his hand to her cheek, and she winced as though she prepared for him to hit her. His hand froze beside her face, not having made contact yet. His eyes squinted in obvious disgust and dislike of her response to him.

Like I would ever intentionally hurt her, Noah thought.

He rubbed his knuckles across her cheek and then cupped it in the palm of his hand. She leaned into it longingly as she savored the feel of his hand on her. He ran his hand around to the back of her neck and pulled her face to his. He covered her mouth with his then his tongue pushed against her lips to ask for access.

She opened her mouth to him, and he kissed her passionately. His other hand came up to meet her neckline. He softly caressed her collarbone before he moved down across the skin of her chest that showed through her tank top. The other hand moved down her back and around to her side before he gripped her hip.

Damn, you feel so good. I've missed you so much, Noah. Brianna's thoughts betrayed her.

Lost in his kiss and her thoughts, she realized too late what he'd done. He pulled her hotel key card out from under her bra strap and backed away from her. He turned to Bull and Rebel without so much as a single word to her.

"Interesting place to keep a hotel room key," Noah said as he handed the card to Bull. Brianna knew her face displayed the shock, then the anger at how easily he'd manipulated her. However, she was glad he had not felt any lower, or he would've found what else she had hidden in her bra.

"What do you want to do with her, boss? Want me to call the police?" The man behind her asked Noah. She didn't know him, and he obviously didn't know her connection to Noah, Bull, and Rebel. She wondered where Shadow was but didn't dare ask.

Noah looked at Brianna as he considered what to do with her. She didn't realize she shook her head from side to side until he spoke.

"No? Don't want the police involved?" It was a rhetorical question. He stared at her for a few seconds longer.

Brianna finally spoke. "I really don't think you want the police involved. Can we decide this somewhere other than here? I'm not sure it's safe."

Noah's anger was in full fury then as he growled. "Put her in the car. Bull, Rebel, you two ride with us."

Bull took Brianna's arm and put her in the back seat of the SUV, behind the passenger seat. He walked around to slide in behind the wheel, Rebel climbed in the front passenger seat, and Noah sat in the backseat with her, his back against the door and his body turned to face her.

"Where to, boss?" Bull asked.

"My house," Noah replied, and Bull put the SUV in gear. Brianna felt Noah's eyes on her as Bull pulled out of the garage. She didn't dare look at him yet. Traffic was light just after one o'clock in the morning, and Bull easily maneuvered into the right-hand lane of the highway. She leaned her head to her left to look around the seat and saw a traffic light a few hundred yards away. Her eyes drifted up to the rearview mirror where she saw Bull watching her intently.

The hatred in his eyes made her shrink back into her seat. She was glad she couldn't see Rebel's eyes, but she knew he wouldn't feel any different. She finally looked over her shoulder at Noah, saw the same look in his eyes, and felt the vise cinch around her heart a little tighter.

She swallowed hard and said, "Look, I know this is…complicated…but it would really be best for everyone if you just let me go."

From the front seat, she heard Rebel's sarcastic tone. "You must be joking."

Trying her hardest to keep her voice even, Brianna answered, "No, I'm not. Let me go. I will leave, and you will never see me again. I won't make any trouble. We were all friends once, weren't we?"

No response, so she continued. "I really tried not to disrupt your lives. When you realized I was really alive, how did you feel at first? Honestly?"

She had seen their faces when they realized who she was and knew they were shocked. But if they were glad to see her at all, she'd use that to try to convince them to let her go.

Noah and Bull answered in unison. "Angry."

Brianna's eyes grew wide, and her mouth gaped open. She had not expected that response at all. She felt as though all the air had been sucked out of her lungs, and the vise around her heart split it in two. She barely choked back the tears that stung the back of her eyes before she managed a response, her voice just above a whisper.

"Angry? You're angry that I'm still alive? You don't even care why?" Her eyes were darting back and forth between Noah and Bull, searching for any sliver of remorse. But she found none—only cold stares.

Softly, and with great difficulty, she choked out, "Rebel? You too?"

He had no response.

She stared out the window, pulled her feet up in the seat, and curled into her legs. As hard as she tried, she couldn't stop the tears that flowed down her face. She had expected Noah to be angry that she hadn't called or come back in the last three years. Mad that he was fooled and that she had been living somewhere else. But being mad because she was alive was just cruel. Even though their relationship had been strained before she disappeared, she never even considered that he didn't care about her welfare at all.

The past three years had been pure hell on her. Noah, her friends, and her family were always on her mind. The love she had for them was overwhelming, and each day away from them made it worse, not better. The loneliness was hard to deal with, but their safety kept her going.

Mostly to herself, she whispered, "I've lost everything." She could see Noah's face in the reflection of the glass as he watched her, studied her, and determined his next move.

"What was that? I couldn't hear you." She knew damn well he heard her. He was just being an ass.

She shook her head. "Nothing."

She didn't turn to look at him. She continued to stare out the window at nothing in particular. The tears continued to flow down her cheeks and her neck, but she didn't bother to wipe them away.

Bull pulled into the left lane to maneuver around a slow-moving car. Just as they passed it, the car sped up and pulled alongside them. Brianna shifted her eyes to look at the driver and saw him point a pistol with a silencer out of the driver's window.

She screamed, "Gun! Get down!"

She hurled her body to the left, landed with her back against Noah, and faced the gunman. She waited for the shattered glass and searing pain of the bullet. She held her breath but didn't move until Noah put his hands on her shoulders, picked her up, and sat her back in her seat. She opened her eyes and saw the glass was still intact. Bewildered, she looked at him, and he simply said, "Bullet-proof glass."

The man shot two rounds at the SUV before he realized his mistake. He then turned and raced down a side street away from them. Rebel called one of the other men in the second SUV to pursue the shooter. Brianna was shaken to the core when she realized that man was probably the one who found her in Colorado.

She looked at Noah. Her voice was watery and quivered, and

she was unable to stop her body from shaking. She pleaded with him. "Please, Noah. Just stop and let me out here. I'll find my way back on my own."

He looked at her as if she'd lost her mind. "A man just shot at us, and you want me to stop and let you out? You want him to come back and shoot you in the head at point-blank range?"

She shot back, "What do you care? One less thing for all of you to be angry about."

Richard and Brianna both show up alive within hours of each other? Noah knew better than to think that was a coincidence, but he hadn't yet figured out the connection.

No time like the present to find out, he thought.

Noah leaned forward, closer to her. "No, I don't think I will let you out here. Maybe I'll just take you to Richard."

Her head jerked to meet his eyes, and he saw complete terror in her eyes. That terror wasn't there before, even after the guy shot at her. That was definitely not the reaction he had expected from her. At one point, he had suspected something was going on between Richard and Brianna. He never really believed she was cheating on him with Richard, but he wasn't sure what exactly was going on.

Noah remembered Brianna brought Richard up frequently in conversation, always asking questions about him. She asked about how they met and about their business dealings. She was careful about the way she questioned him, but Noah was suspicious, nonetheless.

Brianna turned her head to appear as if she was looking straight ahead, but Noah saw her eyes darting in all directions. He could see every muscle tense in her body, and her breathing and pulse rate had increased dramatically. He knew she hit the flight-or-fight mode in an adrenaline dump, and she was definitely terrified of something.

She looked back at him, and the pain in her voice was palpable. "You would really do that to me?"

He let out a disgusted "humph" as his response.

The SUV slowed for a red light as she looked back out the side window. Lightning fast, she grabbed the door lock and the handle, jumped from the vehicle, slammed the door behind her, and ran as hard as she could.

Bull had also been watching her, but he was a split second too late on hitting the automatic door locks. Just as she slammed the door shut, Noah slid across the back seat, but he was locked in, giving her a good head start on him.

Noah chased her down the side street, as Bull honked the horn and finally got around the cars that waited at the red light. Brianna scanned the area ahead as she looked for an escape route. She saw an abandoned house with a fenced backyard. Behind it were a few more houses and what appeared to be an apartment complex.

She jumped the chain link fence and kept going until she reached the apartment complex. She hid in the shadows and stayed close to the buildings. She spotted another main road a couple of blocks down. Fear propelled her. Fear that Noah would really take her to Richard. Fear that she had misjudged him and he was really part of everything she had uncovered.

Why else would he have said that? she asked herself.

Pushing off like an Olympic runner, she headed in the direction of the cars and a crowd of people when she was suddenly engulfed from behind. Big, muscular arms circled her and pinned her arms in front. A long, muscular leg looped one of hers and made it impossible to move.

Noah's deep voice growled in her ear. "You're not going anywhere." The SUV slid into the parking lot in front of them. Bull and Rebel got out of the car and approached them as Noah released his hold on her.

She was boxed in, and there was no way out. She was close to hysterical by that time. She shook her head and held her tied hands out in front of her to keep them at bay. Through her tears, she repeated her plea. "Just let me go."

Noah didn't know what was going on, but he sure as hell intended to find out. He tried to coax her. "Bri. Just get back in the car."

"No! You're not taking me to him!"

The three men gathered around her and led her back to the

SUV. She climbed in the back, Noah sat on one side, and Rebel sat on the other, sandwiching her in the middle. She pulled her feet up on the seat, wrapped her arms around her legs with her chin resting on her knees, and let the steady stream of tears continue to flow from her eyes.

Bull looked at her in the rearview mirror and saw the fear and defeat in her eyes. He was still mad that she had betrayed his trust. With his low, gruff voice, he started, "Sunny, look—"

She quickly cut him off. "Don't. Call. Me. That. That was a nickname given to me by friends, who swore always to be my brothers!"

She could feel all three sets of eyes on her, but she refused to look at any of them. She didn't want to see the hatred in their eyes, feel their icy stares, or sense their indifference toward her safety.

A few moments later, with no emotion left in her voice, she added, "Those men don't even exist anymore." Three of "those men" were in the SUV with her and had all turned their backs on her.

She leaned her head back against the headrest and closed her eyes. God, she was tired.

Once inside his house, Noah walked Brianna to the den and told her to stay there. In case she decided to run again, he activated the security alarm to lock all the doors and windows. Noah, Bull, and Rebel went into the office to watch the security tape again. The camera didn't capture whatever she did in the bedroom, and there was nothing in her hands when she came out.

They speculated that she might have planted something in there, but that didn't seem reasonable since he never used that bedroom. There was nothing in her hands when she went in. They rehashed the events of the night again, trying to make sense of it and come up with a plan.

Rebel's cell phone chirped, and he had a short conversation with the other security team. Hanging up, he looked at Noah. "Dude got away. They chased him, but he abandoned his car and took off on foot. Tags came back stolen."

Frustrated, Noah raked his hand through his hair and let out a loud sigh. "I don't know who's trying to kill her, or what she's up to. But she sure as hell didn't think of me when she brought all this shit to my front door."

Rebel leveled his gaze at Noah and said, "Brother, you know I got your back, but you may be too close to the trees to see the forest on this one."

"What do you mean?" Noah's frustration was growing.

"Man, look. I'm just looking at the facts. One, she tried to get away from you. Two, when the guy shot at her, she wasn't trying to save herself—"

"What the hell do you mean, 'she wasn't trying to save herself'?" Noah growled.

"If she were trying to save herself, she would've lain down in the seat or the floorboard or, hell, man, even just bent over. But she didn't. She used her body to shield you. We are trained to handle that kind of stress—she's not. Most any civilian—and a lot of soldiers, for that matter—would panic in that situation, Reap. I saw her face, man. She didn't know that was bulletproof glass. She was protecting you from that bullet."

Noah put his head in his hands and blew out a breath he didn't even realize he was holding.

"And three," Rebel continued. "She begged to be let out of the car, even after dude tried to shoot her. That doesn't sound like someone who's trying to bring trouble to your door."

A small voice at the door said, "He wasn't aiming at me."

All three men whirled around and looked at her, trying to take in what she said. Then Bull spat out a response. "What the hell did you just say?"

Brianna looked at each of the men, feeling partially afraid of the repercussions she would face for intruding on their male bonding time. She had only heard the last part of what Rebel was saying, but she knew he was referring to the guy who shot at them earlier.

She took a deep breath and said, "He wasn't aiming at me. He was aiming at Noah."

Rebel turned back to Noah and gave him an *I-told-you-so* look.

Noah looked back at the doorway, and Brianna was gone. The three men filed out of the office and back to the den. They found her sitting on the leather couch in the darkened room. Noah turned on a lamp, sat in his recliner, and the other men each took a seat. One sat in the second recliner and one on the love seat.

Surrounded again, Brianna sighed inwardly.

Noah couldn't get used to seeing her with the short, black hair. She always had long blond hair, and he remembered how he loved to run his fingers through it.

She'd lost a lot of weight too, he realized. She was always lean and muscular, but she seemed to be thinner than he remembered. She definitely looked tired. Noah considered it had been a long day for her, but she looked utterly undone. He hesitated to ask her any questions because he was concerned she would shatter to pieces if he did. She wasn't crying any longer, but her eyes were red-rimmed, bloodshot, and swollen.

Without saying a word, he rose and walked to her, squatted in front of her, and took her wrists in his hands to remove the zip-tie cuffs. When he grabbed her wrists, she winced in pain, but she didn't say anything or make a sound. He opened his fingers, her wrists resting in the palm of his hands. He saw the lines of dark purple bruises in the shape of fingertips against her pale skin on both wrists.

"Did I do this to you?" Guilt riddled his voice because he knew the answer. His eyes searched hers for some reaction, but she just pulled her hands away and looked down. He was still outraged and hurt, but he would never physically hurt Brianna intentionally.

"It doesn't matter." There was no self-pity in her voice. She wasn't trying to make him feel bad for what he'd done. She just stated a fact, as if she deserved it.

He pulled a knife from his pocket and cut the ties from her hands. She absently rubbed the indentions they had left on her wrists, and he realized he had zipped them a little too tight. She had never complained about it. He stayed squatted in front of her and watched her, but she wouldn't look at him. He looked at Bull and then at Rebel, but they both watched her.

"Can I please use your shower?"

He didn't know how such an innocent question could hurt him so much. Brianna had had her own apartment when they first started dating, but she had practically lived there with him. She had slept in his bed. She had made love to him all night in his bed, his shower, and most everywhere else in the house. But she was asking for permission to use his shower?

"Sure. Don't even think about trying to run, though." He kept his voice even to hide all the emotions lying just underneath the surface. He stood but stayed in front of her. He offered his hand to help her up, but she didn't take it.

"Thank you." And with that, she quietly left the room as she continued to avoid looking at anyone.

Inside the bathroom, she broke down again, unable to stop the tears and body shakes. During the quiet part of the ride, she'd had time to think and sort through the events of the night. When she saw the man raise the gun and aim at Noah, her heart sank to her knees.

She knew Noah didn't love her anymore. He viewed her disappearance as betrayal, and loyalty was not an option with these guys. Noah didn't understand, and there was no way he would believe her word at that point.

Even with that, and the fact that he was angry she was even still alive, she couldn't stop her traitorous heart from loving him. And she couldn't bear the thought of him getting hurt because of her. She knew what she had to do. But first, she knew he and the others had questions that needed to be answered. She decided to tell them whatever they wanted to know.

She thought solemnly, *What could it hurt now?*

She removed the wig and the hair cap, and the pain behind her eyes let up slightly. She knew she would have one hell of a headache after crying so much. She ran her fingers through her matted hair and started the water for her shower. She made it as hot as she could stand it. She was surprised her colored contact lenses hadn't been washed away with all of her tears.

She tried to wash away the pain and dread of what she knew

was still to come. She shampooed her long blond hair and applied conditioner since it would definitely need it after being under that wig for so long. Once she had rinsed off, she sat on the tile floor with her back against the built-in seat and sobbed until the water ran cold.

After she dried off, she realized she didn't bring any clothes with her to change into. They'd driven straight here, and her backpack was still in the hotel room. She wrapped the towel around her and stepped out into Noah's bedroom. She intended to ask him if he could spare a T-shirt for her to sleep in for the rest of the night, or morning, whatever it was then. She knew he had decided she would stay at his house until he figured out what he should do with her.

She walked by the bed and noticed a pair of pajamas laid out across the bed. Her heart nearly stopped when she thought that Noah's girlfriend had come over while she was in the shower. She never expected him not to date anyone after her "death," but she couldn't be in the same house with them. She couldn't sleep in the next room knowing another woman was in bed with him. Visions of them together played in her mind, and she shook her head to get rid of the images.

She felt like she was about to hyperventilate when something registered in her brain and she realized they were her old pajamas. Noah had laid out a pink cotton tank top with spaghetti straps and pink pajama pants with white polka dots for her. She quickly dressed and towel-dried her hair. She was much too tired to mess with the hair dryer right at that moment. Reluctantly, she made her way back downstairs.

She heard muffled voices in the den and knew the guys were still in there talking, so she went to the kitchen instead. Her eyes and head hurt from crying, so she left the light off and stood at the huge picture window to look at the pool water sparkle from the underwater lights.

The lights changed colors, reflecting throughout the decorative water fountains in the middle of the pool and the waterfall at the other end. Brianna always loved to watch the water at night. Water and waves had such a calming effect on her, and she desperately needed it right then.

She felt the air in the room change, energize almost, with body heat, muscles, nervous energy, and testosterone. She knew that Noah, Bull, and Rebel stood behind her in the dark.

"What do you want to know?" She didn't turn around.

"Everything," Noah said flatly as he flipped on the kitchen light. He turned to look at her and stopped dead in his tracks. Her blond hair was back, still a little damp, but no doubt, it was blond and long again.

Damn, he thought, *she's been wearing a wig this whole time.* He wondered if he'd lost his edge but quickly dismissed it as shock and stress.

He'd suspected she'd lost weight, but seeing her standing there removed all doubt. The pajamas he'd laid out for her fit her perfectly at one time. He always loved how her body filled them out. That night, they hung loosely on her, and she looked so…lost.

She stood with her back to them and stared out the window with her head slightly tilted down. Her arms were wrapped around her waist as if she tried to protect herself. Noah stood with his friends, but she was alone.

A thought hit him so hard it almost felt like a punch to the gut. Has she been alone all this time?

"Where do you want to start?" Her voice came out so soft but strained, as she worked to hold back the tears.

Noah had heard her sobs in the shower when he laid out her pajamas. Her pain sounded so raw, so real, that he almost walked into the bathroom just to hold her. The sounds were faint at first, but as Noah walked closer to the bathroom door, he distinctly heard her pain. Old feelings rose in his chest, and he put his hand on the doorknob, intent to rush in to comfort her. Then he remembered attending her funeral…her fake funeral…and he backed away from the door.

He decided that then wasn't the time to reminisce.

"Is there a boyfriend I need to be concerned about showing up here, looking for you?"

"No."

A snort and a sarcastic comment Noah couldn't withhold. "Oh, let me guess…he probably thinks you're dead, too."

Both heads snapped in his direction as Bull and Rebel looked at him. Reaper nodded and looked down momentarily. Okay, low blow.

She shook her head and paused. "There's no one. There hasn't been anyone since…since you."

Reaper, you are a dick. "Where have you been all this time?"

"Boulder, Colorado."

"Why Boulder?"

"Because that's where the US Marshals put me when I entered the Witness Protection Program."

The three men looked at each other, all puzzled. Noah's jaw dropped, and he couldn't believe what he'd just heard her say. WITSEC only happened in the movies, not in real life. Not for anyone he ever knew anyway. Bull's face showed his complete disbelief of her story, while Rebel was intrigued. Noah couldn't think of anything intelligent to say. He simply asked, "Why?"

Brianna turned to face them and stepped a few paces closer to them. Noah saw her cobalt-blue eyes and realized she'd been wearing colored contact lenses, too. *How did I miss these details about her? Because I have been so busy being angry with her for being alive,* he mentally chastised himself.

She let out a long sigh and considered how to start. "The last story I went on…in the Middle East? I got proof that some of our government officials were guilty of illegally selling weapons to terrorists. One of them tried to kill me by blowing up the plane I was supposed to be on."

Noah, Bull, and Rebel considered her story, but she could tell they were all still very skeptical. She had only given them very vague information. She supplied no names, nothing for them to run any checks on for themselves, and even she had to admit the story was pretty farfetched. Brianna kept her eyes trained on Noah. She refused to look away and give him any reason to think she was lying.

Noah finally broke the silence. "When did you last eat?"

It was Brianna's turn to look puzzled. "Um, I don't know. I guess on the plane yesterday."

Noah's face didn't soften as he asked, "A pack of peanuts? That doesn't count. When did you last eat real food?"

"Uh, I guess sometime yesterday." She glanced at the clock. It was already after two o'clock in the morning. "Well, I guess the day before yesterday, now." She shrugged nonchalantly.

"What can I fix you?"

She eyed him for a second before she resolved she wouldn't get pulled into any manipulation tactics. She said she'd answer his questions. He didn't have to play on her emotions in some cruel joke.

"Look, I don't know what your angle is. You don't have to play mind games with me. I will tell you whatever you want to know. Just be sure you want the truth before you ask the question."

"Right now, my only angle is to feed you."

"Thanks, but I'm not hungry. I don't have much of an appetite."

Noah kept his gaze leveled at her, but there was definitely a change in his eyes. They weren't quite as hard or angry anymore. He didn't trust her, but she didn't see hatred either. She knew his thoughts were about what question he'd ask next. She saw a shift briefly flicker in his eyes when he made his decision. It was then that he seemed to harden toward her again. She felt butterflies in her stomach from the anxiety of what was to come.

"I talked to Richard. I went to his hotel suite to see him."

"Oh? What did you two talk about?" She tried to sound nonchalant, but a small doubt lingered and still nagged her in the back of her mind.

He saw the same signs of terror well up in her again and wondered why Richard's name caused such a change in her demeanor. So, of course, he pushed on.

"Different things. Mostly about you." Noah shrugged.

Her big blue eyes filled with tears, but she fought them back. Noah knew she tried so hard to hold it together, but he didn't know why Richard affected her so much. And that really pissed him off.

"What does he want you to do?" Her voice cracked on her last word, and she swallowed hard.

"What do you think he wants?" Noah knew how to interrogate people and get the information he wanted. He could almost always turn their questions back on them so that they actually answered it on their own. That method gave him more information than anything he could think of alone.

"I'd say that he wants to make a deal with you. A trade."

Noah narrowed his eyes and clenched his jaw so tightly it made his whole head hurt. The muscles in his jaw twitched, and he balled his hands into tight fists. But he remained quiet and knew if he didn't push the questioning too hard, she would fill in the silence for him.

She didn't disappoint him. Her voice was soft but resolute. "I've actually been thinking about this. Especially since that guy took a shot at you tonight."

Brianna took a deep breath to calm her racing heart. She obviously didn't want to continue her current thoughts, but Noah watched her steel her nerves and proceeded anyway. Noah saw the woman he had loved standing before him. He watched her gather the courage he had never given her enough credit for possessing. He marveled at her as she drew her strength to stand tall in front of three large, intimidating men. When she nodded her head after a silent dialogue in her mind, he instantly knew she had made a decision he wasn't going to like.

Brianna took a couple of steps closer to him, wrung her hands, and still tried to fight back the tears that then rolled down her cheeks. Her watery voice quivered as she asked, "If you agree to the trade, will you be safe?"

Noah nodded, but he wasn't sure he could speak, even if his life depended on it. He had a terrible feeling in the pit of his stomach about the direction this conversation was headed. She looked down for just a second, contemplated the information, and then looked him square in the eye.

"Then I want you to agree to it. If you believe Richard, that he'll leave you alone and you'll be safe, you have to agree to it." Unshed tears glistened in her eyes, and Noah could only watch as they fell down her face.

Bull had watched the exchange. He knew what Noah was doing, but had no idea what Brianna meant. Whatever it was couldn't be good, though, so he butted into the conversation. Bull did not attempt to hide his contempt for her. His voice and his eyes were hard as he demanded an answer. "Brianna—what the hell are you talking about? What fucking trade?"

She looked at Bull and stated simply, "My life." Then she looked at Noah. He dreaded the words he knew would follow. "For Noah's."

17

CHAPTER SEVENTEEN

Noah kept his face unreadable, but his heart thumped against his rib cage. He knew going into it that he had a bad feeling about this conversation, but he hadn't considered this turn of events. His mind raced to put the pieces of the jigsaw puzzle together. There was no doubt that Richard was the key to everything. Her initial questions about him, followed by the terror in her eyes when Noah said he'd take her to Richard, and then this new revelation. It all so obviously pointed at Richard, but Noah didn't know what "it" was.

Rebel's deep voice reverberated through the kitchen. "Your life? Reaper, what the hell is going on? What is she talking about?"

Bull chimed in. "There's no way we would let anyone get to Reaper. What kind of bullshit are you up to, Brianna? What are you trying to do to him?" His voice was rich with hatred and close to yelling.

As he stalked toward her, Brianna absently backed up a couple of steps. She felt the pangs of guilt and pain in her heart from the knowledge she'd lost his trust. The angry look on his face scared her. She had never seen him like this before, especially toward her.

Brianna tried to keep her voice calm and not add to the anger that grew in the kitchen. "I know you don't believe me, but I'm not up to anything. I really tried to do what was best for everyone, considering.

"I can't tell you how much I've missed all of you. It has killed me to stay away for the last three years. But I had to because it was the only way to protect you. When I saw Richard came out of hiding, I knew he would come after Noah to get to me. I'm trying to help Noah."

Bull countered. "Bullshit! You're full of shit!" Turning to Noah, Bull continued. "Reaper, man, don't fall for this—" He pointed to Brianna while he considered his next expletive. Brianna's hands were steepled over her nose and mouth, her eyes closed, and her tears increased.

"Enough, Bull." Noah didn't yell, but the curt tone of his voice left no room for argument.

Before a brawl ensued in his kitchen over the bomb Brianna just dropped on them, and Bull's resulting outburst, Noah told Bull and Rebel to go home and get some rest. They all needed sleep, and they would finish the conversation later in the day. Bull and Rebel both gave Noah their secret code look before they left. Brianna didn't know what it meant, but at that point, she didn't think it really mattered.

She had made her decision, and she was at peace with it. There was just one more thing that she really wanted first. It was something that she needed, and only Noah could provide it. She waited at the base of the staircase when Noah reset the alarm system after the guys left.

He turned to her and said, "You found your pajamas. The rest of your clothes are in the guest bedroom closet. You should go on up and get some sleep."

"You-you kept all my clothes?" Surprise echoed in her voice, but Noah couldn't respond with anything more than a nod.

He had kept them all those years. They stayed in his closet until he could no longer stand the sight of them and the memories they held. He had his housekeeper move them to the other bedroom. To this day, he still couldn't bring himself to part with the only thing he had left of her.

Why would he keep them? She questioned if he kept them because he hoped she'd return one day. Maybe it was purely of sentimental value instead. She desperately wanted to ask him, but she was afraid of the answer. She bit her bottom lip and pulled it into her mouth.

He knew that look. She was nervous about something. She only did that when she was nervous.

"What is it, Brianna?"

"I...uh...was just wondering...why you didn't stay at your—" she swallowed hard "—girlfriend's house tonight."

"Girlfriend?" He had a hint of confusion in his voice.

She looked at him with a look that said she knew he was lying. "The girl you were with at the banquet."

He sighed but didn't take his eyes from hers. "She's not my girlfriend. She wants to be, but she's not."

She looked at him and cocked one eyebrow. "I overheard people at the party talking. They said you would be spending the night at Alexa's house again tonight."

He let out a long, loud huff and explained. "I have from time to time, yes. Only at her house. She's never stayed here. She's never been in our—uh, my bed."

Brianna nodded her understanding, but she still looked so sad. He still wasn't sure what to believe, and he didn't know what to feel about her. So many questions swirled through his mind.

Why would she leave me like that?

Why would she let me believe she was dead for the last three years?

Why did she break in to my house?

And if she was the bad guy here, why would she be so willing to give her life for mine?

"Why were you at the gala tonight?" he asked.

She considered lying, but he'd see straight through it, and then he wouldn't believe her at all. Even though she dreaded the backlash, she met his gaze head on and told him the truth.

"I didn't originally plan to. I didn't even know about it until I was on my way here, to your house, and I overheard someone talking about it. Then I saw you leave in your tuxedo, and all the other guys were in tuxes, so I knew your company must be in charge of the gala's security.

"It was stupid of me. I could've used the time to get in and out of your house without being caught, without turning your whole world upside down." She paused. He waited. "The truth is, Noah, I just wanted to see you. I wanted to get as close to you as I possibly could because I've missed you so much. As much as it hurt to see you with someone else, it's been worse not seeing you at all."

He still stood at the alarm pad, his hand on his hip, and he tried to look anywhere but at her. She looked like his Brianna again. Despite everything that had happened, it killed him to be so close to her but feel so far away. He had mourned her for so long and had dreamed that she would show up one day, that her death was all just a bad dream.

But he'd had to move on and get past her. He'd built up his business and was extremely good at it. The thought of her being in witness protection instead of in his protection was a complete insult to him and his abilities. She'd ultimately put her trust in someone else. Someone she didn't know and who didn't love her as he did. Another man who hadn't been forced to live without her for the last three years, who didn't have his heart ripped to shreds, and who didn't want to build a family with her.

His anger had been simmering up to that point, but it suddenly reached a boiling point.

"You know, Brianna, I'm still furious. Do you have any idea what I've been through? The plane you were on, or I thought you were on, exploded! Do you have any idea what that was like to watch the news footage over and over again? To wonder if you felt it, to question if you knew what had happened, to think you suffered and I couldn't be there to help you.

"It killed me to lose you. I died along with you every single day. The first full year, I barely even existed. We had a memorial service for you. Your friends and your family, they were so hurt. But you've been alive and well all this time, hiding in Colorado. While we all struggled to live with your death.

"Tell me something. Exactly how am I supposed to be okay with this?"

Her voice was so low, so soft, and so weak, he barely heard her from across the room. "I never wanted to hurt you. I didn't have a choice, Noah. I don't know what else to say."

"What if that isn't good enough? I deserve a better answer than that. Hell, even Bull and Rebel deserve a better answer than that. You left all of us. But what about me? Me? All I get is 'I didn't want to hurt you.' But you did!"

He knew he was ranting in half-finished thoughts, but there was just too much unfinished business to hold it in. Since he'd opened that old wound, all of his pain and suffering just poured out in the form of rage.

"It would've put your life in danger if—"

He was beyond livid and so very close to completely exploding. "What exactly did I do for a living when you met me? What do I do for a living now? Don't give me that bullshit. You didn't trust me enough to protect you. But you trusted a stranger to do it."

She knew better than to meet the hurt and anger in his tone of voice with her own. Keeping her voice as low as possible, she tried to explain. "I know, Noah, and you're a professional. The difference is you had a good idea of who your enemy was when we first met."

"And now I don't. Is that right? Is that what I'm supposed to believe?"

She crossed her arms over her body as if she were trying to hold herself together in one piece. "Noah, try to remember how it was between us. Before any of this happened. You did not doubt that I loved you then. Did you?"

"I believed you did." From his choice of words, she knew he meant that at the time he believed it, but he wasn't so sure anymore.

"Think about it for just a second, Noah. Knowing how I felt about you, why would I give up everything, everyone in my life, unless I had no other choice? You, the guys, my whole family, my whole life, Noah. Everyone who ever meant anything to me. I gave up everything and have been alone all this time. You know me better than anyone. How could I have done that if I'd had any other choice?"

Noah listened to her words and tried to consider every angle. He felt like he'd been fooled once and didn't like playing the fool. But right at that moment, he couldn't come up with any other reason than the one she gave. Not completely conceding, he shrugged. "I guess."

"Let me ask it this way. What would you have done to keep me safe back when…when you still loved me?" She bit the inside of her cheek to keep from crying again but failed miserably.

Angry that she would even question his love for her, he bit out his reply. "I would have done whatever it took, and you damn well know it."

Nodding in agreement, she replied, "Exactly, Noah. Whatever it took. Regardless of the consequences you'd face. Regardless of the pain it would've caused you. I know you would have. I'd do whatever it took to protect you, too, because I love you."

Noah seemed to accept that explanation better. At least he seemed to consider her reasoning. "I still don't understand why you trusted someone else to protect you, but I get your point about doing whatever it took."

He raked his hand through his hair and then pulled both hands over his face. When he opened his eyes again, Brianna had moved to stand directly in front of him. She was so close he could smell her shampoo and soap, and it reminded him of the many times they'd made love in the shower. And how he'd thought of that very scene every time he stepped into his shower without her over the past three years.

"There's something I want to ask you to do for me. A last request, I guess." She bit her lip again.

She looked so vulnerable and scared, and the man in him wanted to comfort her. He was still so confused, hurt, mad—no, furious—over the events of the last few hours. He tried to make sense out of anything, but he still just couldn't believe she'd hurt him like that.

"Go on." His voice had a questioning tone, and his face wore a guarded expression.

She waited so long to speak again that he didn't think she would finish her request. "You can say no. I don't want you to feel…obligated."

"What is it, Bri?"

His voice almost sounded tender for those few seconds, and she felt a glimmer of hope warm her heart. But she tamped it down because she knew better than to hope for a fairy-tale ending. He was rightfully mad, hurt, and hadn't forgiven her. She couldn't blame him.

"Can you…uh… Will you… Can I have…" Her voice trailed off again, uncertain of how to ask and even more uncertain of how he would respond.

"Just say it."

She searched his eyes for a moment before she stated her request. "For the rest of the night, can you just pretend you still love me?" Her eyes welled up with tears. As she looked down at the floor, her tears spilled over and ran down her cheeks. "I just want to spend my last night in your arms."

Brianna craned her neck up to look at him. She watched the war play out in his eyes. He debated whether he should give in, whether he even wanted to give in. It was at that moment that she knew it had been a mistake to ask.

She watched his eyes harden again, and she recognized that look all too well. His mind was set. Too much had happened, and he couldn't go back. She would spend the last night of her life as she had spent the previous three years. Alone.

She shook her head, looked down at her feet, and backed away from him. "Forget I said anything. I shouldn't have asked that of you. It was really selfish of me. I'm sorry for putting you on the spot like that."

She turned and slowly walked up the curved marble staircase to the second-floor landing. She stopped for a second as she looked down the hallway. At the end of it was the bedroom she had once shared with the man she loved more than anything. She felt the stab in her heart as she realized that she had lost him forever. All the reunion dreams she'd held on to every minute of the past three years crashed and burned before her.

She took a deep breath, walked into one of the guest bedrooms and closed the door behind her. It was symbolic to Brianna. As she closed the bedroom door, the door to her heart slammed shut. She knew Noah was her soul mate five years ago in the desert. It belonged to him, and she didn't want it back.

Noah couldn't believe what she had just asked him. Pretend to love her? He didn't know whether he should feel insulted or complimented at her request. The warring emotions in him tore him apart. On the one hand, he wanted to rush upstairs and tell her he didn't have to pretend to love her—he still loved her more than anything. On the other hand, she had betrayed him in the worst way. She let him believe she was dead. She'd never tried to contact him and still wouldn't have if he hadn't caught her.

Noah sulked. *Just what the fuck am I supposed to do now?*

"I NEED TO KNOW WHY YOU BROKE IN TO MY HOUSE." SHAKING HER shoulder, he said again, "Brianna—I need to know why."

She opened her eyes and startled at the tall, dark figure that stood over her. It took her a second to remember where she was, but she immediately recognized the deep timbre of Noah's voice. She rubbed her eyes and looked at the clock. She'd only been asleep ten minutes. She sat up and swung her legs over the side of the bed.

Confused, she asked, "What, Noah? What did you say?"

"Tell me why you broke in to my house. I need to know."

She looked up into his eyes for a moment as she considered what she should do. She decided then was as good a time as any to give him the evidence she'd collected. She had already decided to give it to him in the morning and explain everything in detail before she went to Richard. She bent to pick up her shoe, reached inside, and brought out a flash drive. "For this," she said as she handed it to him.

He knelt down in front of her, the moonlight streaming through the window directly onto her face. "What's on it?"

"All the evidence you'll ever need is on that flash drive and in the few papers that are still in my hotel room. Keep them somewhere safe. I-I really tried to help you, Noah. I'm so sorry it wasn't enough."

He wanted to ask her what she meant. He wanted her to explain everything from start to finish. But all he could think about was that she was back in his house. After three long years of missing her, she was in a guest bedroom instead of his bed.

"It is password protected. The password is—" she put the back of her hand up to her mouth, blinked back tears, and looked away from him "—the password is Sunny, with a capital S."

Sunny, short for Sunshine.

The nickname that was given to her the night they all promised to take care of her, to be her brothers, just like they were to each other. As he looked at her then, he felt a squeezing in his chest that told him somewhere along the line, they had all let her down.

"Bri." His voice was soft and reminded her so much of how he used to sound when he said her name.

"It's only a few hours until dawn, Noah. You should get some sleep. All of this will be over soon, and you'll be able to put everything behind you. I know I have no right to ask anything of you, but this really isn't for me."

She watched his face to gauge his reaction before she continued. "Please don't tell my parents anything about my coming back. I don't want to hurt them more than I already have. I don't think they could take attending my funeral a second time."

The finality of her words was evident in the distraught look on her face. He knew she intended to see this through to the end, to her end, just as she'd said. Regardless of how hurt and mad he felt about her disappearance, he couldn't deny her genuine anguish.

She was still the same person he fell head over heels in love with so many years ago. She still put everyone ahead of herself, she still loved him unconditionally, and she willingly handed over all the documents she'd worked so hard to get. Those didn't appear to be the actions of someone who wanted to play him.

She was still his Brianna. For better or for worse, that's what he had every intention of vowing before God, friends, and family. That promise had already been made in his mind, carried out in his heart, and flowed in his veins. Their fates were already intertwined and weren't severed even in her "death."

He hooked one arm under her knees, the other under her arms, and started to lift her off the guest bed.

She pushed both hands against his chest to stop him. "Noah, no. You don't have to do this. It's okay. I get it. I've realized something since I asked you for tonight. I can't go through with this now that I know you don't love me. I thought we could pretend it all away for just one night. But I can't do it. I know it'll only hurt worse."

Brianna had no idea what he was thinking, and his eyes didn't let anything show. Her heart broke all over again with his every touch, even just being in his presence. She knew he would never really accept that she stayed away because she loved him more than anything. It broke her heart even more to know that by trading herself to Richard, she would die with Noah thinking poorly of her.

"Brianna, I can't say that I agree with what you did. I don't. At all. You should've trusted me to protect you."

With an exasperated breath, she said forcefully, "Noah, none of it was to protect me. I had to hide to protect you. Everyone who could've hurt you had to believe that I died in that explosion."

Her hand went up to his cheek, and she lovingly stroked alone his jawline. Her teary eyes held his as she continued. "I love you, Noah, more than anything, more than anyone. I've never stopped loving you. Not after I had to leave when I first met you in the desert, and I didn't stop loving you three years ago when I had to stay away from you to protect you. I've loved you with my whole heart every second that we've been apart. I hope that you can believe that—one day."

"You're not sleeping in here, Brianna." With that, he picked her up and carried her to his room. She wrapped her arms around his neck and leaned in to breathe in his scent. She silently vowed she would cherish this moment, no matter how much it broke her heart. As he set her down next to his bed, he saw the deep love that shone in her eyes, and she searched his eyes for even a sliver of reciprocation.

He shook his head, but he never took his eyes off hers as he moved in to kiss her lips lightly. His hand went up to her neck, his fingers gently stroked downward, across her collarbone to the spaghetti strap of her tank top. He pushed it off her shoulder and kissed her along the same line that his fingers had trailed. He felt her shudder under his touch. He moved to the other side and started all over. As he raised his head, he moved his hand to the back of her neck and into her hair.

He grasped a handful of hair, tilted her head, and covered her mouth with his. Their kiss suddenly became feverish and urgent. Her hands flew to his chest. She felt his muscles tense and relax under her fingers. She unbuttoned his shirt one at a time. Her fingers explored every inch of him along the way, memorized every line of his body as they went. Her fingers traced his six-pack abs to the top of his tuxedo pants and watched as they dropped to the floor. He removed his boxer briefs and stepped out of them. She reached for him and pulled him close to her.

She felt his erection on her abdomen, and her hand found his hard, thick length. She began to stroke him gently. He groaned and grabbed her hand to stop her. "Keep that up, and this won't last much longer."

He quickly pulled her tank top over her head and bent as he pulled her panties to her ankles. He kissed and licked his way back up her body. He picked her up and sat on the edge of the bed with her in his lap, while he gently stroked her face.

He couldn't stop the thoughts that whirled through his mind.

...I lost everything...

...She was protecting you...

...I tried to help you...

...My life for Noah's...

"What is it, Noah?" Brianna asked when he suddenly stopped. Her heart squeezed, and she held her breath as she expected him to say he had changed his mind. That he couldn't allow himself to go through with it. That he didn't want to spend the night with her.

He sat her on the bed beside him, rose, and walked to the window. The glow from the lights outside cast beams across his naked body and showcased his dominant form. One of his muscular arms was against the window, bent at the elbow, and his forehead rested on his forearm. Brianna felt exposed and rejected as she sat completely naked on his bed.

He changed his mind, she thought as she pulled the top sheet over her and waited for him to answer.

"You really would give up your life for mine. Wouldn't you, Bri?" The first slight hint of emotion was in his voice, just a sign that he considered she had told him the truth.

"Yes."

He noticed that she didn't hesitate in her answer. He turned to look at her for a moment and then walked back to her. The muscle in his jaw twitched, and uneasy emotions played across his face. He knelt in front of her, pulled the sheet away from her, and wrapped his arms around her waist.

"You already did, didn't you? You gave up your life here to protect me. Like you tried to protect me in the car when you thought that guy was going to shoot me." He wasn't really asking as much as he was coming to a realization. But he waited for her to answer.

She hesitated before replying, knowing the questions that would come next. "Yes."

"But why? What am I missing?"

"It's a long story, Noah. But I will tell you everything later. For right now, can you just believe me?"

"One more thing that's bothering me." She nodded, indicating for him to continue. "Why didn't you trust me? Why didn't you tell me what was going on back then? I would've helped you." His tone wasn't accusing or doubting her. She understood that he just really needed to know why.

"I did trust you, Noah. I do trust you. And I tried to tell you. But you…you got mad whenever I brought up Richard's name. Then, that last day when I tried to tell you, I wanted to tell you. But you were so busy with work. Then I had to leave on assignment before you even got home that night." Her voice trailed off.

He sighed and laid his head on her lap. "Yeah, that I remember." *I remember I was too wrapped up in myself to listen when you tried to talk to me.*

18

CHAPTER EIGHTEEN

She slowly ran her fingers through his hair. It was longer than before and curled slightly on the ends. She loved the silky feel of it as it moved across her hand. Her fingers made long, slow strides through it as she relished the time with him. She caressed his head as her fingers slid across his scalp. He straightened his back as he kneeled in front of her. She was face-to-face with him again after all the time apart, and her heart swelled with love. Every sensation in her came alive when he pulled her hips closer to the edge of the bed, covered her mouth with his, and then turned her head to deepen it even more.

He moved closer to her as he pushed her legs farther apart to make more room for him. He ran his fingers along the taut lines of her stomach. His fingers instinctively remembered the feel of her yoga-muscled body. He kept moving his hand down, between her legs, and his fingers found the warmth of her wetness. He felt his way along her sex. He gently stroked her and savored her soft moans of pleasure. His hand moved to her center, traced her soft wetness before he plunged his finger deep inside her. Her soft moans were enough to drive him into a frenzy.

Slowly, torturously, his hand cupped her mound and wordlessly claimed it as his own. The heel of his palm rubbed against her clit while his fingers moved in and out of her wetness. He felt her tremble as her hips instinctively rose to meet his hand. He knew her first orgasm was imminent, and he felt her velvety walls constrict around his fingers.

Her excitement and obvious need for him instantly made him unbelievably hard. The soft skin of her delicate hand wrapped around him stroked him from the base to tip and pulled his own moans from deep inside. His hips involuntarily moved in time with her hand as she continued to stroke him. His mouth covered hers again and their tongues caressed seductively.

Unable to wait any longer, he repositioned her on the bed. He gently pushed her shoulders down to lie flat on the bed as he covered her body with his. He had planned to take it slow, to make their lovemaking last, and savor every part of her. But her loving touch and submissive sounds made those plans fly right out the window. She opened her legs to invite him in, and he held the tip of his long, hard thickness at her wet center to tease her before he plunged inside her. His hips pushed in, and they both gasped from the incredible feeling of their intimate contact. He stilled his hips as his voice rumbled through his chest.

"Baby, you're so fucking tight. Am I hurting you?"

He pulled back to look at her face just as she gasped. "No, don't stop! Please." Her hands moved down to push his hips and urged him farther into her.

He moved slowly at first as he gave her body time to adjust to his size, mold around him, and fit him like a glove. As he increased his speed and thrusts, he watched her become his Brianna once again right before his eyes. She moaned and raised her hips to match his thrusts, took him to the hilt, and didn't allow him to lessen the intensity.

She screamed, unable to stop her cries. "Oh God, Noah! Don't stop!" Her voice was like an aphrodisiac to him. It pushed him to keep going when he thought he would explode.

He propped up on his forearms, framed her face with his arms, and his mouth crushed down on hers. His tongue dove in and took what was rightfully his. What should have always belonged to him. What he had missed every day for the past three years. His hunger for her was so deep, so primal, and so possessive that it thoroughly owned him. He knew he could never get enough of her.

She wrapped her legs around him and ground her heels into him when he attempted to slow his pace. She wanted him as much as he wanted her, and she showed it. "That's my girl," he murmured in her ear. "Let me hear you."

With every orgasm that rocked her body, the strong pull in her lower abdomen triggered her screams of ecstasy. His name never sounded so good, so right, as it did when it fell from her lips. Her inner walls quivered and squeezed him as he took her over the edge repeatedly. She had always been so responsive to his touch, but he felt the connection was even stronger.

"You feel too good, baby. I can't hold back any longer. Open your eyes and look at me, Bri."

She did as he commanded, and he saw the tears that were held behind her lids roll down her face. He bent his head to kiss her. "Come for me. I need to feel you come again."

He pushed up to straighten his arms and deepen his thrust. He took her over the edge of ecstasy with him, falling in tandem together. He watched her eyes and her face change as she let go, and the way his chest squeezed nearly took his breath away. Their bodies were utterly spent and thoroughly sated.

He relaxed his arms and allowed his massive body to cover hers. When he started to roll over, knowing he was crushing her, she held on and refused to let him move.

He chuckled in her ear. "Bri, I know you can't breathe."

"I'm okay. I don't want to let you go yet."

He rolled over onto his back and took her with him so that she lay entirely on top of him. She turned her head to the side and rested her cheek on his chest. He felt the warm tears as they pooled where her head lay.

"Are you okay? Did I hurt you?"

"No, you didn't hurt me." Her voice was watery and strained as she attempted to talk through the tears.

"Then why are you crying?"

She sniffled but didn't wipe her tears away. "It's just been so hard not to see you, touch you, or hear your voice. Knowing that you were so close, but so far away. I've been so alone."

His hands stroked her back lovingly as he listened to her patiently. He didn't know what to say or how he should reply.

"I'm sorry, Noah, for all of it. Everything. I know that doesn't make up for it."

The sun began to rise before they went to sleep. They made love twice more before they both passed out from exhaustion. Brianna knew she would sleep soundly for the first time in three years, safe and secure in Noah's warm embrace. He spooned her from behind, draped his arm across her body possessively, and kept her as close to him as possible.

Just before he drifted off to sleep, he heard her whisper, "I love you, Noah. I always have and I always will. I hope you remember that after tomorrow."

Noah felt a chill move over his body. He rolled over, his arm stretched out to pull Brianna to him, but she wasn't there. He opened his eyes and leaned up on his elbow as he strained his ears to listen for any sound. At first, he thought she might be in the bathroom.

The faint smell of coffee, bacon, waffles, and hot syrup wafted up to his bedroom, and he smiled. He loved her waffles. He had gained fifteen pounds when they first started living together. He pictured her in his kitchen, in her pajamas, dancing to the radio as she cooked breakfast.

He pulled on his shorts before he headed downstairs to the kitchen. His stomach rumbled from hunger, and everything smelled so good. It felt good to have her home. It felt right. He knew there was still a lot to talk about and pieces of the puzzle he needed to know to find closure, but he couldn't deny how glad he was to have her back.

Bull and Rebel sat at his table as they scarfed down the waffles and coffee. Noah headed straight for the cabinet to grab a coffee cup.

"Morning, boss. Sleeping in, huh?" Bull and Rebel smiled at him and then at each other. They shook their heads and resumed stuffing their palates. Noah looked at the clock and was shocked to see he'd slept past noon.

"Hey." He looked around the kitchen then back to the table. "Where's Brianna?"

They both stopped eating and looked at him. They stared at him briefly before Rebel answered. "Uh, we thought she was with you."

"She was, but she obviously made breakfast. So, where is she now?" He looked at each of the guys, who then looked at each other and back to him.

"Reap, she was down here. She cooked and talked to us for a few minutes, then said she was going back upstairs with you," Rebel answered.

"How long ago has that been?"

"About an hour ago."

Noah ran back upstairs, called her name, and looked through the bedrooms, closets, and bathrooms. She wasn't anywhere to be found. He ran back down the stairs. Rebel and Bull said they had checked the rest of the house but found no sign of her. Noah headed for the front door to check outside, and his heart dropped. He saw a white envelope taped to the door with his name on it. Tied around the oversized doorknob was the black blindfold from the desert—the symbol of her commitment to her brothers.

He strode to the door, jerked the envelope down, and tore it open.

Dear Noah,

This is the hardest letter I've ever had to write. You're probably really mad at me right now, but I hope this letter answers all of your questions and that, in time, you will see I had to do this. I know you never really intended to trade me to Richard. You're too good of a man to do that. But this the only way you'll be protected.

Richard was using you and your company to ship weapons illegally to terrorist groups in the Middle East. Your security firm was the perfect front for them to transport weapons and get them into foreign countries. He set up the contracts with you so that you'd take the blame if they ever got caught. His name is not found on any of the official documents.

This operation actually goes much further up the chain of command than just Richard. The flash drive has the documents that prove your innocence and shows that Richard is coordinating the weapons drops. There are financial records with wire transfers to his offshore bank accounts that match the dates on every contract he made with you in my backpack. When in doubt, follow the money.

On my last trip, Richard figured out I was onto him. I went into hiding after he tried to kill me. When Richard reappeared, I knew he would come after you to draw me out. The only reason he hasn't killed me yet is because he needs to destroy those documents first. But now he's sent someone to kill you and to get the evidence from me. He won't stop until you're dead.

The people involved won't let this information ever see the light of day. You'll still take the fall, and I won't let that happen to you. I found one of your wires and activated the digital recorder. Use the recording to stop him once and for all. He won't be protected once it hits the press. Then you'll be safe, and this nightmare will be over.

Thank you for giving me one last night together. I know you don't love me anymore, and I understand why. You still made last night very special for me, and I can't tell you how much that means to me. I've realized that I can't live without you again—I don't even want to try. The only thing that has kept me going the last three years is the hope we would be together again someday.

I love you, Noah. I love you more than anything. You are the best man I know, and I want you to live a long and happy life. My only hope now is that one day you'll forgive me and remember only the good times we had. That's what I'm taking with me.

Forever Yours,

Brianna

"WHAT THE FUCK IS SHE THINKING?" NOAH'S ANGER REACHED A flashpoint. "She isn't trained for this. She'll get herself killed!" He handed the letter to Bull and paced like a caged animal, ready to pounce and maul someone.

"I don't understand why she thinks only she can save me. How many times do I have to remind her what I do for a living?" Noah growled as he paced.

"From the way this letter reads, she's convinced Richard won't allow her to live knowing what she knows. It's either you or her, and she chose to take your place," Rebel replied. "She left all the evidence with you because she knows they'll bury you both if she tries to use it. Having the additional evidence against Richard for killing Brianna will ensure your safety."

Noah propped his fists on his hips and racked his brain over her decision. He tried to see everything from her point of view to understand her reasoning, but he had the sense there was still something missing. "What did she say this morning?" Noah barked.

Rebel knew he would want a word-by-word relay of the conversation.

"She was cooking when we came in. She said good morning. We sat down and looked at the paper. I commented on how strange it was that she and Richard showed up the same day. That we were told she was dead and he was presumed dead.

"She asked what I meant by he was presumed dead. I told her about that US Marshal Stevens showing up at the office out of the blue one day. How he said he wasn't convinced Richard was on the plane. I explained that he said he didn't have any proof, he didn't really ask us many questions, and then we never heard from him again after that. I asked her if Richard's reappearance meant she was safe and if that's why they released her from WITSEC. She didn't answer me. That's when she said she was going back upstairs with you."

Noah looked at Bull. "And you?"

Bull stared at her letter he still held in his hand when he replied. "I didn't even speak to her, Reap."

"All right, she has quite a head start on us, but we need to get a plan together. Call more guys in, our best only. We have to find her. Send someone to her hotel room to clean out her stuff and see when she was last there. Bull, you still have the key?"

Bull nodded.

"Good, have the area canvassed. We have a recon mission on Richard to do. Find out where he is right now, where he'll be later, who he's with, his known contacts, recent financial transactions, his favorite foods—everything."

"You got it, boss," Rebel said as he walked away to get started.

Bull walked outside, pulled out his cell phone, hit a name, and waited. "We need your help."

19

CHAPTER NINETEEN

US Marshal Stevens told Rebel he didn't think Richard was on the plane. Stevens knew Richard wasn't on the plane, and he's known this whole time.

Rebel didn't realize the weight of his words and how much hidden meaning they held. He had said them so easily that he could've been talking about the weather, but Brianna connected the dots immediately. She knew she'd never fully trusted Stevens for a reason, and then she realized why.

Her mind swirled with the facts and possible scenarios that all of this meant. The questions that she should've asked from the outset, but she was too young, scared, and naïve to see it then. She couldn't think of any reason why a US Marshal would be in the Middle East.

The one reason that made sense was that he was part of the whole scheme. He was actually there with Richard in some capacity. He must work for Richard, to help prevent him from getting caught and to make his own illegal money while he was at it.

Memories of the day that changed her life flooded her mind. She'd repressed them every other time they tried to ambush her because they brought so much pain, longing for something she couldn't have and regret how she'd contributed to her circumstances. She focused on allowing them to replay so she could attempt to figure out what she had missed.

As she left the hotel in Turkey, she ran into Richard—literally smacked into him. She then sprinted to her rental car and immediately drove toward the airport. She still had to wait quite a while before her flight began boarding, but just knowing she was one step closer to going home to Noah would make her feel more secure.

She returned her rental car to the attendant and walked alone through the parking garage toward the terminal. The hairs on the back of her neck stood at attention and alerted her that something was very wrong. The uneasiness of physically feeling someone's eyes on her sent waves of panic through her. Not knowing exactly where the danger lurked added to her heightened anxiety.

Footsteps fell behind her, but she didn't dare turn around to look. She quickened her pace to reach a more populated area, but the footsteps behind her also accelerated. She placed her arms in the straps of her backpack, grabbed the straps to hold it securely against her body, and broke out in a full sprint.

When she exited the garage, she made a sharp right turn and found a covered spot where she crouched down out of sight. She waited to see who came out of the garage next. She reasoned if he stopped and looked in both directions instead of just crossing to the terminal, she'd know he really was after her.

Within a couple of seconds, a large figure took a couple of steps out of the garage and then suddenly stopped walking. He looked in both directions, took a few steps in the opposite direction from her, then suddenly did an about-face and walked a few steps in her direction. She remained crouched in her hidden spot and held her breath.

It was Richard himself, and he searched for her fervently. She'd been so foolish to think she could handle something this big on her own. She was so close to the terminal, so close to the plane that would take her home. But she knew if she stepped out into his sight, she'd never make it home again.

"Any sign of her?" Richard asked as another man approached.

"No. She's definitely fast, I'll give her that," he replied.

"Yeah. No shit. She runs all the time. One of my surveillance guys refuses to tail her anymore," Richard chuckled sarcastically. "Damn it. Find her. She can't get on that plane."

"She'll have to go through security to get on the plane," the other man replied. "She'll have to approach the airport door at some point."

Richard shook his head. "I can't go back until she's found. Deron gave her up easily enough. She has more than enough documentation to bury me, Bosco."

Before Bosco could reply, Richard's phone rang. He glanced at the screen and noticeably tensed before he answered it.

"Hollingsworth."

After an extended silence, Richard's face turned bright red with anger. With gritted teeth, he finally spoke. "Yes, crystal clear."

Richard put the phone back in his pocket and ran his fingers through his hair. Bosco watched him with a wary expression. "What was that all about?"

"That was Sayyaf. He said if I don't bring her to him in the next hour, I will regret getting on that plane," Richard replied.

"Does that mean he plans to—" Bosco's voice trailed off.

"That would be my guess," Richard huffed. "Motherfucker!" he bellowed. "I'm completely fucked if we don't find her right now. Cover the door. I'm going to look around inside for her."

The two men split up, and Brianna remained utterly still, her hands covered her mouth, and her eyes welled with tears. She watched as Bosco briskly walked away and Richard entered the airport. There weren't many places she could effectively hide in the international terminal with one man watching the doors and one watching intently inside.

If she could wait it out another hour, she hoped Sayyaf would demand Richard's presence. She'd be able to rebook her flight and get home undetected. She pulled her phone out of her pocket and tried to call Noah. With every redial, a woman's voice told her that all circuits were busy and to try her call again later. She squeezed her phone in her hand and brought it to her forehead.

"Noah, I need you so much right now," she pleaded. "I don't know what to do."

Brianna leaned her back against the wall behind her and fought back the terror that threatened to incapacitate her. She tilted her head back and looked up at the sky. The stars had just become visible in the evening sky. Her flight should be boarding by that time, and there was no way she could get through security and to her gate before the door closed. She intently watched for Richard to leave the airport terminal so she could rush inside and change her flight to the next available one.

The fates seemed to align in her favor as she watched Richard and Bosco leave the airport. Richard muttered an expletive with every long stride he took. He was obviously disgusted and angry enough to kill someone. Namely her. As the two men passed by, she heard his reply to something Bosco had said.

"Sayyaf called and ordered us to a meeting with him. Right now."

"That doesn't sound good for us," Bosco said, his tone conveying his worry.

"If he planned to kill us, he wouldn't call us to his house. He has other plans for us," Richard replied. "We probably won't like them, though."

When they were out of sight, Brianna stood and sprinted across the street toward the terminal entrance. A large jet appeared over the top of the building as it rose toward the twinkling stars. She stopped to watch it, confident it was the jet she should've been on. Her feet began to move, but her eyes remained glued to the plane as it rose higher.

In a split second, her whole world changed right before her eyes. A giant fireball consumed the plane as she watched in horror. The explosion completely obliterated the plane and sent small pieces of the fuselage in every direction for miles. The noise was deafening, and the fireball was gigantic. But the terror that resulted on the ground was complete pandemonium.

Panicked screams and heart-wrenching sobs came from every direction as onlookers realized what they had seen. Metal scraped on metal as cars crashed into others, the drivers distracted and shocked by the horrible scene. Police and airport security screamed directions in Turkish. They sounded even more terrifying yelling in a language Brianna couldn't understand.

She froze in the street with her jaw dropped open, her eyes wide from terror, and her heart pounded against her chest wall. Through the mass confusion of travelers that rushed from the building, a single voice caught her attention.

"This is US Marshal Stevens. Get Bill Jackman—it's an emergency," he yelled into his cell phone. "Bill, there's been an explosion at the airport. From what I can tell, a plane exploded upon takeoff. Appears to be an intentional attack. The authorities are evacuating the airport. I need immediate assistance and evacuation."

"You're a US Marshal?" she asked, clearly panicked. Still on the phone, he simply nodded, and she continued. "I need help. I'm a reporter from Miami. Can you help me get home? Please."

"Hang on one second, Bill," he said into the phone before he addressed Brianna. "Do you have a passport?" he asked as he eyed her carefully.

Brianna handed him her passport and nervously waited as he carefully inspected it. Her eyes continuously darted around, took in the mass confusion that surrounded them, and watched for Richard to reappear. A wave of relief washed over her when the Marshal spoke next.

"Bill, I have a young lady with a US passport here with me. She appears to be a legitimate citizen. I'm bringing her in with me," Stevens said into the phone.

After a few more clipped responses, he gave her passport back to her. "Come with me. The US Embassy personnel will pick us up, but they can't get into this area. We need to get outside the airport perimeter on foot."

"Let's run," Brianna suggested adamantly. "The sooner, the better."

"If you're sure you can keep up," he replied.

Brianna nodded in agreement, the stiff, quick jerks relaying her urgent need to move immediately. The pair bolted through the throngs of frightened people until they reached the designated area. Two large, black vehicles stopped in front of them, and three US soldiers stepped out of the first one and surrounded them.

"What's your name?" one of the soldiers demanded curtly.

"US Marshal Stevens," he replied, handing over his badge and passport.

"Brianna Tate," she replied as she gave up her passport.

"I'm Major Paul Lowe," he introduced himself. "They're good," he said to the other two soldiers. One of the men opened the back door of the second vehicle, and Major Lowe told them to get in.

As the distance between her and the airport grew, Brianna's nerves became worse. She had to remain in control while she was in the midst of danger. But when she began to feel safe and had time to contemplate on the events, she began to shake uncontrollably. Stevens noticed immediately and watched her suspiciously.

"So, what brings you to Turkey?" he asked.

"A lead for an article that was called in at my newspaper," she replied.

"You flew halfway around the world for a lead?"

"I'm a damn good investigative reporter. I did a lot of research first," she replied defensively. "Everything checked out, and it's a groundbreaking story. It just all went to hell when I got here."

"What do you mean? What went to hell?" he pressed.

She immediately knew she'd said too much and didn't want to add more to an already volatile situation. "My story. My source. Everything."

"I want to help you, Miss Tate," Stevens replied. "I really do. But I need to know what kind of trouble you're in first. You seem like a sweet girl who is a little out of her element in this part of the world. If there is even a remote possibility that your trouble is tied to that plane, you have to tell me. This could be a matter of national security, and I can't let you back into the US"

She considered his words and what it would mean for her if she couldn't get on a privately chartered flight back home. With the airport locked down and security on high alert, she knew there was no chance of arranging that outside of official government channels.

"I was supposed to be on that plane. I don't have proof that it exploded because of me, but I don't believe in coincidences. Two men are searching for me right now. And if they find me, they'll kill me because of the information I have. They're trafficking weapons and using DOD transport planes to hide them."

"You have proof of this? Any tangible evidence?"

"I have copies of the catalog pages that show the shipments of weapons have been received here on a regular basis," she offered.

A voice inside her said to still be careful and leery of everyone, so she didn't tell him about the evidence she had stashed in Noah's house. At this point, she decided no one could be fully trusted. If Stevens could get her home, she'd enlist Noah's help in how to turn the evidence over to someone who could really help.

"That would be a good start," he replied. "If you have, or can get, additional evidence, that would be even better." His statement hung in the air between them on purpose. It was to test her and see how she'd respond.

"As I said, I'm a good investigative reporter. I will keep digging until I have all the evidence I need," she replied honestly.

"Who is after you?" he asked.

"A man who works in the DOD," she replied vaguely.

"If what you're saying is true, you're in serious trouble," he warned her. "If anyone knows about this, or is involved with it, that's treason of the highest order. The penalty would certainly be death. Withholding evidence of this nature is also treason, so be sure of what you say. Are there any other Americans besides the DOD guy involved? Anyone else I need to know about?"

Brianna's thoughts immediately went to Noah and how his company was involved. She couldn't let him take the fall for what Richard had done. The evidence had to be controlled by someone who would protect Noah as she did. "No, no one else is involved in this."

"Does anyone else know about it? If you've told anyone, they could become a target themselves."

"No one knows specifics. Only the general storyline that I'm working on," she replied.

"People involved in black-market weapons trade won't care that you're a young woman. They won't care that your family and friends don't know specific details. If you go back home, these men will find them and kill them," Stevens strongly cautioned her.

"What am I supposed to do, then?" she probed. "Where am I supposed to go?"

"I can get you back to the US and into the Witness Protection Program. If you have more evidence that I can take to the State Department, I can push for arrests of anyone involved. Once we have everything we need, you'll be safe and can return home," he promised.

Sensing her hesitation, he continued. "Why do you think I'm here? I've had to help other Americans get out of here safely because of how dangerous these rebel extremists can be.

"That—" he motioned over his shoulder toward the smoke rising from the burning remnants of the jumbo jet "—is nothing compared to what they do to people they take prisoner. Don't subject your loved ones to that."

Richard was still on the loose and wanted her dead. Sayyaf was evidently a very dangerous man if even Richard was afraid of him. Bosco remained a threat, and she had no idea who else she was up against before the danger was over.

"Okay. Get me back to the US, and I'll keep digging until I have every shred of evidence. As much as I don't want to go into hiding, I don't want my family and friends to pay for my mistakes," she agreed.

Stevens contacted his friend, Palmer, at the US Embassy in Turkey and arranged for her transportation and new identification. When their plane landed, and she handed her passport to the US Customs Agent, Kristina Miller was born, and Brianna Tate ceased to exist.

After Rebel's comments, she realized that Stevens suspected she'd had proof somewhere in the US all along, so he pretended to help her in the Witness Protection Program until he knew for sure.

He hounded her for all the evidence in every conversation they had. She gave him the small amount of proof that she could, but she never gave him the final link to Richard—his offshore bank account numbers.

She called him every week with questions on where the case was and when she could go home. With this information, his refusal to stop asking her for more documentation made perfect sense. He knew there had to be more because he didn't find his name associated with anything. He was somehow implicated in the evidence she gave Noah.

Department of Defense personnel.
US Marshals.
US leaders.
Foreign leaders.
Big business owners.

There were too many high-level people involved for them to leave Noah alone, to leave him out of it, even if she handed over her proof. She had brought this to Noah's door. In her mind, none of this would've ever happened if she hadn't kept digging. She couldn't let Noah pay with his life, or rot in jail for the rest of his life, for her stubbornness in getting the story.

After Rebel's offhand comment, she knew what she had to do. She finished cooking the waffles and excused herself from Bull and Rebel. They barely noticed her absence anyway since they were too busy eating breakfast. Bull hardly even looked at her, much less spoke to her. She missed her brothers, but she couldn't think of that right then. She had to hurry before Noah woke up and stopped her.

She knew the whole interrogation technique he used with his questioning. It was definitely not the same technique he would've used in the field. But he had used that on her too many times during their relationship, especially to find out any surprises she had planned for him. She couldn't keep any secrets from the man. Even though he agreed to trade her to Richard, she knew he would never go through it. Even if he hated her, he still wouldn't have done it because he was an honorable man.

So, she had to make the trade herself in a way that Richard

would be caught red-handed, and his associates couldn't protect him any longer. She decided the premeditated torture and murder of a young woman, who had proof of his treasonous black-market weapons dealings, should be enough to put him away for life. The others involved would distance themselves and allow Richard to take the fall for it all.

She thought of last night and how it felt to be in Noah's arms again. Her heart hurt and tears pricked her eyes at just the idea of leaving him again. She'd watched his eyes when she asked him for her final request and knew it was too late for them. There was no going back to what they had because she had really fucked things up between them. So many regrets raged through her mind. If only she had told Noah about Richard. If only she had made him listen. If only she had stood toe-to-toe with him, fought it out, and made her case known.

If only she had one more day with Noah.

She didn't know why he changed his mind at the last second, but she almost didn't go through with it herself. The thought of him making love to her because he felt obligated in some way was just too much to bear. Once he kissed her, though, all rational thought left her. She was only glad she had that one last memory with him. But at that moment, she had to put all of her thoughts and feelings aside and focus on her plan.

Noah's security firm used state-of-the-art equipment. He had various types of surveillance gadgets and exciting toys that made the jobs more manageable. Most were at his central office in downtown Miami, but a few items always made their way home with him. Some were worn on clothes, placed in a shirt pocket, or the old-fashioned method of taping to the skin. Brianna searched his office and found a remote access digital recorder that was discreet enough to hide in plain sight.

The recorder would be found if anyone screened her for bugs, so she would wait until the last minute before turning it on. It only required a simple touch to make it start recording, but if anyone were watching, they would definitely know what she had planned. She activated the receiver for the recorder in Noah's home office, wrote him a letter to explain everything as best she could, and quietly walked out the front door. She left the blindfold tied to the front door knob because she wanted to leave them with the knowledge that she would never betray them. She had kept that with her all these years, and it seemed fitting to leave it with them then.

She ran all the way back to the hotel where her backpack still waited for her. The clerk on duty recognized her and gave her a new key card for her room. She quickly showered, dressed, and checked out. She knew Noah and a small army of men from his security team would be coming for her soon, but she planned to be well out of sight before they found her.

She took off alone down the street and to hail a taxi at the corner. She knew Richard was still in Miami, and Noah mentioned he'd gone by his hotel suite to see him. It also helped that his return was all over the news feeds. They conducted interviews at his posh hotel suite and jokingly asked how he tolerated the terrible conditions of his current residence. Hailing a cab, she gave the hotel name to the driver.

"The Villa by Barton G."

Next, all she had to do was pull off the tricky part. She needed to find out Richard's plans for the night and confront him. She wanted their meeting to be in a very public place so he wouldn't shoot her on sight. She needed to catch him in the act and make him talk to her first for her idea to work. She planned to spy on a man who was thoroughly trained and highly skilled in reconnaissance techniques. There was also no doubt Noah and his team would employ the same counter-techniques very soon.

Yeah, this will go over really well, she thought sardonically.

She stepped out of the taxi, paid the driver, and walked into the hotel lobby. Scanning the room, she didn't see Richard anywhere, but she kept her face turned from the security cameras as much as possible. She used her "Kristina Miller" identification and government-issued credit card to check in to the hotel. She knew her credit card transactions were most likely traced if what she suspected about Stevens was true. But this was the best way she knew to get close to Richard.

She pocketed her room key and exited the hotel. If she planned to fit in at the swanky establishment, she'd need more appropriate clothes. Her current clothes were nowhere near elegant enough to blend in with the other patrons. She left on foot and went in search of the high-end boutiques for a few new items —dresses, shoes, makeup, and jewelry. She also decided to buy an expensive wig that was made of real hair so it would look authentic.

She spent the afternoon shopping in several different stores to find the items she needed and buying them, regardless of the cost. After today, it wouldn't matter anyway. She was careful to watch for anyone following her as she walked from store to store. After a couple of hours shopping, there was one man who had been at more than one store with her, but he hadn't bought anything. She mistakenly turned down the wrong street and quickly found herself away from the crowds.

Brianna quickened her pace, but it was too late. A man grabbed her from behind, wrapped his hand around her mouth, and pulled her into a side alley. Her heart pounded as she struggled against his hold and tried to elbow him in the ribs. He shoved her into the back seat of an idling car, where another man was waiting for her.

She blinked rapidly and tried to catch her breath as she gave the man sitting across from her a dirty look. The man who'd grabbed her slid into the front seat of the car.

"Stevens? What the hell are you doing? Why didn't you just talk to me?" she yelled.

"Because you are not even supposed to be here. And we shouldn't be seen together in public."

"Then why not have your village idiot here—" she motioned to the other man "—talk to me instead? He's followed me for the last two hours!"

Ignoring her sarcasm, Stevens got to the point of the meeting. "Do you have the rest of the evidence for me?"

She felt completely uneasy being around him after what Rebel said earlier, so she schooled her features and lied. "No, I don't have it. I'm still working on it. I have your number."

"I need you to get it to me as soon as possible. I'll be waiting," he ordered.

Brianna jumped out of the car and hurried back to the more populated area. There were still a few things she needed to purchase before her mission was complete. The bathroom at a gourmet coffee shop served as her changing room as she transformed into a long red-haired socialite. She also made sure her eyebrows matched her new wig color.

She hailed a taxi to take her back to the hotel after her earlier mistake. She couldn't risk being seen by anyone else. She returned to the hotel, bags in hand, and walked in as though she owned the place. She didn't actually feel the confidence she outwardly displayed. She desperately wanted to be back in Noah's arms where she felt safe and secure.

20

CHAPTER TWENTY

Noah called an emergency meeting with a dozen of his best men in the downtown office of Steele Security. He arrived well before anyone else got there, even though every man there had immediately dropped everything and rushed in. The dry-erase board was full of information on their newest case.

"All of you have heard a lot about Brianna over the past three years," Noah explained. "We still have to find out all of the details of what happened, but she wasn't killed, and she's back. As if this weren't complicated enough, the enemy is one of our own. Richard Hollingsworth."

The rumble of expletives used to describe Richard echoed around the room. Every former military man there understood precisely what Noah meant. One of their own, a brother-in-arms, had dishonored himself and, by association, tainted their reputation.

"If Richard sees us anywhere around here, he will immediately make his move to kill Brianna. We have to assume he has a team of undercover agents, just like we do. We need eyes on Brianna and Richard—immediately. If you see Brianna, grab her no matter what. She is your first priority."

Noah concluded his mission speech and motioned for everyone to gear up. It wasn't quite like the forty-pound backpack he carried in the Army, but he was dressed for battle, nonetheless.

Bull, Rebel, and the dozen-man team joined Noah at the whiteboard as they mapped out the area around Brianna's original hotel and around Richard's hotel. The search at her hotel had turned up minimal information. She had checked out and left on foot. The clerk pointed in the general direction she walked, but her trail went cold very soon.

The computer techie of the group, Brad, had a search running on the local taxis, in the event she used a credit card in her name. The chances of finding her were essentially nil since they didn't know her alias name. Brad also worked to retrieve all the information from the flash drive Brianna gave Noah. Reviewing the data, he whistled. "Girl's done her research, Reap. This is huge."

Brad continued with his recount of the evidence Brianna had saved to the flash drive to give them more details than Brianna's letter had given. "None of these contracts are the standard ones you signed, Reaper. Your signature has been forged, and according to her notes, all the escorts you provided were illegal.

"If anyone had been caught, you would've been sent to jail for life...if anyone had let you make it that far. With the names attached to this operation, they would've buried you. She was right. This never would've hit the press. You'd be dead, and the story would've been buried along with you."

Bull lowered his head and swore under his breath. "That son of a bitch."

Noah nodded and shook his head. "With all the escorts I've approved, it could've gone wrong at any time. At best, I would've been hung for treason.

"Richard and I were friends since high school, and he purposely involved me in running guns to a band of murdering rebels," he seethed. "Then when Brianna found out, he tried to kill her. I will have Richard's head for this," Noah vowed.

Bull's phone vibrated, and he glanced down at the name on the screen. Noah looked at him expectantly, and Bull said, "I have to take this, Reap," as he stepped out of the room.

A moment later, he returned and walked to the computer where he changed the search parameters to find financial transactions for "Kristina Miller." The computer returned numerous results at several boutiques. "Got a hit," Bull called out.

They looked at the store locations on the map, and Rebel commented on how close the stores were to Richard's hotel, just as the computer returned a room charge hold for The Villa by Barton G.

"She's at the same fucking hotel. We have to find her before we're too late," Noah growled. He then passed out pictures of her to the other men, but with the charges at the wig shop, he reminded the men that she had changed her looks again.

With everyone briefed on the mission and dressed for urban warfare—meaning suits, button-downs, wireless communication earpieces, and gun holsters under their jackets and at their ankles, the security team climbed into the SUVs and drove to the hotel.

Noah decided he would check in as a guest and try to get eyes on both Brianna and Richard. Several pieces of his security equipment would help them keep watch over all the exits. If all went well, they would also have ears in Richard's suite.

Bull pulled out his cell phone again. He briefed the person on the other end on the plans for the night and ended the call. Noah turned around in his seat and stared at him as he waited for Bull to report in.

Bull said, "Don't ask, Reaper. Just trust me."

Noah stared hard at Bull. "You know I do. But if you're pulling someone else in, don't you think we need to know, so we don't shoot the wrong guy?"

Bull nodded but said, "You probably won't even know he's there, Reaper."

Still sensing the tension, Bull added, "Look, man, I've been too hard on her. Yeah, it sucks that she let us believe she was dead. But she had a damn good reason, and I didn't even give her a fucking chance." He folded his arms over his chest as he took a deep breath.

"I gave my word I'd always have her back, and I let her down, man. I'm doing my damnedest to fix that."

Noah gave him a look and a nod that said he knew precisely what Bull meant.

The drive from Noah's downtown Miami firm to the South Beach hotel seemed to take forever. Noah was anxious to get there and stop her before she could do anything else stupid, or before Richard found her. He walked up to the counter and requested a suite and a meeting room. The team needed somewhere private they could set up for the night, and it would be too conspicuous for the entire team to crash his suite.

With only ten suites in the hotel, Noah was lucky to get the last one available. The concierge showed him to the meeting room, and he called the rest of the team waiting outside in the SUVs. They brought in all the gear and began to set up for surveillance. The hotel had once been a private mansion, and while definitely large and elegant for a single owner, at only three stories, it was small in comparison to other hotels.

Noah scouted the hotel as discreetly as possible. He noticed the people checking in to the suite next to Richard's had just arrived. A young man in a dark suit with a hotel name tag was carrying their bags into their room. Noah picked up a couple of bags and followed the other man into the suite. He discreetly placed a listening device on the wall shared by Richard's suite, just behind the wall sconce so it wouldn't be seen. He knew they wouldn't be able to get into Richard's room undetected, but this room gave them the closest access point that he could get.

The young man thanked Noah for his help with the bags. Noah slapped him on the back and, with a smile, said, "Anytime, kid."

Noah left the suite with no one the wiser. He called Brad to tell him what they had to work with.

Brad replied, "I will try to boost the signal to make it more sensitive. It may mean more distortion on our end, but any bit of information is better than none."

"I'm going to check Brianna's suite now. She's probably not back yet, but I have to see. It's too close to Richard's suite for me to stay here and wait, though," Noah relayed. "I'll be back in a few."

When Noah returned to the command center room, Brad informed him he had just successfully patched into the hotel's security cameras. They had eyes and ears on all floors, elevators, and the front door. Noah breathed a sigh of relief for the lucky break they'd caught. When Brianna returned to the hotel, they would know. He visualized slinging her over his shoulder and carrying her back home. One way or another, he was determined to find her and stop her.

One of the guys had food catered in for the group. To anyone else, they looked like a group of businessmen getting ready for their meeting the following morning. Their computers were all on the tables, and they were engaged in business strategy discussions, using code words only they would decipher. Brad's computer screen wasn't visible to anyone else, so he continued monitoring the cameras. When the hotel staff left the room, he switched it so everyone could see it on the projection screen.

Brianna entered the hotel lobby in the midst of a large group, wearing her red-haired wig, new clothes, and new makeup. When she heard a familiar voice coming from a man a few feet in front of her, she kept her face turned away from him as she listened to his incessant ramble. Richard, she sneered. He continued talking to his companion as though no one else were around.

"Make reservations for dinner at Prime 112 at eight o'clock tonight. I want my table at Mirage by eleven o'clock in the VIP room. I want a bottle of Moët chilled and ready. And make sure they have the security camera feed on the plasma this time."

His assistant was taking notes and just replied, "Got it."

Well, thank you, Richard. You just gave away your schedule much easier than I ever imagined, she thought sarcastically.

Brianna checked her watch—almost six o'clock. She had plenty of time to get ready to go to Miami's most exclusive club. She decided since Richard would have the security feed playing live in his VIP room, she shouldn't have any problems getting in. It was getting out alive that would be tricky. The loud noise in the club would make the recorder useless. She had to get him to leave the club to pull this off.

She settled in her room with the purchased clothes and accessories prepared for later tonight, along with the hidden recorder. When she finally sat on the bed, she felt exhausted to her core. She didn't get much sleep last night, or this morning, thanks to Noah. She smiled warmly at the memory. She immediately felt the sharp pain of regret and loss from losing him yet again.

She shook it off because she knew there was no other way. She ordered room service from her personal butler, compliments of the Villa suite, and retrieved her cell phone from her backpack. She knew she had time to kill since Richard would be getting ready for dinner. There were a few things she wanted to research on the internet while she waited.

She was deep in thought, taking notes, and researching the area when a light rap on her door startled her. When the butler called to her, she held the door open for him as he carried her tray of food to the small table. The smell of food reminded her how long it had been since she'd last eaten, and she suddenly realized she was starving. She sat down at the table and began to eat. Her thoughts drifted to what was to come. Her stomach seized when she realized this was most likely her last meal and she was utterly alone again.

Unable to eat any more, she decided to rest for a couple hours before she went to the nightclub. She set the alarm on her phone to wake her in time to get ready for the club. She lay down on the bed, and even though she should've been too anxious to sleep, her eyes were suddenly very heavy. Her last thoughts before she drifted off were of Noah, just like every night before.

Brianna's alarm on her phone went off just as she was in the middle of the best dream about Noah. She turned the alarm off and sat on the edge of the bed. A sudden wave of intense fear and dread washed over her because she knew what was about to happen. She kept repeating that she had to see this through to save

Noah. That was the only consolation that kept her going. She prayed this would be enough to stop Richard once and for all. She rose, walked to the window that faced the ocean, and opened it. She took a few minutes to listen to the waves lapping on the beach and let the sound calm her frayed nerves.

She showered and dressed to go to the exclusive South Beach nightclub, Mirage, where Richard would be. She carefully applied her makeup and made sure everything was completely perfect. She tried on the red wig but decided against it. She knew she wouldn't walk away from Richard alive. Her last request to herself was to be Brianna for the night. She dried her long hair and styled it with the flat iron, adding curls to the ends to help accentuate her looks.

She had picked out a trendy tight-fitting dress to help her look like she belonged there. It was glittering blue and stopped above mid-thigh. The top tied around her neck, leaving her arms and back exposed. In the back, the tight material began again below her waist, teasing at giving a view of her ass. She moved her hand along the front hem of the dress, felt the small recording device, and breathed a sigh of relief that it was securely in place. She reasoned that it was in the best place to avoid suspicion. She could simply pull on the hem in an act of modesty to make sure the dress covered her, and no one would know what she was really doing.

She put on her open-toe silver high heels, then her earrings, followed up with her necklace. She picked up her small matching clutch to put her license, credit card, and cash inside. She gave herself a once-over in the mirror and decided she looked very nice.

Too bad all this fuss isn't for a date night with Noah, she thought solemnly.

She stepped out of her room and asked the concierge to arrange for a limo to take her to the Mirage. She walked to the front of the hotel to wait for the limo to arrive. Within a minute, a long, black limo came, and the driver opened the door to let her slide in. He was barely out of his teens and was probably working his way through college. She caught him smiling at her while blatantly watching her ass. When he realized she saw him, his smile quickly faded, and his face turned a deep red. She laughed to herself and leaned back against the leather seat as he pulled the limo away from the hotel.

～

STEELE SECURITY SAT IN THE PLUSH MEETING ROOM, WATCHING THE security feed change over to different camera views on the overhead projector. When Brianna suddenly appeared in the hotel lobby, Noah yelled for Brad to switch to that camera view only. Noah watched as she walked toward the front door, then he ran out of the room after her. She wasn't there by the time he reached the lobby, so he continued outside. She wasn't outside either. He looked both ways and saw a limo about a block away.

As he ran back inside, Brad was walking to him. "There's a delay on the feed, boss. I'm sorry, I didn't know they were working on a delay on the cameras until you ran out of the room."

"Damn it!"

They walked over to the front desk and asked the clerk about the types of transportation they offered. She confirmed his belief that the limo had just left with one guest and would be back within twenty minutes. Noah asked to be next on the list for the limo and told the guys to get the SUVs ready. He would talk to the driver and find out where he dropped Brianna off.

If this guy refuses to talk to me, I'll break both his legs, he vowed.

"Twenty minutes, my ass! Where the hell is this guy? It's been forty-five minutes!" Noah bellowed. He paced back and forth along the sidewalk as he grew more and more anxious. He still had his wits about him to watch for Richard, and his team still had eyes and ears on him from the SUVs.

"Boss, he's coming down."

Noah heard Bull in his earpiece and moved out of sight. He watched as Richard left and told one of the teams to follow him and the other team to stay put for the time being. He was still waiting for the limo driver to verify where he took Brianna. As he moved back into the lobby, he saw the limo pull up to the front.

By the time the driver parked the limo, Noah had opened his

door and all but dragged him out of the car. "The lady you picked up from here, where is she?"

The driver, obviously young and scared, was speechless. A huge, muscled man had just yanked him out of the car. He stammered, trying to form a coherent string of words. "I…uh…she's…um…"

"Where?"

"Mirage…nightclub…"

The black SUV slid up beside the limo, Noah jumped in, and Bull sped off to the nightclub. No one said a word as they flew through traffic, dodging cars, and running red lights. Noah fisted his hands and released them, repeatedly.

"Brad, anything on the digital recorder yet?"

"No. Nothing yet."

21

CHAPTER TWENTY-ONE

Brianna enjoyed the smooth ride of the limousine and asked the driver to take his time. She wanted to take in the sights and sounds one last time before going to the club. She had him drive the entire length of Ocean Drive to South Pointe Park. He waited while she walked with her toes in the sand and her shoes in her hand. She stood and listened as the waves crashed, breathed in the salty air, and enjoyed the ocean breeze for several long minutes.

She reluctantly walked back to the limo, climbed in the back, and closed her eyes as he drove her to Washington Avenue. In the back seat of the limo, the memories that she wanted to take with her took over. Her thoughts were always of Noah. She could see him, feel him, and hear him close to her. She felt as the car slowed to a stop, and she opened her eyes.

A long line of people that wrapped all the way around the block waited outside Mirage. Young ladies in various states of dress openly flirted with the bouncer. Their attempts to get in ahead of the hordes of others waiting in line were blatantly obvious, but the bouncer didn't seem to mind their advances. Small groups of guys and girls talked and laughed with each other, without a care in the world, other than having a good time.

Brianna stepped out of the limo and looked directly at the security camera, smiled, and waved. She knew it was a clear challenge that Richard wouldn't be able to resist. She showed up there willingly and waited for him to take the bait. She strolled up to the bouncer, smiled, and waited. She noticed an earpiece in his ear and knew he would soon be given orders. He looked down at his clipboard list, then back up to her, before he opened the red velvet rope and let her in. Several people called out to him to also let them in as she walked into the exclusive club.

The multilevel club was packed with bodies writhing to the music on the enormous dance floor. Strangers chatted and looked for company for the night, others waited at the bar to get another glass of their poison of choice. The DJ was set up in the middle to give everyone a good view of the show. A light show danced with the beat and changed colors on the ceiling and walls. Brianna walked through the crowd on her way to find Richard and politely refused several requests to dance and more.

She reached the VIP room and took a deep breath. It was a smaller room for more intimate gatherings but still large enough for a good-sized party. The room included its own bar and plush leather couches. Richard stood as she walked in. His eyes raked over her, and he had the type of smile that reminded her of a sleazy, snake oil salesman. She swallowed the bile that tried to rise in the back of her throat and stopped in front of him.

"Brianna. I'm so shocked to see you. I thought you were dead." He didn't even try to sound genuine.

"Well, it seems we're both back from the dead, Richard."

"To what do I owe the pleasure?"

"I'm here to ask you to leave Noah alone. Call off your dogs."

"You know what I want, Brianna. When I get what I want, you get what you want." His smile didn't reach his eyes. There was no warmth or compassion there. His eyes were stone-cold, and she knew he was lying, but she played along anyway.

Brianna looked around at the others in the room. There were

several young women scattered throughout the room. They clearly enjoyed the free drinks Richard supplied. There were also several hired henchmen who waited for a reason to pounce on someone. "This really isn't the place to talk about it. Is there somewhere else we can go?"

Like the cat that had caught the mouse, he replied. "Of course, of course." He motioned for one of his men to come over.

They walked out the back door of the club and got into the back seat of Richard's car. As the man drove in silence, she watched the buildings go by in a blur. The people out having a good time were oblivious to her predicament. She took mental notes of the direction they were headed—away from crowds, hotels, clubs, and restaurants. They were headed to a more deserted area where they would have plenty of privacy.

Playing the victim, she looked at the man who drove them, then to Richard. "Where are we going?"

"Oh, just a little place I have acquired. It's a good place to talk. Very private."

They continued to hold eye contact until she finally turned her head and looked out the window. They pulled up to a windowless building made of large concrete blocks. The door was solid steel with an industrial dead bolt lock. The driver got out and opened the door for Brianna, while Richard exited from the other side. The driver unlocked and opened the building door for them and then locked it back when they were all inside.

Richard flipped on the light to reveal a large room with a single chair in the middle of it, and a long, thin table sat against the wall to the right. There was a doorway on the back wall that led to another darkened room. The second room was somewhat smaller than the one she was in, but she couldn't see what was in it.

She turned to Richard and asked, "What is this place?"

Richard didn't answer. The driver walked to the table, picked up a wand to sweep her for bugs, and walked back to her. The wand made no noise as he ran it over her front and back. "She's clean."

Then he walked back and laid the wand back on the table. The sound of a door opening came from the darkened room, and

Brianna jerked her head around. Three more men strolled in and stood silently as they waited for orders.

Brianna reached down, tugged on the hem of her dress in modesty, and pulled it down. She purposely glanced around the room with a nervous gaze. She secretly activated the hidden recording device and then flattened the wrinkles in her dress.

Richard watched her but didn't seem to know what she was doing. The corners of his mouth curved up slightly as if he were amused at her attempt to cover herself in that dress.

"Oh, don't worry. These guys aren't here for that."

"Why are they here?"

With an ominous chuckle, Richard nodded toward the men, and they stalked toward Brianna.

Noah's second team of men had waited for Richard to leave the hotel and tailed his car to Mirage. They watched as the driver let Richard out at the front door, and he strolled straight up to the entrance. The bouncer immediately opened the red velvet rope and let him walk in ahead of the line of waiting partiers.

The driver pulled away from the curb and made a turn at the end of the block. Roman, the man in charge of the secondary team, put his team into play.

"Blake, follow the car around to the back of the building. Put a GPS tracker on it in case they leave again," Roman said as he handed the tracker off. "Watch the back and report back if you see anything at all."

Blake took it and walked around to the back of the building as he followed the path Richard's car took. He watched from the shadows as it pulled into a parking lot behind the building, and the driver jogged back around to the front. Blake moved silently through the parking lot and secured the location device to the underside of the car.

Blake conveyed his status back to the group. "The GPS is ready. There's a parking lot behind the building, and there's a back door.

There's no doorknob, so it's an exit only. I'll stay back here. We'll need eyes on it in case they come out of it."

Roman found a place to park where he could watch the front door. Alex opened the GPS tracking software and confirmed the steady dot on the screen.

"Do we have any intel on this guy? Does he have a team of guys? Or another car?" Alex asked from the backseat.

"We know he has men, but we don't have any other specific info on them. We didn't have time to find out who they are or how many," Roman replied.

"So, we're flying blind," Alex stated.

"Pretty much," Roman chuckled.

"Good. I hate when people spoil the ending," Alex joked, and they both laughed.

After several minutes of waiting, Alex got out of the car and began his perimeter walk. All of the men were on edge and with good reason. They all respected and admired Noah tremendously. If he was worried about this operation, they knew they all had a reason to be worried as well. No one wanted to be the one who let him down and allowed Brianna out of his sight.

Alex walked down the street in the opposite direction from Blake. He scanned the faces in the waiting cars as he watched for Brianna. He turned the corner of the block and continued his stroll toward the back of the building. He checked every possible entry and exit point along his walk. As he reached the back alley of the club, he saw headlights illuminate a gravel parking lot.

Screeching tires, a loud crash, and hysterical screams suddenly filled the night air. Alex urgently called to his team through his communicator as he ran back to the front of the building, in the direction of the screams. "Roman. Blake. Talk to me. What's going on?"

"Almost there," Blake replied.

"Drunk driver in a small car just pulled out in front of an eighteen-wheeler barreling down the road. The car now looks like a crushed aluminum can. Driver and passenger are injured," Roman responded. "I'm calling an ambulance."

An hour after he lost sight of her at the hotel, Noah finally arrived at the nightclub. He found Roman and Alex on the sidewalk in front of the building and Blake walked toward them from the corner.

"We have a situation, Reaper." Blake hated being the one to deliver the bad news to his boss.

Noah's hard stare bored into him, and he clenched his teeth when he spoke. "What?"

He knew his men were professionals and whatever happened was probably beyond their control. But he wasn't very logical where Brianna was involved. Especially when he knew exactly what she intended to do, and he knew Richard would have no problem complying.

Roman spoke up. "We were in place, staking out the front door while we waited for Brianna to show up. Blake put a GPS tracker on the car parked in the back lot.

"There was a wreck between an eighteen-wheeler and a drunk driver in a small car. The people in the car were hurt badly, and we helped the fire department extricate them from the car. Just as we finished, we saw a limo turning at the end of the block. She may already be inside the club."

Noah rudely pushed through a group of people who were in his direct line to the bouncer. With Bull and Rebel close on his heels, no one dared to challenge him.

"Joe, I need to get in. One of my targets may be inside, and I need eyes on the prize at all times for this one," Noah said to the bouncer.

"Anything for my Steele men." Joe smiled and opened the rope to let Noah, Bull, and Rebel pass.

"Blake, go to the back door and keep your eyes on it. Do not let them leave with her," Roman instructed. "I'll keep watch in the front."

Inside the club, Noah, Bull, and Rebel split up to look for Brianna. Noah didn't really care where Richard was. His only focus was to find Brianna. The entire place was packed with wall-to-wall people.

There were multiple rooms with various seating arrangements. There were high-backed booths, soft cushioned chairs, actual beds, and some people were even sitting on the floor. He slowly walked through the crowd, and his eyes scanned everyone as he made his way through.

Rebel and Bull systematically made their way through the lower level of the club until the three men had covered every square inch. They walked up to the second-floor mezzanine and continued their search. They kept on and performed the search again on their way back to the front of the club.

"Damn, where can she be?" Noah asked aloud.

He tried to keep his mind in professional mode and not let his personal feelings enter the equation. Emotions only made it worse and prevented him from thinking logically. The three men stood just inside the front door of the club and watched people enter and leave for several minutes before they walked back outside. As they moved away from the crowds of people, Blake came running around the side of the building.

"West! They're headed west! Let's move!"

Both teams scattered to the SUVs. Their tires squealed as they drove in the direction Blake had last seen the car.

Alex looked at the GPS tracking software and said, "This isn't moving!"

Blake shot his reply back. "They had a second car!" He gave everyone a description of it as they pulled out of their parking area. Traffic was heavy with people going out to the late-night parties. By the time they pushed their way through the blaring horns of angry drivers, they had lost sight of the car.

Noah punched the dash of the SUV. "Fuuuuucccccckkkkkk!"

They split up and proceeded to canvass the area, one block at a time.

"This is fucking useless. We don't even know if they went back to the damn mainland or somewhere else on the island." Noah racked his brain to figure out what to do next, where to look, but nothing came to him. Bull kept watching as he drove block by block, intent to do anything to stay busy.

Noah raked his hand over his face, and his hand stopped just over his mouth. He propped his elbow on the door, and he stared out the passenger window. *"Bri, where the hell are you?"* he asked her silently.

Just then, Brad yelled out, "Reaper, she's activated the bug!"

"Pinpoint her location. Now!"

22

CHAPTER TWENTY-TWO

Richard's men surrounded Brianna and forcefully shoved her toward the chair. The chair was made of thick wood and was very sturdy. It was painted black and had padded armrests. The legs were reinforced with two-by-fours running between each one, on each side, front and back. Once she was sitting, she understood why it was constructed that way. They used duct tape to secure her arms to the armrests, and her feet were duct-taped to the legs.

Without saying a word or asking a single question, one man backhanded her across the face. Her body shifted violently to the left. She saw stars and felt a sudden burst of intense pain in her cheek, before the metallic taste of blood filled her mouth. Her eye immediately started to swell. Still dazed, she turned her face back to the front when another blow rocked the other side.

Blood ran down her cheek and out of her mouth as Richard walked up to face her. "You've caused me a lot of fucking trouble. I want those damn documents back, or you'll hurt a lot more than this."

"What documents?" Say it. Say it, she willed him.

"Don't play coy with me. You know damn well what documents."

She heard a loud "Thwack!" in her ear as something slammed into the side of her head. She knew she'd been hit, but she didn't know with what. A fist? A baseball bat?

Oh God, it hurts! She wanted to scream, but more than that, she didn't want to give him the satisfaction.

Her vision blurred as she struggled to hold her head up. Then she felt blows to her ribs that knocked the breath out of her. She coughed, and her chest convulsed angrily when she tried to suck in oxygen. It hurt to breathe, and it hurt not to breathe.

"You stupid fucking bitch. Give us back the weapons invoices," he growled.

She felt another blow to her head, but she was already so disoriented, she didn't feel as much pain as she had before. Or maybe her brain didn't register it. Whatever the case, she knew she wouldn't get out alive.

At some point, she passed out from the beating. She awoke to one of the men slapping her in the face. "Wake up. Come on. Wake up!"

She tried to open her eyes, but they were both almost swollen shut. Her vision was blurry, and she couldn't make out any faces, only dark figures as they moved around her. She could feel the darkness enveloping her, and confusion overtook her. She lost several seconds of time as their words faded in and out.

"Tell us now, or you die, Brianna." The male voice came from the dark figure directly in front of her. She heard the slide of the gun as he readied the bullet in the chamber. She saw the mysterious figure pull his arm up and straighten it in front of him. She couldn't see it, but she knew he held the gun in his hand.

She heard heels clicking across the floor, and a female voice taunted her. "Give me the damn gun if you can't do it, Richard. I sure as hell can."

Just as she thought it was over, she heard another voice in the room with them. It was a very familiar voice. But in the fog and haze of her battered body and brain, she couldn't quite place it.

"Put the gun down. I already told you, man. This isn't happening."

"Oh, it's happening all right. I'm putting a fucking bullet in her head and feeding her to the damn sharks."

That was Richard. I know that voice, she thought.

"I'm not asking. I'm telling you. Put the damn gun down. This is your last chance."

Who is that?

"Last chance? What? You think you can fucking stop me?"

"Yep."

Brianna saw Richard's dark figure turn from her and face the other mysterious figure that had just stopped in front of her. Richard's arm was down at his side, but she could feel the tension in the room.

"And how the hell do you plan to do that? There's five of us and one of you."

He released a menacing chuckle. "I don't need anyone else with me to take out five men."

She saw the shadow of Richard's arm lift upward, and instinctively, she knew he would soon kill her. The loud pops of gunfire filled the room, and people scurried and shuffled all around her. She heard shouting that seemed to come from everywhere and echoed off the walls. She had lost sight of Richard's dark form. There were so many by that time that she couldn't distinguish one from another. Her eyes became too heavy to keep open, and she was exhausted.

She was still taped to the chair and couldn't shield herself. She heard someone scream and realized it was her. She suddenly felt a white-hot, searing pain in her shoulder. Just before she passed out, she heard a calm voice that soothed her. "Hold on, Sunny. Help is coming."

Noah paced back and forth in the surgical waiting room at Jackson Memorial Hospital. He hadn't seen Brianna since the paramedics left with her in the back of the ambulance. She wasn't awake when they loaded her on the stretcher, and they were frantically working on her in the back of the ambulance as it pulled away. He didn't make many friends at the hospital when he arrived at the emergency room and couldn't find her.

A nurse finally informed him Brianna had been taken straight into surgery upon arrival. He was more than aggravated that he had to fill out registration paperwork on her before the nurse would tell him where to wait for word of her condition. After more than two hours of jumping every time any of the medical personnel walked by, a doctor came into the waiting room and called out. "Tate family?"

Noah, Bull, and Rebel rushed to the doctor. He motioned for them to sit down. "I'm Dr. Sullivan. She's out of surgery and in recovery now. She had a gunshot wound to the right shoulder. The bullet went straight through with minimal damage. We cleaned it out to help avoid infection. She will need some physical therapy to restore full range of motion."

Noah let out a sigh of relief. "Okay. We can deal with physical therapy."

Dr. Sullivan nodded, but the expression on his face showed grave concern. "I'm afraid that's not all. She was badly beaten. She has a significant concussion with large hematomas on both sides of her head, and there is some slight swelling around the brain. That is the most serious injury right now. We will continue to monitor her brain activity and swelling closely. I've asked Dr. Conley, a neurosurgeon, to oversee that part of her care. He's one of our best."

Noah's face drained of all color.

Dr. Sullivan continued. "She also has numerous cracked ribs, along with contusions on both sides of her ribs. Contusions were also found on her arms and legs. This lady has sustained significant trauma to essentially her entire body."

Noah couldn't think of a single intelligent medical question to ask. "When can I see her?"

"She'll be in PACU for at least an hour, more likely two, while we monitor her vital signs and her brain activity. If her vitals remain stable, she'll be moved to the neuro-ICU until we're sure all danger of swelling has passed. Once she's in ICU, you can go in during visiting times, as long as you're family." His eyebrows rose as he silently questioned their relationship to her.

Noah responded. "Yes, I'm her husband." *Maybe not right now, but I plan to be.*

Bull spoke up, pointing to Rebel and himself. "We're her brothers."

Dr. Sullivan nodded and said, "We will inform you of any change in her condition." He advised them to move to the neuro-ICU waiting room to wait for the updates.

The clock seemed to stand still as Noah waited to see Brianna. He paced in the waiting room, and when he couldn't bear the confines of those walls any longer, he paced back and forth along the hallway outside the neuro-ICU door. When the ICU door opened, he tried to look in, just to see her for a second. He saw the nurses station in the middle of a round room and the sliding glass doors all around the perimeter of the room.

She could be in any one of those rooms. Alone. Scared. Thinking I'm not here because I don't love her, Noah thought.

The ICU door opened again, and Dr. Sullivan walked out with another doctor.

"This is Dr. Conley." The two men shook hands as Noah waited for the news. Bull and Rebel walked up to stand behind Noah.

Dr. Conley spoke. "We've monitored her for the last couple of hours, and she is stable for now. She will stay in neuro-ICU until she wakes up. I'm afraid we won't know if there was any permanent brain damage until then. Her vitals have been stable, and we have sedated her to help her body rest and heal.

"You can see her for a few minutes, but I should warn you, she is badly bruised, swollen, and there are a lot of tubes. Right now, she's breathing on her own, but she has been intubated as a precaution. If the swelling in her neck or throat suddenly worsens as the contusions become more apparent, the ventilator may have to do the work for her."

"Thank you, Doctor. I really want to see her. She needs to know she's not here alone," Noah replied.

"I can let you see her for five minutes." Dr. Conley shook Noah's hand and walked off.

Noah stared at the ICU door for a moment. The usually calm former military man was scared of what he would find on the other side. He mentally chided himself for being such a pussy and walked inside in spite of his fears.

A nurse met him just inside the door. "You'll have to wash and sanitize your hands before going in the patient rooms."

"Which room is Brianna Tate in?" Noah asked as he turned on the water.

"She's in room eighteen," she answered.

As he walked up to her door, his breath caught in the back of his throat. She looked so small in that big hospital bed. Her hair had been pushed away from her face and was spread out on the pillow under her head.

Her face was savagely battered. Both of her eyes were blackened and swollen, her right cheek had a line of dried blood from the split skin, and her left cheek was a mixture of black and purple bruising. As he moved closer to her, he saw the swollen contusions on the sides of her head and arms. He realized the blood-red bands across her wrists were where she had been bound.

The blood pressure cuff was wrapped around her upper arm. There were tubes attached to her hand, and one went down her throat. She had wires connected to her chest, and the heart monitor above her bed beeped in time with the rhythm dancing across the screen. A nasal cannula delivered oxygen, and there was a slight hiss as the oxygen flowed through the tube.

He felt someone behind him and turned to see Bull and Rebel standing at the door. Bull's face masked the profound need for revenge that warred inside him. Rebel couldn't speak as he stepped into the room. Noah turned back to Brianna and gently touched her hand. He was afraid anywhere he touched her would cause her more pain.

He spoke gently to her. "I'm here, Brianna. I'll be here when you wake up."

Bull and Rebel left Noah alone with her for the last few minutes he had with her on this visit. They walked out to the hall to wait for him.

"We didn't fucking get there soon enough," Bull growled.

"I know, man. But it could have been worse. They could've killed her." Rebel's voice didn't hold the conviction his words tried to convey.

"They almost did. They still might have. She's not out of the woods yet." Bull fisted his hands. "You saw what they fucking did to her. You heard what Dr. Conley said. If she dies, Richard fucking dies. Painfully." Rebel nodded in agreement.

Noah walked out into the hall, and both men looked at him as they waited for any information. He was obviously upset, but he held it together for her. "Rebel. Go to my house and grab enough clothes to last a few days. I'm staying here with her until she wakes up."

"You got it. Call me if you think of anything else you need," Rebel said as he walked away.

Noah had to go to the police station to make an official statement. Over the years, he had built a good relationship with many of the guys on the police force. Tonight, he was glad those contacts gave him time at the hospital first.

"Bull, stay here and watch over Brianna while I'm at the police station. I can't take a chance that someone will come in and finish what they started," Noah said solemnly. "I'll be back as soon as possible."

"I'm not going anywhere, Reap."

Bull stood at his post guarding the ICU door. He checked the picture on the hospital identification card against the person who wore it to make sure no one got past him. If anyone objected, they didn't dare complain to the intimidating sentinel standing guard.

Noah anguished over whether or not to call Brianna's family in Atlanta. On the one hand, their daughter was in the hospital fighting for her life. On the other hand, this was the same daughter they thought was already dead. Should he deny them the last chance they may have to see her? Or let them move on, having already somewhat accepted her death?

If the situation were reversed, he concluded that someone had damn well better tell him, or someone's head would roll. Having the chance to say goodbye was somehow better than the limbo they'd all felt from not seeing her one last time.

Plus, once she had fully healed, he had plans for their future, and her family would be part of it. It wouldn't be a good idea to start out with this kind of secret. He sighed deeply and punched the numbers on his cell phone.

"Hello?"

"Hello, Evan. This is Noah Steele. This will be an unbelievable shock. I'm not really sure how to even begin."

"What's going on, Noah?"

"It's Brianna, Evan. She's alive, and she's in the hospital here at Jackson Memorial. You and your family need to get down here as soon as possible. She's hurt pretty badly, sir."

"Wh-what did you say?" Evan sounded as if the breath had been knocked out of him.

Noah knew the feeling. He relayed as much of the story as fast as he could, without wasting any time.

"We'll be there within a couple of hours, Noah. I'm having the jet fueled as we speak. Now, I have to tell Diana and the girls."

Noah thought back to the note she'd left him. He left out that part of the story when he talked to her father. He had been turning her words over and over in his head, reading between the lines at what she didn't say. Or more accurately, what he didn't say.

She told me she loved me, showed me she loved me. She answered my questions. She made love to me all night. She waited for me. She sacrificed herself for me.

And I never once told her I loved her. Or even that I missed her.

Noah made a silent vow never to let a day go by without telling her how much he loved and needed her.

Brianna's family arrived at Jackson Memorial soon after sunrise. Every single one of them was in tears and frantic to see her. Noah warned them of her appearance much the same way as the doctor had told him. He knew that no description would really prepare them for what they were about to see. Even putting the shock of her being alive aside, the sight of her battered body with all the tubes, bells, and whistles attached to her would evoke nightmares.

Brianna's parents and her three sisters all took turns visiting her during the time they allowed. Her visits were limited to fifteen minutes at a time to keep the stimulation stress to a minimum.

Her condition was still serious, and she hadn't opened her eyes. They couldn't be sure whether she'd suffer permanent brain damage or if she'd ever wake up again at all. It killed Noah that he hadn't seen her since she first came out of surgery two days ago. He simply reminded himself that her family hadn't seen or talked to her in three years.

At the midmorning visit, Missy told Noah to take her turn. She'd already been in once that morning, and she knew he'd been patiently waiting for his turn. He hugged Missy and went straight to Brianna's room. He sat next to her bed and put his hand underneath hers to avoid hurting her.

Her bruises were slightly better than when he had first seen her. Instead of the angry black and purple bruises, they looked more purple than black, with a hint of green showing. Her eyes weren't quite as swollen, though they were still black. The contusions on the sides of her head were healing, but their presence remained obvious.

"Hey, Brianna, it's me, Noah. You probably can't hear me, but there's something I need to say. There's something I need you to know."

He stopped talking for a moment and hoped to get any type of reaction from her. He needed some indication she was waking up.

"I haven't really been living the last three years. I've only existed. The only time I feel anything is when I'm with you. So you have to get better because I can't live without you. I can't love without you. I love you, Brianna. Only you."

Noah rested his forehead on the bed rail while he said a silent prayer. His head jerked up, and he stared at her. Did she just… "Baby, did you squeeze my hand just now? Squeeze it again. Come on, Bri. Squeeze it for me, baby."

It was weak, but she squeezed his hand on command. Noah

called the nurse and watched as she checked all the vital signs. Noah asked her to squeeze his hand again, and the nurse watched as her hand slightly closed around his and then released it. The nurse smiled and walked off to call the doctor.

Visiting time was over, but Noah refused to leave. He assured the nursing staff he wouldn't be a problem. He explained that he had promised Brianna he would be there when she woke up, and that was a promise he intended to keep. Dr. Conley came in, reviewed her most recent EEG, checked her pupils, and then examined her surgical site and her other wounds.

Noah reached through the slats in the rail and put his hand under hers again. She squeezed his hand lightly, and he stood to talk to her.

"Bri, you're in the hospital. You're going to be okay. You need to rest. I'm right here with you, and I'm not going anywhere. I'm not leaving you, baby." Thank you, God!

Dr. Conley and the nurse stepped back into the room and began to put gloves on.

"What's going on, Dr. Conley?" Noah watched the nurse draw up a syringe and walk to Brianna's IV. "What is that?"

"It's okay. It'll just help her relax so we can remove the intubation tube. We'll monitor her for an hour or so in here. If all goes well, we'll move her to a private room." Noah stepped out of their way but refused to leave the room.

23

CHAPTER TWENTY-THREE

All the events that led up to her hospital stay were still fuzzy to Brianna. She was on her second day in a private room. The first day, she slept a lot. When she had tried to talk, her throat hurt and her voice was still raspy from the intubation tube. Noah was there every time she woke, giving her water to sip on, and assuring her that she was okay. He explained again that she was in the hospital and he wouldn't leave her.

She watched him sleep on the uncomfortable hospital chair-turned-partial-bed beside her. She tried to move in the bed and gasped in pain. The stitches in her shoulder pulled, and her cracked ribs objected vehemently. In a split second, Noah was up and at her side.

"Bri, are you okay? What happened?" His voice was drenched with concern.

She smiled at him. "I'm okay. I just wanted to turn over, but the rest of my body said no."

He smiled and put his hand under hers again. Brianna had a brief glimpse of a memory that was just barely out of reach. Noah watched her face and recognized her puzzled look.

"What is it, Bri?" he asked.

"When you put your hand under my hand just now, I had déjà vu. It was so familiar."

Noah chuckled. "I've done that every time I've been in to visit you. I was afraid I'd hurt you if I held yours, so I let you hold mine."

She squeezed his hand. "It doesn't hurt, honest." They were both silent, looking deep into each other's eyes, but neither was quite sure of what to say.

Brianna started. "Noah, tell me what happened that night."

His face hardened, but he didn't drop his gaze her from her eyes. "Bri, I don't really think now's the time. You're still healing and—"

She cut him off. "Noah, I need to know. Please. I'm stronger than you think."

"That you are," he conceded.

Noah recounted the details from his perspective of what happened, up until she went into that building. He told her about finding out which hotel she'd checked in to, grabbing the poor kid driving the limo she took, following her to the club, and then losing her when they took a different car.

She was shocked to hear him describe how close he was to her at the hotel and the club. Then it hit her.

"How did you find me at the hotel? I didn't use my real name." Her eyebrows furrowed, and her eyes showed her confusion.

He smiled and replied, "Um, how do I explain this?"

She cocked an eyebrow at him. "Um…one word at a time," she mocked him jokingly.

The door to her hospital room opened, and a huge, intimidating man stood in the doorframe. The man was larger than she remembered. The black-haired, blue-eyed giant stood 6'6" tall and had rock-solid muscle on every inch of his body. A beaming smile lit up his face as Brianna called his name.

"Shadow!"

Noah strolled over to the door and gave his friend a manly hug. "Good to see you, brother!"

Shadow closed the door behind him, walked to Brianna, and gave her a tentative hug. For such a big guy, he was so gentle with her. "How are you feeling, Sunny?"

His voice stirred another memory, and the full realization hit her. "It was you!"

Shadow looked at Noah and tried to play coy with her. "Me? What did I do?"

Noah tried to hide his smile.

She eyed them both suspiciously and playfully hit his arm. "You were there that night! You came in and stopped them. I owe you my life." Then tears welled up in her eyes, but they were tears of joy and gratitude.

"Well, I can't take all the credit." Shadow's voice was teasing, but she felt the warmth and love of a brother in it. "Actually, your man, Noah, was the real hero."

She looked at Noah and saw he was no longer trying to hide a smile. His body suddenly went rigid, and that familiar mask overtook any emotions on his face. Shadow looked from Brianna to Noah as he noted the shock on Brianna's face and the emotionless expression on Noah's face.

"Ah. He hasn't told you, has he? Well, you two will have plenty to talk about, then. I just wanted to see for myself that you're on the mend, Sunny." Shadow leaned over and kissed her on the cheek. "Bull, Rebel, and I will always have your back, Sunny."

She kissed his cheek and hugged his neck as best she could with her injuries. She told him she expected to see him again soon as he walked out the door.

"What did he mean, Noah? What have you not told me?" Her eyes searched his, and he felt that familiar squeeze around his heart.

He didn't like to think about that night, much less talk about it. It had only been a few days, but it felt like it all happened years ago. He knew she wouldn't let it go. She was hell on wheels when she was onto a story.

"You asked how I found you at the hotel under your alias." She nodded. "Actually, I didn't. Bull called Shadow and told him we needed help. Shadow works for the CIA now, so he was able to find out your WITSEC alias."

"B-Bull called Shadow? For me?"

Noah nodded and continued. "Since we had a name, we could

track your financial records. Your credit card showed a room charge hold, so we went there to find you. Then we tracked you to the nightclub. We lost you because of a bad wreck that happened in front of the club, and then they took a different car when they left the club with you.

"Shadow had been investigating this group for running guns for quite a while. He pretended to be a dirty CIA operative, and Richard was more than willing to use him. He kept tabs on where Richard would be that night. When you activated the recording device, we finally got a fix on you in that building."

He stopped talking for several seconds. She watched the shadows move across his face and recognized the haunted look in his eyes.

"We were still too far away from you, but we were listening." His jaw tensed, and his jaw muscles bunched as he remembered the sounds. Through clenched teeth, he continued. "We listened to them torture you."

She reached her hand up and took his, squeezing it.

"Shadow wasn't close enough right then to stop it. He walked in just as Richard leveled the gun at your head." Noah's other hand clenched the hospital bed so tightly, she thought the metal would break. "Shadow stalled them until we could get into position, then we stormed the building."

With that, he played it off like he'd finished telling the story. But she could tell there was more, and he was holding back for some reason.

"I remember hearing a lot of people suddenly in the room, or what seemed like a lot. I remember a lot of echoes and what I thought were gunshots. I couldn't really see, and my sense of time was way off."

She continued. "Noah, what are you holding back from me?"

He shook his head and sighed loudly. "You were right. It went way further up the chain than just Richard. The woman you saw me with at the banquet, Alexa Pope. She was involved, as was her father. She was in that building with you that night, and I...I had to shoot her. She's dead."

With that revelation, he turned away from her and walked to the window. She dropped her hand from where it held his, immediately feeling the empty loneliness that had been in her life without him.

He shot the woman they said was his girlfriend. She then saw the effect it had on him. He had shot someone he was involved with intimately. He had said she wasn't his girlfriend, but she was apparently something to him. Her heart broke for him and the pain he was feeling, but more for herself. She knew he would never be able to look at her without seeing Alexa.

"I…I'm sorry, Noah. I didn't know…about her or her father. You seem to care a great deal about her. I don't know what to say. Maybe it would've been better if—" Tears streamed down her face as her thoughts finished her sentence when her voice couldn't… *If it had been me instead.*

Noah whirled around and took a giant step to the side of her bed. "Don't even think that!" He stepped back, one hand on his side and the other raking down his face. "Bri, she had a gun on you. She was squeezing the trigger right in front of me. I leveled my gun at her and yelled for her to stop. She laughed—laughed!

"I pulled the trigger, barely a split second before she did. My bullet hit her, threw her backward, and knocked her aim off. If I had been even one second later, she would've killed you. I've never been so scared in my life."

Leaning over the rail, he took her hands in his. "I love you, Bri. I've never stopped loving you. I missed you every damn day you were away from me. When I thought you died, all I wanted to do was die and be with you again. Living without you has been hell on earth."

Brianna pulled him to her and kissed him through her tears. "I love you too, Noah. I love you so much, and I've died a thousand times living without you."

"I stormed into that building to save you. There was no way I could watch you die again," he murmured against her skin.

He felt her tense underneath his hands. "What about Richard? Did he get away?"

"No, he didn't get away at all. He got better than he deserved—

a bullet right between the eyes," Noah replied and showed no remorse.

Later that day, as Brianna was taking a nap, a light rap on the door alerted Noah. He looked up to see Bull walking in. "Hey, brother."

"Hey, Reap," he said softly as he looked at Brianna sleeping. "I wanted to see how she's doing." He hesitated before continuing. "And I need to apologize to her."

Noah placed his hand on Bull's shoulder and nodded in understanding. They watched her sleep for a minute before she began to stir. She opened her eyes and looked from Noah to Bull, then back to Noah.

"Something wrong?" Noah heard the slight elevation of fear in her voice.

Bull answered, "No, no—well, on second thought, yes, I guess there is. Me. I've been wrong—about you and how I treated you, Brianna. I'm sorry. I should've heard you out. You deserved at least that, and I let you down. I promised I would always protect you, and I let you down."

Brianna considered his words, and Bull waited for her to order him out of her room and out of her life.

"Sunny."

Bull looked confused. "What?"

"My name is Sunny, to you." And with that, she smiled at him. Bull was suddenly at the side of the bed, bending over to hug her.

"Always," he said as he kissed her cheek. A silent understanding that his one-word answer held a promise only a brother could make.

The following day, Brianna was discharged from the hospital, and Noah took her home to his house. His protective instincts toward Brianna were in overdrive, and he was convinced that every other driver on the road was out to get her.

"The ride home was interesting." Brianna tried to keep from laughing.

Noah slowly raised one eyebrow at her remark as he turned off the vehicle. "Are you making fun of my driving?"

"No. I wouldn't dare do that," she replied. "The rest of Miami may have something to say about it, though."

"You do realize that you're defenseless right now, right? That you literally can't defend yourself, and I can do whatever I want to do to you," he threatened teasingly.

"You do realize that I know you better than anyone in the world does, right?" she countered. "And I know that you would never do anything but protect me."

Raw emotion filled his eyes as he slowly nodded. "You've got me there. No one else knows me like you do. And there's no way in hell I'd ever hurt you. However, I will hold you hostage and never let you leave my side again."

"You can't call me a hostage if I willfully and intentionally stay with you," she whispered. "Forever."

Noah leaned across the center console and gave Brianna a long, lingering kiss. "Stay right there. I'm coming around to get you."

He walked briskly around the vehicle, opened her door, and gingerly picked her up in his arms. He carried her to the door and then up the stairs to the master bedroom. He carefully placed her on the bed and arranged the pillows under her head. After he turned on the television, he handed her the remote.

"You are on complete bed rest for the next couple of weeks. Doctor's orders—and my orders. I'm going downstairs to make your lunch, and then I'll be back. Whatever you need, I'll take care of for you." Noah gave her his dazzling, heart-melting smile before he turned to leave the room.

"Noah?" she called after him.

"Yeah, babe?"

"I love you. More than anything in the world. Thank you for loving me."

"Loving you is more natural than breathing. It's life-sustaining. I don't even have to think about it. You're not just a part of me, you're the best part of me," Noah replied sincerely.

From one week to the next, he tended to Brianna's healing wounds, catered to her every need, and reminded her how much she was loved. By the end of the two weeks of restricted activities, she playfully warned him about expectations.

"You know, since you've proven you're capable of spoiling me, I'll expect it all the time now," she laughed.

"That's a promise, sweetheart." He flashed a wicked smile and waggled his eyebrows suggestively. "When you're all better, I'll spoil you in every room of this house."

"I'm holding you to that promise as soon as I'm well enough." She winked.

"That's not all you'll be holding when you're well enough."

When she was first discharged from the hospital, she still experienced frequent dizziness from her concussion. Her sore, cracked ribs also kept her from moving quickly. But after the last couple of weeks of rest and all the doting attention from Noah, the worst of her pain and symptoms had subsided.

All the flirting, overt innuendo, and sexual tension between them pushed her beyond frustrated. Two weeks of rest had her feeling much better, but she knew Noah would still be cautious, afraid he'd hurt her. She decided she had to initiate it and not give him any reason to resist. She had been without him for too long. One night of making love, after three long years of being without him, wasn't nearly enough. She planned out her tactical maneuvers for when he joined her that night.

Once he had settled into bed and was drifting off to sleep, she moved silently until she was entirely under the covers. She licked the underside of his shaft, along the vein from shaft to tip, then around his mushroom-shaped head. He was already semi-hard when she first touched him, but he was fully erect within seconds.

She felt his breathing increase with her touch and heard him moan when she took him entirely into her mouth. Her hand gently cupped his balls as her fingers stroked them lightly, moving up his shaft as her mouth moved down. His hands came around to hold her head, and his hips began to thrust in time with her hand and mouth.

He made a louder moan, then she heard his sleepy, husky voice.

"Bri...ah...damn!" He threw the covers back and raised his head off the pillow to look at her.

She lifted her head and smiled at him like the Cheshire cat. Since he couldn't deny her what she wanted, she gingerly crawled on top of him and stroked him with her wet center.

"Want me to stop?" She purred in his ear, though she already knew the answer.

His alpha-male growl reverberated to her core, exciting her even more. "Hell no, I don't want you to stop!"

She raised her hips and positioned him at her entrance. He gripped her hips with his massive hands. Slowly, she took him inside her. She relished the feel of him as he stretched and filled her as only he could. She moved slowly at first, rocking her hips and finding her rhythm until she no longer felt the soreness of her injuries and just the pleasure he gave her. He sensed her need for more, so he held tighter to her hips and thrust his up to meet hers. His thumb moved between them as he massaged her clit and she screamed his name.

He sat up and wrapped his arms around her, then turned her over to lie on her back while he supported his weight on his arms. He moved very carefully so he wouldn't hurt her, but she longed to feel his body against hers. She wrapped her arms around his back and gently tugged to pull him down to her. He cupped her face in his hands and kissed her, and then he lightly flicked his tongue across her lips. She opened her mouth to invite him in, and he took full possession of it.

He continued his kisses along her jaw, down her neck, and to the taut bud of her nipple. His teeth grazed it as he licked, sucked, and kissed on one side before he started over again on the other side. Every touch heightened her arousal even more, and her moans urged him on. He worked his way down her stomach as he kissed and licked every part of her until he reached her hot, wet core. Fully settled between her legs, he moved his hands under her hips and pulled her knees over his shoulder to put her center fully in line with his tongue.

His dark head moved in to lick her from the bottom of her slit to the top of her clit, where he stopped to suck and tug on it. Her hands flew to his head as she fisted his hair to hold him in place. She felt his chuckle rumble through her from deep in his chest.

He did it again and again until Brianna came apart in his hands. "That's my girl. Let me taste you, baby. It's been too long. Come for me, scream my name." When his mouth met her core again, he didn't stop until she loudly screamed his name over and over.

He moved to cover her body with his and kissed her fiercely. The taste of her arousal was still on his tongue and lips from when he pushed her desire into a feverish state. He bent her knees, and then she lifted and spread her legs to allow him full access. With one swift thrust, he rocked inside her and murmured words of love and ecstasy.

He sat up on his knees, put his hands on the backs of her thighs, and drove hard into her. In this position, he hit the pleasure spot with every thrust and felt her inner muscles clamp down around him as she came over and over. Her extra wetness was his undoing, and with her last cry, he growled her name as his own orgasm pumped into her.

He rolled them both to the side to avoid hurting her, but he didn't let her go. They fell asleep with their bodies still entwined, and he was still inside her.

After her initial night of persuasion, Noah was much less hesitant about her physical abilities.

Noah continued to work mostly from home over the following weeks while she continued to heal. He claimed it was because he didn't want to leave her alone in the event she had any problems post-concussion. If someone were to put a gun to his head, he'd admit that he just wanted to spend as much time with her as he could.

"I will not accept no for an answer, young lady!" Evan's voice boomed at Brianna. "The arrangements have already been made, and that's that."

Noah sat back in his recliner and smiled triumphantly. The

whole family was on his side, and there was no way she was getting out of it.

"Okay, Daddy, you're right," Brianna replied casually.

Evan sat up straighter. "What did you say? Don't patronize me!"

Brianna laughed. "I said okay! What more do you want?"

"An ironclad contract would do me just fine," Noah chimed in, as Brianna gingerly took a seat on Noah's lap and wrapped her arm around his neck.

"Look, I learned my lesson. I won't go snooping around in anyone else's dangerous business anymore. I'm done with the whole investigative reporting thing. I'll take the public relations position for Sterling Luxury Resorts and work for you, Daddy." She kissed Noah's cheek and added, "But I'm staying in Miami."

Evan agreed. "Fine, fine. We're building a new Sterling Luxury Resort in Miami Beach on a piece of prime real estate. You'll be able to garner us a lot of good PR."

Diana had another motive for agreeing to it. "And maybe one day I'll get some grandchildren from one of my daughters."

Brianna rolled her eyes.

After Diana and Evan left, Noah set the alarm, picked up Brianna, and carried her to his bedroom. He'd done the same every night since she was discharged from the hospital. It had been almost eight weeks since she was shot, and she was almost completely healed.

She still had occasional soreness in her shoulder and ribs, but it had become more of a dull ache. At first, Brianna did need his help to climb the stairs. She felt safe and secure in his strong embrace. She was past the point of needing to be carried then, but Noah wouldn't hear of it. *Neanderthal,* she thought and smiled, knowing she secretly loved it too.

She loved her parents, but she needed time alone with Noah. He was still as careful with her as the first night she was forced to seduce him. She smiled at the memory of that big, dangerous man giving in to her "torture tactics," as he called them. She walked into the bathroom to prepare for bed. She dug in the bathroom closet to find more cotton balls when she came across her backpack. With everything that had happened over the past several weeks, she had forgotten all about it. As she emptied the contents, she gasped and inhaled so sharply that she felt a pull in her healing ribs.

Oh. My. God.

Noah had just hung up from a phone call as she walked back into the bedroom. "Who was that?"

"That was Shadow. Seems our friend Richard has gotten a lot of his friends in trouble."

She stepped forward to Noah, touching his arm. "You?"

He smiled and answered. "No, not me—thanks to you and those documents. Shadow and his team have rounded up everyone they could identify from the trail Richard left. They will be sent away for a very long time. Shadow told his superiors Steele Security worked with him on the wire you wore. The recording of Richard admitting he intended to kill you completely cleared me of any wrongdoing."

He reached for her, pulled her close to him, and wrapped his arms around her waist. She locked her hands around his neck as he drew her into a long, glorious kiss. His tongue tenderly stroked hers, and then he pulled away slightly to suck her bottom lip into his mouth before gently scraping his teeth across it. He peppered her jaw with kisses and trailed down her neck.

He grasped the hem of her shirt and pulled it up over her head. He savored every inch of her, tasted her, and he took his time with her body.

"Noah, I really need to tell you something."

"Brianna, I really need to show you something."

She was undone by the need in his voice and the wicked, half smile he gave her. He always made her weak in the knees. He quickly shed his boxers and stepped out of them, displaying his rock-hard erection. His fingers trailed lightly over her breasts, stopping to rub her nipples with his callused fingers, before he left a trail of fire over her stomach.

He reached for her shorts, quickly unbuttoned them, and pushed them to the floor. Then he hooked his thumbs in the sides of her panties, lowered them to the floor, and knelt in front of her.

He licked and sucked on her clit, and she fell back against the wall. Her knees threatened to buckle from underneath her. His fingers found their way to her center, caressed and pleased her, and made her wetter. She ran her fingers through his hair while her other hand dug into his shoulder as he brought her closer to the edge.

She gasped when one of his thick fingers plunged deep into her, her knees bent, and her back arched, and she pulled him in deeper. She cried out when his second finger joined the first one, stretched, and filled her as he prepared her body for him.

He stood before her, and she locked her arms around his neck. He cupped her ass and pulled her up as he pushed her back against the wall. She wrapped her legs around his waist as his mouth covered hers. Their kisses became more demanding and more intense. He grunted with intense need and drove his thick, hard shaft deep inside of her.

He placed his hands on the wall, just under her hips, and continued to pound deep into her, over and over again with fierce intensity. "Look at me, baby." She opened her eyes and felt the connection to him deep inside her chest, her love for him over-flowing from her eyes.

She relished every thrust and every feeling with him. Her hands roamed everywhere over his body. Her fingernails dug into his thick muscles with every orgasm that rippled through her. Her moans, screams, and utterances drove him on even more. Unable to hold back any longer when she climaxed again, he let go and allowed her body to milk him dry.

Through heavy panting and continued sweet kisses, he held her against the wall, with her legs wrapped around his waist. "I love you so much, Bri, so fucking much. God, you just don't know how much I love you and have missed you. I will tell you and show you every day. I never want to be without you again, not even for a day."

She cupped his face in her hands and kissed him. "You are my life, Noah. I will never leave you again, no matter what. Whatever the future holds, we'll face it together."

He carried her to the bed and carefully deposited her on her pillow before he climbed in beside her and held her in his arms for the night. He pulled up close to her, molded their bodies to fit each other, and softly asked, "What did you want to tell me?"

"It can wait until tomorrow." She wanted to tell him, but he already sounded half asleep, and she knew this news would probably keep him up all night. Wrapped in his arms and his warmth, she drifted off to sleep, completely sated and completely happy again.

24

CHAPTER TWENTY-FOUR

She stood looking in the bathroom mirror. "Okay, Brianna. This is major. You're going to walk downstairs and tell him. Just tell him."

She stared into her own eyes. "I can't do this."

"Yes, you can. Quit being a coward."

Great, now my inner dialogue is coming out!

While she still had the courage built up—and before she talked herself out of it—she walked toward Noah's office. She called out to him as she turned the corner toward his office. "Noah, we really need to talk abou—" then she realized he was completely engrossed in his work.

He didn't look up when he said, "Uh, okay. Just a sec, babe."

"Oh, I'm sorry, Noah. I shouldn't have bothered you."

She turned to leave, but before she was even through the doorway, his arms came around her waist and gently stopped her. She hadn't even heard him get up. *How does he do that?* she mused.

"You never bother me, Bri." He tenderly nuzzled her ear. He turned her around then he sat on the back of the chair that was directly in front of his large desk. "Now, what did you want to talk about?"

"Noah, it can wait, really. You were deep in thought, and I didn't mean to interrupt you. I know you're busy."

"I'm never too busy for you. Ever. I made that mistake once, but it'll never happen again." His tone was resolute. She couldn't stop the butterflies it gave her to know how sincere he was.

She wiped her palms on her shorts, suddenly aware that they were sweating, and she felt really nervous. Her eyes darted around the room as she tried to think of the best way to tell him.

He immediately noticed how she chewed on her bottom lip, a sure sign that she was nervous. He tried to remain calm because they were in a better place in their relationship. Still, it put him on full alert to see her worried demeanor.

"Um, look. I'll understand if you get mad at me when I tell you this. But I really didn't do it on purpose," she began.

The words were flying out so quickly that it was as if she had to spit them out or hold them in forever. Her tone of voice pleaded with him, and he knew she was scared——of him, of how he would react, to whatever it was.

He stood up, took her hands in his, and kept his tone gentle. She had been through enough, and he vowed he would never be the source of her insecurity again. "Bri, you never have to be scared of me—to talk to me or to tell me anything. Whatever it is, we'll work through it together. Okay?"

She nodded and bit her lower lip again. He kept holding her hands as he stroked the tops with his thumbs to give her reassurance. She continued. "You see, the thing is, with everything that's happened… I didn't even expect to see you, much less anything else to happen… Then I got shot, and I was in the hospital."

Noah smiled reassuringly. "Bri, just tell me what's going on. Let me help with whatever it is."

"I just realized last night that I, um, haven't been on my birth control pills." She spoke each word slowly to watch his reaction.

"Since? When, exactly?" His face became the unreadable mask again, and his thumbs that had stroked her reassuringly suddenly stilled. His whole body went as rigid as stone. Brianna was afraid she'd hyperventilate before she could answer him.

Take deep breaths. Breathe! "Since that first night you caught me here in your house. My bag was still at the hotel. Noah, I'm late."

He was silent. Too silent. She was about to hit full panic mode. It wasn't that she didn't trust him. She did—with her life. He wasn't the type of man who would turn his back on her when she needed him the most, and he definitely wasn't the type of man who'd turn his back on his baby.

The issue simply was that she knew he didn't trust her yet. Their relationship had just started to get back on track. They were becoming closer and felt more comfortable with each other again, but sometimes she sensed his resentment from what she'd done. An unplanned pregnancy tended to make some men feel trapped. She didn't know how she'd survive losing him again.

Since he still hadn't spoken, she felt the need to fill in the silence. "Look, Noah. I didn't do it on purpose. I swear. I may not even be pregnant. It could just be all the stress I've been under lately. I planned to go to the store this morning to get a pregnancy test. Just to be sure, but..."

"Damn it. Should I not have told you yet? I just didn't want to keep something that big from you. I don't want to keep anything from you. I didn't want you to think I went behind your back if I took the test without you. Maybe I should've made sure before I said anything?"

I'm in full panic mode, and he's just standing there! She knew she was rambling, and she couldn't stop herself. His lack of response rattled her more than if he'd been mad and yelled at her about it.

"Noah, say something—anything. Please. Are you mad?" She hesitated before asking the next question. "Do you want me to leave?" She looked down at her hands and chewed on her lip.

"Woo-hoo!" Noah yelled as he scooped her up in his arms and twirled her around. "We're having a baby!" He beamed as he kissed her, and then he sat her back down.

"Noah, wait. We don't know for sure yet," Brianna said with a nervous laugh. But she quickly saw that it was useless even to try to tell him. He grabbed his keys off his desk, pulled her hand, and headed to the car.

"Well, let's find out for sure. Right now!"

Back from the store and with the pregnancy test in hand, Brianna walked into the bathroom. Noah desperately wanted to follow, but he thought he should give her a little privacy to pee on the stick.

How long can it possibly take to piss? He paced impatiently outside the bathroom door, hesitated with his hand on the knob several times, then she finally opened the door to let him in.

"Well?" Like a kid on Christmas morning, he could hardly stand to wait.

She laughed. "Noah, I just now took it. It takes a couple of minutes for the results to show."

He stood over the stick for what seemed like hours. After a couple of seconds, he asked, "Are you sure you did it right?"

"Yeah, it's kind of hard to pee wrong, Noah." She laughed and shook her head at him. She took a couple of steps away and sat on the edge of the enormous garden tub in his master bath. And waited.

After an eternity, Noah turned to her and knelt with his perfectly chiseled body snuggled between her legs. His eyes held the passion and feelings that he usually kept buried and hidden from others.

He lifted her shirt, slowly bent his head to her stomach, and kissed it. "You're carrying my baby."

At Noah's insistence, Brianna made an emergency appointment with a doctor nearby. She drove separately so Noah could go to his downtown office after the appointment. As she glanced around at the other women in the waiting room of the obstetrician's office, she noted their various stages of pregnancy. She tried to picture how she would look as her pregnant belly expanded.

Brianna had explained her worries to the receptionist when she made the appointment. She wasn't sure how many weeks it had been, she had been under anesthesia and given other medications. She and Noah just wanted reassurance that her baby would be healthy.

The receptionist scheduled her for an ultrasound and told Brianna to bring the medical records from the hospital so the doctor could review them. Noah was ready to tell everyone about the baby, but Brianna convinced him to wait until after the first office visit when they'd have more information. The nurse called Brianna's name, and they followed her down the hall to the exam room. Brianna changed into the paper gown and sat on the examination table.

Noah rummaged through everything in the room while Brianna and he waited for the doctor. He opened the cabinet doors, rifled through the supplies, and flipped through the magazines on the counter. Finally, the doctor strolled in the room, said hello, and then motioned for her to put her feet in the stirrups. He performed his usual physical exam and tapped on her belly. Brianna watched his face for any sign of worry. Not seeing any evidence of it didn't make her feel better, though.

"Well, what do you say we have a look at that baby?" he asked.

The nurse had gathered the materials for the ultrasound and squirted lubricating gel into a condom. She picked up the ultrasound wand, put the condom on it, and handed it to the doctor.

Noah's eyes locked on to it and grew wide. With his threatening tone, he asked, "Where are you putting that, exactly?"

The doctor chuckled. "The baby is too small at this stage to see it by regular ultrasound. We only need to insert it just past the tip. It looks worse than it really is."

Soon the black-and-white picture appeared on the screen. The doctor pointed out the baby from all the various lines and squiggles on the screen. The doctor began taking measurements of the size of the baby, the size of her uterus, and the volume of amniotic fluid. Noah moved to Brianna's side, kissed her cheek, and grabbed her hands. Together they watched in amazement at the images on the screen.

"Well, from the measurements, it looks like you're somewhere around six to eight weeks. I can only give you an estimate right now, but we'll do more measurements as you get further along."

Brianna did a quick calculation and realized conception could've occurred just before she was battered and hospitalized, or just after her release from the hospital. Just those few days could make such a huge difference.

The doctor told her to get dressed and meet him in his office so they could talk about her medical records, what to expect over the next several months, and any other questions they had. Brianna's hands were shaking as she dressed because she was so nervous.

Noah put his arms around her and pulled her close. "It'll be okay, baby." He kissed the top of her head, and they walked to the doctor's office.

The doctor was friendly, but matter-of-fact, as he spoke. "We try to give as little medication as possible to pregnant women, especially in your first trimester. I can't guarantee anything, but I don't see any medications that alarm me."

Brianna let out a sigh of relief and felt Noah squeeze her hand. She looked at him and saw his unfaltering smile. His strength seemed to move through his hand and into her. She had to believe that everything would be fine, that the baby would be healthy. Once outside the office, she began to breathe easier and felt truly happy.

"I have to go into the office for a meeting now. Will you be okay?" Noah's voice was laced with concern. She could tell he didn't want to leave her yet.

"Yes, I'll be fine. Quit worrying about me and get to work." She replied in a teasing and playful tone.

Noah kissed her goodbye, climbed into his truck, and drove off toward his downtown office. He really didn't like leaving her, especially after their first doctor visit. He wanted to take her home and spoil her for the next fifty or sixty years. He knew it was somewhat irrational to worry so much about her. He couldn't seem to shake the feeling that there could still be some repercussions after the fiasco with Richard.

Brianna walked across the parking lot to one of the Steele Security SUVs she drove until she got her car. Out of the corner of her eye, she saw a full-size SUV drive slowly behind her. She reached for the door handle when a man grabbed her from behind, covered her head with a black cloth, and pulled her into the back of the SUV.

He tied her hands and growled into her ear. "Don't fight if you want to live."

She sat motionlessly, trying to calm herself and figure out what to do next. Her voice couldn't hide her fear as she asked, "What do you want with me?"

She felt the car move and knew they were on the main road. She tried to figure out where they were headed, but her sense of direction was off under the hood she was wearing. Thoughts of Noah and their baby kept her from going into complete panic mode. She tried to keep her stress levels as low as possible, but at the moment, she didn't feel very successful.

After several stops, starts, and turns, she heard the vehicle's engine turn off. Rough hands grabbed her from the back seat, yanked her out, and pushed her forward. One hand grabbed the back of her arm and guided her in the darkness. After more turns and pushes, she was guided to what felt like a soft chair. She asked again, "What do you want?"

His angry, hushed voice responded. "I want those documents, Brianna. Give them to me, or your family will get you back in pieces."

Her hand went instinctively to her lower abdomen to protect her baby. Bile rose in the back of her throat, and she fought to push it back down.

"I-I don't have them."

His voice held disgust and disdain for her. "Then what good are you?"

Keep him talking. "I don't have them with me. I can get them."

"Can you now?" He didn't believe her.

"Yes, just…don't hurt me."

He didn't answer, and she knew he was considering his options.

"If you let me call Noah, he can get them. He can meet you somewhere, or he can leave them somewhere. You can let me go. Just take the documents and let me go."

She recognized the man's voice as US Marshal Stevens's. Over the last couple of months, Noah had told her about several high-ranking officials that had been arrested during Shadow's investigation of Richard's scheme. She hadn't heard Noah mention Stevens's name, but she had just assumed he'd been arrested too.

That was a stupid assumption to make, Bri. Now you're here with him… wherever here is, she chastised herself.

He didn't answer her, but she heard him move around the room. She heard him rummage through something, but his movements were so fast she couldn't figure out what he was doing. She heard muffled sounds as items moved, then cabinet doors opened and closed. At one point, he talked to himself. She strained her ears with every sound for clues that would tell her what he was doing.

How long until Noah realizes I'm gone? she wondered.

CHAPTER TWENTY-FIVE

Noah finished his meeting at his office in downtown Miami and was very pleased with the new contract he'd acquired. Shadow had done his best to keep Noah's name and his business name out of the negative press. His old friend had been instrumental in helping him recover from the potential backlash that scandal could've caused.

Noah's new client owned a significant computer software business and had offices located throughout the nation. The owner wanted a security detail at each location for the next twelve months as they worked to develop a new product line. This contract would put Steele Security on the map like no other before it. The best part was it was entirely legitimate.

After his meeting ended, Noah worked on planning for resources to staff that many locations in his first long-term contract. He was so engrossed in his work that he quickly lost track of time. When he finally looked up, he realized he had been at it for hours, but Brianna hadn't called him once. He grabbed his cell phone to check for missed calls, but there were none.

He tapped the screen and dialed her number. It rang several times before rolling to voice mail. He tried the house phone, but no one answered it either. Don't panic. She could be busy or taking a nap or… He turned to his computer, tapped a few keys, and checked his home security system. It hadn't been turned off or rearmed since they left the house together that morning.

"Bull. Rebel. Can you two come here for a minute?" he called down the hall.

"What's up, boss?" Rebel asked.

"Brianna isn't answering her cell or the home phone. I just checked the alarm system, and she hasn't been back since we left early this morning. I have a bad feeling," he explained.

"Reap, she's probably out shopping or something. Give her a little time and space. I guarantee she won't leave you again," Bull assured him.

Noah blew out an exasperated breath and considered what he was about to tell them. If he was wrong and she was fine somewhere, she would have his head. But he couldn't face the alternative.

"Brianna's pregnant. We just found out this morning. We haven't told anyone yet, not even her family, because we just went to the doctor today to confirm the baby's healthy. She'll be pissed at me telling you without her here, but if anything has happened to her…"

Bull and Rebel were visibly stunned.

"Congratulations, Reaper." Rebel beamed. "That's awesome news. So she's probably out buying baby stuff, then. Fifty bucks says she has her arms full and can't answer her phone."

Bull laughed with Rebel, but he knew Noah was worried. "Let's find out where she's blowing your money, Reaper. Wasn't she driving one of our SUVs today?"

Bull pulled up the GPS tracking software for their fleet of Steele Security SUVs on the computer. Every vehicle had been fitted with a tracking device so employees could be found in case of an emergency. He located the one assigned to Brianna and looked up the address where it was parked.

He turned to Noah, the worry visible on his face. "Reaper, she never left the doctor's office this morning."

The three men sprang into action. Rebel called in backup as

they walked toward the parking garage. They'd start at her last known location and determine their next step from what they found at the doctor's office. The ride from the downtown office to the doctor's office took no time with Bull's driving.

As Bull had stated, the SUV still sat in the parking lot exactly where she'd met Noah that morning. He looked all around the car but found nothing to help them. He used the spare key to check for car trouble, but it started without a hitch and had a full tank of gas. Noah went inside to talk to the receptionist and learned Brianna didn't come back into the office.

Running back across the parking lot, he called Brad. "I need you to hack into the area traffic cameras, and any other security cameras at this location, and find out what happened to Bri. Now!"

Bull had his phone out and called Shadow to have him stay on alert. Shadow was back in Miami, and they all decided to meet at Noah's house, including Brad, to search for Brianna. Noah called Brianna's phone several more times, but it rolled to voice mail every time. He knew without a doubt that she was in danger.

Brad's tone of voice startled Noah from his thoughts. "Noah, I got something here!"

Noah rushed to his computer as Brad played the video again. He watched as a man in a black mask grabbed Brianna, dragged her into the back of an SUV, and sped away with her. The camera caught the direction the vehicle traveled for another twenty seconds before it panned in the opposite direction.

"I'm working on cleaning up the image for the license plate."

"Email that image to me," Shadow commanded.

Within a few minutes, Shadow had an email back from his contact at Langley. The email was a clear picture of the SUV, the license plate, along with the owner's name, address, and all known phone numbers.

US Marshal Michael Stevens.

"He was Brianna's handler when she was in the WITSEC program," Shadow added.

"Hey, wait a minute." Rebel recalled a conversation and worked to put the pieces together in his head.

"What, Rebel? You know something? Talk to me!" Noah's agitation was evident in his tone.

"That morning she made waffles. I told her that US Marshal Stevens came by to talk to us. He told us that he didn't think Richard was on that plane and he thought Richard had been taken hostage.

"She didn't say he was assigned to her. She must have figured out that this dude was dirty. How could he not be if he knew Richard was still alive? They never reported he was taken hostage until he showed up. This one guy knew they were both alive."

"And he knows Brianna was the key to the investigation." Noah was beginning to realize what they were dealing with and how much danger Brianna was in with Stevens.

Noah dialed the cell phone number from Shadow's email. He was surprised when the man answered.

"Stevens."

"You took something of mine today, Stevens. I will tear you limb from limb with my bare hands if even one hair on her head is missing." Noah's voice was calm but low. He was serious and determined to get Brianna back and carry out his threat against Stevens.

"And you have something I want. How about a swap?"

Noah didn't like Stevens's cocky tone. He sounded so sure of himself and not at all threatened by Noah's statement.

"What do you want?"

"I want the documents Brianna collected. Every single piece of it. Save it all on a flash drive. I know you still have a copy of it."

"Let me talk to her first. I want to know she's not hurt."

"Noah?" Bri called to him.

"Bri—I'm coming to get you!"

"Not until I get what I want, you're not."

"Just say where and when, Stevens."

He gave an address where he wanted to meet in one hour. As expected, he told Noah to come alone. Brad saved a copy of the documents from his computer to a flash drive and gave it to Noah.

They geared up for battle. This time in their work fatigues, guns and knives, communication devices, stun guns, smoke grenades, and mace in various holsters and hiding places. Noah sent one team to the address listed in the email Shadow received, just in case Stevens was sending them on a wild goose chase. Shadow called his friends at Langley to initiate a search for any other local addresses that were even remotely associated with Stevens.

When I get my hands on him, he won't have to worry about going to prison. He'll be going to a morgue, Noah vowed. There was a reason why his nickname was Reaper, and he was determined to put it to good use.

"Come on. We're going for a ride," Stevens said as he yanked her up from the chair.

"Stevens, you don't have to do this."

"Do you know how much trouble you've caused me over the last three years?" he asked as he pushed her into the front seat of the SUV.

As he closed her door, she felt something at her feet and quickly leaned over to touch it. My purse! She quickly grabbed her cell phone out of the side pocket. As he slid into the driver's seat, she tucked it between her right thigh and the edge of her seat, as far away from Stevens as she could get it. She kept her hands at her sides and only moved her fingers as she unlocked the screen.

With her head held just right, she could barely see the touchscreen of her phone from underneath her hood. She quickly hit the speed dial button for Noah's cell and let the phone stay on. She hoped he could somehow track her cell phone signal and find her. She at least felt better knowing he was on the other end of the line.

"Where are we going, Stevens?"

"Oh, I'm going to meet your boyfriend and be done with all this shit," he replied nonchalantly.

"And what do you plan to do with me?" she asked tentatively.

"You'll see soon enough."

Is he seriously enjoying this? "How did you get involved in this? You're supposed to be one of the good guys."

"Good guys finish last, sweetheart. Haven't you heard? Hollingsworth screwed me over after I helped him. He owes me."

"But your name didn't even come up in any of those documents. You were safe."

"He screwed me over. That's why my name wasn't there. At first, I thought you were playing me when I kept asking for them, and you never gave them to me," Stevens shared.

"I wasn't playing you. I didn't know you were even involved."

"Yeah, I figured that out. Richard cut me out completely. He took all the money for himself, but you have all the offshore bank account numbers."

"So you can take all the money and just disappear," she concluded.

"Such a smart girl. Unfortunately for you, you're too smart for your own damn good."

Stevens felt very confident in his plans. He gloated about how he had beaten Richard after he'd tried to screw Stevens out of his cut. A brilliant thought had come to him when he realized that Brianna didn't know of his involvement.

While the feds are busy arresting and scheduling trials, I'll clean out the bank accounts and never be found again.

He was confident that this plan would work out perfectly for him. He only had a couple of minor details to take care of first. One of those was Brianna, and the other was Noah. They both had to die for him to be able to disappear.

He laughed to himself at the thought of how love-sick Noah would come barging in to rescue his damsel in distress, only to find out what genuine suffering meant. He had planned every detail of this scenario in his head, over and over, for the past three years.

He knew Brianna would eventually run straight back to Noah and straight back to the evidence. He didn't know where the stupid bitch had hidden the documents, but he knew she didn't have them on her. He had searched her townhouse plenty of times while she was out on her runs.

She didn't even know he was the one who'd convinced Richard's buyers there was a "new weapon" in the making. His brilliant schemes even surprised him sometimes. That thought brought a real smile to his face. Richard and that Alexa Pope bitch were both dead, her old man was arrested, and every day he heard of someone else in the circle who had been caught red-handed.

Maybe Richard cutting me out of the circle did me a favor, he mused, *since now everyone's money will be mine.* And as Brianna had pointed out, no one even suspected he was part of it.

In a few minutes, the only two people who could delay my departure from the country will be dead, he sneered. *I'll take the account numbers from Noah's cold, lifeless hands and disappear.*

He had secured Brianna to a wooden post in the old farmhouse that had once belonged to his grandmother. It had long since been condemned, and she moved in to a nursing home. He'd held on to the property in hopes that it would be worth something one day.

He laughed at his own witty self again. Tonight, this condemned house will be worth hundreds of millions of dollars. It would be valued at more than any other property in the world. The house was made of wood—old, rotten wood. It would burn to the ground with a single spark. And there was no doubt that there would be sparks.

All around the room, he had set trip wires that crossed over another. No matter which way Noah rushed in, he'd set off the small bombs Stevens had crafted. His time spent on the LAPD bomb squad paid off in the end. He'd learned how to dismantle bombs, but in doing so, he also learned how to build them.

The ones he set in the house were little more than Molotov cocktails and didn't take any real genius to rig. The trip wire would ignite the flares that sat beneath the rag hanging from the gasoline bomb. It was a short rag, so it would be a short fuse to burn. Once one went off, the whole house would catch fire, automatically igniting the others. With a fire burning that hot, everything should burn away without a trace. He knew there was no way Noah would leave Brianna in there to die alone.

Stevens left Brianna inside as he quietly moved around the side of the house. He crouched down in the darkness as he waited for Noah to arrive. He planned to kill Noah first, take the flash drive from him before dragging him inside the house. Once the flares went off in the house, they'd both burn beyond recognition. Then, he would just drive away and never be seen again. Such a perfect plan.

∼

Noah jerked the phone up when he saw Brianna's name light up his screen. He hit the button, heard her conversation with Stevens, and knew exactly what she was doing. He put the call on mute and transferred it to the vehicle Bluetooth link so the team could listen through the speakers.

"Brad, track her cell phone and find her!"

Brad was already on it. He was sure what he was doing was illegal, but Shadow gave him the nod to continue. He hacked in to the cell carrier's website and identified the towers that returned the pings from Brianna's phone. A few calculations later, he had triangulated her position within a few hundred yards.

Noah listened as Brianna continued to talk and kept Stevens talking. That was a small consolation, just knowing she was still alive and didn't sound hurt. But Noah had also heard Stevens's comment and his tone of voice. Stevens wasn't leaving any loose ends, and Brianna knew too much just to let her go. He planned to kill her as soon as he got the bank numbers.

Noah sped to the location Brad indicated and saw the SUV turn into a long, gravel driveway. The house couldn't be seen from the road, so the team would be forced to go in blind. There was a row of trees on either side of the driveway, and they ran parallel with the road. He pulled over and told the guys to work their way up to the house. He was instructed to show up alone, and he would, but they would be close behind him.

The other men quickly disappeared into the night, and Noah drove on alone. He carefully took in the scenery as his SUV crawled along the gravel drive. He looked for any signs of traps. He knew what to look for since he had both set and been in enough of them in his military career. *Just like riding a bike,* he thought. *Some training never really leaves you.*

A single light shone through the window in the house at the end of the drive. He knew better than to think rescuing her would be that easy. He caught a glimpse of movement outside, on the other side of the house, and knew it wasn't any of his men. They would approach from the opposite direction, and they couldn't have beaten him here. Stevens was lying in wait for him, and he would be damn sure Stevens was disappointed.

He stopped the car in the gravel driveway. He left it far enough away from the house that it wouldn't be seen but would completely block the only exit. He turned off the dome light of the SUV and silently slipped out the door. He crouched down beside the wheel as he searched the perimeter of the house. His gun was drawn at his side as he ran toward the house. He stopped to look in Stevens's empty car before crouching beside the front of the house.

He raised his head slightly to look in the window where the light was on and saw Brianna sitting on the floor. His eyes quickly scanned the room, but it took a moment to comprehend. When his mind registered what he saw, his heart stopped in his chest.

That fucking bastard is already dead. He just doesn't know it yet.

Noah knew his men were within radio range and, as quietly as possible, whispered, "He's mine." He moved silently along the front of the house toward the direction he saw Stevens going. As he turned the corner of the back of the house, he saw a dark figure crouched by a large bush in the backyard. His eyes scanned the area around Stevens, looking for anything out of the ordinary. He caught a movement in his peripheral vision. His men were setting up for an ambush.

Noah stole up behind Stevens, as silent and deadly as the Grim Reaper himself, caught him in a headlock with his left arm and the barrel of his Glock against his right temple. "Make a move, asshole. I dare you."

Stevens went rigid and stilled his movements. Noah had hoped for more of a fight than this. He didn't like to kill anyone in cold blood if he didn't have to. But this one time he might make an exception for Stevens. He also might just enjoy it. Stevens's hand shot back, and a brief glint of moonlight reflected off his Bowie knife.

Noah was too close to avoid the nine-and-a-half-inch knife entirely. He jumped back and to the left, but the blade sliced Noah's right side and left a gaping wound. Burning pain tore through him as his left arm dropped to hold his injured side, and Stevens whirled around to face him. Charging, Stevens extended his arm and stabbed the knife toward Noah again. Noah's powerful roundhouse kick knocked the knife out of Stevens's hand. As he dove for it, Noah shot at him. The bullet hit him in the side of his chest, and this time, Stevens didn't get up.

Noah gave him a hard kick in the side, but Stevens didn't move or even groan in pain. If he were still alive, he wouldn't have been able to take that kick. Especially since Noah strategically placed it right at the bullet's entry wound. Noah walked away from Stevens while still holding his wounded side. Noah moved quickly to get Brianna out of the house before it went up in flames.

The other men watched the interaction between Reaper and Stevens, but no one interfered. They understood Reaper's innate need to handle Stevens on his own. Reaper briefed the men on what he'd seen in the house, and even though he didn't need to, he stressed to every man to be careful where they stepped inside the house. They carefully entered the dilapidated house and stepped over numerous trip wires. Blake and Roman worked on removing as much of the threat as possible while the others helped free Brianna from her bonds.

Once she was outside the house, Brianna saw Noah's blood-soaked shirt. She looked up at him with fear in her eyes. Not for her own safety, but fear of losing him. "Oh my God, Noah! You're hurt!"

He tried to relieve her fears when he gave his best smile and boasted, "It's nothing. I've had worse."

She knew better than to believe the wound was nothing. One of the guys gave her his shirt. She folded it and held it firmly against Noah's side, putting pressure on the wound to help stop the blood loss as much as possible. She wrapped her arm around his waist to help him walk to the vehicle.

A noise from behind them startled her, and when she glanced over her shoulder, she saw Stevens lunge at Noah with his large knife. With her free hand, she grabbed the gun from Noah's holster. She quickly turned to face Stevens, squeezed the trigger, and watched as the bullet hit him right between the eyes.

She felt Noah take the gun from her shaking hand as she stood staring at Stevens's dead body. Bull walked up beside her, put his arm around her shoulders, and quipped, "Our little sister doesn't miss when she aims her gun."

"My brothers trained me well." She gave Bull a weak smile and leaned into him briefly. She stepped back into Noah's embrace to assist him into the SUV. "It's time to take you to the hospital, Noah."

26

CHAPTER TWENTY-SIX

"I don't know about that, Noah. I'm sure going to miss him being in the CIA," Brianna teased in her Southern drawl as she curled another strand of hair.

Noah had just told her that Shadow was turning in his notice at the CIA and coming to work for Steele Security. He half jokingly said to her that Shadow saw more action in the time that Brianna was up to no good than in all his years with the company combined. The truth was Shadow knew he was going to be an uncle soon, and he wanted to be with his family. Noah was thrilled to have him join his security firm.

Brianna was preparing for their date night. She stood in the bathroom in her camisole and matching lacy panties. Noah walked to her, rubbed his hand across the little bump on her stomach, kissed her, and then knelt to kiss the baby. She loved when he did that, and it had quickly become a daily ritual.

∼

She said she would be right down, Noah thought for the twentieth time. He called up the stairs from the foyer, where he'd been waiting for the last fifteen minutes. "Brianna! Don't make me come up there and get you!"

She appeared on the second-floor landing, looked down at him, and quirked her eyebrow up. "Oh, and just what do you plan to do with me?"

He flashed his wicked, half grin at her. He knew how that smile made her blood boil in the best way possible.

Finally dressed and ready to go, she walked down the stairs, and he never took his eyes off her. Her baby bump had made most of her clothes a little too tight for comfort. She'd shopped for new clothes to wear on their date night. At Noah's insistence, she had someone from Steele Security close on her heels at all times. There were still people who wouldn't be happy with being implicated in the scandal she broke, and Noah refused to take another chance.

She'd picked an elegant aqua blue dress to wear out. The straps made a V up from the center of her chest and looped around her neck. It was gathered and belted below her breasts to draw the eye to them. The flowing material hung down over her bump and stopped at mid-thigh. She wore her long hair pulled up in an elegant ponytail, with small wisps of curls that hung down strategically around her face. Her white-gold bracelets adorned her arms, and matching earrings twinkled when she walked. Her slingback silver heels matched her silver purse that hung over her shoulder.

"Wow. Maybe we should just stay home, after all." He was only half serious, but if she agreed to it, he wouldn't argue. His eyes moved slowly up and down her body, and she could feel him undress her as she walked down the staircase toward him.

"Not a chance, Mr. Steele. You are taking me out tonight." Brianna smiled as she approached him, put her hands on his chest, and lovingly stroked the hard muscles underneath. "You look very handsome yourself, Noah."

Noah had made reservations at the most romantic spot he could think of for her. He knew her love of the water, any kind of water, and he had arranged for a four-course dinner on a private yacht. A small band would be onboard to supply the romantic music. She took his arm as he led her out to the waiting limo.

He watched her face as they drove toward the marina. Confused, she looked at him, but he just shrugged his shoulders. She knew she wouldn't get any information out of him, so she snuggled up to him and enjoyed the ride. She really didn't care where they went, as long as she was with him. Anywhere was better with him by her side.

She looked even more puzzled when they boarded a small boat and sped out into the dark ocean, but she complied. His pride swelled when he realized she didn't question him at all; she just completely trusted him. When they approached the yacht anchored just offshore, her eyes grew big. She looked at him so lovingly and with the biggest smile on her face.

He smugly gave himself a mental pat on the back. *Oh yeah, score one for Reaper!*

He helped her board the large vessel, and the crewman led them up the stairs to the top deck. The table was set with white linens, china plates, and crystal champagne flutes. There was no alcohol for her, though, but she savored every bite as the staff brought out one delicious dish after another. The band played slow, romantic songs, and just before dessert, Noah stood and asked her to dance with him.

On the dance floor, she wrapped her arms around his neck, as he wrapped his around her waist and pulled her close to him. He whispered in her ear.

"You are so beautiful." He kissed her neck and along her jaw until he reached her mouth. "I love you, Bri."

Looking up into his eyes, she said, "I love you so much, Noah. This is all such a wonderful surprise. Thank you."

He leaned down and kissed her tenderly, loving the feel of her fingers playing with the hair at the back of his neck. Noah thought about how right it felt to hold her again. He knew he was the luckiest man in the world to have a second chance at creating a life with her.

The staff brought out their dessert plates, and he led her back to the table. Under the lid, a small black velvet box sat propped open on her plate. It held a three-carat round-cut diamond solitaire, set in a white-gold band, with fourteen diamond side-stones that wrapped around the band. She gasped, and her hand flew to her mouth.

She looked up to find Noah down on one knee beside her. He picked up the box and held up the ring.

"Brianna, I can't spend one more day without you by my side. I've loved you from the moment I met you. Will you give me the greatest pleasure of going to sleep in my arms every night and waking up in them every morning, of having my children, and taking my name?"

With tears streaming down her face, and smiling from ear to ear, she jumped into his arms and yelled, "Yes! Yes! Of course, yes!"

Noah helped her back to her seat as she continued to stare at her engagement ring. "It's gorgeous, Noah. I absolutely love it. You didn't have to pick out the biggest one they had, but it's too late to take it back since it's mine now."

Noah laughed at Brianna's honesty and humor. "I'll never take that back, Brianna. That promise will last a lifetime."

"I completely melt when you whisper sweet nothings like that to me," she replied. "You spoil me so much more than you should, but that's not why I love you. Your devoted heart owns me. Your sensual touch commands me. You protect me, help me, calm me, and excite me all at once."

"I do aim to please." He winked.

"Your aim is dead on, then, because you definitely please me."

"Well, I'll make sure the neighborhood knows that when we get home."

"Share your dessert with me so we can get out of here faster." Brianna stretched her arm across the table and helped herself to his plate.

"I love when you take charge," Noah chuckled. "Now I'm taking you home, where my heart can own you, and my touch can command you. I need to try these new features out."

~

BRIANNA AND HER SISTER, MISSY, HAD A GIRLS' DAY OUT SHOPPING. Missy was as excited about the wedding as Brianna was, and they finally had a chance to spend the day as sisters and enjoy each other's company. Missy insisted Brianna try on every wedding dress she could find until they found the perfect one. Then the perfect veil. Followed by the perfect shoes. Next was the perfect jewelry. Add to that too many bridal magazines. By the time Brianna got home, she was exhausted.

"Have fun with your sister today, baby?" Noah greeted her as she walked in.

"Yeah, I really did. I've missed her. She's so excited about the wedding." Brianna's face lit up when she saw Noah. He was barefoot, and his jeans hung low on his hips. He was shirtless and showed off his sculpted chest, arms, and abs. She'd never get tired of looking at him. He held his arms wide open, and she walked straight into them.

She had dropped all her bags, except one long garment bag. "Is that what I think it is, Brianna?" Noah asked as he took the bag from her hand.

"Yes, that's my wedding dress." She beamed, but then her smile fell.

"Hey, what's wrong, Bri?"

She let out a small chuckle and said, "I look fat. In every dress I tried on, I looked fat. It's a girl thing, I guess."

After he hung the garment bag on the coat rack, Noah knelt in front of her, lifted her shirt, and splayed his hands across her belly.

"I think this little bump is so sexy, Brianna. I love that my baby is growing inside you."

She ran her fingers through his hair as he kneeled in front of her. He looked up at her with intense desire in his eyes, and she felt her knees go weak.

As Noah rose to stand, he lightly dragged his hands up her body as he went. He pulled her shirt up over her head and tossed it aside. Then he gently stroked her cheek before his fingers lightly brushed down both sides of her neck to her collarbones. His hands flowed over her skin and left goose bumps in his wake until he reached her bra. He quickly unhooked the front clasp and let out a guttural growl as her growing breasts sprang free. He rubbed his thumbs over her sensitive nipples before leaning in to take one in his mouth.

She gasped as he sucked and pulled on her, and her back instinctively arched into him. One hand continued to rub the other breast, while his other hand left a heated path across her stomach to the button of her shorts. He swiftly unbuttoned them, pushed them down to her ankles, and she readily stepped out of them. He moved to take her other breast in his mouth. She pulled him closer to her and demanded that he take more.

His hand continued its exploration over her lacy panties to the heated pool of liquid between her legs. He could feel her wetness through them, and his already full-grown erection throbbed painfully.

"Damn, Bri, I will never get enough of you." His deep voice was husky, filled with desire for her. Before she could respond, he removed her panties, his finger explored her sensitive folds, and he found her small nub of pleasure nerves.

She dug her fingers into his shoulder and moaned in pleasure. He increased the pressure with his thumb as his fingers plunged deep inside her. With a sharp intake of breath, she cried out, "Oh, Noah!"

He felt her inner walls quiver as he increased his speed. He knew she was close to climaxing. Her normal breathing turned into rapid panting, and her hips moved in time with his fingers.

"Mmm, don't stop!" Her raspy voice pleaded with him.

"Come for me, baby. Let me feel you come."

She felt his hot breath in her ear as his deep voice whispered and urged her on. He felt her entire body tense as her head dropped back. She gripped his shoulders harder, and he felt the ripples roll through her, clench around his fingers, and drench them as she cried out his name. "Noah!"

As she raised her head and opened her eyes, she saw the smug, sexy smile on his face just before his mouth covered hers. His tongue pushed into her mouth as he slowly and tenderly caressed her tongue. She raked her fingernails over his chest, down his abdominal muscles, to the top of his jeans.

She slipped one finger under his waistband, lightly rubbed across the hypersensitive skin, and just skimmed across the top of his erection. He groaned into her mouth. She quickly unbuttoned his jeans and slid her entire hand in to grasp him.

The kiss soon became urgent and demanding, as she stroked him up and down with one hand and pushed his clothes off him with the other hand. He pulled away from the kiss, quickly lifted her, and carried her up the stairs to the bedroom. Setting her in the middle of the bed, he stopped to look at her beautiful naked body and began to lower his head to make love to her with his mouth and tongue. She grabbed his face in her hands and barely breathed out, "I can't wait, Noah. I need you inside me, now!"

"Okay, Brianna, but just this once." She felt the deep rumble of his laughter through his thick chest. He moved his body to cover hers. Using his knee to part her legs, he settled between them and framed her face with his forearms. He paused at her wet opening, stared into her eyes, and she wrapped her legs around him as she tried to push him forward while she moved her hips toward him.

He laughed again.

"My baby is so impatient." He pushed deep into her. She cried out in pleasure and arched her back. They soon moved in time, his hips surged, and hers rose to meet him. He was amazed and quite pleased with himself that with her every orgasm, she wanted more and more.

At last, she cried out, "Noah, I can't take anymore! Come with me, baby."

He thrust into her and felt her excitement as it built. Her inner walls milked him as they squeezed and quivered around him. He let go as he whispered words of love and emptied himself into her.

He rolled off her to his side, pulled her close to him, and rubbed her small baby bump. He nuzzled his face into her hair as he murmured, "I think I'll just keep you pregnant all the time. I really love how you can't get enough of me."

She felt him smile against her, and she responded, "I don't have to be pregnant not to get enough of you, Noah. That'll never happen." Then she added playfully, "I'll be glad to let you try to make me, though."

He loved her challenge. "You got a deal, and I'm holding you to that."

Brianna smiled and rolled to her side, snuggling into Noah's body as his arm wrapped around her. They drifted off to sleep, sated and happy.

She awoke in the middle of the night and walked to the bathroom. When she returned to bed, she had to admit that maybe the pregnancy hormones were adding to her libido, because she couldn't go to sleep until she had him again. He slept soundly as she planted featherlight kisses along his jaw, down his neck, and then took him in her mouth. He groaned in pleasure, and his hands went into her hair.

"Damn, woman, are you trying to kill me?" His tone was playful, but he was aroused and more than willing. He pulled her head up with a groan, and she rose to straddle him.

She held him at her core and intentionally impaled herself on him slowly. She watched him as he watched her. She rocked back and forth slowly as she enjoyed the ride and the feel of his thick length entirely inside her. She moved one hand up to her breast and pulled at her nipple.

His eyes darkened, and the look on his face was feral as his hands gripped her hips and forced her to move faster. As she increased her speed, he thrust up into her. She ran both of her hands down her torso, then one hand held tight at the base of his erection as she moved up and down, while the other hand reached around to gently stroke his balls. She felt it as he shot into her, and she climaxed with him.

Both of their chests heaved as they tried to catch their breath. They rolled onto their sides and snuggled. Noah confirmed his original plan on a pant. "Oh yeah, I'm definitely keeping you pregnant from now on."

Noah woke early the next morning, eased out of bed to let Brianna sleep, and went down to the kitchen to cook her breakfast.

The smell of bacon and coffee woke her, and she smiled when she realized where he was. She picked up his T-shirt that was on the chair beside the bed, pulled it over her head, and watched as the hem fell to midthigh. In the bathroom, she ran her fingers through her hair, brushed her teeth, and then made a beeline for the kitchen.

Noah looked up as she walked in, and she recognized the hunger in his eyes and the gruffness of his voice. "You look good enough to eat. Seeing you wearing my shirt turns me on."

She stood on her tiptoes and planted a heated kiss on his lips. "I'll let you show me just how much later in the shower."

She turned toward the coffee and heard him growl. Suddenly, she was lifted in the air, seated on the counter, and Noah stepped in between her legs. She wrapped her legs around him and pulled him in close to her. The look in his eyes was one of pure love. It was so warm and inviting that she felt it reach deep inside her.

He cradled her face in his hands. He opened his mouth to say something but stopped short. She saw raw emotions in his eyes and knew he wasn't the type to easily share his innermost feelings.

Brianna put her hand on his, leaned her cheek into his palm, and patiently urged him on. "What do you want to say, Noah? It's just me—you can tell me anything."

He moved his hands to her hips but didn't take his eyes off hers. "I need you to hear me out, okay? So I can get it all out at once." Brianna nodded in agreement.

"When I first met you, in the desert, I knew it was a bad idea to get involved—the secret missions, and we lived literally a world apart. But I couldn't stay away from you, and I really tried. I fell completely in love with you out there. I found you on purpose that night in the bar. That wasn't luck or coincidence. It was luck that some guy didn't have his hands on you when I walked in, because I would've killed him."

He took a step back from her, inhaled a deep breath, and raked his hand over his jaw before he continued. Brianna didn't interrupt. She knew he wasn't finished, but her heart lurched over the distance he suddenly put between them.

"When you started asking me a lot of questions about Richard, I got jealous. It seemed like you were talking about him all the time, and I started thinking maybe you were cheating on me with him. Really thinking that you were, Bri, and I pulled away from you."

He took another step away from her and leaned against the island. "That day you came to me wanting to talk, I was so wrapped up in my own bullshit, I couldn't think straight. I said I was too busy with work, but I wasn't. I was afraid you were going to say you were leaving me. I've never run from anything in my life, Bri, but I ran from that."

She nodded that she understood what he meant and looked down at the floor. She'd never even considered that he thought she would cheat on him. She suddenly noticed he was quiet, so she looked back up at him. He was waiting for her full attention, and he was giving her time to digest what he'd said.

"Then you left for your assignment, and you didn't come back. When they called to tell me you were dead, I…" His voice trailed off, and his hands were balled into tight fists. "I didn't think I would make it. I was on suicide watch. I don't know how long Bull and Rebel stayed here with me because I didn't want to live without you."

Brianna didn't speak, but the tears steadily flowed down her cheeks as his words created the mental images. She'd often wondered what exactly had happened, but hearing it was more painful than she'd thought possible.

"They say time heals all wounds, but that's not true. Time made it worse. Time reminded me of all the things that we would never do together. I learned to live with the pain, but it never left. The day you came back, I was torn between being so damn grateful that you were alive and so fucking mad that you were alive."

He saw the hurt flash in her eyes again and immediately realized how the words sounded.

"Not mad that you were alive. That came out wrong. I was angry that you stayed away from me all that time—three long years. I mean, how could you have ever loved me if it was so easy for you to live without me, you know?

"Anyway, when you stayed with me that night, you told me and showed me how much you loved me in so many ways. When I got up the next morning, I actually felt better. I smelled the waffles, and it was like those three years were just a bad dream. You were here with me again."

He next spoke through clenched teeth as he held back the anger and myriad other emotions that swirled in his eyes. "And then I realized you were gone again. I know why you did it. But, Bri, while I was searching for you, all I could do was listen while they beat you and threatened to kill you. I ran into that building just as she was squeezing the trigger. The gun was point-blank at your head… One second later and I would've watched you die!"

He started pacing the floor but kept his eyes on hers as he kept talking. "Brianna, you willingly gave up your life to save me—twice! You are so much stronger than I ever gave you credit for being. I thought I was strong, but you seemed to be just fine without me. I need to understand how that is."

27

CHAPTER TWENTY-SEVEN

Brianna was still and silent as her tears continued to flow. When she heard Noah describe what he went through, the pain she put him through, it tore her heart out. She wanted to explain, to give him some consolation without making excuses. She thought the best way to do that was just to state it.

With a watery voice, she started. "I'd appreciate it if you'd hear me out now. I will tell you whatever you want to know. I want you to know that I don't mean for anything I say to sound like an excuse. I'm only trying to explain my thoughts and feelings, okay?"

Noah nodded and closed the distance between them when he moved back between her legs and rested his hands on her hips. He kissed her forehead and waited for her to gather her thoughts.

With a small smile, she explained. "I'm sure you knew, but I was head over heels in love with you when we first met. I had to leave before you returned from your mission, and it killed me to wear that blindfold. Thinking I might pass you on your way back, get just a glimpse of you, or maybe a wave before I left. And it wasn't luck that I wasn't with another guy when you walked into that bar, Noah. It was love. There was no one else for me after we made love that night in the desert."

He cocked an eyebrow in disbelief, but as agreed, didn't say anything.

"There wasn't. I had offers, a few guys asked me out, but I never went. No one else even held a candle to you. And I'm sure you know this by now, but just in case, I never cheated on you with Richard. Or anyone else, for that matter. Not even in the three years we were apart. That day I went to talk to you and you were busy, I thought you were about to leave me. I had no idea you thought I was seeing him."

He knew she was telling the truth, but he still couldn't believe his ears. *Did she remain faithful to me all that time?* He didn't have to say anything for Brianna to know what he was thinking.

"My heart still belonged to you, Noah. No one else could ever take your place. And even though you didn't know, I still thought of myself as, well, yours, and I would never betray you like that."

"I know it feels like I did betray you, and I can't blame you for feeling that way. I guess, in a way, you're right. I let you believe a lie, even if it was meant for your good. Richard was there when I went on that last assignment. I didn't even know that at first, though. I met my informant, and Richard showed up to kill us both. Then I rushed back to my hotel."

"Richard had already figured out I was investigating him, and he knew I had evidence that proved his guilt and your innocence. He tried to kill me over there. All those innocent people on the plane died in my place. Before I went to Turkey, I had a bad feeling, and I didn't take the evidence with me. I hid it here in the house before I left. I don't know why I did that. I'd never done that before, but something just told me I needed to."

A shudder ran through her body at the thought of what would've happened had she taken it with her. "Anyway, I escaped from him and rushed to the airport. I was running back to you—to tell you everything that had happened. But Richard and his hit man got to the airport before I did, and I couldn't find a way in without them seeing me. So I missed the flight. I was hiding outside the airport, crying as I watched it leave without me. Then it exploded."

She was silent for a minute, tears flowing for all the people who died on that flight, when that explosion was meant for her alone. Noah sensed her pain and lovingly rubbed her arms while he patiently waited for her to continue.

She sniffled and took a deep, calming breath. "At the time, I didn't think about how strange it was that a US Marshal walked out of the airport in the Middle East. My first thought was just that he could get me home to you. So, I gave him the condensed version of what had happened. It wasn't until later that I realized he asked me if I had the evidence on me.

"When I said it was still in the US, that's when he agreed to get me home. But he wouldn't let me come back here to you. I was so scared after everything that had happened. He spun a great story of why I had to go into WITSEC to protect you, especially since you were heavily implicated.

"The Marshal kept asking for all the evidence the whole three years, but I didn't know why until recently. He didn't believe I had given him everything, because I never found his name in it. Well, you heard the rest of that conversation when I was in the car with him. But Richard knew I still had it, too and he wanted it.

"Stevens knew Richard wasn't on the plane, even though he showed on the manifest. I didn't know that for sure until that morning when Rebel said Richard was presumed dead, but not from the plane exploding. When Richard showed up in the paper, I knew he'd found me. And since I was already 'dead,' the only way he could get me to cooperate was through you.

"'I'm sorry doesn't even begin to make up for what I did. There are no words even to explain how sorry I feel for what you went through. I wish I could take it all back. I wish I had run to you anyway and figured out something else. Those three years were pure hell for me, Noah.

"Knowing that you were only a plane ride away from me haunted me. I cried myself to sleep every single night. I wished you were there with me, I wondered whom you were with, and I knew you had to move on with your life. The only thing that kept me going was a small hope that we could be together again one day.

"I was just so alone, Noah. I thought you were leaving me. We had become so distant in those last few weeks before I left for Turkey. I wanted to talk to you and tell you everything, but you barely talked to me. You had even quit sleeping in the bed with me. You started taking night shifts and staying gone. I didn't think you wanted me to live here with you anymore. Then I was in some third world country, and everything went wrong."

She shook her head. "There's still no excuse for hurting you like that. I just want you to try to understand that I couldn't let them destroy you because of me. You would've gone to prison, or they would've killed you. It would've been entirely my fault.

"I believed they would leave you alone if everyone thought I was dead. I thought you were leaving me anyway, so I guess I didn't really think you would've taken the news that badly. I only wanted to protect you, Noah, because I love you so much."

Noah leaned in to kiss her, but she gently stopped him by putting her palms on his chest. He felt her back as it went straight as a rod and her muscles tensed.

"You asked me to marry you, to have a family with you, and there's nothing I want more. But there is something I need to know now. I need you to be honest—with yourself as much as with me."

He nodded and then asked, "What do you need to know?"

"I need to know if…" Her mouth was suddenly dry.

She didn't want to finish the question, because she was afraid of his answer. It could change everything. Her hand went to her stomach as she instinctively protected their baby that grew inside her. Tears filled her eyes as she looked at his handsome face and felt the same anxiety rise in her chest that she felt every night she had slept without him.

Noah tried his best to figure out what was on her mind that had upset her so much. He saw her hand move to her stomach as if she was shielding their baby from something hurtful. He saw the tears well up, even as she tried to fight it. He kept his voice low and soothing. "What, baby? Tell me what you need to know."

She had to know for sure before they could move forward. She knew she had to get the words out. "I need to know if you can forgive me."

Noah didn't answer, but his eyes silently questioned her.

She took a deep breath. "I know you love me and care about me. I know you want our baby. But love isn't all it takes to make a happy marriage and a happy home. If you can't forgive me, if this is always between us, we can't ever really be happy. Everything has happened so quickly with us since I came back here. Maybe you should take some time to be alone and think about it. I will understand if you do."

Noah finally answered. "You're exactly right."

She tentatively asked, "About?"

"We can't be happy without forgiveness. There hasn't been one day that I haven't loved you. Not one day that I didn't want to be with you. I've never wanted you to leave, Bri. Forgive me for ever making you feel that way."

Brianna stared at him like he had lost his mind. That sexy smile crept across his face.

"And I will forgive you if you promise to never, ever, leave me like that again." His face turned serious, as he punctuated each word. "Brianna. I. Can't. Lose. You. Again."

"I promise, Noah. I promise," she cried as she pulled him to her. He kissed her and pulled her into his strong arms.

"NOAH?" BRIANNA'S TONE WAS CAUTIOUS WHEN SHE APPROACHED him as he was working in his home office.

He looked up from his computer screen and smiled. "Hey, baby. Come here." She walked to him, and he pulled her into his lap. He wrapped one arm behind her, and the other hand rested on her baby bump. He kissed her and asked, "What's on your mind?"

"I was just working on the wedding invitations. I know you've never wanted to talk about it before, but I just wanted to ask. Are you sure you don't want to invite your family to the wedding?"

Noah looked down at his hand as it rubbed her belly. "The only family I need is already right here with me." Brianna's hand gently lifted his chin up to look at his eyes.

Noah explained. "Every family has a black sheep, right? In my family, I guess that's me. When I chose the Army over a career in my father's business, he told me never to come back, so I didn't. You, our baby, Bull, Rebel, Shadow, and the rest of the guys—the ones who are always here for me. That's who my real family is, Bri."

Her heart broke for him as she tried to put herself in his place. She tried to picture how she would've reacted if her father had disowned her when she refused to work for him and became an investigative reporter instead. She couldn't imagine her father ever saying she could never come back, then she immediately thought of the baby growing inside her. What kind of parents could do that to their child?

"Do they even know where you are?" She pulled back and looked at him, as he answered.

"Couldn't say. But they don't live too far from here. If they really wanted to find me, my dad has the resources to do it." Noah's voice was flat, but Brianna could feel the undercurrent of hurt in him.

"I was just thinking about how excited my parents are about the baby. After all this time, I bet your family would be thrilled to see you and find out they'll be grandparents soon."

He shook his head. "I don't think so, baby."

She put her arms around his neck and held him tight as she promised, "You will always have me, Noah." She felt his arms tighten around her. "And if you ever decide to talk to them, I will be at your side."

BRIANNA'S WEDDING PLANNER ARRANGED THEIR LATE AUGUST wedding with little effort. Brianna chose a barefoot beach wedding at sunset. Her mother, Diana, and her sister, Missy, both helped Brianna get ready. Brianna loved spending this special time with them. She was about to marry the man of her dreams, and she had her entire family there to share the big day.

"An outdoor wedding. In late August. In Miami. Whose idea was this anyway? I can't do anything with my hair!" Missy had been in front of the mirror for twenty minutes working on the same section of uncooperative hair.

Brianna laughed and threw a hair clip at her. "It was my idea, thank you very much!"

Missy picked up the clip and pulled back the section of hair. With the snap of the clip, she said, "Perfect! Thanks, sissy!" Looking at the time, Missy touched Brianna's shoulder, and her voice hitched when she spoke. "Bri, it's time to get your dress on."

When Brianna looked up at her sister, tears sprang to her eyes when she saw tears glistening in Missy's eyes. Blinking back tears, Brianna chided Missy teasingly. "Don't cry! You're going to make me cry, and I just finished my makeup!"

Brianna stood and hugged Missy. Within a couple of seconds, their mother had wrapped her arms around them both. "I love my girls!"

Missy helped Brianna put on her wedding gown. It was sleeveless with a straight A-line fit and stopped about midthigh. The folds in the fabric lined each side of the dress, starting just above her breasts and extended to her hips in a rounded pattern. The folds gathered at her midline, just below the V-shape in the neckline, by a diamond-encrusted pearl pendant.

Diana took Brianna's hands in hers and held her arms out to the sides as she beheld her daughter. "You look absolutely elegant, Brianna." Tears spilled over Diana's eyelashes, and she dabbed them with a tissue. "I can't tell you how blessed I feel—to have you back, to see you get married, and to know I'll be a grandmother soon." She pulled Brianna in for a tight hug as she whispered, "I'm so proud of you, and I love you so much, Bri."

Brianna couldn't speak. It took every ounce of energy to fight back the tears. So she hugged her mom even tighter.

Diana spoke for her. "Momma knows, Bri." She smiled as she

pulled back from her. "I know, I know—you just finished your makeup."

Just when she thought she would get out of her dressing room without crying, her father showed up at the door. "You are absolutely gorgeous, Brianna. Noah is a very lucky man." Brianna saw water shimmer in Evan's eyes, and the first tears fell before she could stop them when he finished speaking. "How can I give you away? You were my girl first."

Brianna's arms flew around his neck, and she squeezed him tightly. She managed to squeak out, "I'll always be your girl, Daddy."

"All right, enough of the waterworks! You're going to be late for your own wedding!" Missy was back in charge and shooing everyone out of the dressing room. She quickly touched up Brianna's makeup and reassured her. "You look perfect. Ready?"

"Ready."

Brianna and Missy joined Evan outside the dressing room and walked to the staging area, where the wedding coordinator, Emily, waited with Brianna's other bridesmaids—her sisters, Jessie and Ashley. They hugged Brianna just as Bull, Rebel, and Shadow walked up.

The three men pulled Brianna to the side. Bull kissed her cheek as he started. "Sunny, you are glowing. Really. We have a gift for you, and we thought you might want to wear it for the ceremony."

Shadow pulled a square velvet box from his pocket and opened it. Brianna gasped when she saw the necklace. The elegant dog tag hung on a white-gold chain by a diamond-studded lobster clasp. The front of the dog tag was polished white gold, the edges were lined with diamonds, and an infinity symbol was engraved in the middle.

Rebel removed it from the box and said, "Read the back."

"Out loud," called Missy, who had evidently eavesdropped on their conversation. Everyone laughed and gathered closer to Brianna.

Brianna turned the dog tag over, and her hand flew up to cover her heart. She read aloud. "A brother's love never ends." She looked at each man, tears brimming again, unable to speak for a moment. "I love it. I-I can't thank you enough."

She hugged each man, thanking each individually. With a kiss on the cheek, she whispered, "I love you."

Bull then took the necklace and clasped it around her neck. "It looks great on you, Sunny."

Emily said, "It's time, everyone." She motioned for the music to start and sent Jessie and Rebel down the white carpet toward the minister. When Jessie was a quarter of the way down, Ashley and Shadow followed. Bull held out the crook of his arm to Missy, she slipped her hand in, and they started their walk down the aisle.

The music changed to announce the bride as Brianna slipped her arm around Evan's. He looked at her and asked, "Ready, sweetheart?"

She took a deep breath and said, "Ready, Daddy."

They walked out, arm in arm, and Brianna witnessed the perfect sunset. The sky was different shades of pink and purple as the sun shimmered on the water and hung just over the horizon of the ocean. The slight ocean breeze made the humidity and heat at least tolerable.

As they turned the corner to face Noah, Brianna's heart leaped at the sight of him. Noah wore a sky-blue short-sleeve button-down with white cargo shorts. His dark tan against the blue shirt made him look even sexier than usual. She could feel his eyes move over her, take her in, and she saw the admiration in his face. She smiled as she walked toward him and her future.

Noah couldn't move or breathe when Brianna stepped into his line of sight. Everyone else faded away when he saw her, as if they were the only two people in the world. She was more radiant than anyone he had ever seen. And she was all his. His chest swelled with pride as she walked down the aisle, to him, to be his, forever.

Evan had a visibly hard time releasing her when the minister asked who gave her away. His voice was strong as he responded, "Her mother and I do."

But Noah saw Evan squeeze her arm tighter as he said it. As Evan's eyes met Noah's, the unspoken message was unmistakable.

"*Take care of my daughter, or I'll take care of you.*" Noah nodded, hiding his smile, and took Brianna's hands.

After a few words from the minister, he said, "I understand the bride and groom have written their own vows." He nodded to Noah to start reciting his vows.

Bull handed Noah the ring as Noah spoke. "Brianna, I promise to be the best husband I can possibly be. You will have all of my love, all of my heart, and all of me for the rest of my life. I will do everything in my power to protect you, provide for you, and make you the happiest woman in the world, every single day. I love you today, tomorrow, and forever." Noah pushed the ring onto her finger as she watched breathlessly.

Tears brimmed in Brianna's eyes as she took Noah's hand and slid the ring onto his finger. "Noah, since the first day we met, you have been in my heart, on my mind, and my only love. I promise to stand by you, be your soul mate, and support and love you in every way possible. My life starts and ends with you. From this day forward, you are my everything. I will freely give you all of my love, every day, for the rest of my life."

The minister declared, "You may now kiss the bride." Noah took Brianna in his arms and kissed her deeply as the guests cheered. After what felt like forever of taking pictures, the wedding party moved to the reception area. Their friends and family watched as Noah and Brianna took the floor for their first dance as Bryan Adams's song "(Everything I Do) I Do It for You" started playing.

Noah wrapped his arms around her waist as she slipped her arms around his neck. He pulled her as close to him as possible and leaned his head down to whisper in her ear. "I love you, Mrs. Steele. I can't wait to get you away from all these people."

The low timbre of his voice and warm breath so close sent shivers down her spine. She turned her head slightly and kissed him lightly at first, then more passionately. As she pulled back, she whispered, "Let's go find a broom closet somewhere." She felt his chuckle rumble through his chest.

They managed to stay through the rest of the reception before they made their exit. The guests showered them with birdseed on their way to the limo waiting to take them on their honeymoon.

No one noticed the lurking figure watching from the shadows.

Ready for more Steele Security?
Keep reading for a FREE sneak peek at Wicked Ties AND a sneak peek of Fine Line!

WICKED TIES SNEAK PEEK

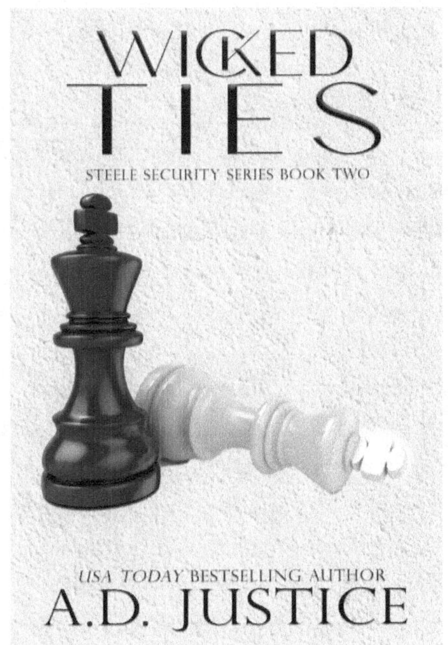

PROLOGUE

"Colt! Coming to you, buddy! Get ready!"

Colt widened his feet and slightly bent his knees, getting into his stance as the batter took a swing. Just as his coach predicted, the ball flew in low toward him in his shortstop position and bounced off the ground once before he caught it and whisked it to first base.

"Out!"

"Great job, Colt!" Colt heard his father call from the stands but he didn't take his eyes off the field. The sun was in his eyes but his baseball cap helped some in shielding his face. The bright spring day was perfect weather for a game. The vividness of the tulips, pansies, and daffodils in bloom colored the landscape. The slight breeze kept the sun from being too hot, but the heat didn't matter to Colt. He played all summer in the sweltering heat and loved every second of it. But this, this was a perfect spring Saturday for baseball with his dad watching.

Colt punched his glove a couple of times and took his stance again as the next batter swung. He loved this—the smell of the dirt, the feel of swinging the bat, and the sting of catching a line-drive. He was only seven, but he knew he wanted to be a professional baseball player when he grew up. That would make his daddy so proud.

"Let's get 'em, son!" He knew his dad's voice anywhere. He could pick it out of the crowd of parents on both sides of the dugouts with his eyes closed. He loved the game, he loved the crowds, he loved everything about baseball—but none of it compared to how much he loved his father.

His father, John, worked a lot of hours and had to travel frequently, but he never failed to make time for Colt. Every day that he was home, John spent time doing something—anything—with Colt. He taught him everything he knew about baseball in their backyard. They had just started working on football, too, since Colt was close to being old enough to start playing on the local recreation league team. But Colt insisted that baseball would always be his first love.

John also made it a point to teach Colt from an early age how to treat a lady. Even at seven years old, Colt could see how much John and his mother, Beth, loved each other. They unfailingly showed one another complete respect and trust. They were affectionate with each other and with Colt—keeping their small town Alabama home as cozy as possible. Colt felt loved, safe, and secure with his parents.

After Colt's team won the game, John took the family out for the standard celebratory dinner of pizza and ice cream. Afterward, John and Beth strolled hand in hand toward their home on the oak-lined street of their small town. Colt was secure on John's broad shoulders and thoroughly enjoyed being able to touch the lowest branches of the trees as they walked and chatted.

Late that very night, Colt heard voices coming from the kitchen. Sneaking out of his bed, he crept down the hallway, crouching low against the wall to keep out of sight. Just as he reached the opening to the kitchen, he heard his parents speaking in hushed tones. He could tell they were concerned about something but he couldn't hear what they were saying. When they started moving toward him, Colt rushed back to his room and jumped in the bed. Several minutes later, John knelt at Colt's bed, ran his fingers through Colt's hair and whispered, "Just remember I love you. Always, son."

The next morning, he woke to his mother's quiet sobs. Walking softly to his parents' room, he saw his mother holding a piece of paper. He silently crept closer and closer to her until he could read the note over her shoulder. She never knew he was there and he silently made his way back to his own room.

He was only seven, but he could read the one line the note contained. And he knew he was forever changed because of those eight little words.

"You and Colt are better off without me."

CHAPTER ONE

The reception for the newlyweds, Mr. and Mrs. Noah and Brianna Steele, was in full swing. They intentionally kept the wedding small, with only immediate family and close friends invited. Some of the close friends in attendance—like Shadow, Rebel and Bull—were all also employees of Steele Security, Noah's security firm located in downtown Miami. The unbreakable bond was sealed between the "brothers" when all the men served together in the Army as Rangers, and finally in a remote area in the Middle East in the clandestine Delta Force unit.

Noah and Brianna exchanged vows at sunset on the beach, with the bride radiantly glowing in her early pregnancy and the groom smiling from ear to ear, like he was the luckiest man in the world. Noah and Brianna's relationship had been through hell and back over the past several years. But with Brianna's return to Miami, they managed to pull the pieces back together and move forward as man and wife, stronger than ever.

Engrossed in their nuptials and having eyes only for each other, neither Noah nor Brianna noticed the figure lurking in the shadows. The one person who tracked their every move, while keeping out of sight of the guests, the wedding planner, the caterer, and other workers. The one uninvited guest, who had crashed their private party, but remained unannounced, unseen, and unheard. The one who patiently waited for the right opportunity to make a move toward the happy couple.

When the wedding party moved inside an outdoor event tent, the uninvited visitor patiently waited outside. There were plenty of ways to blend into the background—to be invisible and silent—when it was absolutely necessary. This was one of those times. It was absolutely necessary to keep quiet and stay hidden. The intruder's sole focus was to wait them out, knowing that they eventually would *have* to leave the sanctity of the tent and head for their waiting limousine.

The intruder patiently waited as the wedding guests danced, laughed, and thoroughly enjoyed themselves inside the fully air-conditioned tent. For everyone except the blushing bride, the champagne flowed freely.

Bull, Rebel, and Shadow all met Brianna in the Middle East when she was on assignment as an investigative reporter. They were actually her assignment, but in a short span of time, they developed a close relationship. They became her brothers, in the same manner that Noah was their brother, and they each took that unspoken oath seriously.

Bull's commitment to Brianna and Noah was unconditional and unwavering. As Brianna and Noah's brother, he felt a keen responsibility to keeping them safe, watching their backs, and being available whenever they needed him. He loved Brianna like the little sister he never had and she had more than proven her worth in his eyes.

Brianna shared dances with her new husband, Noah, and then with Shadow and Rebel, throughout the evening. But Bull waited until the end of the evening to request his dance. He viewed his relationship with Brianna as a special one. He didn't easily trust people and she had earned his trust—actually twice in one lifetime. *No one* had ever lost his trust and then won it back again. No one until Brianna, that is.

"Can I have this dance?" Bull's smile lit up his handsome face as he leaned down and offered his arm to Brianna. She had just taken a seat next to her husband to rest her weary, swelling feet when Bull approached.

When Brianna first met the team, it was Bull who was the hardest for her to get to know. She knew right away that he regarded loyalty and trust as the ultimate test of friendship. If anyone failed that test, they would never get another chance. For those who passed the test, they would never find a more loyal friend.

"I don't know if that's a good idea, man. Her feet are-," Noah started to respond, but Brianna cut him off.

"It's okay, Noah," she patted his arm and turned to Bull, smiling warmly. "I would love to dance with my brother. I thought he'd never ask." Brianna smiled as she stood and walked to the dance floor with Bull.

Noah smiled proudly as he watched one of his best friends walk off with his glowing bride on his arm. There was no jealousy in their relationship. Noah knew very well how Bull viewed allegiance, honor, and trust in their tight-knit group. He knew when he met Brianna in the desert that he would one day marry her. There was absolutely no reason to ever question her love and faithfulness to him. She'd already proven that to him with everything they had been through.

Bull was hurt when he thought Brianna had betrayed him. His trust in her was temporarily shattered. After she revealed the truth, and Bull understood all the events of the past, he realized he had been wrong about Brianna's intentions.

When Noah thought about it, he had to admit to himself that he was relieved that Bull was able to forgive Brianna for her breaching his trust—even if it was for a good cause. It would've been hell living between the two strong-willed, hard headed people he loved had Bull not relented.

Arm in arm, Bull escorted Brianna to the dance floor and gently twirled her around to face him as they began swaying to the slow music. Bull looked around the tent, taking in all the happy faces, the toasts and cheers accompanied by glasses clinking. The bride and groom's deep-rooted love was evident to anyone who even glanced at either of them. He knew his friends would have a perfect life together. Not that there would never be problems, but their trials had only made them stronger and better prepared to face whatever the future may bring.

Bull had accepted long ago that he would never have *this*—a wife, someone who holds his heart, someone with whom to share his thoughts or someone he could trust with every facet of his life. He was happy for his friends but it just could never be in his cards. That decision was made for him—inside him—long ago. He didn't share his feelings, dreams, fears—or his love—with anyone outside of his group. He sure as hell didn't give his heart away to anyone who could hurt him.

"You look gorgeous, Sunny," Bull said, referring to her with the nickname she'd earned when she first met them while on assignment. "It was a beautiful wedding and Noah is a lucky man. I can't wait to be an uncle and help Noah teach that baby boy a few hand-to-hand techniques."

Brianna burst out laughing and put her forehead on Bull's expansive chest. His high school football coach gave him that nickname because of his enormous and formidable stature. Following through on his duties was tantamount to his sense of honor—and one of his duties was to be an uncle to the baby growing inside of her. And his honor would not be impugned.

Brianna shook her head in only slight disbelief at his statement and asked, "What if it's a girl?"

With an equally serious face and tone of voice, Bull answered. "She can learn, too."

When Brianna laughed, Bull finally conceded and laughed along with her. "Seriously, Brianna, I am looking forward to being an uncle. You and Noah will be great parents."

"Thank you, Bull. That's so sweet of you. I mean that," Brianna responded before straining on her tiptoes to kiss his cheek.

"I want you to have fun on your honeymoon, but I want you to be careful, too, Bri. Don't leave Noah's side if you can help it. I don't want anything to happen to you. *Promise me.*" His smile was gone and so was any glint of humor. He was instantly back on soldier duty and she was his charge.

Bull's sudden seriousness and frankness caught her by complete surprise. Bull was normally a man of few words, but when he did find it necessary to issue a command, he meant what he said. For him to specifically ask her to stay close to Noah and be careful meant he knew something she didn't know. She'd learned that much about him, and she also knew better than to quiz him about it. Years of working on a "need to know" basis made him keep information to himself much more than the average person.

Still, Brianna searched his eyes for any trace of worry or any other sliver of information she could use later to pry everything out of Noah. Bull felt her penetrating stare, knew what she was looking for, and steeled himself against it. The last thing he wanted was to add undue stress on her, especially while she was pregnant, but he learned to rely on his instincts many years ago. Those instincts had kept him alive in many hazardous conditions.

Realizing she would have better luck penetrating Fort Knox than penetrating Bull's thoughts and feelings, Brianna nodded in agreement. She responded, "I promise, Bull. I don't intend to leave Noah's side the whole two weeks unless I absolutely have to."

Satisfied with her word, Bull escorted her back to Noah, who waited patiently at the bride and groom table. As they approached, Bull watched Noah's eyes take in his new wife. He was amazed with how they instantly filled with love and admiration every time Noah looked at Brianna. They also demonstrated how possessive and protective he was of Brianna.

He became even more possessive and protective of her after he learned of her pregnancy. In honor of the love that flowed between Noah and Brianna, Bull made a silent oath to do whatever it took to keep Brianna safe. He meant what he said—he was looking forward to being an uncle and he would use any means necessary to protect his family.

Noah's eyes reluctantly left Brianna and met Bull's. Brianna saw the immediate shift in Noah's demeanor—the crinkling of the outer corners of his eyes, the hard set of his jaw, and the deep breath he inhaled that drew Noah up even taller than his normal Greek-god self. She knew he saw something in Bull's countenance that set him on guard. Noah and Bull had worked together for too long and had too many full conversations without ever saying a word for Noah to have missed it. She just wished *she* knew what it was.

Noah took Bri's hand and pulled her into him for a full body embrace. Since he towered over her, Brianna couldn't see the looks he and Bull exchanged or even guess at what the looks conveyed to the other. When she pulled back, Noah lowered his head and gently brushed his lips on hers, his hands on either side of her face, then deepened it to kiss her thoroughly and completely.

It really didn't matter how many times he'd kissed her in exactly that manner, every time made her weak in the knees and gave her heart palpitations. Mr. Noah Steele was one fine specimen of a man, and she was so thankful that their lives were reunited.

"It's time to go on our honeymoon, *Mrs. Steele*. Let me take you away from here now," Noah whispered seductively to Brianna. Brianna knew full well that his words held a triple meaning. It actually was time to leave, he wanted to get her alone, and he knew something was wrong and he wanted her as far away from it as possible. She decided to go with the meaning that she liked the most.

"Take me away, Mr. Steele. *Take. Me. Away*," she replied as she wrapped her arms around his neck, stretched on her tiptoes, and kissed him back. As his strong arms wrapped around her, she forgot about Bull's warning. She forgot about the guests who were most likely watching. She forgot about anything and everything else that the world wanted to throw at them.

It was time for her honeymoon with the man she loved.

Keep reading here: Wicked Ties (Book 2)

FINE LINE SNEAK PEEK

Prologue

A Terrible Idea
Nick

"For the record, this is a terrible idea."

My director, Calvin Montgomery, locks his angry eyes on me while speaking to the handler who will be assigned to me—if Calvin approves the operation, that is.

"Sir, Special Agent Nick Tucker has repeatedly proved what a valuable asset he is in the field. He's one of our best. He has outscored most of his peers in both field and psychological profile tests—even those who have previous undercover experience. We can't deny the man has the skills we need on this assignment. He deserves this chance."

"Yes, I can read the reports as well as you can, Jack. But Nick doesn't have any true undercover experience—not even on short-term cases, and the others do. Maybe they didn't score as well on the psych tests because they're already accustomed to living among the criminal element and acting as one of them. Did that ever occur to you? We both know how hard this life is even for a few months, but the case you're asking me to put Nick on is potentially a multi-year mission."

Calvin turns his penetrating gaze to me, constantly assessing my every reaction, looking for a weakness and a reason to deny my involvement. I've been in hectic firefights before and kept my cool, though. My time in the military, working for Steele Security, and providing private security for billionaire Dominic Powers before joining the DEA prepared me for most every perilous situation they can throw at me. Drawing on my inner strength, I keep my expression passive, my breathing regular, and my instinct to remind him he's driven a desk for too many years to remember what working in the field is actually like under wraps.

"You'll be cut off from everyone you know, Nick. You'll essentially divorce your entire life—for years. Your friends, your family, wife, girlfriend, boyfriend. *Everyone.* You hear me? And that's the easy part of the job. Even contact with Jack will be sparse, especially due to the group you'll infiltrate, so you'll be making decisions on the fly. Any outside affiliation will be scrutinized—and these guys won't ask questions first. They'll shoot you in the head and replace you with the next guy in line. I'm not convinced you truly understand what you'll have to do to be one of them."

"I can assure you, I do understand."

"Is that right? This UC op has been issued special permission to break the very laws you've sworn to uphold. Your psych profile shows a strong sense of duty and a penchant for following the rules to the letter. So, you'd be fine if they order you to force some young kid to sell drugs on the street corner and bring you every penny of the money he made? Then rough him up if he doesn't bring you enough?"

The visual that pops into my brain before I can stop it makes my heart rate increase instantly, the artery in my neck jerking and giving away my reaction.

"Or maybe it's not a him. Maybe it's a her. You'd willingly force a young woman into prostitution, selling her to any Joe Blow off the street, who'll do whatever the fuck he wants to do to her? You can make them believe you don't care about her at all, just how much money she brings in for getting her John's rocks off? What if that means her customer gets to beat the shit out of her just because he has mommy issues? I mean, as long as he doesn't kill her and she can perform for her next trick, what the fuck does it matter, right?"

My stomach churns with disgust, and the room around me turns red with my rage. But I tamp down those feelings inside my chest until they form a mangled ball full of drive and determination to see this through to the end.

"I'll do whatever the fuck I have to do to stop these bastards. The longer we sit here repeatedly arguing the same points and imagining hypothetical situations, the more time they have to commit those very crimes. Sir."

"I'm sure I don't have to remind you we're after the major charges to shut them down for good. Small-time hoods are a dime a dozen. We want the source—their suppliers. Local reports say this group is using a prescription drug that hasn't even cleared the FDA yet. It's highly effective and lethal in the wrong hands. That's in addition to the influx of opioids and other controlled substances from their Mexican drug cartel affiliation. We can't blow the entire operation because you feel the need to feed your savior complex over every sob story you hear. Most of those women asked for it anyway—they probably even enjoy it."

"I'm well aware of what we're after and how to do my job." Inside, I'm seething; outside, I display a calm demeanor.

He's testing me, that much I know. His last comment was to gauge my knee-jerk reaction because that's exactly how this gang thinks. If Calvin approves my request for undercover work, the group I'll join will say and do a lot worse to me than my director has ever even thought about. If I can't handle my boss yanking my chain inside the comfort of his office in our secure, air-conditioned building, I have no business being an undercover agent where anything and everything can go wrong.

Will go wrong.

Something always does.

To stay alive, I have to think fast on my feet, improvise, and give an award-winning performance.

No time like the present to start earning a few of those golden statuettes.

"Sir, I can handle anything they throw at me. I've been in intense situations in my career, starting in the Army, through private details, and in my time with the DEA. I'm ready to take my career to the next level, and I need undercover experience to do that. This wasn't Jack's idea—I requested to be assigned to this case."

The muscles around Calvin's eyes contract, crinkling the skin until only small slits remain. He draws a slow circle around his mouth with his thumb and forefinger before resting his chin on his hand. With my gaze locked on to his, I wait for him to make his decision. The first one to blink will be Calvin, because I am all in.

"All right, Special Agent Tucker, you've convinced me to give you a chance. On one condition."

"What condition is that?"

"If at any time you suspect your cover is blown, or your gut warns you that something is off and they've turned on you, get out of there. To hell with the case and the charges. Call Jack, get to the safe house, do whatever it takes to extract yourself from the situation."

"I appreciate your concern, sir, but it won't come to that. I'll see this through till the end."

"All right. We'll get your name, background, and criminal history established. Congratulations, Nick. You have the distinct honor of pledging to one of the most notorious motorcycle gangs in the world. The Devil's Dominion rules their LA territory with an iron fist. I only hope they don't turn that fist on you."

"Thank you, sir. I won't let you down."

~

Six Months Later

"Are you sure you're ready to approach them, Nick? No need to rush things." Jack paces in his kitchen while I sit at the table and finish my coffee.

Jack Collins fits the bill for a retired biker. He is a handler, but he's curated his entire life around the motorcycle club lifestyle to avoid arousing any suspicions. He hasn't pledged to any outfit, but he is known by enough bikers that no one questions his presence, and no one crosses him. He has the don't-fuck-with-me air down pat.

His long black and gray hair is pulled back in a low ponytail. His sun-weathered skin bears the ravages of years on the open road—the deep-set wrinkles, the sunspots, the year-round dark tan. His brown eyes are keen, assessing a man and his intentions with a quick glance. The skin on his hands matches his face, but his grip is as strong as a man half his age. The long span of his career gives him advantages others could only hope to attain one day.

"It's time, Jack. You're my handler, you know I'm ready, and you know that shit is escalating out there. My hair has grown out, along with my beard. All my ink is finished—nothing overly distinguishable but still believable. My criminal background is airtight, and my stints in San Quentin and Pelican Bay legitimize my badass felon status."

"You can't use words like *legitimize* around these guys, Nick." Jack scrubs his hand down his face.

"I can talk real dumb too, Jack. Like I ain't got no schooling or nothing."

"Make fun of this all you want, Nick. But I'm telling you, these guys have a grittiness about them, a certain way they talk, a language all their own. It's a combination of the motorcycle gang lingo and prison slang."

"Trust me, I got this. I've mastered how they speak, the motorcycle gang terms, and the prison slang. I've memorized my background and rehearsed how I became a badass ex-convict, looking to join the baddest MC club around. One point that is pure genius on your part is showing I was part of a Tijuana-based gang before I was sent to prison. Thanks for that."

"Anything I can do to keep you from having to murder someone as part of your initiation. Because that's what they usually require—and could still order you to do it. But we'll cross that bridge when we have to. If you can patch in, you won't have to do the lowly probie bullshit. That'll at least give you a leg up in earning their trust and working your way up the chain faster than most.

"If you have to improvise and add anything to your history, don't forget to tell me immediately. We can build your experience around whatever you need, but it could take a little time to get it on paper. And don't say gang. You know how one-percenters feel about that word."

"Striking the word gang from my vocabulary now. And I'll try to keep the improvisation to a minimum, but I'm sure it'll come up. My documented history is solid, but that doesn't account for the things I never got caught doing. If you happen to have any former gang members in your back pocket, that would be useful too."

"I'll see what I can do. You never know, this old dog may still have a few tricks you don't know about."

One thing about Jack Collins, he always has another trick up his sleeve no one else knows about. How he stayed one step ahead of the agents under his charge when he went weeks without hearing from them is a mystery in our world. He takes his job home with him every night, and the safety of his agents is his first priority. I know I am in good hands.

"Thanks for the coffee. I'm heading back to my dinky little apartment to get into character. They're having a party at their clubhouse tomorrow night, so I'll use that opportunity to make my presence known."

"Good luck, kid. Don't die."

"That's the nicest thing you've ever said to me, Jack." I smile over my shoulder as I leave his bachelor pad and climb onto my bike.

My new life waits for me, in the gritty, dirty underbelly of the criminal world. Getting the approval for this level of undercover work is a boost to my ego and a rush to my senses. The heightened danger, constantly surveilling my surroundings, and testing my ability to decipher friend from foe within a matter of seconds will take my career to the next level.

I feel as if I've found my purpose in life. Finally.

~

Major Mistakes
Savannah

The woman staring at me looks familiar, but I don't know her. Not anymore anyway. Her red hair is longer than when she was younger. Her deep green eyes hold so many secrets, ones she'll never tell. She's also much thinner than she used to be—a telltale sign of stress and depression settling in over the long haul. The sad fact is, I used to know her very well. But now she's only the outer shell of the vibrant, bubbly personality I remember from just a couple of years ago. The light in her eyes is dim now, barely perceptible even when I'm searching for it.

"When did this happen, exactly? How did I become *this* woman?" I stare into the hollow green eyes reflected in the mirror, talking to myself. Again.

A loud bang on my apartment door abruptly ends my one-sided conversation. My heart drops, and a groan escapes from my throat. Dread covers me like a lead blanket. There's only one person that can be…the one person I really don't want to see, much less spend the evening around. But I don't have a choice. I'm trapped, like a frightened, timid animal in a cage.

After removing the door chain and unlocking the multiple bolts I had installed, the door swings open before I can even grab the knob.

"Why the fuck do you have the door locked like that? Who are you hiding in here?" Butch pushes past me, moving from one room to the next through my apartment as he searches for the invisible man.

"There's no one here except me. Just like last time. And the time before that. You know I always keep all the door locks in place when I'm here alone."

It's a phobia I have—an intense fear that drives me to check the locks several times before going to bed every night. He knows this about me, because he's complained about it every time he's stayed at my apartment. Thankfully, that hasn't happened in a very long time.

He stomps toward me in his heavy leather boots, the ones he wears every day because they best protect his feet and ankles while he's riding his motorcycle. It's strange how what I initially thought was intriguing, dangerous, and sexy about him when we met are the very traits that make me want to run away and start a new life somewhere else today.

I just haven't figured out how to get away from him yet.

"Pack all your shit. We're leaving."

"What?" I whirl around on my heel and stare at him, completely dumbfounded.

"We're moving. Prez is sending me and a couple of other guys to DC to induct a smaller club into ours. We have to try them out, see if they're worthy enough to wear the Devil's Dominion colors. This is my chance to show him I'm officer material and get on the voting ballot to move up in the club. I've been waiting years for this day."

The only thought in my mind is that my opportunity to get away from him is finally here. The day I've been waiting to come for far too long. There's no way I can move from LA to DC—they're at completely opposite ends of the country. Literally from one coast to the other. My entire life is here in LA, including my job and the few friends I had before I started seeing Butch.

Maybe my friends will take me back when I get rid of him.

"That's great news for you, Butch. I'm glad the president finally sees your potential in the club, and I hope they make you an officer soon. But I can't just up and move across country with you. My job is here—my entire career I've worked years to establish. I also have a lease on this apartment I can't just break."

I'm listing every logical reason I can think of, no matter how lame it will inevitably sound to him. He doesn't care about excuses—he only cares about results. More specifically, he only cares about the results he wants to see.

"Wouldn't that just fucking thrill you? Wouldn't you just love for me to go across the fucking country for the next six months and leave you here alone so you can fuck every swinging dick that crosses your path? Of course you're going with me, you stupid bitch. Who the fuck do you think is gonna drive the truck behind us and haul our shit across the country? All our stuff won't fit on our fucking bikes, you moron. Now, pack your shit like I said."

With his final command, he shoves me and slams my head into the wall, catching the edge of the doorframe with the full blunt force of the impact. Even with my eyes closed, I can feel the room spinning. Nausea settles into my gut and the bile churns, threatening to work its way up my throat. The pain in my skull makes me whimper. His only reply is a disgusted huff.

"Now, rent the fucking moving truck, pack your shit, and let's go to DC before I'm too old to ride my damn bike anymore."

After I hear the door open, he hurls one last threat at me. "If you even think of trying to get out of this, I'll kill every single person you love. All your fucking friends from the hospital. Your mom. Your sister. Try me, bitch. I dare you."

He stomps out, the chains on his boots and belt clinking with every step, growing fainter until I hear the engine of his bike roar to life. Funny, or not funny, how it reminds me so much of his own terrible roar. After he rides away, I open my eyes and gingerly move off the wall where he left me.

The door to my apartment is standing wide open.

He knows my paralyzing fear of leaving the door unlocked. Irrational or not, it's still there.

I want to rush to lock every bolt, but the first step in that direction reminds me of my head injury. The disorientation, nausea, and I are not new friends. With slow movements, I lift my hand to feel the goose egg forming behind my ear. I'm not even surprised to find blood on my fingers when I lower my arm again.

My walk to the door is slow as I calculate each step and how much farther I have to go. My chest is heaving from the building anxiety. When the door is finally locked—every bolt is secured and every chain is in place, my pounding heart slows enough so I can breathe normally again.

After I put a cold compress on the back of my head, I slide onto the couch and carefully lie back on the throw pillows. I waste a few minutes daydreaming about never leaving my apartment again, never unlocking the door again, while waiting for the throbbing in my head to subside. As often as I dream about this, I should've already found the master plan for leaving Butch in my dust.

Since nothing else I've tried so far has worked, I pick up my laptop and rent the moving van as the asshole commanded. A one-way trip to Washington, DC coming up, sans the excitement a cross-country trip should elicit. The only way I can describe how I feel about what I just did is I'm positive I've just signed my own death certificate.

In fact, the longer I'm around Butch, the more I realize that outcome is inevitable—it's only a matter of time. The odds there will come a day when it's him or me increase with our every encounter. I let my eyes drift up to the ceiling, staring at nothing in particular while thinking about my situation. My job as an emergency room nurse is stressful and adrenaline-filled, but it pales in comparison to a single interaction with Butch. In an ironic twist, I would be required by law to report potential domestic abuse if one of my patients presented with the same signs I bear.

He wasn't always like this. When I first met him, the tall, muscular, brooding man was much sexier. His brown hair was longer than other men I'd dated before, but it gave him an edgier appearance. Eyes so brown they're almost black sparkled with playfulness and teasing. But it was all a charade—he was pretending to be someone he wasn't. And he was so good at it for so long—long enough to ensure I fell for him. Long enough to ensure I was caught in his trap. When I look at him now, all I see is the ugliness inside. Any desire that once burned for him has long been doused.

Thankfully, those nights with him have dwindled to an occasional visit—and only when he needs me to do something for him. He disappeared for a couple of weeks one time, and I thought he'd found someone else to prey upon. Selfishly, I hoped he had—but then I immediately felt bad for wishing him on anyone else. Unfortunately, one day, he simply walked back into my apartment as if he'd been here all along. No explanation. No questions.

His visits have been sporadic since that day. Usually when he's drunk and looking for somewhere to crash after a night out with his friends. He passes out in my bed, and I sleep on the couch, unable to stand being in the same room with him any longer than absolutely necessary. His insane jealousy makes no sense to me whatsoever. We are not a couple and haven't been for a very long time, yet he calls me every name in the book when he accuses me of seeing other men.

Not that I'm the least bit interested in even trying to date. I still can't get rid of the last mistake I made.

Now he shows up and demands I move across the country with him. I'm having a hard time wrapping my head around this one. It's not like either of us wants to be with the other. That much is clear. But I believe he'll make good on his threat to kill everyone I love. In fact, I have no doubt he will.

One problem at a time, though. Before we even reach the East Coast, I have to survive the actual 3,000-mile trip with him and his buddies. That should be fun—waiting for them to pass out on the bed from the abundance of drugs and alcohol so I can grab the extra linens and sleep on the nasty floor. But I prefer the floor over touching any of them. Maybe I'll sleep in the truck…with the doors locked…under the guise of protecting our belongings.

A few hours later when I walk into the hospital for the night shift, my heart is heavy, and all my feelings show on my face. My coworker takes one look at me, and her face falls.

"What has Butch done now?" Stella puts her hands on her hips and draws in a deep breath. She already knows she won't like the answer.

After explaining the series of events and the commandment Butch issued, I watch her face for the disappointment I know will come. On one hand, I completely understand it, and I was even the same way…before I became the abused and battered victim. Life is now divided into two sections: BB and AB. Before Butch and After Butch.

Before Butch, I said no man would ever lay a hand on me and live to tell about it.

No man would ever abuse me in any way—physically, mentally, or verbally. I would leave him in a heartbeat.

No man would replace my job, my dreams, or my friends—the sacred relationships I'd always held so dear.

After Butch, I withdrew from my friends.

My dreams took a back seat.

Self-esteem was what others had, but not me.

I miss the Before Butch version of myself. But now I feel as if I'm in too deep and can't claw my way out. One thing I've realized after looking back over the past eighteen months is none of this happened suddenly. He chipped away at the very core of me little by little, bit by bit, day by day. Until the very spark that made me *me* disappeared. And I allowed him to do it.

It's my fault.

If I'd been stronger, smarter, faster…maybe I would've seen the warning signs for what they really were.

Huge signs that flashed "Bridge Out Ahead."

But his apologies were so sincere at first. So heartfelt. He was remorseful and promised those bad things would never happen again.

He'd drunk too much. He always liked to fight when he drank. Such a man's man.

He was under too much stress. Work was a constant sore spot. His coworkers or his boss never liked him. They always made up a reason to get rid of him.

Of course, that was before I found out the truth about him. Before I understood what being in a one-percenter motorcycle club really meant. When I made the mistake of calling his club a gang during a heated argument, I saw stars after he backhanded me for disrespecting his brothers.

That was the day the apologies stopped and the real threats began. Old ladies didn't leave bona fide club members. Ever. It wasn't the woman's decision whether to stay or go. She just did what she was told and lived with what she got. He warned me to be glad I wasn't a sheep—one of the women they pass around to each other indiscriminately, using at will for any hedonistic pleasure they wanted to indulge in at the moment.

Ignoring the pleas and concern in Stella's eyes, I continue updating her on my plans. "I'm turning in my two-week notice tonight. That date was the earliest I could get a moving truck big enough for my stuff plus theirs anyway. I'm so glad it has a towing hitch for my car too."

I leave Stella, disappointed expression and all, to start my rounds and focus on the emergency cases. I wish I could stop time so my shift would never end. But working in busy emergency rooms always makes the time go by faster than the slower pace, comparatively, on the medical-surgical floors. Before I know it, the sun rises and a new day dawns, and I have to face the unpleasantness of packing all my belongings.

Two weeks will pass in the blink of an eye.

～

The Initiation
Nick

"You ready for tonight?" Jack's serious expression gives away his thoughts. Unusual for him after the years of handling undercover officers.

"I'm as ready as I'll ever be." I slide my arm into my cut and complete the persona of Renegade.

Turns out, the idea to convince them I was part of a Tijuana-based club was a stroke of genius on Jack's part. The Devils' ties to the Mexican cartel are already in place, but with my joining them, the full backing of the cartel is implied, giving them more muscle than they already have. An ATF agent has been working a few members of that gang over the last several years, so interagency cooperation kicked in, and my alibi was instantly airtight. With my background in prison and ties to the Mexican cartel-sanctioned motorcycle club firmly in place, I approached the Devils with an offer they couldn't refuse.

The Devils' already long reach just increased with no effort on their part. At least as far as their reputation with rival clubs is concerned. Keeping those other clubs at arm's length while the Devils conduct business is vital to maintaining their dominance in the territory. When the club president realized the possibilities I could bring, the dollar signs in his eyes were so bright, they rivaled the neon signs of the Vegas strip.

Headbanger, also known as Bobby Blalock, is the club president. He has a rap sheet longer than my leg, along with countless other crimes he's never been charged with committing. Or ordering. His officers and many other members are all too eager to carry out plans on his behalf. They're brothers in colors, but they're also all vying for the attention of one man. The one who can make or break them in the club.

Tonight is initiation for a few new prospects who are on their way to becoming full patch members. The ceremony to patch in is a big deal to these guys—it seals their identity and their place in the family.

I've been riding with the Devils for the past two weeks. Hanging out with them in the clubhouse provides a completely unique perspective on the inner workings of a notorious outlaw gang. Some of the guys have done hard time, and it's a miracle most aren't still in prison. I've had to bite my tongue way too many times already—something my director knew about me before he approved the assignment.

My moral compass always points due north. Always.

Their skewed sense of right and wrong doesn't mesh well with me. In fact, we're like oil and water at the very core. The only peace I have is when we're on the open road, the wind whipping around me, and the road rushing by under my wheels. The sense of freedom on a motorcycle is the sole only thing I have in common with these guys. It's the only time we're even remotely on the same page.

The long ride to the initiation grounds in the hot, arid desert of Southern California gives me time to get myself back into character. Jack stressed over and over how I have to be part of the group to avoid suspicion. Because of the high stakes, I've been given special clearance to break the laws I've sworn to uphold. But there are oaths I've taken, and I have no intention of reneging on them.

There are lines I refuse to cross.

There are rules I refuse to break—even for the greater good and the thrill of closing the case.

But I have to act like there are no lines I won't cross. To be convincing, I have to put Nick Tucker away and be Renegade to the bone. In my mind, I have to think of Renegade as a completely different person. It's the only way I can pull this off.

He's an ex-con, fresh out of a maximum-security prison, and that has to be my persona. As a convicted felon on parole, I can't legally cross the border to ride with my old club because the pigs will nab Renegade immediately. I can't exactly drive my motorcycle through the underground tunnels to cross the border. Of course, as Renegade, I have the contacts, so I could find an illegal way, like a fake passport or hidden in a caravan. But I'd take that risk only for a golden opportunity, a sure thing.

Renegade has talked a good game in his two weeks with the Devils. Tonight, Prez will present me with the final piece of my colors—the top rocker panel for my cut—because I scored the largest shipment of meth and negotiated the best deal for the club he's ever seen. Compliments of my DEA and ATF friends.

When I finally roll up to their private hideaway in the desert, my Renegade character is in full swing. After grabbing a couple of beers from the cooler, I stroll over to where the officers are hanging out with a few of the lifers—the men who have been part of the club for so long, they aren't required to attend all church meetings and outings anymore, but they're every bit a part of the club as any other member. They can come and go as they please, though most stay more than they leave. This is the only life they know.

"Good of you to bring me a beer, Renegade." Axle reaches for one of the longneck bottles I'm carrying, so I hand it over without a fuss. He's one of the most respected lifers in the group. His experience combined with his naturally level head makes for a powerful ally in a group of trigger-happy thugs. Despite Axle's advanced age and lack of officer status, no man in this group wants to tangle with him.

"You know I always got your back, Ax."

"Back atcha, kid." He takes a long pull from the bottle but keeps his eyes locked on mine. "Heard about that big score you got for us. I'm impressed—and I don't impress easily. Good job."

"Appreciate it, man. Just glad I could help out."

"Well, well, look who's coming our way. The new prospects are here, and they brought their offerings to the Devils with them." Nutcrusher, the club vice president, stands and rubs his hands together, eager to get down to business.

When I glance over my shoulder at the approaching prospects, my stomach drops to my knees and my empty hand curls into a tight fist.

Their "offerings" are new sheep, women being shoved into the midst of the already rowdy scene. The three prospects are each forcing a woman to walk in front of them. The women alternate from stumbling ahead a few steps to digging their heels in to try to stop, only to be shoved from behind and start the process all over again. Their eyes are wide and full of fear. Their faces are tear-stained and their hair is disheveled—and not from the ride here since they arrived in the club van.

I'm positive these three women have already been used as offerings before the new patches ever brought them to meet the brothers. Before I consciously realize I'm moving, my feet develop a mind of their own and take a step forward. Then I feel a hand on my shoulder, holding me back.

"What you see tonight will test your mettle, boy. You've never been around anything like this, I can already tell. But I guarantee, if you blow your cover now, you'll never see anything at all, ever again."

Shocked by his words, I whip my head around and meet Axle's knowing gaze.

"Use it, kid. Use everything you have to see and do as a member to take them down. As shitty as it sounds, you can't save these women and do what you came here to do at the same time. Keep your eyes on the end goal, son, and make them pay for their crimes when it's all said and done."

"What are you talking about, Axle?" He knows. We both know he knows. But I'll be damned if I'll blow my own cover.

"I'm CIA, Nick Tucker from the DEA family. I've been on this case for a long time, waiting for my foreign target to make his move so I can take him down. I told you, I got your back."

"The CIA can't operate on US soil, Ax. Everyone knows that."

His grin resembles one connected to an inside joke. Everyone else is clueless, and one person holds all the aces in his hand. "Sure we don't. I'm on loan to whichever agency wants to take the credit for the bust when it goes down. If you're still here when it happens, maybe that'll be the DEA."

Before I can reply, the shrill shriek of a woman's scream combined with ripping fabric fills the air, making my guts churn with disgust. Any man who would lay a hand on a woman in anger or abuse is no man at all. He's a pussy who knows he couldn't stand toe-to-toe with a real man.

The crowd that gathers around the three women—to watch, to encourage, or to participate—are the worst of the underworld. Preying on the defenseless and taking advantage of those who are hanging on by a thread as it is.

"Come with me, Renegade. This is as good as this scene gets. It's all downhill from here, and I don't think you can stop yourself from intervening yet." Axle guides me away from the ruckus.

I can still hear their pleas to stop. Their screams that echo through the desert air. Their cries for someone to please help them…to make it stop.

But I do nothing.

What kind of man does that make me?

"When they finish with the girls, they'll take them back to the clubhouse, and the club doctor will patch them up. They'll use them as sheep, or they'll cycle them into the prostitution ring and run them on the streets. They're not easy on them, but they don't permanently damage them either. Headbanger has a strict rule on that part since it affects his cash flow."

"Axle, your explanation doesn't help me one fucking bit. Do you even hear yourself? Of course they're permanently damaged now. Maybe not in the way you meant, but they still are." He nods in understanding, and he knows he can't say much more to justify what we've witnessed. "Where did they get those girls? Did they kidnap them?"

"No. They pick up hitchhikers or strays. Bring them into the family. Give them food, a place to sleep, and the protection of a notorious motorcycle club. But they expect the girls to earn their keep one way or another. This may be the first time you've ever seen this, but it won't be the last. It won't even be the worst thing you've seen by the time your undercover operation ends."

The silence between us only seems to amplify the mixture of screams and catcalls behind us.

"Talk to me, Axle. Tell me about life in the CIA. Were you in the service? Anything, man. Talk about the fucking weather. I don't care."

"This gets easier, kid. You'll learn to compartmentalize shit like this. Picture those assholes in prison orange, enduring the same fate they're subjecting those girls to right now at the hands of a big, angry brute in their cell, where they have nowhere else to run. Then make that your end goal and sole mission in life. Find what gets you through the rough spots one day at a time. Your assignment will be over before you know it. Then you can put all this bullshit behind you."

I don't see that happening.

~

Chapter One

Savannah—Two Years Later

"We're moving you out of that apartment today. I've been waiting for this day forever. No more excuses about waiting until your lease is up." Karen slings her backpack over her shoulder and jingles her car keys in her hand. "Let's go do this."

"What if he's still there?"

"That's why my husband and his friends are meeting us. We need their muscles to carry your furniture, and the fact that they're all cops doesn't hurt either." Karen smiles broadly, knowing Butch wouldn't dare start something with them around. "You know, you're welcome to stay with Spencer and me anytime you want. For example, if you wake up in the middle of the night scared and don't want to be alone anymore. Or if you just want to have a slumber party full of alcohol and junk food. Just show up at my house and make yourself at home."

"That sounds like so much fun. I don't know how to thank you for this, Karen." The shame of my situation is almost unbearable. All the time I've wasted, being afraid of Butch and what he'd do if I said or did the wrong thing when he was around. Not living my life to the fullest, enjoying every minute of every day. Not doing all the things I've wanted to do when I wanted to do them. Not spending time with my family so I could keep them as far away from that bastard as possible.

Being controlled and dominated by a cruel man.

"You can thank me by staying away from him for good. By calling the police if he comes anywhere near you again. By asking for help if he finds a way to back you into a corner again. I will get you out—one way or another. You are not alone in this, and you are not to blame." Karen grabs my arms to emphasize her words, and I consciously avoid wincing in pain from the pressure on my bruised skin. She doesn't know the bruises are there; I've hid them well.

Guess old habits do die hard.

"You have my word. Once I'm rid of him, it will be once and for all. There will be no going back or letting him in again for any reason. I've honestly wanted this for a long time, but I never could make it work. I think this time will definitely be different. For the first time in a long time, I have hope for a better life."

"It's all yours, babe. All yours for the taking. Once we get you moved, we'll work on finding you a real man. I'm sure Spencer has at least one single, handsome friend we can set you up with."

"Oh, no. No, no, no. I'm not interested in anything remotely resembling a man in my life. I'll just borrow your husband and his friends for heavy-lifting duties and scaring away bad guys. That's as close to having another man as I want to get."

"Woman-to-woman…friend-to-friend…I have to be brutally honest with you, Savannah."

"Go ahead. I know you. You'll explode if you don't get it out."

"It's not you I'm worried about as much as it's your poor, neglected, prune-shriveled va-jay-jay. I mean, it's seriously been three years since you took it out for a sit and spin? No squats in the cucumber patch? No gland-to-gland combat? We're both mandatory reporters, and you are definitely way past neglecting the old bearded clam. I think I need to turn you in to the nearest hot policeman."

Before meeting Karen, I'd almost forgotten how good it felt to simply laugh with a friend. To say whatever crazy thought came to my mind without fear of ridicule or reprisal. To have someone on my side, in my corner, standing by me no matter where the chips may fall. Stella was the last person I was semi-close to, but my friendship with Stella was nothing like the one I now have with Karen. We tease each other relentlessly, and I always tell her she elbowed her way into my heart, never taking no for an answer.

And saved my life in the process.

Now she's adding fun, love, and laughter too. Maybe the old me will emerge like a butterfly coming out of a cocoon.

We arrive at my apartment complex and find Spencer is already here waiting for us with his own small army. He pulls Karen into his arms, a warm, sweet smile on his face as he looks at her and kisses her hello. He's not at all shy or embarrassed by public displays of affection—or showing how completely and utterly in love he is.

Watching the two of them embrace, I'd swear the depth of their love for each other is their source of strength.

Butch insisted love was a weakness. A way other people could use you without explanation or a chance for retribution. He didn't believe anything that exposed your vulnerabilities could possibly make you stronger.

Butch was wrong.

I see it so clearly now, watching my friends. They give me something to aspire to reach in relationship goals—one day, possibly. The way I feel right now, I'd never trust a man enough to feel safe with him. To give him all of me and believe he'd do the same. Perhaps I'll find that man at some point in my life, but I plan to focus on myself first.

My goals.

My hopes.

My dreams.

I've put them on the back burner for a man who wasn't worth even a second of my time. Today is the first day of the new me.

"Hi, Savannah. Good to see you." Spencer turns his attention to me, keeping his arm wrapped around Karen's waist.

"Thank you for doing this, Spence. I don't know how to repay your kindness—and all your friends. I wish you'd let me pay you for your trouble." My gaze drifts to each of his friends standing by the moving truck—and I immediately regret it. Though they try to mask their thoughts, I see the judging stares and disgusted glances.

I can't exactly hide the black eye I'm sporting, though it has mostly faded to light green bruising.

They're asking why I've stayed so long.

They're questioning what I've done to deserve this.

They want to know why I'm so weak and spineless to let someone treat me this way.

I've experienced these reactions so many times from other people. Until they've walked a mile in my shoes, they'll never understand what it takes to be able to get out of a situation like this. Now that I've lived it, I can honestly say I didn't have a fucking clue what I was talking about when I used to pass those same judgments on other women.

"You're not paying us one single penny. We're happy to help." Spencer releases Karen and steps toward me. "Can I have your keys? Jake and I are going up to your apartment to make sure it's safe. Stay here with Terry, Jarod, and Trent until you hear from us. Then you and Karen can pack your things and we'll get you away from this asshole." Jake steps up next to Spencer and inclines his head at me as Spencer speaks.

"Sure. This one is the door key, this one is to the top bolt, and this one is the bottom bolt." I hand the keys over, feeling guilty for allowing complete strangers to stick their necks out for me. They're off duty, doing this as a favor to Spencer.

"I sure hope he's up there. And I hope he puts up a fight. At the very least, a little resistance. All I need is one good reason to take him down." Jake cracks his knuckles and sneers his lip. "I'm more than willing to pay him back on your behalf, Savannah."

Could I have been wrong? Could their expressions I took for judgment against me have been disgust with Butch instead? Have I read others wrong too?

"I appreciate the offer, Jake. But I don't want you to get in trouble because of me."

"You're looking at it all wrong, sweetheart. All he has to do is touch me wrong one time and he's assaulted a police officer. That's a serious offense, one he'd be hauled away in handcuffs over." Jake smiles, hopeful for the chance to arrest Butch and avenge me in one fell swoop.

One can hope he's in my apartment. Right?

Both fortunately and unfortunately, Butch wasn't in my apartment, and he never showed up while we were there, packing and moving all my belongings out, cleaning up afterward, and leaving the complex without a trace we'd ever been there. While I would've enjoyed seeing him hauled away in handcuffs by a few of DC's finest detectives, I'll take the stealthy approach we pulled off over a confrontation with him any day.

My new home is actually in a newer apartment, but the rent is affordable, and the neighborhood is on the trendier side. This area is nice and safe. I spotted a small coffee shop down the street. Cozy and quaint, it looks like the perfect place to work on my secret project. Something I've decided to do just for myself as much as for others.

"This place looks great!" Karen walks in like she lives here— after unlocking all my locks and bolts with the extra key I gave her —and I wouldn't have it any other way. "You must've been up all night, unpacking and decorating your new place."

"I couldn't sleep. I was too excited to close my eyes."

She drops her purse on the couch, places her hand on her hip, and quirks one eyebrow up at me. "For the record, I'm letting you get away with that abbreviated answer because there is some truth to it. Don't think for one second you'll get away with that shit in the future, though."

"Fine. I was also checking the door and window locks every five minutes and thirty-six seconds. And my ears were oddly in tune with every loud engine that drove past, regardless of the hour."

"I knew I should've spent the night with you last night, even though you insisted you'd be fine. It's really too bad Butch didn't show up yesterday. I would've enjoyed seeing the guys take care of him. But that also means he has no idea where you are now. There are over six million people in the DC metro area. You could live in Virginia or Maryland now for all he knows."

"But he knows where I work. He could follow me home from the hospital." With that thought, I can't help but glance nervously around my small condo, even knowing he isn't inside it. It's a reflex, as if mentioning his name will actually conjure the man out of thin air. "And it's not like you can just move in with me, so enough of the guilt trip for not spending the night."

"Let's devise a plan in case he does show up at the hospital or spots you on the road on the way home." Karen gives me her undivided attention. "Watch your surroundings at all times. We'll alert human resources and arrange for a security guard to escort you to your car every morning. If you think anyone is following you, don't go home. Drive straight to the police station and call me on the way. I'll get Spencer and the guys on the case immediately. Stay in public sight, and never yell for help. Always yell 'Fire.' That draws more people faster than screaming for help does."

"You are definitely married to a cop."

"I need to ask Spencer about self-defense classes. I'll go with you. We can do it on our days off." The wheels in Karen's head are spinning, making plans and mental to-do lists. All to ensure my safety and security.

My best friend is the best person.

"Have a seat. I'll get us a couple of sodas from the fridge, and we'll just bask in the newness of my new little home." True to her nature, she refuses the seat and checks out my decorating skills instead.

"You have great taste, Savannah. I don't know why you chose the noble but overworked profession of nursing over interior design. You could star in your own remodeling TV show by now." Karen pops the top on the Coke can and sips as she strolls to the master bedroom. "I love how you arranged this. You need to come over to my house and help me figure out how to rearrange and redecorate."

"You want to change your bedroom?"

"Oh no, not just the bedroom. My house. I want you to redo my whole house."

"That's more than just a weekend project, Karen."

"Yeah, I know. I'm good with however long it takes. Gives me time to parade Spencer's friends around and see which one you mesh with best."

"Sit. Stop with the matchmaking. Talk to me about more important topics."

We settle on the couch, facing the floor-to-ceiling windows that let in all the natural light I could ever want, and stare at the landscape of Meridian Hill Park only a block away. A light dusting of snow covers the bare trees, shrubs, and grassy areas. The temperatures haven't dropped enough for the snow to stick to the pavement yet, and the cold wind hasn't stopped anyone from enjoying the park.

"You know I only want you to be happy and loved, right? The way Spence loves me and puts me first in everything he does. I want that happy home life for you too." Karen's unusually serious tone makes my breath catch. I swing my eyes up to read her expression. Should've known I'd only find kindness and compassion there.

"I do know that, Karen. Sometimes when I watch you and Spence together, I'm overwhelmed by how much I wish I had what you two have. It's not envy—it's a goal I've set for myself. But whether the man for me is one of Spencer's friends or not doesn't make a difference right now.

"I've lost myself over the last three years. Butch was a different man when I first met him, though I should've recognized the warning signs and red flags for what they really were. The blinders I wore were my fault, and I accept the blame for that. But when the switch flipped and the abuse started, it wasn't just physical injuries. The mental damage he caused nearly destroyed me. Before I even consider looking at another man, I have to be okay with looking at myself in the mirror again.

"There's a fine line between love and hate. I need to find my way back across that line."

"You know I don't judge you for staying with him as long as you did. The threats, the violence, and being in the constant state of fight-or-flight takes a terrible toll on your overall well-being. But I am so thankful you're away from him now, and I'm so proud of you for finding the courage and strength to do it. Just to be clear, though. I will have you committed on a seventy-two-hour psychiatric hold if you let him back in now. You have all the support you need from me, Spence, and a host of DC's finest."

"That seventy-two-hour hold kind of sounds appealing. A little vacation. I could use a long weekend away. Can you arrange for that evaluation to be done in the Bahamas?"

"Your sarcastic humor is what first told me we'd be best friends.

You know you're not going off to a Caribbean island for a mental-health check and leaving me here to work your shifts. We go mental together, or we don't go at all."

"Good to know your priorities are in order."

"Did you expect anything less of me?" A sly smile spreads across her face.

"No. In fact, I would've been very disappointed in you if you had replied any other way."

"You know me too well. There's no mystery left in our relationship…no hidden gems for you to uncover."

"I haven't met all of your personalities yet. I'm sure you have plenty of mysteries left for me to figure out."

Days bled into weeks with no sign or word from Butch. Over that time, I began to find purpose in my work again. Meaning in my life. A new direction to take and a way to use what I've been through for good. The exciting prospects of new projects, secret plans, and shifts at the hospital consumed my time. I fell into bed every day completely exhausted and thoroughly content for the first time in years.

"Have a good day. I'm off for the next four days, and I am not coming in for anyone or anything." I've already briefed the incoming day nurse on the status of each patient and completed all my charting from the night shift. All that's left is to clock out and stroll through the doors.

The snow flurries swirl in the wind outside and the skies are a gloomy shade of gray, but nothing can dampen my mood today. My neighborhood has a quaint little coffee shop at the end of the block. The scents and the scenery are calling my name. My laptop, a table with a view, and a piping hot cup of coffee are all I need to work on my life-defining purpose—a new business venture to help other women in my predicament. I'm writing a book for women in abusive relationships, and I need time and inspiration to add another chapter to the hardest story I've ever told.

My own.
No time like the present.

READ THE REST OF FINE LINE NOW!

BLURRED LINE & HARD LINE ARE NOW AVAILABLE!
SPEND MORE TIME WITH NICK, SILAS, AND ROMAN!

BOOKS BY A.D. JUSTICE

Steele Security Series

Wicked Games (Book 1)

Wicked Ties (Book 2)

Wicked Nights (Book 3)

Wicked Intentions (Book 4)

Wicked Shadows (Book 5)

Crossing Lines Series

Fine Line

Blurred Line

Hard Line

The Vault Series

Precarious: Warning, Part One

Insidious: Warning, Part Two

Treacherous: Warning, Part Three

A HOMETOWN NOVEL

Intent

All I Want

All I Need

Entice (coming soon!)

The Crazy Series

Crazy Maybe (Book 1)

Crazy Baby (Book 2)

Crazy Love (Book 3, Free Short Story)

ABOUT THE AUTHOR

A.D. Justice is the award-winning, *USA Today* bestselling author of several series and stand-alone romance novels in various romance genres, including romantic suspense, contemporary, and paranormal.

When she's not writing, she loves spending time with her alpha male husband in the Northwest Georgia mountains. They're living out their own HEA, frequently on horseback with a dog in tow.

She is also an avid reader of romance novels, a master of procrastination, a chocolate sommelier, a twister of words, and speaks fluent sarcasm. An avid animal lover, she has two horses, two cats, and two very spoiled dogs.

She loves chatting with her readers. You're welcome to stalk her across all social media!

Connect with her online!

Newsletter
Facebook Reader Group
Website

facebook.com/adjusticeauthor

instagram.com/authoradjustice

bookbub.com/authors/a-d-justice

amazon.com/author/adjustice

pinterest.com/adjusticeauthor

ACKNOWLEDGMENTS

I want to personally thank those who specifically helped with this book.

First and foremost, I want to thank my Lord and Savior for His continuous grace and love.

My husband for believing in me and supporting my endeavors, my long nights, and the days I missed with him.

My friends who stuck by me: T.K. Leigh, Michelle Dare, and Tabitha Stokes. I love every one of you!

My editor, Lisa Hollett, for her gift of words and her sense of humor.

My readers, love, like, or hate this book, thank you for giving it a chance!

An extra special THANK YOU goes to the very special bloggers who are part of my blogger group. I appreciate your help and support so very much! You are my trusted few who get first dibs at any book I write because I know it's in good hands. MUAH!!!

www.ingramcontent.com/pod-product-compliance
Lightning Source LLC
Chambersburg PA
CBHW031141120726
47905CB00006B/1776